TOMB WORLD

TOMB WORLD

JONATHAN D BEER

BLACK LIBRARY

A BLACK LIBRARY PUBLICATION

First published in 2025.
This edition published in Great Britain in 2026 by
Black Library, Games Workshop Ltd., Willow Road,
Nottingham, NG7 2WS, UK.

Represented by: Games Workshop Limited – Irish branch,
Unit 3, Lower Liffey Street, Dublin 1,
D01 K199, Ireland.

10 9 8 7 6 5 4 3 2 1

Produced by Games Workshop in Nottingham.
Cover illustration by Svetlana Kostina.

A CIP record for this book is available from the British Library.

ISBN 13: 978-1-83609-378-7

See Black Library on the internet at

blacklibrary.com

Find out more about Games Workshop
and the worlds of Warhammer at

warhammer.com

Printed and bound in the UK.

---

*With thanks, as ever, to Paul, for hauling me across
the finish line once again.*

For more than a hundred centuries the Emperor
has sat immobile on the Golden Throne of Earth.
He is the Master of Mankind. By the might of his
inexhaustible armies a million worlds stand
against the dark.

Yet, he is a rotting carcass, the Carrion Lord of
the Imperium held in life by marvels from the
Dark Age of Technology and the thousand souls
sacrificed each day so his may continue to burn.

To be a man in such times is to be one amongst
untold billions. It is to live in the cruelest and
most bloody regime imaginable. It is to suffer an
eternity of carnage and slaughter. It is to have cries
of anguish and sorrow drowned by the thirsting
laughter of dark gods.

This is a dark and terrible era where you will find
little comfort or hope. Forget the power of technology
and science. Forget the promise of progress and
advancement. Forget any notion of common
humanity or compassion.

There is no peace amongst the stars, for in the grim
darkness of the far future, there is only war.

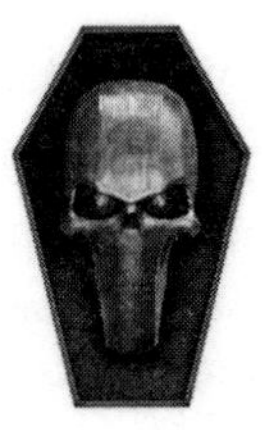

PROLOGUE

The Imperium of Man stretches across the galaxy. A million worlds, each turning beneath the vigilant light of the God-Emperor.

Orymous is one such world. Billions of souls live out their lives upon its surface, serving His design. They huddle together in its cities, vast stains of rockcrete that spread along coastlines and over mountain plateaus. They labour in its fields, enormous agri-complexes that cover continents. They plumb the depths of its indigo oceans for promethium, the lifeblood of the Imperial machine. They live, as untold trillions do, praying to the Holy Throne of Terra for salvation from all that blights them.

The void above Orymous teems with vessels, great blade-tipped craft put forth from the shipyards of the Adeptus Mechanicus. They come and go in their multitudes, carrying soldiers and arms and machines and the immense produce required to sustain them all. Orymous is a mustering world, a gathering place for the God-Emperor's armies. Wars of conquest, of reclamation and of retribution have sallied forth from this planet, carrying the Imperium's wrath across the stars.

But Orymous has not always been a human world. Indeed, Orymous has not always been its name.

ACT 1

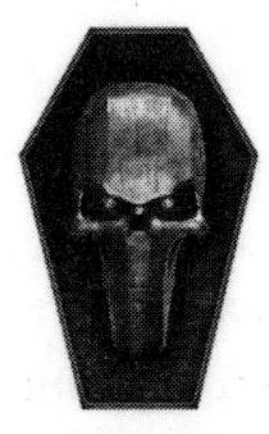

CHAPTER 1

A fire burns beneath a metal grate. Above the fire is a sigil, carved from polished onyx, wreathed in oily smoke.

The sigil is the icon of the Triarch, known to every witness gathered about the fire for it is affixed upon their bodies. These bodies, formed of living metal, are aglow from the light of the fire, and aglow from within.

Placed at intervals around the fire are other objects, grains of sand and shards of brass. The fire is unnecessary, as is the sigil and the rest. In truth, almost all of the sorcerous adornments placed about the chamber are unnecessary. Kamoteph has ever scorned the trappings of 'magic', the cloak-and-shadow lies that many practitioners of the cryptek arts employ to conjure mystery and conceal the true source of their powers.

But the trappings have their uses.

Lord Hekasun watches all that transpires with rapt attention. His sharp-edged skull twitches left and right in the manner of an avian as he struggles to comprehend that which is beyond him. Each of Kamoteph's smallest gestures draws his sponsor's gaze, his copper oculars glowing like banked coals within the depths of their sockets.

The fire dances along the planes and edges of the cube, the only object that is truly needed for the ritual's success. It is smooth, no larger than the cryptek's clenched fist, cradled at the peak of a pyramid of metagold struts. A work of uncommon artifice, the tesseract labyrinth is an example of the necron mastery of space and time. It can serve as repository, archive and receptacle for anything its bearer chooses to place outside the strictures of reality.

In this case, it is a prison.

A chant echoes from the stone walls, stirring the air that has been pumped into the chamber to serve as fuel for the flames. It is an ancient language, drawn not from memory but from the texts of a dead empire. The twelve most gifted of Kamoteph's acolytes form a circle about him, though between them stand the impassive forms of Lord Hekasun's lychguard. Mandulis, the lord's vargard, is closer at hand, a bare pace from his master and rigid with restrained violence.

Kamoteph's dominion-link with his apprenteks make them extensions of his will, subordinate to his needs. In the driest, most mechanical sense, Kamoteph has linked their processing power with his, expanding his capacity to interrogate the gargantuan reams of data that exist within the cube's matrices. In the arcane sense, which is at once more true and more false, he has slaved their meagre abilities to his, sustaining him as he explores the labyrinth's dimensionless interior.

Kamoteph stands hunched over the fire and sigil, arms and hands moving occasionally between ritual poses. He is bent almost in half, his spine a heavy arc of necrodermis that forces his head low, a bare cubit from the sigil and the flames beneath.

Kamoteph the Crooked is the name he has been given by unfriendly courtiers, a mocking sobriquet to which the cryptek is entirely indifferent.

He draws metal hands together, digits shifting into the seventh configuration of Olm. Kamoteph has been at work for thirty-one days, his mind bound to the infinite medium of the labyrinth. Such endurance offers no challenge for his god-wrought body, but it is not his body that has been taxed.

It is like casting a noose around smoke. Slowly, infinitely slowly, the cryptek shapes and sculpts the mist, sifting each speck of unreality for a trace of what he seeks. Those he finds, he husbands with deft gusts of power, drawing each fragment together from the diffuse nothingness in which they dwell.

This analogy is good enough for Hekasun's stunted imagination, but it is also wrong in every way that matters.

'Well?' Hekasun interrupts, not for the first time. It is fortunate that much of the ritual is purely for show, as Kamoteph's lord and master is an impatient and querulous creature.

Lifting even a fraction of his attention from the miasma of the labyrinth is a trial, but Kamoteph does so. 'I am drawing near, o lord.'

He is. His task requires immense focus and sublime skill, but Kamoteph possesses both. The ephemeral sense of a consciousness, of metal and fusion and a functioning mind, are all coalescing from the labyrinth's innards.

'I name you, Khemet.'

Kamoteph speaks the words aloud. This is not for show. The cryptek is summoning a thinking mind from a void, beckoning it to remember itself. He can feel it respond. The ephemeral is becoming enduring, the diffuse becoming whole.

'I name you, Khemet. I call you. I seek you, and bind you, and pull you near.'

The chanting grows in strength in response to Kamoteph's unspoken command.

'I name you, Khemet, and I call you forth.'

It happens in a rush. Like hauling a boulder up one side of a mountain, eventually the stone reaches the peak and tips.

Atoms remember their bonds with one another. Crystalline synapses draw together, firing in sequence. Fragments of matter bind, becoming metal bones, metal limbs, metal sinews. The caged star that burns at the centre of each necron remembers its strength, and a blaze of jade light erupts within the labyrinth's surface.

Now is the critical time. He is the conduit, the path out of the maze. Kamoteph must hold himself together. He is the beacon, the lighthouse, the flame in the darkness.

The apprenteks' chant reaches a furious pitch in response to their master's need. Their core-flux vents blaze with the effort, each taxed to their limits. In the sconces the flames rise, dancing in time with the chant, and the shadows lengthen. At Kamoteph's side, all but forgotten, Hekasun leans closer, entranced by the occult magic at work.

An apprentek succumbs. His reactor core gutters like a candle in a gale, and he collapses to the godsteel deck with a discordant crash of metal that is lost beneath his brethren's chanting. Kamoteph ignores the death, drawing harder on his bond with those that remain. He must endure. If he falters now, all that he has done to reach this point shall have been for naught.

Something stirs in the labyrinth's depths. It comes as though from a great distance, growing from the merest flicker of movement. Clouds part, making way for viridian light that banishes the shadows of the chamber. It burns from the labyrinth cube, illuminating every plane and edge of Kamoteph's face, shining with a ferocity that eclipses all other light.

It is only in the final fraction of a second that Kamoteph is able to perceive what it is he has summoned, and a shiver of fear racks his metal frame.

For the longest time, she has been nothing.

Less than nothing. Whatever was thrown into the labyrinth has not survived its torment. She has been broken. Torn apart by the relentless march of time. Riven by utter and total absence.

And now, without warning, she is restored.

Existence is incomprehensible. Nothing is as it should be. She feels metal where there should be flesh. Her thoughts are shards of arithmetic calculation, not the lightning storm of consciousness.

There is a void where her soul should reside.

It is too much. Whatever kernel of self that still lies at the centre of her being rebels. She cannot endure the horror of the real, and so she flees back into the oblivion that has been her sanctuary.

The thing that emerges can barely be called a necron.

It writhes, a flailing tangle of metal that bursts from the blaze of light that shines from the labyrinth's surface. It crashes through the fire, scattering charred wood and casting the priceless cube from which it has escaped into the farthest corner of the room.

A wordless moan pours from a maw that gapes open, a cry of utter horror that lashes at the chamber's walls. Its jaw grows wider to unleash the scream, drooping under its own weight until it detaches and crashes to the floor. Necrodermis sloughs from its limbs as its morphic field falters, leaving a skeletal under-structure that thrashes in purposeless fury. Jade light explodes from fractures that open in its torso, so much so that Kamoteph fears that all his work to pull the creature from the labyrinth will be wasted in a gush of unchained core-flux. But it holds itself together, scrabbling against the godsteel floor in a snarl of limbs.

Hekasun steps back, horrified, and his vargard takes his place. The brace of lychguard that flank the ritual stamp forwards with their warscythes levelled, replacing the apprenteks, who falter in their chanting and scatter in terror.

Whatever shred of consciousness the benighted creature possesses detects the threat. With a swirling crash of struts and spars it hurls itself towards the vargard's blade. Mandulis catches the leap with the staff of his scythe, throwing it aside.

It lands in a heap, only to scuttle back to all fours and take off. It moves in an uncoordinated shambles, throwing itself forwards to catch itself on emaciated hands and feet. The sound of broken knives clattering against steel fills the room, beneath the moan that continues to howl from the ruin of its face.

'Seal the chamber!'

Hekasun's order comes too late. Despite its disordered gait it moves with unnatural speed. The entrance to the chamber is a low archway, lit by the soft glow of power conduits from the corridor beyond. A pair of warriors stand before it, gauss flayers crossed to bar the way.

The thing crashes through the meagre barrier and lopes beneath the archway's lintel. The sound of violence and horror echoes away as it charges, heedless, into the bowels of Kamoteph's ship.

'What madness have you unleashed?' Hekasun rounds on the cryptek.

Kamoteph does not breathe, but he is breathless, exhausted by the final rush of effort necessary to draw the object of his search from her prison. He steps into the strewn wreckage of the ritual fire and retrieves the carved onyx sigil of the Triarch.

'I have released her, my lord.'

'As one would a plague?' Hekasun stabs an accusatory finger towards the cryptek's faceplate.

'Hardly, my lord.' Kamoteph is not accustomed to error, and

exhaustion and pride make his reply sharper than is wise. When Hekasun's oculars narrow, the cryptek bows low in apology. 'I had not anticipated such a degree of synaptic degradation.'

'It was folly to allow you to convince me of this course. Now I must hunt and eradicate a feral warrior through the decks of the ship.'

Kamoteph starts forwards in alarm. 'I beseech you, lord, do not. Khemet has what we require. Everything hinges upon her.'

Hekasun stares at the cryptek. 'We do not need her.'

Kamoteph bows low again. 'With the greatest respect, my lord. We do.'

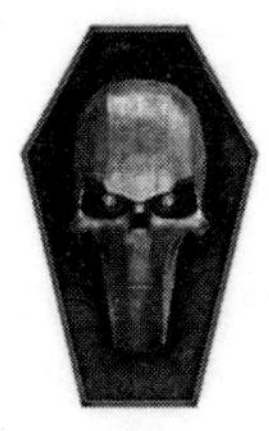

CHAPTER 2

She runs, without understanding the act of running, nor from what she flees or to where.

Whatever is left of her mind is all but gone, ragged and thrashing like torn sailcloth in a gale. It is pure instinct that drives her body's motions, instinct and the hundred thousand background processes that regulate the power levels of her core reactor, the actuators in her joints, the processing language of her neural mesh.

what am I what am I what am I what am I

There are flashes of memory – images and sensations and the code-facsimiles of emotions – that erupt as knife-edged shards out of the misfiring operating cores of her brain. A figure towers over her, and betrayal stabs at her centre. A crown is cold and distant, and supreme. Pride lifts her, and she soars over a battle-field that spans the stars themselves.

She is dying. Whatever strength is propelling her is waning, falling away with the clods of silver metal that melt from her skeletal limbs like candle wax. Alarms add their wail to the chaos of her colliding thoughts, and alert-glyphs dance in her sight. Each one is another barb to her sanity, driving her further into the recesses where she can escape the horror of her being.

She does not run in search of succour. The place she finds herself in is dark and barren. The walls and floor and roof are sheer faces of black stone, veined with geometric lines that pulse with a sickly light. She knows that nothing lives in such places. She is a gheist, haunting the tunnels of a tomb.

She rounds a corner and there are figures ahead. Six of them, stick thin, their bodies reflecting the poisonous light from the corridor's walls. Fear rises as they march towards her, and she sees their appalling mockery of life. Eyes that are green coals burn in deep sockets. Their mouths are slits cut into metal faces, immobile and thick with malice.

They hold long, sharp implements in their hands, glowing with the same bilious radiance that emanates from behind their open ribcages. She knows these things. They are weapons, made to kill, made to strip the flesh from the living.

She throws herself upon the closest, bearing it to the floor beneath the force of her impact. There is no skill or martial art in her attack, just wild fear escaping in undirected violence. The creature emits an electronic grunt of protest, but it is Khemet who screams when she looks into the eye of a monster and sees herself in its reflection.

This is what she is. She is kin with these creatures, these constructs, these false imitations of life and strength, these…

Necrons. We are called necrons.

The realisation awakens something, forces a connection with a ravening flash of heat and pain. She is a necron. A soulless intellect bound to an immortal frame by the duplicity of spiteful gods.

The fragile essence that is hiding from all that assails her finally breaks under the assault, and in the breaking Khemet is freed. The horror of her existence is too great to behold, and so she does not see it. She smothers her dread, burying it to scream and wail and shudder in its revulsion. But the greater part of her rises, deaf and blind to the aberrance of her being.

She is a necron. And, what is more, she is powerful.

She is still dying, but she can save herself. Senses Khemet has forgotten she possesses reach out and into the warrior, into the hollow cavern of its brain, and override its core functions. She grips its faceplate with a hand and the metal deforms, binding itself to her fingers. Khemet leaches the necrodermis from the warrior's frame, metal flowing like water from its gaunt body to hers.

It is over in moments. Its body has been withered to its skeletal essence, its strength siphoned away. Something like a muted scream barks from the dying warrior's faceplate, and then the light of its appalling eyes grows dim.

Khemet stands.

The theft of the warrior's metal has invigorated her, or perhaps it is the awareness of her nature. In either case, the erratic firing of her thoughts has calmed, if only by a fraction.

Her name is Khemet. She is a necron. She possesses strength, or can steal it from others. All else is still a swarm of sparks, shorting and colliding and corrupting any focus she might grasp.

And while her body is partly restored, she is far from whole.

A viridian beam glances from her shoulder, ripping away some of her stolen necrodermis. The other warriors advance, gauss flayers levelled, undaunted by her consumption of their kinsman.

Khemet turns and hurls herself into their midst.

'If this continues, she will tear the ship apart.'

Hekasun speaks mildly, affecting disinterest. But Kamoteph can hear the concern behind the words.

'It is entirely possible, lord.'

They observe Khemet's rampage through the eyes of the *Senusret*. The sensors that line the ship's corridors show them her progress, and her brutal encounter with the first squad of warriors sent to contain her.

Neither show the least concern for the eviscerated serfs. Such disinterest is the birthright of necron nobility, but they also know that the warriors are not truly lost. At the moment of their death, the *Senusret*'s reanimation circuits capture their engrams and spirit them away. In ordinary circumstances the reanimation protocols would also capture their broken bodies, stealing them from the battlefield for molecular deconstruction and repurposing, the same minds implanted into the same, reforged bodies. This is the great strength of the necrons – destruction is rarely absolute.

'Then again,' says Kamoteph thoughtfully, 'perhaps not.'

He is watching the creature he has summoned. As Khemet consumes each warrior, her stance changes. She rises from her bestial crouch. Her movements become less feral and more fluid, displaying the surety of a warrior. She still lashes out, batting aside any weapon that swings towards her, but with strikes that show directed anger, not untethered madness.

Eventually she can take no more. The wasted remains of six warriors litter the corridor's floor and Khemet stands restored. Except, he sees, for her right hand, which has stubbornly refused to regenerate. Her arm ends in two jagged spars of metal where a wrist articulator should be.

Her hand's absence is a curiosity Kamoteph intends to explore, if he is given the chance.

When Khemet realises that she can drain no more metal from her victims, she pauses. It is only for a second, but Kamoteph sees it clearly. She halts, considering what she will do next. She too notices the absence of her hand, staring down at the truncated wrist. Then she takes off, plucking a gauss flayer from the deck as she goes.

'I believe I can end this, my lord,' says the cryptek.

Whatever she may have been when she emerged, Khemet persists, her instincts and identity buried beneath the scars of the labyrinth. Thus, it is a matter of freeing herself from wherever she resides – no different, in many ways, to liberating her physical form.

'I demand it,' says Hekasun imperiously. 'Your folly unleashed her, so you must cage her once more.'

'As you say, sire. But I shall require the use of your vargard.'

Behind his lord, Mandulis hefts his warscythe.

Her body has shaped itself into a vessel of power. Her limbs are strong and her torso is heavy, far bulkier than that of the warriors she has slain. There is potential in that weight of metal and mechanism, but she has no time to explore it. While her body is mostly restored, Khemet's mind is still far from whole.

Her missing hand is a nagging, gnawing pain. Not a physical pain – Khemet has been unaffected by the dozen incidental wounds the warriors inflicted in their death throes – but there is a deeper hurt, a scar that is etched across her circuits. She knows not why it is lost, or how. Whenever she turns her focus to the question a bitter flash of regret and loss and white-hot hate blows up with a hurricane's force, threatening to corrupt her fragile sanity. Like so much else, her hand's loss and its meaning are locked away behind mental firebreaks to preserve what stability she can muster.

Her passage through the dark corridors has become less frenzied, though no less swift or violent. At every junction there are more warriors to bar her way. Where she can, she batters them aside, but the threat of their gauss flayers sends her plunging down other paths when she finds them waiting for her.

There are no halls or chambers, no greater spaces, just a maze of narrow tunnels. At intervals she passes what appear to be lintels, stone arches that stand proud from the walls as if to suggest entrances to other spaces, but they are blocked by the same black stone.

She is being herded. She has recovered enough of herself to know this, the way a prey creature senses the approaching hunter. At the junctions she is directed one way or another in accordance with some will. Part of Khemet rages at the arrogance, but her newborn intellect is content to go where she is being sent, if only in the hope of learning more of her hunter, and herself.

Finally, the warren ends. There is only one hallway left, opening onto a larger chamber. Sharp lines of viridian light pulse through the walls, seeming to beckon her onwards.

Khemet could stop here. Turn and run back into the maze, confront the cohorts of warriors that have dictated her path. But there are no answers that way.

She enters, passing beneath a slab of rock that seems to reflect no light. Beyond is an open space, high-ceilinged and occluded by shadow. There are no furnishings, no seats or consoles or glyphs to indicate the chamber's function.

those are the trappings of life there is no life here there is only stasis

One wall is dominated by a vast window, a sharply angled rhombus of transparent crystal set into the stone. There are pinpricks of light moving beyond the window.

Stars. We are in the void.

From where she draws these concepts – the mighty spheres of crushing gravity and fusion that are stars; the immensity of the emptiness between them that is the void – she does not know.

The starlight is not what claims her attention. A single necron is waiting for her, standing unwavering in the centre of the chamber. This, she sees, is a true warrior. The others, the thin, slow and bitter creatures she has killed and run from were thralls, stamped from the same press in their multitudes. The construct facing her is a soldier, a killer, hulking and clearly lethal. His eyes and the smoky outgassing of his ribcage too mark him out from those others, alight as they are with fuliginous copper rather than poisoned emerald. He holds an immense warscythe in both hands. A weapon wielded by kings, and those who would protect them.

The warrior offers no words, and nor does she. For whatever reason, the power that directed her here desires to see them fight, and in her ignorance and fury she will oblige.

They come together in a shower of jade sparks. The slender flayer cannot match the warscythe's weight, particularly as Khemet is hindered by her absent hand. A single swing of the scythe would carve her long barrel in two if she met the blade directly, so she does not. Khemet catches the first massive cut with a counter-strike that hits the flat of the warscythe and deflects its passage. The warscythe slashes past her head, captive energies humming within. She thrusts in turn, driving the warrior back, using the flayer's length as a spear to deny him the warscythe's advantage.

They are fast, she and the warrior, and strong. Each meeting of blades shivers up her arm, absorbed by kinetic buffers and muscle-fibre bundles. Her body was built for this, built for combat, built for war.

Built to execute.

She wields a weapon of surpassing craft, and ends thousands in blasts of viridian fire, scouring them from existence. She sees necrons forced to their knees by their own bodyguards, presented for her to end. This is her function, her reason for being. Khemet is an executioner.

The memory boils up from the cauldron within her, and the loss of focus almost ends her. The warscythe catches the flayer and hammers it aside, and only a desperate roll beneath its backswing prevents Khemet from being cut in half.

The warrior presses, swinging the great blade in huge arcs that Khemet can only weave between. She backs away but the wall is close behind her, impassive and unyielding. She can flee no more, so must attack or die.

Khemet lets the next swing pass her, close enough that the tip of the warscythe drags its way through the surface of her chest, and then she strikes. She stabs forwards, the gauss flayer held by its pistol grip. The knife-blade barrel slides into a gap between two ribs and Khemet fires. A flash of gauss erupts from the weapon's end, and the warrior's core bursts in a gout of orange fire.

He sags to his knees, dead instantly. As the warrior slumps to the deck his body fragments, segmenting into prismatic blocks that dissolve into finer and finer particles. What strikes the floor is a cloud of sand that melts away to nothingness. In seconds there is no trace of the warrior she has fought, merely an empty chamber and Khemet, no wiser.

She spins, expecting a blade in the back. But there is no other, only the open viewport to the stars beyond the transparent crystal.

The protocols of combat that took control of her recede as quickly as they came. This is something else she has learnt about herself. She possesses wells of not merely knowledge but skill, experience, ability – whole partitions of her being that can devote themselves to a task with singular focus. It is only in fighting that she has found them. One part of herself rose up to become dominant, quieting the rest, letting something like calm come over her.

But that clarity is slipping. There is still too much she does not understand about herself, about the place – the voidcraft – upon which she has awoken. Without the locus of combat the kaleidoscope of memories and questions returns in full force, crashing through the ordered thoughts like a breaking wave. Khemet clutches at her head, a bodily act of self-preservation that is entirely involuntary.

After what feels like seconds, but could be hours, the warrior returns. He comes not from the open archway but through the stone of the wall to her left, the spiteful eyes and cruel faceplate emerging first from the solid matter. Khemet finds herself oddly unsurprised – this, she knows, is something they can do. Necrons mastered the art of manipulating reality long before her birth.

birth we were born we lived we are not this we are not these monsters

The growl of actuators in her neck is loud as Khemet shakes her head, clearing the aberrant thought, pushing down that frightened nub of self back into its vault.

It is the same warrior she has just fought, identical in every detail. His metal is pristine, unblemished, showing no trace of the wound her gauss flayer inflicted.

The calm returns. This is a test. For whatever reason, the unseen hand that brought her to this place requires that she remain, so it presents an opponent against whom she will be tested, again and again.

Without knowing why, without knowing who she is or how she fights so proficiently, Khemet hefts her gauss flayer and attacks once more.

Kamoteph has never found the exertions of warriors particularly engaging, either as spectacle or a technical exercise. Even so, he watches Khemet and Mandulis duel, not to appreciate the artistry of their violence but to observe the storm-racked disorder of Khemet's thoughts.

He is several decks away, fingers interlaced in the second alignment of Ahtekh, but his mind is with Khemet as she parries

Mandulis' every blow. He has steadily threaded his consciousness into hers, using the *Senusret*'s interstitial network as a bridge. He sits, silent and unseen, amid the appalling chaos of her broken mind.

Four times Mandulis has entered the chamber, and four times he has been destroyed. When he attacks, Khemet counters his strength with a speed that cannot be equalled. When he allows her to attack, she dictates the combat so thoroughly that she dances around his massive swings. During their third engagement the greater weight and reach of his warscythe almost tells, battering aside the slender gauss flayer, but she abandons the weapon, and with a great heave rips his skull and spinal column from his body. As his corpse sparks into death, Khemet plucks Mandulis' weapon from his body, preventing it from phasing away.

The decision to switch weapons – to make a conscious judgement, weighing multiple options – reassures Kamoteph that there is some rational, thinking part of Khemet that can be saved.

Finally, he determines that he has seen enough, and begins to act.

During each duel the great discordance of Khemet's mind calms, displaced by the protocols of combat that are deep-seated in her being. In that calm Kamoteph can search, in much the same manner as he sifted the labyrinth. With care and subtlety he finds and assembles the fractured algorithms and logic gates, dredges for what snatches of identity he can grasp, and steadily begins to piece together Khemet's sense of self.

His aid swiftly tells. He cannot improve on the tranquillity she achieves during combat, but in the interim periods, the scant moments it takes for the *Senusret* to seat the vargard's consciousness into a new body, Khemet retains more of her battle-calm. The clashing discord of memories is still there, still waiting to draw her into their depths, but Khemet's conscious mind is lifted above them, observing rather than being swept up in their thrashing cacophony.

It is slow but steady work, difficult but far less taxing than extracting Khemet's body from the labyrinth. But when the seventh Mandulis is slain, the scales tip.

'Get out!'

Kamoteph is shocked, so much so that he almost loses his footing within Khemet's mind. He had not imagined that she would be capable of perceiving his presence. He imagined himself an invisible hand, working without her knowledge. It would have been better, he thinks, had she attributed her recovery to her own resilience.

He ignores her demand. Khemet's grafted ego is far from stable, and it requires considerable effort on his part to maintain.

When the eighth copy of Mandulis dies, Khemet tries again to dislodge Kamoteph.

'I see you. I will give you nothing.' It is less an interstitial sending and more a grunt of will given words.

After some thought, he replies. *'I do not intend to take anything.'*

When the ninth dies, Khemet speaks to him clearly. *'Show yourself.'*

Finally, the guiding hand emerges.

This one is no fighter. He leans heavily on a blade-topped staff. His segmented vertebrae are deeply curved, and the metal of his shoulders and cervical spine has grown up and around his skull, forming a crooked hunch that bends him almost to Khemet's waist. A single outsized ocular dominates his faceplate, which draws down into a pronounced mandibular crest.

A curtain of small tiles hangs from the arm that holds his staff, like the pinions of a moulting bird. Khemet is certain she knows the symbolism of the shards of metal and ceramic that clatter gently as the creature moves, but she cannot form the connection.

With him comes a host of scuttling metal constructs. They follow in the creature's wake, a tide of scarabs and scorpions, wyrms and arachnids. Several ride upon the creature's shoulders, clattering across his arms and along the curved length of his spine. The largest stands to the height of Khemet's waist, a beetle with an iridescent black shell and wickedly curved mandibles. They are vaguely threatening as a collective, moving with a disconcerting unity of purpose.

The one who brought Khemet to this place enters alongside the tenth copy of her slain opponent. The hulking warrior towers above the creature, though his gaze does not leave Khemet. He is clearly restrained, leashed by a greater power. Khemet does not move, nor does she lower her stolen warscythe.

'I am Kamoteph.' The bent-backed creature speaks, a deep growl accented by the metallic tones of his vocaliser. He gestures behind him. 'This is Mandulis.'

The warrior does not respond to his name, and Khemet is equally impassive. Their duels have been hard-fought and bitter. And, of course, she has dismembered him in nine different ways since first they met.

'I thought you should know the name of your assailant,' continues Kamoteph. There is a mocking edge to his voice, but Khemet cannot tell at whom it is aimed.

She still says nothing. In truth, she is unsure whether she can speak. Though she has felt the burden of madness lifting, she can feel it waiting, lurking. What spills from her vocaliser could be the nonsensical gibberings of the damned.

'And you are Khemet,' says the hunchback.

'I know.' Her vocaliser makes a cracked, metallic wheeze. These are the first words she has spoken for… some time. She cannot say how long, and she does not wish to try.

'What do you remember?'

Far too little. Her memory is still a jumble of conflicted images and sensations, ill-defined and out of sequence.

'What are you?' she challenges instead.

'I am a cryptek.' The title means nothing, though he speaks it with clear pride. When Khemet does not react, he explains. 'A worker of the arcane. A technomancer, by vocation.'

'Magic.' The word occurs to her suddenly, prefigured with glyphs of distaste and mistrust.

Kamoteph scowls. 'My "magic" pulled you from the labyrinth.'

A spike of alarm runs through Khemet's core. Now she has a word to put to that feeling of absolute dread. The cause of the abyssal emptiness in her mind, in which her memories swirl and collide and seep away.

'The labyrinth,' she repeats.

'Your prison. A most cruel form of punishment, even by the standards of our lords and masters.'

'Why was I imprisoned?'

Kamoteph takes a few cautious steps towards her. 'Can you not recall?'

Khemet tries. She truly does, but she cannot endure venturing into the scalding swirl of memory. There is the flickering sensation of a blow to her chest, the shock of her hand being cut from her arm, and a blaze of rage that falls away into oblivion.

Kamoteph sees her struggling. 'I can aid you.'

Khemet snarls in reply, a harsh grunt of electronic noise. 'I need no aid.'

'I can restore what you have lost.'

'I have lost nothing.' But that is not true. There is an absence. She looks down at her truncated arm. It is not the hand that is missing, but what it is meant to hold. Something of immense value, and authority. A symbol, of something greater and more terrible than herself.

'What am I?'

The words escape her, utterly shameful but impossible to stop.

The question seems to please Kamoteph, who takes another step forwards. His staff strikes the stone like the report of a herald's trumpet. 'You are a praetorian.'

Embers of pride rise within her, but unmoored from any context.

'I do not know what that means.'

'If you will refrain from slaying any more of our servants, I will help you remember.' Behind him, Mandulis is a statue, his warscythe held utterly still.

After an age of hesitation, Khemet lowers her blade.

CHAPTER 3

Lord Hekasun does not relish the times when he must venture into Kamoteph's lair. He much prefers the martial austerity of the *Senusret*'s command deck, his natural place aboard the vessel. But there are times when he must lower himself to secrecy, and thus he must go where no others will tread.

Kamoteph's laboratory is in the prow of the ship, at the very centre of the two sweeping wings that project forward of its hull. Hekasun knows he is growing nearer by the increasing presence of scarabs and other canoptek beasts. The creatures are a common sight on any necron craft or world, their scuttling activity a background noise that Hekasun has long since learnt to ignore. But the profusion and variety of the constructs that Kamoteph surrounds himself with goes beyond function, straying into the macabre.

They are the cryptek's vocation. Every follower of Kamoteph's creed has one, a passion – insofar as the C'tan left their deceived followers the capacity for passion – that they explore with the diligence and patience of the immortal. Kamoteph is a techno-mancer, which as far as Hekasun's limited understanding goes concerns the use and function of the canoptek constructs that serve and maintain necron technology.

The green light of power pulsing through the *Senusret*'s walls reflects from their carapaces as Hekasun walks into their midst. Scarabs and beetles of every size and description cling to the floor, walls and ceiling, parting for him if they might impede his progress towards their master.

It does not occur to Hekasun that they would not part if he were unwelcome into their master's midst.

It seems to Hekasun that the ship's illumination grows dimmer as he enters the cryptek's domain. The decks are lit more and more by the sickly glow that emanates from the constructs' eyes. Dozens of jade-green circles, each cluster unequal in number and placement, stare at him as he passes.

Hekasun finds Kamoteph at one of the many workstations in his lair, his hunchbacked body bent over a spyder that he has opened and spread across the metal bench.

'My lord.'

Kamoteph, as is proper, abandons his work the moment Heka-sun enters.

The cryptek leans heavily on his staff and walks with a pro-nounced limp, in abject defiance of the god-given strength in his limbs. Hekasun has encountered many such unfortunates. Though they had walked – or been hurled – through the furnaces of biotransference and emerged clad in powerful frames of living metal, their minds have stubbornly clung to the frailties of their consumed bodies. Some are cognitively enfeebled, unable to accept the full potential of their new mental faculties, whereas others cannot shed the physical infirmities that had plagued their former selves.

Kamoteph is one of the latter breed. Hekasun pities him, so far as he is able. But the cryptek has proved his value to the noble many times, in spite of his psychosomatic impediment. That, after all, is how they have come to this situation.

'Have I erred in trusting you, Kamoteph?'

Hekasun offers no preamble, and Kamoteph is unfazed by his blunt challenge.

'My assurance remains, lord. Khemet will achieve all we require of her. I ask that you extend your trust a while longer.'

'You ask for too much, cryptek. She is half feral.'

Kamoteph does not reply immediately. He shuffles away towards another workbench and another half-built construct, finding an excuse to retreat from Hekasun's presence in his lair.

'There is time before we reach Qeretesh,' he says. 'I had anticipated that Khemet would bear the scars of her imprisonment. The labyrinth's damage can be undone.'

'If there is anything of the praetorian left in her.'

'That is what I shall determine. I have seen inside her mind, lord, and shall see deeper in the course of rebuilding her.'

The lure of power Kamoteph offers is a naked attempt to divert Hekasun's misgivings. The secrets of the praetorian order are a prize indeed, but Hekasun is not so easily put off.

'Have you considered what it is you seek to rebuild? The servants of the Silent King are not known to be biddable.'

Kamoteph nods. 'That is true, lord, at least in my limited experience.'

Hekasun allows the silence to stretch out between them.

'What do you ask of me, o lord?' Kamoteph asks finally.

Hekasun resents the need to speak his commands so plainly. 'Restrain her. Bind her. In the course of remaking her, insert the means to destroy her. My destiny will not be impeded by the whims of an honour-bound relic.'

Kamoteph bows low.

'As you command.'

Khemet drifts.

No. Drifting implies movement, and there is no movement. There is nothing. There is no direction, no orientation. There is no light, and no darkness. There is only absence.

Khemet fights. She flails, lashing out against the nothingness, groping blindly for something, anything, that is tangible. But if her limbs respond she does not feel them move. They have been shorn from her, her mind ripped from her body. There is nothing left of her but a displaced intellect, cast into the void.

'There is no value in dwelling on that,' says Kamoteph.

And yet it is all Khemet can think of. Whenever she strains to recall, whenever she attempts any exercise of thought more complex than determining the arc of a sword's swing, her mind finds the labyrinth's boundless desolation.

Kamoteph sits on a stone chair, his staff resting across his knees. Around him, a dozen scarabs click and scuttle in idleness. She has learnt that he is never without them, canoptek constructs of various design and function. Some, the size of her clenched fist, he allows to clamber along and across his body. He appears indifferent to their presence, but since Khemet acquiesced to his offer of aid she has never seen him without them.

Khemet paces. The cryptek has given up attempting to have her adopt a meditative pose. She cannot endure stillness. Even a second's immobility sparks a riot of error codes and frantic action, limbs lashing out in spasmodic terror.

She has been assigned quarters, and the room shows the evidence of these outbursts. A pair of Nikah Dynasty tapestries, ancient beyond measure, are torn rags strewn across the floor.

The walls are scarred by metal hands that have ripped at their surfaces, clawing sensation from the stone. Anything Khemet can do to force a connection with the present, to feel the inputs of her body, she has done.

'Think. Remember.'

For six days Kamoteph has sat with her, slowly rebuilding her conscious and subconscious minds. He has released a swarm of nanoscarabs into her skull to reforge the billions of crystal synapses, reset the shorting logic engines, and rebuild accumulators worn down by a century of abuse.

that is no mind it is a cage a prison a mockery of a thinking soul

The renewal of her cognitive processes, Kamoteph has said, is only half of the task. His microscopic constructs can repair the frame, the scaffolding along which her thoughts can run, but Khemet must populate it with her sense of self, her identity. And thus, Kamoteph demands that she reach into the black well of memory, summoning the storm that threatens her sanity.

'What is a praetorian?'

This is the question he repeats, never offering answers. He claims to be at work, using his occult powers to suppress the worst of her mind's outbursts so she can search its depths. Khemet does not enjoy the connection Kamoteph has forged between them, nor the knowledge that his miniscule pets are at work within her head.

In truth, she does not enjoy anything. Khemet has emerged from the labyrinth to find an existence that is harsh and joyless. She occupies a body designed to excel only in destruction, to take pleasure from nothing. The closest she has come to joy was the peace she found in hacking Mandulis apart in the observation port.

The vargard – an elite warrior elevated to the responsibility of guardianship over a noble, she now recalls – is stationed beyond the walls of her quarters, a precaution against a relapse into madness that Khemet finds at once insulting and insufficient.

'What is a praetorian?' Kamoteph asks, persistent as only a machine can be.

'I do not know.'

Evidently the cryptek's patience is running thin. He lifts his staff and slams its end against the stone floor.

'Then use your imagination! By the dead, if you cannot remember the least detail of your existence then at least consult your lexicon and contemplate what the title implies.'

She looks up sharply from her aimless pacing. 'Do not mock me.'

'Why not?' The hunchbacked creature leans towards her. 'You are nothing. You possess no power, no authority. I have no need to fear you.'

She crosses the chamber with swift strides to loom over the crooked figure. 'You have every reason to fear me, cryptek.'

The threat unlocks something. The swell of potential violence within her unbars a gate, picks at a loose thread, parts the clouds. All these and more are inadequate to describe the shock of realisation, of clarity blazing like a sunburst through her discordant thoughts.

Primed by Kamoteph's relentless pestering, Khemet opens herself to the memories that pour forth.

The Unclean come, and Khemet throws them back.

Across the expanse of time and space, Khemet fights. She has been a warrior for countless aeons, a defender of the only empire worthy of the name.

She has faced all that the relentless hostility of the galaxy has to offer. The upstart species, mere millennia from the comfort of their primordial pools. The ancient enemies, the Old Ones and the aeldari and the enslavers. The C'tan, the truest foe of all necrons. It matters not; Khemet has slain them all.

The memories of all the fighting Khemet has faced rush over her. The duels she has fought. The battles directed. The wars waged, and campaigns won.

She staggers, overcome by the volume of all that she now remembers. The engrammatic vault from which they came now lies open to her. The temptation to delve into it, to relive the triumphs she has won, to revel in the feelings of indomitable strength, is overwhelming.

Satisfaction glows in the cryptek's oversized ocular. 'At last.'

Irritation at Kamoteph's intrusion stops her from plunging back into the ocean of memory. She steps away from him, fighting another twitching outburst that gathers in objection at her restraint.

He leans back in his chair. 'But tell me, is that all that a praetorian is? A fighter? A pugilist with little thought to honour and duty?'

'No.'

The expression of physical power is not her purpose. She can feel – she knows – that it is merely a means, a necessity of her function. She must be formidable, not merely to the enemies of the necrons but to the necrons themselves. She possesses the strength to match the power of any lord or phaeron so she can wield the authority granted to her. To permit her to execute her judgements as she sees fit.

With an emerald blast of energy, she ends the life of High Adjudicator Ferenzik.

The metal body, devoid of its torso, topples backwards to be caught by a swarm of canoptek scarabs. The swarm immediately lifts these remnants and hauls them away, a paragon of industrial efficiency. Later, the constructs will disassemble the body and repurpose its necro-dermis for the needs of those who are still functional.

They are brought before her screaming, or raving, or silent and immobile. Khemet has been at work for three days, bringing peace to the broken house of the Zathanor Dynasty. They failed to endure the rigours of the Great Sleep, and so death is the only mercy they can receive. As a praetorian, this is her most solemn duty, and Khemet bends to her task with patient diligence.

This rush is tinged with more complex emotions, and an immensity of knowledge.

Khemet is, at her centre, an executioner. The realisation does not bring shame, but pride. She is entrusted to enact the ultimate sanction against those who fail to uphold the honour of the Infinite Empire. Those who fail the many tests the galaxy presents, or succumb to the many temptations that power brings.

The honour codes of the necrontyr unfold within her. They have their own partition within her mental architecture, accorded such prime importance that their expression and interpretation are hard-coded upon her being, much the same as the techniques of swordwork and the stratagems of war. These are the tenets upon which her existence is based, that she exists to enforce.

we are the necrontyr we are not these hollow things these necrons we were a great people we were betrayed

Kamoteph is watching her. If he is aware of the occasional eruptions that emanate from her suppressed hindbrain, he makes no sign of it. Khemet, to her dismay, is growing numb to them, dismissing them as swiftly as they occur.

No, it is not that she is dismissing them, but rather that they are swept up in the tidal wave that crashes over her.

For many hours, they are both silent. The release of so much data is overwhelming. Khemet can feel her mind's engines working, striving to process and index all that she has seen and done. It is a task that will takes years, decades, even if she were to sit in perfect stillness and devote the entirety of her energies to its undertaking.

'When did you awaken, Kamoteph?' She breaks the silence without warning. This is the first idle question Khemet has asked, and she can see the wariness come over the cryptek.

'A little more than seven centuries ago,' he replies.

'Early.'

'Not as early as some.' There is resentment there, but Khemet does not care to probe it now.

'I did not sleep,' she says instead.

Kamoteph nods, but she is not speaking to him. She is barely conscious that she is speaking at all.

'I… have endured. Persisted. For millions of years. For as close to an eternity as one can name.' The pressure of so much existence piles up within her.

'How did you do it?' the cryptek asks.

Khemet stands motionless, watching Ghenenekh's twinned suns chase one another across the sky.

She has decelerated her chronosense to its minimum, speeding her perception of time to permit weeks to pass as minutes, and years as hours. Her body's other senses are still alert for intrusion, and her chronosense will crash back to normalcy should the tomb world's innumerable canoptek constructs detect the slightest anomaly. But to any outward observer, Khemet is no different to the dozens of stone statues that line the tomb's esplanade.

She has done this many times across the aeons of her immortal life. When she has explored all possible means of diversion, all the sundry ways her mind can be kept active and engaged, Khemet

*has sought refuge from the creeping passage of time by stepping
out of its path.*

*Khemet considers it a form of sleep, the closest any praetorian can
come to true respite. Not for Khemet and her peers the long, long
embrace of the tomb. No, it is their duty, their penance, to forgo
the oblivion of the Great Sleep and stand as sentinels over slumbering billions. The younger races of the galaxy will rise and fall, but
through the tireless vigilance of Khemet and her order would the
necrons awaken once more, and reclaim the stars that were theirs by
right of ancient conquest.*

*Khemet stands motionless, watching suns chase themselves across
the sky.*

Alerts suddenly wail. In pursuing the memory she has relived
it, settling into the same immobility she adopted on Ghenenekh, and at countless other times throughout the millions of
years of her existence.

She can feel Kamoteph moving, acting, directing her consciousness to push ahead, to look beyond the memory to another. Part
of her fights him, reflexively. But then she feels the shape of where
he is sending her, and Khemet reaches for it hungrily.

*She moves for the first time in seven centuries. An accumulated rind
of calcified stone shatters as her limbs flex. The grey dust of Ghenenekh is scorched to ash as the exhaust vents of her core reactor burn
with revived strength.*

*Her chronosense has returned in an instant to its baseline. Such a
sudden lurch in her perception requires even Khemet to pause, allowing her mind's processing centres to reconfigure themselves.*

*For a moment – truly just a moment, now – Khemet wonders
what has awoken her. But then her cognitive train works through its
buffer, and she understands.*

There are intruders in the south library.

Canoptek wraiths have already engaged them. The tomb vault's autonomous spirit has pulsed a warning that triggered her preset alerts, and is now feeding Khemet a stream of data across its interstitial network. In her mind's eye, she sees a ferocious battle of particle casters and razor-edged metal. Lithe bodies clad in sculpted plates of psychically sensitive armour vault and caper, dodging the snapping mandibles and blazing transdimensional beamers of the tomb's automated defenders, lashing out in turn with energised blades and arcane weaponry.

Aeldari.

This world is guarded by four other praetorians, peers in whom Khemet has a trust that can only come from millions of years of shared duty. She receives terse notifications from each of them, alerted as she has been by the vault's spirit. They stride into dimensional doorways at points scattered across the globe, and emerge an instant later from a shimmering emerald portal less than six khet *from the besieged library.*

Khemet herself sets off with a measured stride, giving her body's actuators a moment to test themselves and ensure optimal function after her idleness. From her position on the tomb's western terrace, it will be swifter for her to approach from the exterior of the complex, and tactically advantageous to engage the aeldari from the rear.

With a flourish, she recalls her rod of covenant from its pocket dimension. The stave enters reality in a burst of jade energy and settles comfortably in her waiting hand. Its bladed head is sculpted in evocation of the ankh of the Triarch, the same symbol that burns upon her metal chest and proclaims her allegiance, above all else, to her absent king.

After centuries of inactivity, the promise of a pitched battle ignites a gratifying fire in her central reactor. Periods of rest can be useful, but Khemet lives for her duty.

The gravity displacement pack that forms the upper portion of her torso flares into life, carrying Khemet up into the sky and towards her enemy.

Khemet surfaces as though from beneath an ocean's waves. Error codes still dance in her sight, and are slow to subside.

'Such weakness.'

When Khemet realises the comment is directed at her, anger burns away much of the turmoil. She looks over at him, still sitting upon the room's sole chair, as though he requires the carved stone's respite from a day's exertions. As though every stick of furnishing were not alien to him and to the necron existence.

'You dare speak to me of weakness? You, whose flaws extend to mastery of your own form?'

Kamoteph rises, and despite his stoop he seems to tower over Khemet, his presence outstripping his dimensions.

'My flaws are my own, praetorian. But I expected more from you. The labyrinth was a harsh domain, no doubt, but you are a disappointment. The Silent King's favoured servants should not be so fragile.'

With the gates thrown open, this comes easily. In a great cascade, an avalanche of renewed emotion, Khemet sees the figure whom she has served all the years of her long life.

She stands in silence, illuminated by the light of a poisonous star and the unyielding gaze of an imperious monarch.

Every praetorian in the galaxy stands beside her. They are arrayed across the decks of thousands of ark-craft in serried ranks, unconcerned by the chill of the void. They bask in the presence of their lord, but mourn the reason they have been brought together.

Szarekh, the Silent King. The deceived sovereign and conquering saviour of an empire.

He looks down from his dais, bathed in the baleful glare of their home star, the virulent orb that laid its curse in the bones of every necrontyr. At his back, suspended like jewels in the azure rays, are the vessels of his armada, the craft of the honoured millions who will accompany their king into his self-imposed exile.

The greatest jewel of all is the Song of Oblivion, *pre-eminent among the vessels sent forth by the necrontyr. It was from the throne of its majesty that the Silent King cast down the gods and shackled them to his will, slaves to those they had enslaved. Now the mighty ship will carry him into the lightless expanse beyond the galaxy's edge, an eternal penance for his failure to perceive the lies of the C'tan.*

Khemet looks up, aching in whatever facsimile of a soul the treachery of biotransference left her. The fault did not lie solely with her king. Khemet, as with all the praetorians of the Triarch, are the appointed guardians of the empire's spirit. She, as much as any other, bears the shame of accepting the star gods' honeyed words while blind to the hunger in their eyes.

Szarekh says nothing, for he is the Silent King. But Khemet needs no words, no parting oaths or gestures. That he has taken this brief moment with them, a final conclave between a master and his most devoted servants, is all the acknowledgement she requires.

His dais completes its long, slow drift across the face of their formation. Szarekh halts, fewer than a hundred khet from Khemet's ghost ark. For the briefest moment, Khemet thinks that he will break the tradition of millennia and raise a hand in farewell. Or, perhaps, he will violate the ancient taboo and speak some parting word, a last order that would sustain Khemet through the ages to come.

He does not.

With the briefest flare of light her king steps through a dimensional doorway, departing to take the helm of his palanquin for the voyage to come.

None move to follow him. For the praetorians there can be only one duty. As long as their monarch is absent from his realm, they will guard it. While the rest of the Silent King's subjects march in lockstep into their stasis vaults, they will stand as sentinels over the tomb worlds. They will defend a sleeping empire against the grasping claws of the Unclean, and chronicle all that passes in the domain the necrons have abandoned, but not relinquished.

For inherent in the purpose of the Great Sleep is the promise of awakening – that the necrons will once more bestride the galaxy. Khemet clings to the hope bound up with that promise – that the hour of their rising will also be the hour in which their all-conquering king is returned to them. When he is returned to her.

The engines that will propel the master of an empire into exile blaze into life, their brilliance fit to eclipse the cancerous sun. Slowly, but with growing speed, the fleet turn their prows to the emptiness and depart.

Khemet watches until the last glimmers are swallowed by the darkness of the void.

'Remarkable.'

The word escapes Kamoteph, and Khemet crashes back to the now.

The cryptek has seen all that she recalls. Intruded upon a moment of the gravest sanctity, and after his scorn and mockery. None outside the praetorian's order were present to witness the Silent King's departure, and now that most solemn memory has been tainted.

Kamoteph backs away, staff gripped suddenly tight, as if that could ward off her rage.

Khemet has no weapon to level, and so can only express her fury as a fist raised and poised to strike.

'Withdraw your creatures from my head, and end your voyeurism of my thoughts.'

Kamoteph backs away awkwardly, his canoptek pets scuttling from beneath his feet. 'You still need my aid.'

'Then you will give it without prising open my brain.'

The cryptek nods, dropping his long chin in submission.

The faintest sensation, like a stream of sand, trickles down the nape of her skull and along her arm. A knot of grey, no larger than a fingernail, forms on the back of her clenched fist. Kamoteph extends a hand and sweeps it over Khemet's, and the nanoscarabs are gone.

There is no matching sensation for Kamoteph's retreat from her thoughts, but when she runs a diagnostic she finds her interstitial nodes untouched by outside influence.

'Now get out.' Khemet points towards the far wall.

She has learnt enough of Kamoteph in the few days she has been free to know that it is not in him to endure her dismissal without comment, so she is unsurprised when he pauses at the threshold.

'Your progress pleases me, praetorian. You may yet serve your purpose.'

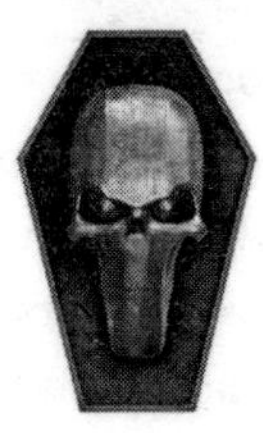

CHAPTER 4

'Why have you freed me?'

This is the question Khemet asks each time Kamoteph comes to her.

Khemet has been given the freedom to roam the *Senusret* by Hekasun, though she has yet to encounter him or be invited to his presence. She has not sought out that audience, though she knows she should.

After the first flush of pleasure in her returning sense of self, her recovery has stalled. So much of her cognitive processing is taken up with the effort of containing all she now recollects, Khemet finds herself slow-witted. Worse, she is distracted, robbed of the purity of focus her cursed metal existence should bring.

The reason is not complicated. Her time in the labyrinth was spent drifting between her memories, retaining what little sanity she had left by reliving all that she has said and done in the course of her age-long existence. That path into her engrammatic vaults is well-worn, and too easy to slip into. It is not merely a temptation, but a compulsion, to escape the constant trials of the now by disappearing into the triumphs and tragedies of the then.

But to give in to such compulsion is an intolerable weakness. Thus, Khemet has taken to roaming the ship in search of other stimuli.

She has quickly exhausted the novelties it can offer. She has walked its dark halls, and stood among its crypts. She finds a measure of peace by looking through viewports at the passing starlight. She has observed the chained fragment of a star god whose immense power is siphoned to drive the *Senusret* through the void, but she finds little interest or satisfaction in its torment.

Kamoteph seeks her out in these places, or in her quarters. Though he has become more cautious in his handling of her, the cryptek continues to urge her always to confront her fear and reach into her memories, in spite of the risk she feels lurking among them. He is fixated upon restoring her, awakening the parts of Khemet that still remain out of reach. While she is just as eager to be free of the unbearable weakness that plagues her, his interest plainly goes beyond altruism.

'Why did you free me?' she asks. He has found her in one of the practice halls near the rear of the *Senusret*, one of many such spaces whose function was rendered unnecessary by the C'tan's treachery. No necron, regardless of their station, has any need to practice the forms of war. Khemet had been using the empty space to test her capacity for stillness, but the cryptek's arrival sets her to pacing about the hall.

'We were bade to release you by the overlord,' Kamoteph replies.

'Which overlord?'

'Do you not recall?'

The urge to lash out boils up, and Khemet forces it back down. 'I have cautioned you before, cryptek, to be wary of mocking me.'

He inclines his head. Khemet has learnt that a pretence of sub-mission is Kamoteph's habitual response to reproach. 'Speak to me,' he says, 'of Lord Anrakyr.'

He is called the Traveller.

The ceaseless crusader, the phaeron so driven by a vision of necron supremacy that he gave up his claim to his own crownworld so that he might raise an empire from its torpor.

The wandering vagrant, who plunders the strength of the worlds he stirs from the Great Sleep before their time.

'He is an overlord,' she replies, after the momentary shock of successful recall subsides.

'Not merely *an* overlord,' corrects Kamoteph. '*Our* lord, to whose service we are pledged.'

'I serve only the Silent King and the Triarch.' The words are automatic, not heartfelt as they should be. But Khemet has no heart, and while the bonds of fealty are hard-coded in her, they are unmoored from the experience of time and deed.

'That,' says Kamoteph carefully, 'is not entirely true.'

This time, he is prepared for the violence of her reaction. As Khemet strides towards him, hands clenching in the absence of a weapon, Kamoteph retreats into the swarm of canoptek constructs that have accompanied him. They do not attack her but they foul her steps, requiring that she either stamp them into shrapnel or halt her approach.

'I bid you think,' he says quickly. 'I do not question your devotion to our king, from whom all light and power flows.' The cryptek touches the ankh of the Triarch emblazoned in his chestplate. The same glyph marks the necrodermis of every necron in existence, placed there at the moment of biotransfer-ence to mark them all as subjects of their king.

'But you were alone for so much of the Great Sleep. Millions of years, a lone sentinel against the Unclean.'

In spite of all that he has done for her, Khemet resents Kamoteph's intrusion into her thoughts. He has seen all that she has remembered, every war and judgement and condemnation. Khemet has never shared that kind of intimacy with anyone, not even her fellow praetorians, with whom – despite what Kamoteph says – she shared the long years of the Sleep.

'It is only to be expected that as your isolation ended, as the dynasties awoke, you sought out… direction.'

She remembers. She is ashamed, but she remembers. For so long, Khemet's duty was her own, to enact as she saw fit. She stood watch over silent tombs, battled the ravening encroachments of the Unclean, without any guiding hand.

And then she found the Traveller.

Khemet has heard of him long before his fleet enters the blighted skies above Menouthis. In recent centuries Khemet has been constantly at work, racing between the stars to shepherd the early awakenings of isolated tomb vaults, near-forgotten fringeworlds, and gilded crownworlds. For many thousands of necron nobles, Khemet's faceplate has been the first they have seen in sixty million years.

In the course of her fleeting passage she has encountered the signs of the Traveller's passage. Tomb worlds that had been overrun by the Unclean for millennia, now scourged of life for their sins. Newly risen coreworlds, their overlords in a state of outrage that they had been roused only to have whole flotillas and legions claimed as a tithe by the one who had woken them. Others of her order who have been drawn into his orbit, who serve as outriders of his coming and custodians of the noble courts he stirs from their age-long rest.

Khemet's scythecraft detects the coming of its greater brethren as they enter the solar system, giving her time to rise from the depths of Menouthis' vaults to greet him. The Traveller's fleet now drifts in orbit, a hundred pinpricks of light even with her oculars tuned to their maximum magnification.

She stands at the tomb's great gate, staring up into the ink-black night. It is sheer happenstance that her presence coincides with his coming, but it is a fortuitous conjunction. Her curiosity has been piqued by rumour, and this way he has brought himself to her, rather than requiring Khemet to seek him out.

She is not kept waiting. A new speck appears in the firmament and grows quickly into the familiar stooping crescent of a Night Scythe. The scout craft is chased by a fiery tail as it drops through the atmosphere, joined seconds later by a long, bellowing roar of displaced air. Its descent is fast and steep until it is only a dozen khet from the sea of sand, and then it pulls up in a lazy glimmering arc that brazenly defies gravity's grip.

The scythecraft comes to rest before her, unleashing a brief hurricane of gritty particles that batter at Khemet's immobile form. The craft is a study in restrained decadence, the swept wings chased with metagold to pick out the glyphs of its master. Its godsteel hull sighs as it shrugs away the heat of atmospheric entry, vitrifying the sand to glass beneath its bulk.

A blaze of light and energy makes Khemet's oculars dim, as the wormhole in the Night Scythe's hull forms a bridge between its orbiting flagship and the desert floor. From the jade beam comes the familiar sound of metal feet marching in lockstep on hard-packed sand.

At the head of a phalanx of warriors strides their overlord, a vision of necron majesty. For all their duplicity, the C'tan had honoured the caste structure of the necrontyr when they fashioned their cages of living metal, giving the grandest and most powerful forms to the phaerons and their heirs.

The overlord towers over Khemet, his body literally built to a grander scale than even that of the Silent King's most favoured servants. His breadth and stature are emphasised by the crest that rises transverse from his head, a crown that Khemet might consider disloyal if it were anything more than a simple bronze crescent. Her concerns are allayed by the ankh of the Triarch, the brand of allegiance that unites the grandest warlord with the lowest warrior, proudly emblazoned at the centre of his chestplate, alight with the same cerulean glow that is barely contained within his thoracic cage. A skirt of heavy bronze plates sweeps the sand at his feet, and a warscythe's butt hisses through the black grains as he approaches her.

'Well met, praetorian,' says Anrakyr, called the Traveller by admiring allies and embittered foes alike.

Khemet lifts her rod of covenant in both hands, holding her badge of office before her. She does not bow; a praetorian bows only to the Triarch.

'Hail, lord. I am Khemet. Welcome to Menouthis.'

He acknowledges her with a single arm pressed against his chest-plate, observing the rite of greeting with microscopic accuracy.

An honour guard of two-score Immortals follow in the overlord's wake, their double-barrelled gauss blasters held in tireless arms. Khemet considers the immaculate warriors. Anrakyr has brought too few to pose a threat to the massed legions of the tomb world, but suf-ficient to demonstrate the calibre of the legions he could call upon. A well-judged bodyguard for a first meeting with an unknown dynasty.

Khemet, for her part, stands alone before the gates of Menouthis. The glyph upon her chestplate and crowning her staff are all the defence she requires, even from a phaeron.

Anrakyr inclines his head quizzically. 'I had expected to be received by a delegation of the nomarch, or another of the Zathanor Dynasty. Not, of course, that the presence of one of the Triarch's honoured emis-saries is ever a disappointment.' He possesses a kingly voice, strong and mellifluous, well suited for the giving of compliments and the issuing of commands.

'Nomarch Benekhir did not awaken, lord. She and her court have succumbed to engrammatic decay.' Khemet is blunt; there is little point attempting to conceal the broken state of the tomb world's rulers.

The Traveller is sanguine, though he pauses for a moment to give Khemet's words their due gravity. 'The entire court?'

Khemet nods. 'The flaws in their stasis coffins are significant and extensive, very likely embedded at their point of construction. There is no hope of recovery.' She hesitates. 'All those who have awoken thus far have required the rite of silence.'

Indeed, that is the duty from which the Traveller's arrival has summoned her. Under the watchful oculars of the Zathanor's crypteks, and restrained by the same lychguard who had been their guardians sixty million years before, the insane lords of the Zathanor have been put to death by blasts from Khemet's rod of covenant. Isolated by Khemet from the tomb world's reanimation protocols, it is a true death, though not as quick as Khemet would prefer.

Her hesitation does not arise from distaste. The euthanasia of necron nobility whose sanity has not endured the Great Sleep is the most solemn duty of the praetorians, and Khemet is not daunted by the act. She is, however, curious how the overlord will react to the execution of his noble peers.

'The Zathanor were ever paupers.' Anrakyr's tone is forgiving, not contemptuous. 'What of their warriors?'

Khemet can hear the hunger in his voice. 'Initial reports from the crypteks suggest that the failure rate for the commoners' vaults will be within expected norms.'

The necron body is ill-equipped to express emotions without words, but nevertheless the overlord's relief is palpable. He leans back slightly, planting the butt of his warscythe firmly in the sand, evidently considering how best to continue. Khemet does not interrupt him; there is a form to what they both know will play out next.

'It was my understanding,' the Traveller begins, 'that Menouthis is the last bastion of the Zathanor.'

'Indeed. Their crownworld was lost to stellar detonation seven million years ago.' Khemet knows this for a fact; she witnessed the moment the Zharetkh star became a supernova. 'They had few other holdings. Those that I am aware of have been lost or overrun by the Unclean.'

'And with your culling of its last members, would you agree that the house has run its course?'

Khemet cannot smile, but even if she could she would not. In spite of the necessary pantomime both she and Anrakyr are playing out, it is no trivial act to pronounce the death of a dynasty.

'I would.'

The Traveller, for his part, does not outwardly revel in his unexpected and bloodless triumph. 'What, then, will become of their thralls?'

With his stately voice, Khemet can almost believe that he is expressing true concern.

'In the absence of any extant leadership, and without the prospect of one emerging, I have dissolved the dynastic claim upon Menouthis.' Khemet makes Anrakyr wait, examining his demeanour. But the overlord is patience itself.

'I render this world to your care, lord,' she says finally.

With a thought, she transmits the command protocols for the entire tomb world to the Traveller, which she had claimed by Triarchal fiat upon her discovery of the court's corruption. The act, at a stroke, gifts Anrakyr dominion over all but the most independent minds within its vaults.

This is no small thing. She has erased an ancient, if minor, house of necron nobility, and granted all that is left of its holdings to the Traveller. Menouthis, for all its impoverished status, holds tens of millions of necron warriors in its depths, to say nothing of its precious seraptek constructs, war machines and voidfaring vessels. No matter how large his legions, this will no doubt swell the overlord's ranks to new heights.

And all of it sanctioned by a praetorian of the Triarch, whose judgement can be overturned only by the will of the Silent King.

'I accept this honour and burden.' Satisfaction burns in the azure outgassing of Anrakyr's central reactor. He turns, and with a curt gesture dismisses the Night Scythe still hovering at his back. The doors and portals of Menouthis are now open to him; he has no need of the scythecraft's wormhole to return to his fleet.

Khemet doubts he will linger, beyond ensuring that the resurrection of his new cohorts has been set in motion. The Traveller, if all she has heard is true, is a crusader, not content to sit idly in lordship of any single world. Menouthis will likely be turned over to one of his favoured allies to govern, to ensure the steady supply of awoken troops for his campaigns.

'In which case,' he says, 'I believe I will review the disposition of the vaults, and ensure the crypteks are equal to their task.' At an interstitial command, the Traveller's Immortals begin their march once more, their formation splitting smoothly to pass around their master and Khemet.

'As you will, lord.' Khemet takes a single step back, ceremonially opening the way for Menouthis' new overlord.

'And what will you do?' he asks.

This time, Khemet does regret her inability to smile. 'I will accompany you, lord.'

'By all means.' There is genial warmth in his voice. He sets off after his Immortals, and Khemet falls into his wake. As they pass beneath the great lintel stone that marks the entrance of the tomb, Anrakyr turns slightly to address her.

'I believe this may be the beginning of a prosperous relationship, Praetorian Khemet.'

Kamoteph is watching her, though denied his prying window into her mind. She is glad of this; she is not proud of the Zathanor's dissolution.

She recalls her conviction in the moment, the necessity of their destruction. But now, with distance from the act, she is ashamed by the transactional manner in which she entered into the Traveller's service. The ending of a dynasty is a solemn deed, and Khemet traded their holdings to Anrakyr without hesitation to prove her value to his enterprise.

She serves.

Khemet is a part of the Traveller's court, attaching herself as others have done to his crusading host. She is Anrakyr's outrider, a harbinger of his approach. She smooths the way for his entreaties with nomarchs and lords. She is warden of the worlds that are swept clean of the intruder races, and shepherd to the nobles who rise from their caskets. At times she is his nemesor, commanding armies in his name.

She becomes his most trusted proxy, and she is content. The Traveller's quest aligns with her praetorian's duty, and she finds much to respect in the overlord. He is the consummate phaeron, adept in matters of both war and state. The codes of honour that bind the strata of necron society are enforced within his court firmly yet fairly, and often by Khemet's own hand. After millions of years of wandering, of isolated acts of service to an abstract ideal, to have her course set by the will of one whom she trusts is to shed an immense burden.

For a time, she is content. But then her duty takes her to the crownworld of Lazar.

'What is it?' He sees her stutter, even going so far as to stretch out a hand in aid.

'None of your affair.' She will not share this with him. She can feel the memories lining up, the engrams queuing in her buffer to be replayed, experienced afresh. She can feel them, and she knows that the shame that is to come is inescapable, because it has already struck.

* * *

The enemy charge again.

From atop her Stalker Khemet observes their advance, their lumbering movements captured by the war machine's scrying tines and fed directly into her mind.

She sees their advance and blunts it. Gauss beams lance from unmasked batteries, peeling away atoms of armour and flesh layer by layer. Canoptek wraiths melt from shrouded bastions, seeming to rise out of the ground itself. Khemet adds the weight of her own weapons, raking the Stalker's particle shredder across the face of the warriors' formation. A stream of antimatter meets matter, and the humans are enveloped by elemental fire.

But for each clutch of armoured figures who meet their doom, more press in from the flanks.

They wear a riot of conflicting heraldry. Khemet has identified five distinct factions, their gaudy armour bearing icons of rampant beasts, stooping avians, and a profusion of human heads bleached of flesh. The most numerous call themselves the Silver Skulls, and the light of gauss volleys ripples across their burnished armour.

The Adeptus Astartes, as she has learnt they are named, are the finest warriors the race of humans can produce. They are exemplars of that upstart empire's strengths and flaws. Brutish creatures, dogmatic and proud. Tactically proficient, though after ten thousand years of incidental engagements Khemet knows the vast majority of their sects to be hidebound and limited in their doctrine.

Sadly, that doctrine is often bluntly effective.

The Stalker takes two small steps, shifting its weight as the ground roils beneath its slender limbs. The humans are bombarding the crownworld from orbit, unleashing crude munitions of enormous weight that bore and burst through ancient rock. Interstitial reports have already told Khemet what she feared – the bombardment is breaking through to the tomb vaults beneath the earth, annihilating tens of thousands of warriors before they can be summoned from their crypts. Worse, their destruction extends through the vaults and down into the world's crust, triggering tectonic instability that will destroy more than the Adeptus Astartes themselves ever could.

Khemet does not know what summoned the humans to the Lazar crownworld, but she has wasted a significant proportion of her cognitive capacity cursing the accident of their arrival. The crownworld had awoken only eight years prior, the latest dynastic holding to receive the Traveller and his fleet. Its stasis vaults are replete with millions of warriors, to say nothing of the hoards of treasure, artefacts, and antiquities of the bygone age of the necrontyr. Khemet had been left to oversee its animation, another bastion of the resurgent necron empire.

Or so it was meant to be. With fifty more years of work by the crypteks Khemet could have met the humans' champions with a world's worth of warriors, and sent them mewling back to their polluted crownworld and its crippled king. But with so little of Lazar's strength awoken, Khemet could not contest the landing of their troops, nor the bombardment of the planet's surface.

This, Khemet knows, is a battle she will lose.

But while the first clash will belong to the Silver Skulls and their allies, the war's outcome will be a different matter. Khemet commands a rearguard action, buying time for all that can be saved to be spared from destruction. Beneath her feet, the crypteks are bypassing all safety protocols to force warriors from their sleep. Capable of following only the simplest of instructions, they are marching in endless ranks into portals spread across the besieged world. These portals carry them in an instant to the crownworld's brethren, the moons and minor planets that circle the Lazar star.

Even now, the humans' vessels will be registering the surges of power erupting from the dozen planetoids of the stellar system. Khemet allows herself a brief moment to imagine their horror at the readings of their scrying screens, and the dawning knowledge of the wrath they have awoken.

Not that she can take any satisfaction from what is yet to come.

Though she will save what she can, the loss of the crownworld is a grievous blow.

For now, all she can do is punish these augmented humans who have been arrogant enough to assault the necron empire. Khemet grips the Stalker's controls, and unleashes a blaze of arcane anger.

The shame of defeat is a tangible thing, a knot of recursive code that Khemet cannot purge. But the worst, she can sense, lies ahead. She must follow where this leads.

'Well met, praetorian.'

The Traveller sits upon his throne. Tapered digits grip the godsteel arms. Sapphire oculars do not waver from Khemet's faceplate. His great warscythe stands beside the throne near at hand, held erect by subtle magics.

'Khemet. I had not expected to return so soon to the Lazar worlds.'

The Traveller's court looks on. In the course of Anrakyr's crusade he has taken more than just warriors in tribute. Lords and nobles drawn from dozens of tomb worlds now accompany the Traveller, some as admirals, generals and advisors, others merely hoping to achieve such status. They range, in Khemet's estimation, from the truly capable to the entirely useless, fit only to be hostages against the good manners of their more able dynastic brethren.

The court stands in clusters on the periphery of the chamber, lurking in the shadows of noctilith columns. A few whisper jibes and slander to their neighbours, their vocal emitters pitched at a volume that she can just perceive. They are the bold and the foolish, the ones willing to risk her retribution in the future. Many more, she knows, will be exchanging snide remarks across their interstitial networks, outside her awareness.

The Traveller does not appear to heed their murmurs. He sits, rigid as only a necron can be, oculars fastened on Khemet.

'But the worlds seem changed since last I passed this way. Depleted, somehow.'

She does not object to his sarcasm, ill-deserved though it is. Khemet knows that she has done all that could reasonably be expected with the force at her command. She has spared much from the wrath of a potent enemy, and bled that enemy through two years of attrition that the human empire could ill afford. The Traveller's judgement is unfair, unjustified, ignorant of all that she has achieved in service of his ambitions.

But she does not beg for forgiveness, or plead that hers was an impossible task. Stained as she is by failure, before this lord of hosts and before this assemblage of her race's nobility, Khemet will endure her chastisement.

Few of the gathered lords and viziers would show such stoicism, such is the distance between her people's highest aspirations and their conduct. But Khemet's role is to be the paragon, to uphold their empire's codes of honour in both word and deed.

'I placed a crownworld in your care, Khemet. The centrepiece of a dynasty. And look what you have allowed to pass.'

The Traveller rises from his throne, a vision of necron majesty. The bronze crest that rises from his crown shimmers in the torchlight. The azure furnace of his central reactor blazes, in contrast to the emerald-green glow that burns within Khemet's own thoracic cavity.

'I had such trust in you.' He takes a slow pace towards her, and another. Each footfall strikes the deck with the chime of an abyssal bell. 'But I see that this is my error. All that we have achieved together. All that you have done for me. It blinded me to the simplest of facts.'

He comes to a halt a single step from Khemet, forcing her to tilt her head back to meet his gaze.

'You, my most loyal praetorian, who wears the weight of your years so heavily.'

There is no forgiveness in his tone, no compassion. But neither is there mockery. His manner is that of a forbidding patriarch disappointed in a wayward child.

'You have laboured for so long. It is only to be expected that you would one day falter.'

This, finally, is too much. The pride of a praetorian can only bear so many insults.

Before she can speak, the Traveller raises his steepled fingers to his faceplate, a picture of imperious contemplation.

'Yes. You should rest.'

Khemet does not see the threat before it is too late. So certain is she of her position, so inviolate is her rank and role amid the overlord's court, that she fails to recognise the danger in Anrakyr's movements. Her familiarity with his proximity blinds her to his intent.

The Traveller extends one hand. His warscythe leaps from its place beside his throne to slap into his open palm. Its jade edge describes a glimmering arc as Anrakyr brings it round and up, cutting towards Khemet's chestplate.

As the warscythe ascends, light flashing from its edge, Khemet's chronosense awakens in a violent lurch. The overlord's movement slows to a crawl, his rising blade less than a cubit from her body.

Through the shock of betrayal, she sees that the strike is not directed at her head or central reactor. Anrakyr does not aim to kill her, but disarm her. Outrage is layered upon the shock that still grips her.

She can do nothing as the blade carves through the necrodermis and reinforcing spars of her forearm. The limb falls away, Khemet's rod of covenant still clutched in its grip.

A familiar blaze of light floods the chamber, reflecting from the leering faceplates of the Traveller's court. Khemet does not need to turn to know that a tesseract labyrinth has opened behind her, a portal to a nether dimension of its master's choosing. Banishment to these prison-realms has been the Traveller's favoured punishment for centuries; Khemet herself has hurled many unfortunates into their *lightless depths. In the dilated seconds before she meets the same fate, the irony is not lost on her.*

Anrakyr lashes out with a silver foot, and a monumental impact crashes into her chest. Her thoracic cage buckles, setting off countless alarms that demand but fail to claim her attention.

As she staggers back, lifted from her feet by the force of the blow, Khemet cannot look away from her rod of covenant. The dilation of her chronosense makes it seem to hang in mid-air. The pain-signal of her severed hand has not yet reached her, but Khemet's outrage at the loss of her icon of office is instantaneous.

In the final moments before she is consumed by the labyrinth's glare, Khemet locks her oculars on those of the Traveller.

And then there is nothing.

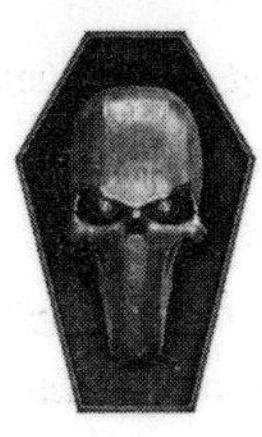

CHAPTER 5

Khemet's hand is re-forming.

Now she knows the cause of its loss, whatever mental or mechanical block that had prevented its restoration has fallen away. In deference to her restored calm, Khemet has secured the use of a maintenance scarab, rather than stealing the necrodermis from the body of a fellow necron. The construct has clamped itself to her forearm and is steadily extruding a string of living metal from between its mandibles to knit with Khemet's body. Her morphic field readily accepts the material and shifts it to where it is needed – in a few days, Khemet will be whole again.

Or, at least, her body will be restored.

She has been left undisturbed for several shipboard cycles. Kamoteph has, mercifully, been detained with other duties, leaving her to process all that she now recalls of her imprisonment, and the events that led to it. Though her thoughts are turned inwards, Khemet has returned to her idling, undirected roaming of the *Senusret*. She still abhors any form of stillness.

In the days since her release Khemet has been plagued by a cold, abstract kind of anger. She had believed that her fury arose from the shame of her debilitated condition, a manifestation of her frustration and corrupted neural pathways. And while that undoubtedly is the case, now that Khemet has access to her most recent memories and can recall at will the betrayal that cast her into the labyrinth, she has a far more potent and justified cause for her rage.

The injustice of Anrakyr's actions is a hot coal in her core. She is a praetorian, an agent of the Silent King. No one, not even a phaeron, may elevate himself above the servants of the Triarch. The Traveller violated the gravest laws of the necrontyr when he placed himself in judgement over her. What is more, he has compounded his crime by robbing Khemet of her rod of covenant, her staff of office that marks her as a praetorian of the Triarch.

In her isolation, Khemet has found a new kind of solace from the persistent flaws and failures of her cognition – imagining the forms her vengeance will take when she next meets the Traveller.

'*Khemet. Your presence is desired by Lord Hekasun.*'

The interstitial message arrives fully formed, as though Kamoteph walks beside her.

'I told you to leave my mind, cryptek.' She snarls the words, grateful for a target against which to turn her attention.

'*I assure you, praetorian, I have made no unsolicited entrance to your thoughts. The interstices are merely the simplest means of contacting you while continuing with my work.*'

Khemet chooses to hold on to her anger in the face of Kamoteph's conciliation.

'Does Lord Hekasun give any consideration to my desires?' This, she knows, is simply contrarian pique. She has been planning to force an audience with the commander of the *Senusret* for several days, the first step on her imagined path that will lead her to Anrakyr.

Khemet has not paused in her wandering at Kamoteph's contact. As she turns a corner, stone giving way to more stone, she finds her way blocked. Mandulis stands across the passageway's width. Much like their first encounter he is armed, and says nothing.

'*I am afraid not,*' says Kamoteph into her mind.

That Hekasun chooses to insult her by dispatching his vargard to usher her to him is telling of what is to come, though she takes some pleasure in recalling Mandulis' destruction at her hands. A warden who has been defeated by his ward is not a potent form of intimidation.

'Very well,' she says aloud.

Mandulis turns on his heel and sets off. He does not wait for Khemet, but after a moment's petulant hesitation she follows.

She waits for anything further from Kamoteph, but he is silent. She is glad; despite his protestations to the contrary, she does not trust that the cryptek will honour his promise to leave her thoughts alone.

As she walks, the digits of her intact hand begin to drum against the metal of her thigh, a manifestation of her trepidation at returning to the company of other necrons. It is only for a moment, her fingers producing a handful of dull notes that barely go beyond her. But it is enough for Mandulis to notice; Khemet sees the vargard tilt his head slightly towards the sound.

'You are Lord Hekasun's vargard,' she says, as cover for her dismay at showing her impairment to another. 'Were you always in his service?'

He does not answer.

'How many times have you been destroyed?' she tries instead.

He does not answer.

'Do you even know?'

He halts abruptly, turning so that his copper oculars can fix upon Khemet's.

When the C'tan crafted the slave-bodies for their deceived servants, they made their faces cruel. Heavy brows sit above deep sockets, lit by bitter oculars that stare out of the darkness. The sharp planes of their faces draw down into sneering, lipless mouths. The necron visage is cold, callous, spiteful.

Mandulis' face is all this and more. His necrodermis is flawless, but there is an unmistakable air of time-worn malice in his stare. This is a warrior who has endured much, and who remembers every slight and scorn.

The vargard, his point made, resumes his marching pace. Khemet nods to herself, struck by a surprising pang of regret for her mockery. Reanimation is the greatest gift that biotransference bestowed, but it is not faultless. Every body-death, every mind's pass through the reanimation circuitry of tomb worlds and ships degrades that mind further. Serfs and nobles alike are slowly worn away, a little less of themselves restored to their newly crafted bodies.

Mandulis, she suspects, is evidence of this. His silence is not a choice. His brain and body have been rebuilt so many times, with flaw compounding upon flaw, he has lost the ability to speak.

The vargard leads her into a part of the ship she has yet to explore, further forward within the ship's narrow superstructure. The *Senusret* is a Dirge-class warship, a slight and swift grade of vessel most often found escorting its greater brethren. Now, however, it sails alone.

Khemet has been aboard many such ships, and would have had no difficulty finding her way to its command deck unescorted. That familiarity is her undoing. As she turns a corner her perceptual centres fail. With a lurch akin to vertigo a wave of memory crashes over her, laying every time she has walked through a hallway such as this upon her senses one atop the other, until the signals of her inputs are all but swamped and she cannot tell where memory ends and the now begins.

She looks around at the pattern of marbling within the stone. The glyphs carved within their columns. They are all alike, all the hundreds of times she has stood in this spot. Her vision blurs, unable to distinguish between what she is seeing and what she has seen.

Khemet stumbles, her equilibrium lost. As she staggers, the tip of her foot strikes the wall, leaving a short, shallow scar across its smooth surface.

In an instant the vertigo passes. The violence of its departure leaves her even further off balance, until she realises how she had broken the spell.

The scratch she made in the wall is new. This is the only version of this corridor that is marked this way. She has changed it. She has acted upon the world, rather than reliving what she has already done. This is the dividing line that she needs, the means of fixing her broken perceptions in the moment.

Khemet stares at the faint scuff as the last of the overlapping memories recede to their vaults. It is only then, when she feels she is back on firm ground, that she glances up.

Mandulis has not paused in his stolid, inexorable march, and is a dozen paces ahead of her. If he noticed her stumble, he gives no sign of it.

She sets off once again, now barely seeing the corridor and the shades of darkness in the noctilith, all her attention turned inwards. After several paces she reaches out and lets her hand brush along the cold, unyielding surface at intervals. Occasionally she digs the tips of her fingers in, faintly scarring the stone, marking the world. Feeding her mind a pulse of fresh sensation to keep her chained to the now.

The corridor opens abruptly into a squared archway, a pair of warriors flanking the entrance. They stand at either side with spears bared and crossed to block her path. At Mandulis' approach they sharply withdraw their blades, adhering to the protocols of authority without thought.

The command deck of a necron vessel is a multi-tiered affair. Crew stations project from the blackstone walls, and are sunk into geometric depressions. Each station is an arrangement of sharp-edged consoles, illuminated by the unhealthy jade glow of information passing across their faces. In ages past, each cluster of consoles would have been attended by a collection of serfs, honoured far above the standing of their birth to serve aboard a voidship.

At the rear of the deck is a throne, raised by a series of stepped platforms to place the vessel's commander far above their thralls. The arrangement of the deck's levels, which to an uneducated eye seems random, is in fact a mathematically perfect disposition to ensure the occupier of the ship's throne has an uninterrupted view of each serf and their station.

Of course, such architectural considerations had been rendered unnecessary by biotransference. A necron lord receives thousands of sendings per second from every part of their ship's systems. They can cast their consciousness directly into the head of any warrior to see what they see and take charge of their limbs. Visual surveillance of a crew slaved to a commander's will is an anachronism.

Yet it does not stop some from adhering to the old ways. As Khemet enters she observes a cohort of lychguard making their slow rounds along the walkways between the crews, oculars sweeping over vacant serfs. The warriors are largely idle, staring with blank incomprehension at controls that do not require them. The only real activity is undertaken by a few apprenteks scattered amongst the serfs, slender creatures marked out by their bracelets and necklaces of attainment tiles.

Khemet's arrival goes unnoticed, or at least unremarked, by both the crew and the few knots of nobles that litter the deck. There are a dozen necrons of various ranks clustered at the foot of the throne's pyramid. The vents of their central reactors glow in shades of jade, copper, sapphire and amaranth. They, like the lychguard, clearly have no role in the function of the *Senusret*, serving merely to clutter the deck.

It is clear which of the nobles is in command. He sits atop the throne, occasionally deigning to give his attention when a group of sycophants request it. This is a familiar scene for Khemet. Few necron lords, whatever their true rank and standing, would be without a train of subordinates to reinforce their status, and Hekasun is evidently no exception.

She watches Hekasun, as Mandulis abandons her and drifts loyally to his master's side. Kamoteph has told her that he was present for her release from the labyrinth, but Khemet does not recall him. He is a broad figure, as powerful and well sculpted as any of the necrontyr nobility beneath him. A pair of sickle-bladed swords hang on either side of his stone seat, close at hand, but that means little. Every noble, regardless of their rank and function, carries the skill and knowledge of necrontyr warcraft in their minds.

Khemet has hovered on the periphery for too long – her hesitation will be noticed if she lingers any longer.

As Khemet enters their midst, the press of figures parts as though she carries a contagion. She halts at the foot of the throne's ziggurat. She suddenly feels the absence of her rod of covenant. So many times has she stood as she now stands, at the centre of a hostile court and beneath the gaze of an arrogant lordling, but bearing the sigil to which all must heed.

'You asked for me,' she says after a long pause. All audible conversation has paused at her approach.

Hekasun stares down at her. 'I did not ask for you,' he replies. 'I summoned you.'

After so many days of Kamoteph's blandishments and cajoling, Hekasun's honest aggression is surprisingly refreshing.

'It pleases me to see you restored, praetorian. On our last meeting you were in a far more… inchoate state.'

'For what purpose was I summoned?' she asks. She will not indulge his petty impulse to perform for his cronies.

Hekasun's gaze sharpens. 'Kamoteph. I think you explain it best.'

The cryptek shuffles forwards. He has been standing silently at the base of the throne's pyramid, proximate to but clearly separate from the fawning nobles. He plants himself before Khemet, leaning heavily on his staff, and waits until she shifts her attention from his lord to the cryptek. If he regrets his role in Hekasun's pageantry, he gives no sign of it.

'Praetorian Khemet,' he begins, in a sonorous tone. 'By the judgement of Overlord Anrakyr, to whom this court is pledged, you are *duatekh*. Condemned. Your existence is forfeit.'

Evidently Kamoteph has been commanded to demean her before Hekasun's cadre of lesser lords. Khemet's extant hand clenches into a fist.

'But our overlord is merciful. He would see you serve once more.'

Again, the Traveller sets himself above Khemet. Above even the Silent King. Khemet's thoughts of retribution stir, awakening her combat protocols. The flames of her core-flux shift in response, burning hotter and harder.

'You have been released into the custody of my lord Hekasun,' Kamoteph continues. 'He holds your leash. If you perform as you are required, my lord is empowered to consider you redeemed. If he judges otherwise, you will return to the labyrinth.'

She can feel her self-control slipping. No force in the universe would compel Khemet to return to that prison, and the mere threat of it is enough to send sparks racing along her neural net.

It takes all of her restraint to remain still. 'What would you have me do?'

Hekasun rises from his throne, an image of imperious command.

'You lost the Traveller a world, praetorian. Now, you will win him one.'

Realisation dawns like a shattering crystal, each shard knife-edged with perfect clarity. This is the answer to her question to Kamoteph, to why she has been freed from the labyrinth.

As a praetorian, Khemet is empowered to override the command precepts of a tomb world. She has done it before. She gifted the world of Menouthis to the Traveller, and there have been others, those isolated and forgotten worlds that Anrakyr's host came upon in their tireless campaign. Entire stellar systems, like the Lazar crownworld, have awoken from the Great Sleep to find that they serve an entirely different master, their dynastic lords displaced and their loyalties remapped to the Traveller and his generals.

'Do you understand the task you are charged to perform, duatekh?' Hekasun demands from his dais.

Khemet understands that she has been freed merely to serve as a tool of theft, with as little honour or nobility of purpose.

'I do.'

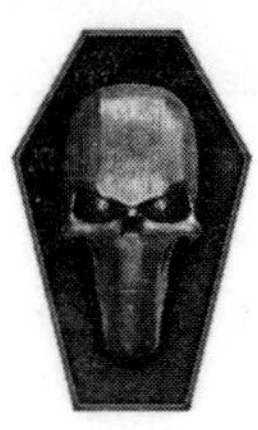

CHAPTER 6

Her humbling delivered, Hekasun returns to conversation with his court, beckoning several up the steps of his throne so they can praise his commanding display. Kamoteph gives Khemet the briefest of bows, a fractional dip of his head, before retiring to his place in the shadows.

For a time she observes, feeling the pulse and rhythm of the deck. The lychguard pace, alert for hints of disobedience that are impossible for the vacant warriors they oversee. Kamoteph's mentees work, though in truth there is little a crew is required to do aboard a necron craft.

Khemet goes purposefully ignored. This in itself is not unfamiliar; few would purposefully attract the attention of a praetorian, and so she is used to a degree of studious inattention.

There is so much that she does not yet know. The Traveller has tasked Hekasun to wake a slumbering world, but she does not know which world, or from which dynasty they will be stealing. When questioned, the *Senusret*'s autonomous spirit is unhelpful – the ship is indeed decelerating, but it will not share its destination with her.

Their objective is not the only mystery. During her idleness she examines the medley of necron nobility Hekasun has chosen to accompany him on this mission, and she is left even more confused.

It was not simply the great dynasts who formed the aristocracy of the necrontyr. Nobility was a station to which one was born, not a rank awarded through distinguished service or merit. How the scions of the dynasties employed themselves had varied greatly in accordance with the size of their house, the scale of their dominion, and their personal proclivities. The sons and daughters of phaerons and overlords were raised to rule, but the lesser houses were as destined to serve as the commoners, albeit in significantly greater comfort.

A creeping realisation settles upon Khemet. The glyphs engraved upon the courtiers' bodies display allegiances to a motley assortment of lesser houses, and some that even Khemet does not know. These are not the lords of the Traveller's legions. These are not his nemesors, or admirals, or the wisest of his counsellors. No, these are the disowned. The assemblage of nobility is made up of those who have been cut loose from their dynasties. They are the dispossessed, the embarrassments, the burdens their overlords could not afford and were happy to lose. They are the members of houses who were content to render them up to the Traveller as hostages.

She looks up at Hekasun. An overblown lordling commanding a single vessel, with a court of second-rate hostages for companions and a bent-backed cryptek for a vizier.

It is becoming apparent to Khemet that this mission does not rank highly among the Traveller's priorities.

'Absurd, are they not?'

None of Hekasun's lackeys have yet approached her, either

out of fear of Hekasun's judgement or – she hopes – fear of her. The first necron to do so is a deathmark, who appears with the silent tread of her profession from around the corner of a pillar.

'None of them have commanded so much as a parade, and yet they preen as though they are about to break the heavens themselves.'

Khemet had not noticed the deathmark as she had entered, but that is hardly surprising. Those Khemet has known are as fleet of foot and subtle of manner as any necron can be.

'Hail, praetorian.'

'Greetings, assassin,' Khemet replies.

She speaks the title with no great venom. Though there are many in her order who consider any use of those who bear the deathmark to be a grave violation of the codes of war, Khemet is more open-minded. She has never and will never sanction their sly ways in conflicts between dynasties, but the necrons have loathsome and treacherous foes. The concealed blade has its purpose, and Khemet has never baulked at deploying the deathmarks to sever the head of an Unclean army when that is the swiftest path to victory.

'I am Ahnuret,' she says, stepping from the shadows.

'Khemet.'

'Khemet.' Ahnuret's voice is an atonal burr, but it does not mask the faint amusement in her repetition. 'An esteemed name.'

She ignores this. The root of her name is *kemmeht*, an ancient term for the most sacred ground of the necrontyr. The parents Khemet can no longer recall presumably chose it out of piety. For Khemet, it is just a name.

'How did you come to be here?' she asks instead.

'I am a member of Kamoteph the Crooked's hierotek circle,' says Ahnuret flatly.

'The Crooked?' It is rather blunt, but such epithets usually are.

'It is well earned, and not simply for his stature. Be wary of him, praetorian.'

Khemet glances over at the cryptek, and sees that he has noticed her conversation with his assassin. He is watching their exchange with undisguised curiosity.

'If you have something to say, speak plainly.'

Ahnuret is unwilling to be drawn in front of her master. 'I offer only words of advice. Caution is rarely unwise.'

Khemet cannot argue with that.

Several hours pass, during which the *Senusret* slows from its relativistic pace to a more sedate glide. Its passage describes a gentle arc through the void, curving in towards a dull red star and an unremarkable stellar system.

The vessel's pilot, a lychguard hardwired into its station on the deck's forecastle, suddenly speaks. 'We have arrived, my lord.'

The courtiers' conversations cease at the announcement, and all turn towards the visualising plates mounted about the deck.

A dense cloud of rock drifts serenely, several thousand khet ahead of the *Senusret*. At its centre is a vast mass of base metals – the core of a sundered planet, Khemet sees, surrounded by the shattered remnants of its crust.

'This was Amenset,' announces Kamoteph. 'A coreworld of the Urgenesh Dynasty.'

Khemet has never visited this world. 'What became of it?'

'The Unclean,' answers Hekasun. 'Humans, to be specific.' There is an edge of mockery in his voice. He is enjoying this moment of superiority over her, enjoying the possession of knowledge she does not have. 'The Imperium of Man laid claim to Amenset in our absence. They came. They built their little buildings and their statues. They *bred*, spreading like a cancer.'

Hekasun pauses, amusement dying with his description of humanity's desecration of one more necron world. On the far side of the chamber, Ahnuret has emerged from the shadows. Her hands clench and unclench around the grips of her disintegrator pistols.

'Their profusion was their undoing,' Kamoteph says, taking over the telling from his master. 'The tyranid genus is drawn towards any great weight of biology. The aliens came to feast. In their terror, the humans obliterated their cities, and the planet beneath, to deny the beasts their meal.'

'And in their ignorance destroyed the tombs of my cousin dynasty,' adds Hekasun.

Khemet says nothing, returning her attention to the scrying feed. The borderless vista, with its scatter of rock in constant motion, is a soothing sight, even with the knowledge that each boulder is a gravestone for the necron world.

One of Hekasun's sycophants asks the question Khemet will not. 'For what purpose have you brought us here, o lord?'

The self-satisfaction returns to Hekasun's aura. 'Well, technomancer? Do not keep us in anticipation.'

Kamoteph nods slowly. His hands make practised motions, and the scrying feed shifts. Khemet's gaze is drawn to one of the greater fragments, its surface pockmarked from impacts with its lesser kin. It is vast, an entire tectonic plate set free from its planetary core. As it turns, Khemet can make out the shattered remains of a mountain range, upthrust along a fault.

The feed takes her closer, and closer still. Broken rock resolves into peaks and valleys, trenches and plains, all bleached by radiation. Khemet's imagination paints the lost landscape onto the shattered plateaus: snow and grass, scree and stone.

The *Senusret* peers further, until finally the feed comes to rest above the ridge of a low mountain. Some quirk of geology had carved an enormous amphitheatre from the rock, hundreds of khet across. The feed shifts slowly, in deference to the rotation and drift of the tectonic plate through the void.

Embedded within the mountainside's bowl is a vast slab of noctilith. Once precisely cut, it has clearly been eroded by aeons of exposure to the climate that was annihilated by the humans. The slab is mounted atop two pillars made of the same black stone, each as worn as the crossmember.

For a moment, Khemet does not recognise what she sees. Time and trauma have passed since she last saw such an object – a creation of such surpassing rarity that she had thought herself aware of each and every example in existence. But it appears that she is wrong.

It is a dolmen gate.

It has been an age since Khemet last set her gaze upon a dolmen gate.

They had once been the most precious tools and treasures of the Infinite Empire. They were doorways to the under-realm, breaches into the inexplicable matrix the Old Ones had constructed within the empyric domain that lies behind reality.

Its makers had called it the webway. Through its tunnels they had moved armies and armadas about the galaxy with a rapidity the necrontyr could not match. The creation of the gates, permitting the violation of the webway, had been the turning point of the War. Millions of warriors had marched beneath their vast lintels, carrying death to the hated foe.

Like so much, the dolmen gates had been the gift of the C'tan. The star god Nyadra'zatha, the Burning One, had taught the art of their making to a select cabal of the Silent King's most able crypteks. Each had been the work of decades, requiring every resource of the newly immortal necrons.

Unlike all else the C'tan had pressed upon the empire they had enslaved, Nyadra'zatha had asked for nothing in return. The screams of the Old Ones and their child races had been all the payment the cruel entity required.

Now, in the era of awakening, the dolmen gates were incalculably rare. Were any cryptek with the understanding of how to construct them to rise from their tomb, they would command a power such that any phaeron would grant them the greatest portion of their fiefdoms in return. Even the locations of those that remained would obtain a price to elevate any astromancer to the status of an overlord.

Khemet aches with sudden curiosity, but she is unwilling to deepen her position of ignorance. How Hekasun – or, more likely, Anrakyr – came to know of this gate is something she will learn later.

The lordling leans forwards in his throne, as enraptured by the sight as every other in his court.

'Kamoteph. Open it.'

The cryptek bows his head. 'As you command, my lord.'

He shuffles towards a station at the centre of the deck, enclosed on three sides by the sharp-edged panes of interface consoles. With no small amount of effort, Kamoteph levers his hunched form to its greatest extension, arms raised as though in praise of the dread being that brought the gates into existence.

And he begins.

A signal spills from the *Senusret*, a soft warble of aethermancy. Kamoteph moves with ritual precision, hands curled into claws to sculpt the signal that whispers from the lodestones set within the ship's body.

Through the scrying feed, Khemet sees the gate come to life. It begins slowly, the faintest thrum of power rising from the base of each pillar. The *Senusret* sees the gathering energy, drawn from within the matrix of the gate itself, and paints an image of viridescence glowing in the void.

The power builds, travelling along ancient veins set within the noctilith. Of all its valued properties, the greatest quality of blackstone is its resonance with the realm that lies beneath the mundane dimensions of the galaxy. It could repel, annulling the empyrean's unnatural influence upon the soul-bound species, or it could amplify.

As the gathering energy reaches its apex, Khemet hears the harmonics radiating from each megalith across the vastness of the void, and through the godsteel of the *Senusret*'s hull.

The gate opens.

Khemet corrects herself. A dolmen gate does not open. It punctures.

The power summoned by Kamoteph and channelled by the esoteric mechanisms of the dolmen stones is spent in a fraction of a second, drawing in and somehow *down*, funnelling towards the epicentre of the gateway's arch. A blaze of light erupts, the by-product of arcane interactions that Khemet, even with her epochal lifespan, cannot begin to comprehend.

The light does not fade. Indeed, it grows, shifting from lambent jade to strident gold. Tongues of colour flicker and mingle in an interface that expands by the moment, drawing open in the manner of an iris pulling back around an ocular.

The skin of reality is clawed apart, cubit by cubit. Within the arcane storm is a void, revealing the alien realm Khemet last saw over sixty million years before.

The bare rock between the menhirs of the dolmen gate has disappeared, obscured by the black expanse that the *Senusret*'s perceptory tools cannot pierce. Faint wisps of phantasmal energy curl from the opening, the occasional flare of aureate power lashing from its edges to strike the dolmen stones.

'The way is prepared, o lord.' There is no strain in Kamoteph's voice, only triumph. The ancient power of the gate has done its work – the cryptek simply provided the key.

Hekasun's hands grip each arm of his throne. 'Then let us take it.'

The brace of lychguard slaved to the ship's navigation consoles lights the engines. The *Senusret* accelerates smoothly, diving towards the opening.

Khemet has no breath to hold, but the weight of anticipation nevertheless sits heavily upon her. She resents the nagging prickle of rethreading necrodermis around her incomplete hand, a distraction from the solemnity of the moment.

There is a single, pregnant pause as they pass through the threshold, and then the *Senusret* and its occupants abandon the material plane.

CHAPTER 7

Blades made of lightning hunger for her soul, and go wanting. Shards of porcelain fill the air, and chip and shatter against her limbs. It is still new, this awful prison of metal, and though Khemet's thoughts echo with her own screams she revels in the strength of it. She revels in the tears of the Unclean who throw themselves at her, and break upon her fury.

There is so much she cannot recall. No matter how she reaches for them, the details are lost to time's corruption.

She remembers marching in lockstep with her brethren, all servants to a single will. The Silent King watches them from atop his dais. He watches her. This she remembers with absolute clarity – the intoxicating, terrifying awareness of her lord and master's eye upon her.

Mist coils about her legs as she duels with Unclean heroes, the spawn of their creators' arrogance and desperation. The mist is burnt away by shafts of fire that flay the ground itself. A realm is broken by the stride of seraptek constructs, and the unchained warcraft of attacker and defender alike. The echo of shattering porcelain is matched only by the shriek of gauss and the mournful cries of the defeated.

The power of an empire has come to the webway, enriched and impoverished by the treachery of slavering gods. An epoch of the galaxy ends in almighty war, the greatest war, that burns with the strength to end the stars themselves, and at its climax it is the necrons who stand atop the cinders.

Khemet and her people sold their souls for this victory. There is hate enough left within her to consider it a price worth paying.

Khemet sheds the swirl of sense-memories in a state of panic, furious with herself that she lapsed within sight of Hekasun and his court.

That panic dies when she looks about the chamber and sees every other necron lost in the same memory. Passing beneath the dolmen stones has awoken something in them all, a need to relive the greatest triumph of the Infinite Empire.

'Close the gate, technomancer.' To her surprise, Hekasun is the first to shake off his reverie. Khemet can sense his attention return to the scrying feed, and the courtiers follow his lead.

'In progress, lord.'

Hekasun's order, and Kamoteph's response, are curt. But their discourtesy arises from fear, not arrogance. In a way Khemet's people have never been able to ascertain, the webway is sentient. Or, at least, it is capable of responding to breaches in its walls, sensing the violation of the dolmen gates and reacting to stem the entrance of foreign bodies. It will seal itself, cauterising the wound even at the cost of a piece of itself. Any force that enters via a dolmen gate must swiftly close it, or move rapidly to penetrate the webway to a depth that cannot be severed. Whole legions had been lost in the necrons' first assaults before they learnt that lesson.

Presumably those lost cohorts are still active, in the severed branches of the webway. The thought sets an uncomfortable chill in Khemet's mind.

The battle of energies through which they have passed is suddenly ended, sealed by an inversion of the key that Kamoteph used to open the gate. Khemet judges they have been swift enough. Their entry is a minor incision in the webway, rather than a grotesque wound.

With the portal closed, the *Senusret* is swallowed by a darkness that its many eyes cannot pierce. Hekasun speaks first. 'Why are we blind, Kamoteph?'

The scrying feeds show absolute nothingness. Khemet's mind flees the feeds, a lurch of self-preservation and fear that almost rocks her on her heels.

On the other side of the chamber, Ahnuret continues to watch Khemet.

'Permit me a moment, lord.' Kamoteph's attention darts from console to console, augmenting the work of a trio of apprenteks at other stations further forward of their master.

'All stop,' Hekasun commands, fearing a collision with the walls of the webway.

Quite apart from their struggles, Khemet is fighting her own battle. Tentatively – and furious that she has become so timid – Khemet rejoins the *Senusret*'s data streams. The darkness of the visual feed is too much, so she shifts her focus to the data assembling from the ship's proximity sensors. Or, more precisely, the absence of data.

They can see nothing because there is nothing to see.

The *Senusret* is suspended in emptiness. There is the faintest trace of atmospheric particles, but the wraithbone walls that form the borders of the webway are absent. They appear to have pierced a lightless, fathomless void.

'I require an explanation, technomancer.' There is a touch of alarm in Hekasun's demand.

Kamoteph is more sanguine. 'Allow me to supply one, lord.'

Khemet's senses suddenly lurch as Kamoteph shifts to the long-range sensors, which scry not on the order of khet but on the scale of light-minutes.

The webway is a vast and changing landscape, a true realm of its own nature. Khemet knows this from experience. She has fought in capillaries that were narrow enough for a single warrior to hold up an advance, and tunnels so vast that there were no walls, simply a single enormous surface that curved up and around upon itself. In the air above the cities nestled in the webway, necron scythecraft and aeldari interceptors had duelled without any fear of collision with its boundaries.

It is said, though Khemet has never seen them for herself, that there are passages so broad as to permit the greatest vessels of the aeldari to traverse the webway. These craftworlds are the last outposts of the once-proud race, as immense and sedate as planetoids in their movements. To accommodate such craft, the webway's channels would need to stretch for tens of thousands of khet.

This tunnel – though such a word is unequal to the vastness of the cavern in which the *Senusret* hangs – is one of them.

They have forced their way into one of the great trunks of the webway.

For the briefest moment, Khemet forgets herself sufficiently to feel genuine awe. No matter that it is the work of her people's most ancient enemy. No matter that the Infinite Empire has built wonders of its own, fit to eclipse any achievement of the Old Ones. This is an edifice beyond mortal scale and mortal ambition.

'What now, my lord?' asks a noble, breaking the spell.

Hekasun radiates icy, fragile calm. 'We press on.'

* * *

This domain is unnatural.

Of course, so is Khemet's own soulless existence. But she is intimately accustomed to the contradictions of her second life, to the point that she gives them no thought at all. The webway is a challenge all of its own.

She has encountered scattered testimonies from the younger races which tell of their experiences of the webway. Whether through the intercession of the aeldari or through their own cunning, many humans and other Unclean have found their way into the realm over the millennia, and some – a few – have lived to document their ordeals. All speak of the unsettling effect it had upon their spirits, the attenuating of their focus and strength that seem to leach away into the ever-present mists.

Khemet had thought herself immune, not least by the absence of a spirit within her metal form. She had not experienced this feeling of creeping dread during the great battles that had shaken the webway to its foundations. She spent years fighting through its galleries and tunnels, and had never known anything other than calm, adamant purpose and the thrill of triumph.

Perhaps it is the webway that has changed. Perhaps the destruction of the Old Ones robbed their realm of some vital element, permitting entropy to enter its bones and veins. No doubt the aeldari have some florid poetry to express what Khemet is ill-equipped to describe.

It may be that the webway is the same, but it is Khemet who has changed. The lurking trepidation that stalks her could be a symptom of her imprisonment, another manifestation of the weakness that has taken root in her psyche.

However, she feels confident that she is not alone in these feelings. The triumphal spirit that had animated the courtiers has waned since their entry. Many of Hekasun's confederates have turned away from the scrying feeds and left the hall, to pass the time in whatever idleness amuses and distracts them. They feign boredom, but it is plain to see that they feel the same unease that nags at Khemet.

Lacking any shipboard duty, Khemet remains on the command deck. Her hand regrows, joint by joint. She fights the urge to fidget, to give in to the nagging fear that immobility will provoke a relapse into memory. She has passed untold centuries in perfect stillness; she can survive a few days' enforced idleness.

Hekasun also remains, a hunched and brooding figure, but Khemet is certain that he retains his throne only to avoid relinquishing control entirely to his vizier.

The *Senusret* has left the great trunk behind. Khemet suspects that fear of encountering one of the aeldari's leviathans drove Kamoteph to abandon the impossible space. The tunnels in which they now glide are still vast, hundreds of khet across, but their boundaries are now comprehensible to Khemet's senses.

Kamoteph is their navigator. The cryptek has remained at his station since awakening the dolmen gate, though there is little enough for him to do. For much of their journey the *Senusret* follows the gentle curves and inclines of each channel. But whenever they reach a junction within the labyrinthine passageways, it is Kamoteph who supplies the direction, following a course evidently known to him by some undisclosed means.

'Whose vessel is this?' Khemet asks Kamoteph on the second day. She sends her question across the interstitial network so as not to vocally undermine Hekasun. It is also a tentative exploration of her ability to connect her mind with another. Despite her reluctance to open herself in such a way, the interstices are a vital tool for any necron, and Khemet yearns to shed the fragility that infects her.

She is careful to conceal her anxiety from the cryptek.

'This craft is under the control of my lord Hekasun,' he replies, showing no sign of surprise at her sudden contact.

'*But who is its master?*' Khemet persists.

'*I am.*' Kamoteph's sending is veined with the merest hint of amusement. '*The Senusret was placed into my care as payment for my services by High Admiral Namurat around six centuries ago. But your question has many answers. I possess the Senusret, though I am pleased to place it at my lord's disposal. He, in turn, acts with the authority of the Traveller.*'

'*Who commands only by the pleasure of the Silent King,*' Khemet adds.

'*Quite so. We are all servants, my dear praetorian.*' Kamoteph settles himself back into his station, hunched over the consoles.

Hekasun, at least, does not appear to be taken in by the cryptek's obsequious manner, as evidenced by his continued presence on the ship's throne. While Hekasun delivers imperious orders to the technomancer, it is clear from his cautious manner that this is merely the pantomime of lord and servant, maintained to preserve Hekasun's authority amongst his court. They are aboard Kamoteph's ship, following a course set by the cryptek, and it was he who held the key to the dolmen gate.

Khemet is not surprised. Those who explore the mysteries of the universe are ambitious creatures by their nature, and are easily led by hubris to desire temporal, as well as arcane, power. As useful as their arts can be, it is a foolish overlord who places unquestioning trust in his wizards' loyalty.

On the third day, having exhausted her scant capacity for stillness, she stirs from where she has stood and approaches Hekasun's throne.

'What world have we been tasked with waking?'

It takes a fraction of a second before the noble registers her question. She suspects he had slowed his chronosense to speed his perception of their passage.

'It is named Qeretesh,' Hekasun says, though a twist of distaste modulates his voice. 'It is a coreworld, under the dominion of the Zathanor Dynasty.'

The name sparks a connection in Khemet's vaults. Raving nobles, dragged before her by their own lychguard. The Traveller's hunger as she dissolved their dynasty, and passed the keys to a world into his hands.

'I was not aware that any of the Zathanor's holdings had endured the Great Sleep,' she says.

'This one has.' Hekasun is staring towards the main scrying screen, disdaining her presence at the foot of the pyramid.

Khemet wonders if there is some coded meaning in the selection of this world. Has the Traveller chosen a forgotten outpost of a house she rendered defunct as a reminder of her failings? For judging too swiftly?

At least there will be no concerns regarding its mastery, although there may be some issues with the world's leaders still in stasis, assuming they have endured the aeons better than their peers.

'Is there anything further?' Hekasun asks. Khemet is lingering while lost in thought.

'What is the condition of Qeretesh?'

'The humans have claimed it.' The noble tries to speak with indifference, but there is tension that he is unable to hide.

Khemet pauses again, though now it is simply to choose her words. 'Are you aware of the use to which they have put the world? The humans breed like lice, and you do not lead a sizeable force.'

'It will be sufficient.'

'Lord Hekasun–' she begins, drawing on her patience.

'Cease your pestering, duatekh!' Hekasun's command is spoken with a whipcrack, the lordling finally deigning to lock oculars with Khemet. 'I permit you free rein aboard this craft, but I will not suffer your taint to sully me.'

Khemet is startled by his sudden rancour. She had thought

Hekasun to be nothing but an arrogant upstart – who knew such strength of feeling dwelt within him?

She lingers long enough to make a point of her defiance, gaze fixed upon him, then she turns away. She resumes her chosen position at the far edge of the chamber, considering all that the brief and fraught conversation has told her.

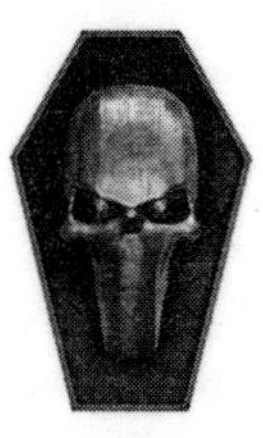

CHAPTER 8

The *Senusret* bursts into realspace, expelled in a blaze of shimmering radiance the equal of that with which it had entered.

The ship emerges from another dolmen gate, built into another mountainside on a world far from their place of entry. How Kamoteph found their door in the barren twilight of the webway is a mystery he does not share. When the cryptek announced that they had reached their exit, Khemet could see no difference between that point and any other on their silent, meandering route. And yet, when Kamoteph had raised his hands and summoned the aethermantic relays of his ship, the way had opened. They had surged into a portal of scintillating, conflicting energies, and then the *Senusret* was once again surrounded by stars.

The ship's autonomous spirit tells her that in the five days they have been immersed in the webway they have travelled across more than a tenth of the galaxy's diameter. This fact sets a brief but jagged spike of anger trembling in her core. The Old

Ones, a curse upon their shattered bones, had built something of undeniable magnificence, and Khemet hates them for it. She hates that she feels awe, boundlessly begrudging as it is, for any achievement of her people's ancient foe.

A defeated foe, all the same. For all their might and majesty, the necrontyr empire laid the Old Ones low, and their great work is emptied of life. That thought warms her.

The *Senusret*, now unrestrained by concerns of careful navigation, accelerates smoothly. With its inertialess drive unchained, the *Senusret* rapidly reaches relativistic speeds. They depart the nameless world in moments, and enter the emptiness of the interstellar void in a few short hours.

Now they have returned to the familiarity of the real, Khemet abandons her place on the command deck. She has exhausted all possible means of passing the time. Khemet knows this should be no impediment to her. She has used her chronosense on many occasions throughout her long life. Most often in battle, to gain precious moments to contemplate how best to defeat her enemy. But she has never before feared to accelerate her chronosense, and step out of time's path so she might be spared its sluggish pace.

Now she does. In the tesseract labyrinth, time had been one more dimension that was stripped away from her, and Khemet fears what will happen to her fledgling mind if she pushes too far, too fast. It is a shameful, cowardly impulse, but one that Khemet has yet to overcome.

She returns to exploring the ship. The *Senusret* is an exemplar of its pattern and she knows it intimately. Nevertheless, she goes in search of stimulus. She walks every passageway and corridor, considers every tapestry and stele. She stares into the white heat of the ship's engines, and for days afterwards radiates energies that would be lethal to any organic creature. She avoids the populated areas, where Hekasun's court congregate, and tells herself that it is right for a praetorian to remain aloof and reserved. She inspects the condition of Hekasun's borrowed warriors, immobile and undeterred by their impassive state of living death.

Everywhere she goes, imperceptible scuffs, scars and scratches mark the walls and floors.

It is another week of aching, arduous time before the ship begins to slow. But finally, as she stands at an observation point and looks at the ship's sweeping crescent wings, she is summoned back to Hekasun's throne.

The *Senusret* returns to a more measured pace, giving Khemet and the handful of courtiers who have joined Hekasun time to consider the object of their mission.

Qeretesh is the innermost planet of an unremarkable stellar system, a speck of blue and green only visible through the scrying feed's magnification. It has three neighbours, each a swollen gas giant at the centre of its own dance of moonlets and icy rings. The yellow star at the centre of the screen is barely brighter than the billions of others that surround it, but it gains in strength with every moment.

As it does, many hundreds of lesser lights come into view. Each light reveals a voidship, shining from a burning engine or glinting from a metal prow.

Human vessels crowd the system. Their provenance is unquestionable – the *Senusret*'s spirit knows the sharp-nosed, slab-sided craft of the so-called Imperium of Man, matching them with patterns of design that it has encountered over the millennia since its waking. Most, it says, are fat-bellied transport craft, ferrying whatever goods this world requires and produces. But many are warcraft, knife-prowed vessels whose spines are topped with crenellations and whose flanks are studded with weapons.

None, individually, could begin to threaten the *Senusret*, itself one of the slightest class of craft built by the necrontyr. Yet the trouble with humans was that they did nothing individually. They swarmed in fleets and armies, millions of tons of iron and arrogance whose weight could crush the admiral or nemesor that was foolish enough to face them directly.

As the *Senusret* peers closer, yet more voidcraft come into focus, static defences that drift in Qeretesh's orbit. They lack manoeuvrability, but the scrying feed picks out potent energy reserves and weapons that equal the power of those aboard the human warships.

'Shroud the ship,' Hekasun orders. Kamoteph is already acting, extending a veil of shadow to cloak the *Senusret* from sight. They are still on the fringes of the system, crossing the orbit of the outermost gas giant, but the consequences of detection are too great to ignore. With the spell of silence enveloping its engines and emissive systems, the ship is undetectable by the humans' crude means. Even visual identification is next to impossible; to the outside observer, the *Senusret* is a shadow against the black of the void.

The stillness of the shroud extends into the command deck for a handful of moments, until Khemet strides towards the pyramid at its centre and glares up at the throne's occupant.

'Where have you brought us, Hekasun?'

'Lord,' he corrects her, his gaze no less sharp or furious. 'You will remember that, duatekh. I am your lord, and you are my servant.'

Khemet imagines the way the lordling would die beneath a blast from her staff. Necrodermis would peel back from metal bones. His reactor core would chip, splinter, and shatter in a blaze of copper light. The arrogance in his oculars would flee, replaced by fear.

'This is Qeretesh,' she says, pushing the image aside.

'Indeed.'

'It is overrun.' It is not a question, but an accusation.

Khemet is gratified to sense that she is not the only one who has been kept unaware of the condition of the coreworld. The collection of courtiers who have come to witness their arrival are evidently as surprised as she.

'They call it Orymous,' Kamoteph says, stepping from his place at the base of the pyramid. 'It is a place for their armies to be marshalled and made ready for their "wars".' He sneers the word – the humans have no conception of the scale and horror of a true war, waged against formidable enemies and baleful gods. 'Many millions of humans under arms, served by billions more.'

The scrying feed shows that this is true. Population centres are picked out against its surface, accretions of ugly structures in whose warrens run the hordes of the Unclean. Each city, and there are dozens, is a blight upon a world that had once been blessed to be a cornerstone of a dynasty.

'This is not a backwater.' Khemet throws the accusation at Hekasun. 'This is a bastion of their domain. They have fortified it. They fill its skies with defences, and no doubt they infest its surface.'

Hekasun stares back, anger turning to scornful disdain. 'Do you fear them so greatly, duatekh?' he asks softly.

Khemet's reactor vents flare, a brilliant explosion of jade that coruscates around her ribcage. She places a foot upon the lowest tier of Hekasun's pyramid. This is a violation, an insult to his authority so grave that, had she been any other, it would earn a swift death at the hands of Hekasun's lychguard.

'I fear nothing.'

Hekasun does nothing to acknowledge her encroachment

upon his dais. 'And yet you mewl and cry at the sight of their ships and their guns and their warriors.'

'I have seen first-hand what the humans can accomplish when they have gathered their strength. They are crude, they are dull, but they are many. And you seek to overthrow their grip upon this world with the meagre force we carry with us?'

Hekasun leans forwards. 'No, praetorian. I do not.'

Qeretesh is orbited by a pair of moons. One teems with humans, huddled together within subterranean tunnels that thread their way through its rock. The other is barren, an irregular hunk of ice that drifts in a wide elliptical track. The humans appear to have little interest in it, so that is where they hide the *Senusret*.

Kamoteph's pilots settle the ship in the depths of a canyon hundreds of khet across and thousands long, a fault line that almost entirely encircles the satellite. Between the canyon's walls and the ship's shrouding field, the *Senusret* will be amply concealed. The humans, all but deaf and blind as their craft are, will have to collide with the necron ship in order to detect it.

Khemet joins Hekasun and his court as they depart the command deck. He bids her follow him as one would order a hound to heel. Khemet conceals her fury, carrying herself with the austere reserve that is her habit.

They march down into the belly of the ship, metal footsteps echoing from stone ramps and stairways. As they pass archways and chambers more of Hekasun's lackeys emerge, forming an impromptu train of necrontyr nobility. Though only a few – the keen and ambitious, those who had wished to be seen to be present – had witnessed their approach to Qeretesh, none would miss making planetfall. Khemet notices that even Ahnuret has joined them, though the deathmark shows the same distaste for close proximity with her fellow necrons as Khemet.

The *Senusret* possesses several marshalling chambers. They are caverns within the ship's body, places for its cohorts and phalanxes to gather in preparation for battle. The warriors themselves rest in stasis-caskets throughout the ship. It is a rare corridor in the *Senusret* that does not have a series of coffins inset within its walls, each holding a slumbering warrior awaiting its master's call.

A necron Khemet does not recognise awaits Hekasun's procession in the closest chamber, standing on a platform that projects a short way into the air high above the blackstone floor. They bow deeply to Hekasun, arms spread wide in supplication.

'Rise,' the lordling commands. 'This is Ptah,' Hekasun adds, for Khemet's benefit.

Ptah is not one of Kamoteph's acolytes, but a cryptek in their own right. They stand tall, slight and thin-limbed. Their chain of essence-tomes hangs about their neck as a triangular plastron, its final tile resting just above the ankh of the Triarch on their chest.

Ptah, Khemet notes, possesses fewer tiles than Kamoteph. The tension between the two is unmistakable. The technomancer pointedly crosses to the far side of the platform, peering over its edge in his crooked pose.

The chamber is a dozen khet across, lit by jade power conduits running through its floor and ceiling in geometric patterns. The walls on either side of the platform are built into tiers and lined with sarcophagi, emptied and unpowered. Their contents have been disgorged, and stand in readiness beneath them.

Four hundred warriors, arrayed by rank and file, newly awoken and ready for war.

As one, they salute their master. Perfect precision, born of unthinking obedience. Hekasun offers the slightest wave in recognition of their automatic act of supplication.

'Your troops are ready, lord,' says Ptah with another bow, hands rising to their faceplate in a gesture of the greatest respect.

Hekasun nods. 'Very good. The failure rate?'

'Tolerable, lord.'

Kamoteph emits a snort of indignation, which through his vocaliser emerges as a snarl of electronic ire. 'The *Senusret*'s caskets are in perfect condition. Any synaptic failures among the waking lie solely with their waker.'

Hekasun interposes himself between the two magicians before Ptah can respond, stepping close to the platform's edge to survey his cohort. 'It matters little. Attrition will be the least of our concerns when this day is done.'

The noble pauses, contemplating the rows of warriors waiting for his command.

'Kamoteph. Open the gate.'

'As you command.' The cryptek's acolytes have gathered on the chamber floor and now hurry to obey, moving swiftly to the rear of the space where the sharp pillars of an eternity gate stand proud from the wall's surface.

The gate is tall, ten times taller than is needed to permit even the greatest necron to pass beneath its lintel. A phalanx of warriors could march abreast between its pillars, to emerge wherever a counterpart gateway could be found. The gates are an integral element of necrontyr warfare, carried within monolithic war machines to permit the rapid deployment of force to wherever it was required.

As Kamoteph's creatures work, Khemet's gaze is drawn to the warriors in their rows. They are, to be charitable, less than pristine. Each one's necrodermis is chipped and stained, their oculars dull and listless. Leaking fluids gather at their joints, and the flux of their reactor cores burns with an unclean haze.

Khemet has never enjoyed observing the line warriors of necron phalanxes up close. To consider them with care, to examine the unique patterns of scars and corrosion that mark each one, is to be reminded that they were once individuals. Bakers, carpenters, water carriers – the great mass of serfdom upon whose servitude the necrontyr empire had been built. Better to think of them as a singular mass, undifferentiated, each a tiny and indistinguishable fraction of the mighty whole. Better to think of them as constructs, rather than necrontyr. Rather than as the billion members of a people robbed of their souls and consigned to living death.

Khemet checks her descent into maudlin recrimination. The truth was that the lock-brained warriors before her had been little different before the treachery of the C'tan chained them within their metal skeletons. They had lived, they had died, and neither act had meant anything of consequence for them or for the galaxy.

'It is a shame that the Traveller did not provide a complement of his Eternals,' Khemet says. The memory arrives, unbidden, of flawless warriors marching into a hurricane of fire and shrapnel. The Pyrrhian Eternals, hailing from the phaeron's home world, were an elite legion, hardened and respected troops that had carried their reputation and ability through the treachery of biotransference.

Hekasun ignores the implied insult she gives to his warriors. 'He offered, but I deemed them unnecessary. We will soon have all the might we require.'

Eagerness makes him forget his habitual scorn for Khemet's contributions. His gaze remains hungrily locked upon the eternity gate, as though through will alone the lordling will bridge the leagues between his ship and his prize.

Kamoteph's apprenteks complete their manipulations of the control consoles beside the vast pillars, and at an unspoken command from their master prime the gateway. The *Senusret* reaches out, questing across the void, through air, through rock, until it finds its match far beneath the surface of Qeretesh.

Khemet feels the briefest pulse of electromagnetism, a slight tug at her carapace, and then the chamber is flooded with emerald light. The quantum tunnel has latched on to another eternity gate, somewhere within the tomb world's galleries and vaults.

Such doorways had once reminded Khemet of a waterfall she had witnessed on a nameless primordial world. She can remember the feeling, the soft pleasure she had taken in watching the flow of energies across its face evoke a cascade of water over a mountain's edge.

But now she feels nothing. This new Khemet sees merely a tool, one of many wonders her people forged and mastered in ages past.

Mandulis has detached himself from his lord, and now leads a squad of lychguard out from beneath the observation platform's lip. These warriors show no sign of the degradation that mars their lessers, the gift of their heightened synaptic powers. Unlike their serf-born peers, lychguard possess sufficient self-awareness to maintain themselves, and even take command over limited elements of a wider battle force.

The royal warden glances up at his lord, and Hekasun waves his vargard forwards. Mandulis and his unit do not hesitate, and set out with gauss blasters held low and ready for use. They reach the threshold of the eternity gate and step forth into its tumult. They are swallowed in an instant.

Slow seconds tick by as Hekasun waits for an interstitial report from his warden. Despite herself, Khemet finds herself gripped by anticipation. It has been too long – far, far too long – since she has walked the corridors of her people's worlds.

The discordant click of scarab legs warn Khemet of Kamoteph's approach. The cryptek is bent even lower than usual, hardly able to raise his head and meet Khemet's ocular.

'Praetorian.'

'Cryptek.'

'It has pleased me to see your recovery in these past weeks. I flatter myself to believe that I played a part in those first days.'

Khemet has no desire to be reminded of her enfeebled state, nor to indulge Kamoteph's vainglory.

'And yet, if you will permit me, I still sense some reticence in you. A hesitation to embrace your full power.'

She turns towards him, intent on demonstrating how wrong he is. But the cryptek speaks quickly to forestall her hand.

'Fortunately, I have something that I believe will address that.'

He passes a hand over his hip, fingers moving in sequence. He summons an object from his pocket dimension, emerging into reality with a soft blaze of light. It is a long and slender staff of godsteel, of a height with Khemet. Each end is bladed, its head crowned with a gem of sublime power and sculpted into the ultimate symbol of authority – the ankh of the Triarch.

It is her rod of covenant.

Khemet moves without thought. She extends a hand and the rod leaps from Kamoteph's grip and into hers, the shaft slapping her metal palm with the clang of a cracked bell. The blade whirls, and comes to rest with the tines of its sigil enclosing the cryptek's thin neck.

'This was not yours to keep.'

Kamoteph bends lower, the segments of his spine extending in its crabbed arch. 'It was placed into my care by the Traveller, to hold in readiness for your restoration.'

Khemet is tired of those who presume to judge her. She is their judge, their arbiter. With this staff she has ended dynasties, pronounced the fate of worlds, destroyed untold Unclean foes. And yet she is forced into the service of the petulant, the petty and the vain.

'It was not yours to keep.' She lifts the blade from his neck.

On the far side of the platform, Hekasun has received an affirmation from his vargard. He leans forwards, and speaks a single word to his warriors.

'On.'

As one, the phalanx turns away. Their long axe-tipped gauss flayers rise in their grip, coils glowing, and rank by rank they set off. Khemet cannot begin to count the times she has watched warriors stride forth in this manner, stalwart as only the wholly subservient can be.

Hekasun contains himself until the last rank is enveloped by the gateway's energies, then gestures to his court.

'Let us depart.'

He leads the way, descending from the observation platform at a pace calculated to project dignity and strength. The nobles behind him march with far less poise and order than their minions. Several have armed themselves with glaives and scythes, in keeping with the martial air of the moment. Hekasun himself wields nothing save the arrogant self-possession that advances before him like a bow wave. In ones and twos, his court cross the chamber floor and disappear into the curtain of viridian light. Kamoteph, with his circle of apprenteks and thrall guardians, and the cryptek Ptah stand ready to follow.

Hekasun stops at the threshold. 'Duatekh. Attend me.'

Khemet has not joined in the noble's advance. She lingers atop the platform, her hands slowly turning her staff about her. She watches its bladed head, alight with power. This weapon has been with her for sixty million years. Yet it is far more than a weapon. It is a symbol, which she has carried through the darkest and emptiest nights of a galaxy that grew to forget the necrontyr. To forget the empire that conquered it.

'Praetorian.'

Khemet deigns to answer Hekasun's petulant call. She lights

the anti-gravity pack in her torso and drifts down to meet him. It is the first time she has woken her powers of flight since her release, and the sensation is potent. This is her place, looking down upon Hekasun and his lackeys, staff in hand.

'You have one purpose,' says Hekasun. 'Do you comprehend it?'

'Entirely. You ask that I give you a world.'

Hekasun glares up at her. 'You are to claim for me what is mine. You are a key. A tool. Nothing more. Do not forget that.'

He turns and disappears into the gate. His servants follow.

Khemet lands. The gateway's face towers over her, boiling with energy, a cascade of power rendered mundane by ancient arcana. It is as familiar as her own faceplate – a doorway to yet another world.

She could remain here. Abandon Hekasun and Kamoteph to whatever fate awaits them on Qeretesh. To face the humans, and their crude and engulfing form of war. She could remain here, abstaining from her duty to defend the tombs of her people out of pique and injured honour.

Khemet looks up at the gate, and steps into its current.

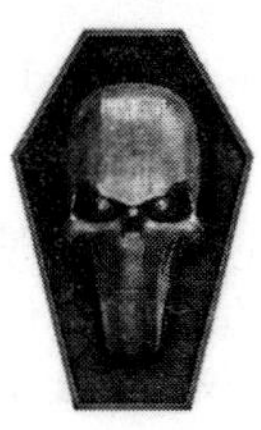

CHAPTER 9

Khemet staggers as she emerges from the curtain of energy, undone not by any enemy but by a wave of relief so palpable it makes her senses blur.

She is home. She has never set foot upon Qeretesh, but she is a praetorian of the Infinite Empire, and every world of that great domain is her home.

A weight she had not been consciously holding rises, a recursive thread of anxiety that has unknowingly wormed its way through her active and passive processes. She is back, returned to the immensity of blackstone halls, the silent peace of the tomb.

Her relief lasts all of a fraction of a second, as Khemet peers into the chamber's depths and sees the battle unfolding within sight of the eternity gate's threshold.

The light of the dimensional doorway blazes into the vaulted tomb, illuminating the struggle. The backs of Hekasun's warriors shine with a dirty green glare, each rib and spar sharp against the darkness. The canoptek constructs they are fighting emerge from the twilight, a chittering horde scuttling and swarming forwards on pincer legs.

The air is alive with the skitter of sharp talons on stone and the shriek of gauss rending metal. Constructs in the forms of spyders, scorpions and wyrms hurl themselves at the thin line of warriors, double-ranked and bent in a crescent with the eternity gate at their back. The chamber in which they fight is small, no more than a dozen khet across, open only on the side facing the gate. The single archway is a hundred cubits high but barely twenty across, constricting the flow of canoptek beasts that seem to come without end.

Khemet has only moments to examine the battlefield before the gate closes, unleashing a plate-glass crash of unchained energies that pushes Khemet away from its breaking face. Tongues of viridian lightning arc into the surrounding stone, and then the only light in the chamber comes from the blaze of necron weaponry.

Khemet's oculars momentarily struggle to adjust to sudden blackness, streaked through with searing blasts of gauss. A hundred shafts of virulent energy puncture the darkness with each second, each one peeling away metal from the carapaces of the constructs. In reply, kaleidoscopic beams of particle casters lash the necron formation. From above, scorpion-tailed acanthrites trace cutting lances over the bodies of their scuttling kin.

Kamoteph is ahead of her. He has conjured a summoning plate from a pocket dimension, and from its jade face spills a tide of canoptek creatures. Spyders and scarabs, locusts and hawks tumble and fly from the surface of the arcane stone. Kamoteph's creatures throw themselves into the fray, matching talon with claw and thermal lance with particle beamer.

The intellect behind the constructs that oppose Hekasun's arrival is clear to Khemet. Each tomb world, like each ship of the necron fleet, is imbued with an autonomous spirit. It is the intelligence that holds the complex together, regulates its function, directs its canoptek servicers to renew its workings and monitor its slumbering occupants. The spirits, even more than Khemet and her fellow praetorians, have been the shepherds of the necrontyr through the long years of the Great Sleep.

Unfortunately, after so long, some spirits are reticent to give up their power.

'Cease your defiance, Qeretesh. Your lord is come.' Hekasun's voice rises above the fray, imbued for the first time in Khemet's hearing with a fragment of true nobility.

'NO,' the tomb world replies. It speaks its denial from vocalisers built into the jaws and mandibles of every construct that assails Hekasun's force. The single word hammers Khemet's aural receptors, reverberating from the walls of the tomb itself.

'Still all defensive constructs. Submit to my dominion.'

'INTERLOPER. INTRUDER. USURPER.'

The would-be lord stands rigid, one hand extended in the manner of a cryptek casting a spell. Mandulis and his lychguard encircle Hekasun, twin-barrelled gauss blasters shrieking destruction into the acanthrites and scarab swarms that dive and scuttle towards the noble. Fragments of segmented tails and broken mandibles tumble in a metal rain that clatters from the shoulders of the lychguard.

Khemet is impressed; despite his command to her just moments before, Hekasun's arrogance has led him to challenge the tomb world's spirit himself.

The noble's fist is clenched, ocular shields closed, all his energies turned inwards. Khemet is not privy to the battle in which Hekasun is locked, but she knows it well enough. It is not a simple matter of speaking a prescribed word or forcing a coded command past the spirit's ire. Hekasun is matching wits with an intelligence whose mind is powered by the molten core of an entire world. Scenarios and riddles, conundrums and paradoxes. Across an interstitial link Hekasun is countering puzzle with answer, enigma with solution, hoping to prove cubit by cubit that he holds the authority to command Qeretesh and all it holds.

'I come vested in the power of the Zathanor. I bear their sigil. I speak their rites.'

Every construct bellows the tomb world's dissent. 'YOU ARE NOT MY LORD.'

Hekasun stands firm. 'But I will be.'

Khemet has broken the will of a tomb's spirit, severed of its master's hand. It was a malignancy that had shed its purpose and forced its way into the minds of those whom it was meant to serve. The effort had almost broken her in both mind and body, and she had sacrificed an entire legion of warriors to shield her from the tomb world's death throes.

But this is not the case with Qeretesh. Khemet can feel it, as she tentatively stretches out into the interstices. Qeretesh is not a severed world, maddened by aeons of isolation and lashing blindly at all who approach. It defends its hearth from intruders, lords of foreign dynasties intent on plunder and usurpation. Qeretesh is acting precisely as its directives require.

The blinding beams of particle casters lash at the noble's warriors, stripping living metal from their skeletal forms. As Khemet watches, the warrior closest to her drops, its leg severed at the hip. Its fire stutters, but from the ground its gaunt head rises, and its flayer follows the warrior's gaze. A beam of jade light coughs forth from its end, and the broken creature continues its fight.

'Praetorian.' Kamoteph's call pierces Khemet's mind like an arrow from a bow. 'Will you join us?'

The cryptek is right. She has been a spectator for long enough. Khemet lights the anti-gravity pack that forms the greater part of her torso and leaps into the air.

A flight of acanthrites immediately change their course, void-blade tails lunging for her. With three broad slashes she carves the constructs into halves that tumble to the ground. Khemet stills her lifting pack, and allows the ballistic curve to carry her over the warriors' line and into the midst of the charging torrent.

She lands with her rod of covenant outstretched, and thrusts into the cognitive stem of a lunging wraith. The blade shears through its skull and the construct crumples. More come, and more are destroyed, hacked to shards. The energised top and tail of her staff describe a whirling arc about Khemet's body, dismembering all that approach. A wraith leaps high over its kin, whip tail extended, and Khemet unleashes a blast of energy that burns through the construct's thorax in an instant.

This is not how she imagined her return to the cauldron of combat, but it is undeniably cathartic.

Khemet hacks her staff through the abdomen of a spyder, then spins aside as a wyrm charges with the aim of smashing her to the ground. As Khemet recovers herself, an azure beam of light stabs down from somewhere far above her and punches through the skull of a leaping locust. The praetorian deftly steps aside as the construct crumples into a heap, inertia throwing it head-long into the front rank of the phalanx. More shots lance out of the darkness; Ahnuret has joined the fray.

To her left, one of Kamoteph's raptors catches a wraith by its snaking tail and hurls it over the heads of its peers, only to be borne down onto the stone by a brace of spyders. To her right, Ptah wields the glowing shaft of an eldritch lance, blasting a torrent of plasma into any construct that approaches. Behind the line of warriors, Hekasun's court fire thermal lances and throw out particle whips, participating loyally if not particularly effectively.

If Hekasun cannot overcome the tomb's spirit, they will all die here. The tomb world's reanimation circuits will reject the engrams of the interlopers in its midst. The complex can call upon millions of constructs, and swamp Hekasun's warriors beneath a tidal wave of claws and blades and rending jaws. It is only a matter of attrition.

But Khemet can prevent that.

For a moment, Khemet allows herself to indulge in the swell of power this knowledge brings. The choice is hers. Continued existence, or permanent death for Hekasun, Kamoteph, and all his minions. Now she is truly restored, not by the rod of covenant in her hand but by the decision set out before her.

She allows herself the moment's indulgence and then, as she must, Khemet reaches into the interstices.

A shadow envelops her, vast and total. It swallows her, consumes her, draws her down into the place where darkness is born, permanent and absolute.

Or so the tomb world's spirit would have her believe.

Khemet has entered its domain, and it is fighting back. She is stripped of form, reduced to a mind persisting in the darkness. This is the reality of Qeretesh, its experience of existence – alone in the void, forever.

Khemet is undaunted by the black depths, because she has been here before. This is not the first tomb world she has confronted. She is ready for the bleak loneliness that tries to swallow her being.

More vitally, Khemet has faced oblivion. Within the tesseract labyrinth there was not simply darkness, but true absence, where even all-consuming shadow would have been a blessed relief. For all that Qeretesh has persisted for uncountable millennia, it cannot conjure true emptiness. The weight of the planet around it is too real for the tomb world's spirit to imagine anything greater.

Khemet reaches out, projecting herself through the interstices. Her will meets the tomb world's. Opposing visions, opposing mindscapes meet, but only one can assert itself.

A light, harsh and cold, pierces the darkness. Khemet knows that if she turns the light will still be behind her, forever out of sight. It is her duty to go forth from the light, but she cannot bask in it, no matter her desire to feel it upon her face.

The darkness retreats, the tomb world's power faltering in the face of her overwhelming mandate.

As the black recedes she discovers Hekasun ahead of her, insofar as distance can apply to this place.

In his reality, the impossible landscape is a throne room, a mosaic floor stretching away to infinity. At the centre of that floor is a crown, sitting upon a stone pillar, as one might display a bauble or antiquity. Hekasun is reaching for it, striving for it, bending all of himself to the task. But no matter how hard he strives, he can come no closer to it.

The noble appears to her as a figure made of golden light, reaching with outstretched fingers to grasp the circlet he so desperately seeks. But the darkness fights him, denies him, closing about his golden hand to rebuff each lunge. The walls and ceiling of his imagined chamber are shrouded in shadow, and close in by the moment. Hekasun lacks the knowledge he needs to defeat the tomb world, and so is attempting to push the world's spirit aside with pure force.

It is only now, seeing Hekasun laid bare to his essence, that Khemet understands the lord to whom she has been leashed. Whatever Hekasun may pretend, he does not seek to claim Qeretesh in the name of the Traveller. That may be the mandate under which he has come, but Hekasun desires the crown for himself. He wants to rule.

Khemet dismisses Hekasun, erasing him from her mindscape. His desires and pride are irrelevant to her.

In her sight, the crown is instead a sceptre, a simple rod of meta-gold shaped into the ankh of the Triarch. It seems to float before her, its face and edges made sharp by the azure light behind her.

This, the tomb world cannot deny. It was built by those who bear the sigil of the Silent King upon their bodies, who owe their existence to his will, and to his folly. Qeretesh is unable to resist her. It was made to obey that sigil.

Khemet reaches out and plucks the sceptre from the darkness.

Khemet rises from the illusion in time to weave aside from a scarab's attack. The battle has not abated in the moments of her vision. Warriors are still being pulled down by a tide of chittering bodies, and sliced apart by streams of energy.

With a wave of her hand, and a wide-cast command across the interstices, she ends the wasteful exercise.

The Qeretesh constructs freeze, all motion halted in the same instant. Wraiths and spyders stand rampant, bladed limbs halted in the act of plunging into reactor cores. Several are destroyed as scythe swings cleave through suddenly inanimate objects. Gauss blasts shatter others, until Hekasun issues a silent order to his warriors to still their wrath. Kamoteph's own canoptek creatures continue to rend their peers to scrap for a few moments more, until the cryptek calls them to heel.

Hekasun unbends from his rigid pose, sagging all at once as though he had endured the rigours of a foot race. With one hand against a knee, the noble looks up into the twilight depths of the chamber.

'It is done. I claim the succession of the Zathanor. I am the master of this place. I am the master of this world.' Each declaration echoes in the sudden silence, rising into the chamber's darkest reaches.

As one, the lords and warriors that Hekasun brought to Qeretesh bow before him.

'No, you are not,' Khemet says softly.

Hekasun turns with a crackle of servos, triumph banished by fury. 'You deny my victory.'

Khemet meets his gaze. 'This is not your doing, Hekasun, but mine.' The lord's anger turns to confusion. Khemet can almost see his mind at work. He searches his command precepts for what he believes he now possesses, and discovers that he does not.

'Insolent wretch! You are duatekh. Give me what is mine!'

The petulance of his demand only confirms that Khemet has chosen the right course.

'Speak that word again, Hekasun, and I shall erase you from existence.' She walks towards him, raising her rod of covenant to bring its sigil-topped head into Hekasun's sight. 'I am a praetorian. Power over this world is not yours to claim, but mine to bestow.'

Hekasun's core-flux is incandescent, burning with the heat of hatred. At an unspoken command Mandulis and his lychguard leave Hekasun and encircle her, holding a ring of gauss blasters ready to rend her body to atoms. A fleeting memory of green blades and a ghostly moan rise out of her vaults, but she pushes it aside.

'Destroy me, and you have nothing.' Mandulis and his warriors halt, as she knew they would. 'I am a servant of the Silent King. My existence is inviolate. If you break the gravest law of our people, you will dishonour yourself and condemn your cadre to an eternity beneath the rock of this world.'

Khemet steps towards Mandulis, but looks past his baleful gaze towards his master. 'Without me, Qeretesh will not obey you. No lights will shine. No warriors will wake. No doors will open. You will be consigned to shadow and silence, to blindly walk the halls of the world you were sent to claim.'

Hekasun glares at Khemet. But she knows his mind. His intention was to use her, as he said, as the key to open Qeretesh to his control, and then he would have destroyed her. The arrogance is astonishing, yet not at all surprising.

'But,' says Khemet, 'I will grant you a portion of the power you seek. We will use it, together, to claim this world, and rid it of the pestilence that infects its surface. And when that is done it will be my judgement, Hekasun, that will determine whether you inherit Qeretesh in the name of your absent master. You shall prove yourself to me.'

For all Hekasun's venality, Khemet knows that this is the path she must take. This world must be woken, and the humans purged from its soil. It is not Khemet's role to claim power for herself. She is an arbiter, charged to instil it in others. Or strip it away.

Hekasun lowers his sickle blades. At least he has the wisdom to know when he is beaten. 'I accept your terms, praetorian.'

Khemet nods.

One by one, the lights of Qeretesh flicker into life.

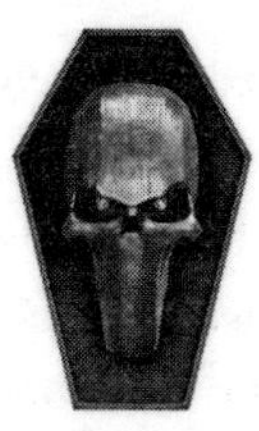

CHAPTER 10

They assemble at the roof of the world, in a grand chamber beneath the planet's polar cap.

Two days have passed since Khemet took possession of Qeretesh. In that time Hekasun and his court have fled from her sight, seeking to escape the shame of capitulating to the one whom they had sought to use. Khemet, naturally, has monitored their progress as they have gallivanted around the tomb world, moving from gate to gate and from vaulted chamber to high hall to survey their new holdings. The coreworld's treasuries have been opened, and its arsenals of monoliths and seraptek constructs and voidcraft inspected. The first of its many stasis vaults, with its legions of coffins, crawl with Kamoteph and Ptah's apprenteks as they catalogue how many warriors and nobles have survived the Great Sleep.

Khemet has left them to their amusement. She has been studying and planning what is to come.

The senses of the tomb complex extend throughout the roots of the world, and its autonomous spirit, now that it has been brought to heel, has been most obedient. The breadth of data it has provided Khemet is enormous, and she has immersed herself in all it can tell. She has learnt much about her enemy, but now Hekasun's marauding and Khemet's study must end. They have a world to win.

The Zathanor, as Khemet well knows, were not a grand dynasty. Their holdings were never extensive nor rich. It is highly probable that had Khemet not ended their line, another house would have engulfed them in time. Nevertheless, a tomb world is a vast construction, veining through the bedrock of a planet. If Khemet so desires, she can walk from one pole of this world to the other without ever leaving its halls, though the tomb world's spirit has spoken to her of areas that have suffered decay and collapse during the millions of years of its slumber.

Khemet has chosen this place at the very top of the complex for their conference as it sits closest to the world's surface. Barely fifty khet of ice and rock cover the chamber's blackstone roof. Though there are many routes that could take them from Qeretesh's depths to stand beneath its sky, this antechamber is the nearest. Though she has no desire yet to march forth, she felt the symbolism appropriate. Khemet and her people will emerge, and take war to the humans.

Hekasun enters the chamber via an eternity gate, stepping from the electric blaze of energy trailed by Kamoteph and Mandulis. She sees that Hekasun has adorned himself with a diadem he has found in the course of his pillaging, a band of metagold that has merged with the necrodermis of his skull. A gem – a vast and flawless ruby – is mounted at its centre, surrounded by an artfully arranged collection of minor jewels.

Khemet considers this vanity. There is only one necron deserving of a crown, and he is far from here.

'Do not presume to summon me,' Hekasun says by way of greeting. 'What is it you require?'

'I have considered the disposition of this world and its occupants,' Khemet replies. She stands at a broad holographic plate, lit by a chrysoprase orb projected from its surface. She holds a small plate in one hand, with which she can manipulate the image of Qeretesh before her.

Hekasun and his company draw closer. The forbidding countenance of the necron visage is only heightened by the pallid light of the projector, sharpening the angles of their metal skulls and deepening the shadows around their oculars.

'Speak,' commands the would-be lord of Qeretesh, one hand toying with the gem embedded in his forehead.

Khemet puts the control plate down carefully. She has anticipated that Hekasun would resist the change in their interactions that she has made.

'I remind you, lord, that I am a praetorian of the Triarch. Think well on how you speak. I do not expect you to be humble, or abase yourself before me. I do not desire or seek that – you are a lord of the necrontyr, and I would have you act as one. But I also expect you to recall this – I am judging you. Consider this should you feel the urge to issue further commands to me.'

He takes her reprimand well. Hekasun's core-flux brightens as he processes his indignation, as does that of his vargard. Mandulis may be mute, but his fury on behalf of his chastened lord is clear to see.

Hekasun's hand strays to the diadem fused to his brow, clicking each digit against its jewel in turn. 'Very well. Please, praetorian. Share your analysis.'

Khemet is willing to overlook his sarcasm for now; she has shaped enough nobles to her will to know that they must be bent, not broken.

'Put simply, if we force an encounter with the humans before we are prepared, we will lose.'

Hekasun pauses in his idle tinkering. 'I had not imagined a praetorian could be a coward.'

He speaks the insult quickly, without consideration for the reasoning that brought her to this verdict. Khemet revises her previous judgement – some degree of breaking may be necessary.

'I have brought more worlds to heel than you have walked upon. Tell me, Lord Hekasun, have you fought the humans?'

Hekasun meets her ocular, but there is a new wariness in his gaze. 'They are weak.'

'Individually. But their strength is in their multitude. A single human war machine is trivial, but they will bring tens of thousands. A single human warrior is nothing, but they will call upon millions.'

'We have millions of our own,' says Kamoteph. The cryptek has been as wary of Khemet as his master since their arrival on Qeretesh. She has yet to decide whether Kamoteph was aware of Hekasun's intention to destroy her. In either case, she suspects that her decision to withhold the full power of the tomb world's command from Hekasun surprised him. If so, that is his error to bear, along with whatever consequences Hekasun chooses to mete out.

'Indeed, technomancer, indeed.' Hekasun looks up and around, as though seeing through the rock to the many legions of the tomb world that he can now call upon.

'Our forces will take years to awaken,' Khemet replies. 'And in that time, if we are rash, the humans will detect our presence beneath their feet. The seismic disturbance of troop movements and power generation will make it unavoidable.'

Hekasun glances briefly to his cryptek, who gives the slightest gesture of agreement.

Khemet continues. 'And thus they will bring a weight of fire and a weight of numbers down upon us that will choke our tombs before our armies can march forth.'

'*My* armies, praetorian. Mine.' Hekasun aims for imperious, but achieves petulance.

'We cannot meet them in open battle until we are ready,' she repeats. If they are to achieve their goal, and win this world for the Traveller as Hekasun has been commanded, then he must be made to grasp this point. If he chooses to indulge his new pride and begins rousing Qeretesh's legions prematurely, the same disaster that befell the Lazar crownworld will occur here.

'What, then? If we cannot take war to the humans, in what way do you propose to cleanse my world?'

Khemet extends one hand up, pointing far into the hall's dark upper vaults, to where Ahnuret has been watching their conversation from a distant balcony.

'Her way.'

If the deathmark is alarmed by their sudden attention, she shows no sign. The assassin has dogged Khemet's steps these past days, haunting the highest places of the tomb complex as Khemet has worked. For what purpose she has attached herself to Khemet's shadow, she still does not know.

Hekasun and Kamoteph follow Khemet's gesture, and understanding begins to dawn.

It will be a quiet war. A hidden war. A war that will break the humans long before the legions begin to march, fought far from the places that will become battlefields.

It will be a war waged from the shadows.

ACT 2

CHAPTER 1

Queen of the North is flying tonight.

The mile markers emerge from the darkness and disappear in a flash of grey rockcrete, a little more than once a minute. The cabin rocks gently as the locomotive follows the subtle undulations of the track. The hiss-thud of labouring pistons beats a tattoo that is as familiar to Vanda as the thump of her own heart.

Enginseer Third Echelon Vanda Gerig's eyes are half closed. She is sitting on the top of the breaker box, a tiny ledge of metal just deep enough to let her take the weight off her aching feet. She is as comfortable as it is possible to be while on duty. The box is located at the perfect confluence of the heat of the engine's reactor furnace and the cool air rushing along the locomotive's flank. She has recently eaten. There is little for her to do except monitor the coolant temperature dials and listen to the rhythm of her machine.

And, most importantly, she cannot smell the conveyor's cargo.

The three engines of Conveyor Sixteen-Red have been on the

same route for thirty-two years, and Vanda has been with them for every year and every mile. First south, laden with bricks of starch and slab collected from the agri-fields and the great tangle of processing plants, as foul and dangerous as any manufactorum on the planet. Half the bricks offloaded at the equatorial voidports, to go up on the lifters to feed the masses aboard the orbital plates, to be replaced by troops, tanks, and whatever goods the Munitorum sees fit to bring down to Orymous.

Then west, far to the west, through the belt of coastal billet-cities before turning north for the brutal sprawl of Verongyl. The entire stage takes eleven days, with pauses to unload and load at each city. Vanda hates that leg, hates the stop-start pace and the strain it puts on the *Queen* and the other locomotives. It takes the conveyor six hours to heave its way from a standstill to its running speed, engines roaring against the immensity of their carriages. It takes eight to gradually throttle back, the universal law of inertia doing far more of the work than the brakes. This was the first lesson she had been taught, before Vanda had even stepped aboard the *Queen*. A hundred thousand tons of metal and freight do not stop on a whim.

The final phase of the route takes Vanda back into the north. It is a long haul, but a simple one. No breaks, no pauses, just an uncomplicated exercise in mechanical effort to climb up the curve of the world to return to the agri-fields, loaded with the foulest of cargos.

On their westward run, each billet-city disgorges a bounty of cylindrical silos. Every silo is triple-sealed and welded shut, and yet their contents inevitably leak out. Human waste, the collected run-off of the cities' sewer systems, is hauled away by Conveyor Sixteen-Red to be used as fertiliser for the agri-fields. In her more philosophical moments, Vanda considers it fitting – she and the *Queen* deliver the bounty of Orymous' great plantations to the soldiers and civilians who are packed like cattle into the billet-cities, and return what becomes of that fare to the fields to sustain them.

Vanda can afford to be philosophical about their cargo. By dint of seniority over the other engines of Sixteen-Red, *Queen of the North* is the lead locomotive, and thus Vanda, as engine-captain, is spared the worst of the stench. Further back, aboard *Veredictum* and *Honour of Orymous*, Vanda knows that it is unbearable. Almost every enginseer assigned to Sixteen-Red has requested and received augmetic olfactory sensors, allowing them to at least be blind to the miasma that penetrates their clothes, hair, and skin with every mile of the northern passage.

Loaded with the manure of millions, Conveyor Sixteen-Red charges on through the night.

The door at the rear of the cabin swings open with a clang. 'Coming up on the hour, third echelon,' says Matejo Azahan.

Vanda blinks, her half-slumber abruptly banished. On the far side of the control cabin, wedged between the wall and the brass frame of a cogitator, Second Echelon Nikas Radomen rolls his eyes.

Vanda glances at the chrono. 'You do it.' She is comfortable atop the breaker box, and the vox-horn is wired into the cabin's centre console.

Matejo takes her laziness as an honour, a show of trust in him. He is a recent addition to the *Queen*'s crew, the single bar of first echelon newly tattooed over his right eyebrow. Vanda thinks he will work out, if he can shed his youthful desire to please all those around him.

The young man primly lifts the vox-horn and thumbs the activation stud. 'Conveyor Sixteen-Red, this is the hourly vox-check. All engines, report your condition.'

There is a pause, then a loud crackle of static. *'By the Throne, boy, it's the noctis shift. Would it kill you to pull that stick out of your arse for just a minute?'*

Vanda does not hide her chuckle. Matejo blushes, but finds the sternness within him. 'Report your condition, *Honour.'*

'This is Honour *of Orymous, at oh-three-hundred hours,'* says Hirve Donisas, third echelon of the *Honour,* in a bored monotone. *'All readouts are green. Coolant temperature nominal. Hydraulic pressure nominal. She's running like a dream, even with the nightmare of shit we're hauling.'*

'Noted, *Honour.'* Matejo does indeed diligently key Hirve's report into the cogitator console. *'Veredictum?'*

The rearmost engine of Sixteen-Red does not respond.

'Veredictum, come in.'

He waits another few seconds, then holds out the vox-horn in mute appeal.

With a heavy sigh, Vanda tips herself forwards from her seat and crosses to the vox-unit. She takes the horn from Matejo's outstretched hand.

'Come in, *Veredictum.'*

Again, silence.

Vanda scowls. With her free hand she reaches forwards to one of the control panels and flicks a switch. A tiny pict screen, no larger than Vanda's palm, hums into life. It shows nothing until she turns a dial, clicking through until she finds the feed for *Veredictum's* cabin picter.

There is no one on the footplate. No one, indeed, in *Veredictum's* control cabin at all.

She thumbs the vox again. 'Damn it, Alwyn, if you don't return to your post in the next three seconds I'm going to have to record this in the route log.'

The seconds tick by, and Alwyn Handr does not appear.

'Throne of Terra,' Vanda mutters. She clicks the dial through the other pict feeds aboard the locomotive. One returns only static and the other, the feed from the interior of the engine's reactor furnace, is occluded, showing only a thin smear of light between blackness.

'Hirve, go and check on him.'

She is not panicking, not yet. It is strange that all three of *Veredictum*'s on-duty crew have absconded, but there are reasons why all three would abandon their posts.

None of them are good, though.

Vanda's gaze shifts to the hatch to her right. There are twenty indentured serfs at work within the furnace of each engine. They are criminals, saved from the horrors of Servitude Imperpituis only to endure a more immediately lethal fate. Few last more than two or three years; the radioactive overspill from the engine's reactors turns their bones to powder and their organs to liquid. Their lives, more than the radiological material that fires the furnace, are the fuel on which *Queen of the North* runs.

It is rare for the serfs to rebel, enfeebled and chained as they are to the machine they serve, but it is the fear of every engine-captain.

'*Don't make me, Vanda,*' Hirve Donisas says over the vox.

'Do it, and take your goad.'

Enginseers work unarmed, aside from shock goads intended to keep the serfs in line when necessary. She can hear Hirve turn serious. '*All right. I'll call in from* Veredictum.'

More than a mile of shit-streaked silo cars separate *Honour of Orymous* from *Veredictum*, and it is a perilous walk along the exterior gantries. It will take him time, Vanda tells herself.

The minutes pass slowly.

'Should we report this?' asks Matejo.

'We're due a check-in with the terminal in eighteen minutes. I'll tell them then.' Vanda doesn't want to report Handr.

Dereliction of duty would mean the loss of his captaincy, and he has been driving for almost as long as Vanda.

The chrono continues to spin. Vanda clicks back to *Veredictum*'s cabin pict feed, waiting for Hirve's lean form to appear at the open door.

The chrono's needle ticks round to twenty past. Hirve has yet to appear.

'Hirve?' she asks into the vox-horn, hoping that his name will summon the fellow engine-driver to appear. Beside her, Nikas looks as worried as Vanda feels.

An impact like the fall of a trip-hammer, or the chime of a monstrous bell, shivers through the *Queen*'s superstructure.

'What in the name of Terra was that?' All three drivers spin to the rear of the cabin, Vanda's grip tight on the vox-horn.

The rear of the engine holds the crew quarters. The *Queen* has bunks for two, along with a tiny galley and ablutorial, and then the hatch leading to the conveyor's exterior. The door through which Matejo has come is closed, but the latch is not locked shut.

Another strike, softer but still heavy. Then another.

'Hirve?' Vanda asks. The rhythmic stamp of metal on metal draws closer. They are footsteps, unmistakably, although too far apart and far too heavy to be any of her crew.

An unnatural, superstitious fear takes hold in Vanda's belly. The tales of monsters and aliens she had learnt as a child come back in a rush. They had always given her nightmares, even though every story ended with the mighty legions of Orymous crushing the Imperium's enemies. Her father had been too good a storyteller, painting Vanda's dreams with vivid images of green-skinned barbarians and cruel, dancing aliens.

But it is none of these horrors that appears at the cabin's door.

The metal flies open, hurled back on hinges that squeal suddenly.

Vanda screams in fright at the sound, but the cry dies in her throat at the sight of the thing that threw open the door.

An enormous creature looms above her. A metal skeleton, hideously broad, peers into the cabin. It has a face, an inhuman metal face, with a green orb embedded in the centre of its head.

The hatch is too low and too narrow for the creature to enter. It bends on thick legs, the action sickeningly human, and curls metal digits around the hatch bulkhead. It pushes and the metal crumples, torn like tin. It stoops, a broad shoulder tearing through an overhead storage unit. A weapon, its blade as long as Vanda's leg, is held in one hand. The curved sword glows with sickly radiance, painting the cabin's black walls a vile green.

Vanda Gerig feels the vox-horn slide from her hands.

The engine's shock goads are locked in a slim cabinet just beside the rear hatch. Matejo Azahan lunges for the armoury strongbox, forgetting that he has not been entrusted with the code. This act of bravery, as noble as it is pointless, brings him closer to the metal monster, and for this he dies first.

Khemet kills quickly, efficiently. After the first human hurls himself on her blade none of the others find their courage. One attempts to throw herself out of the locomotive's cabin, but Khemet is much, much faster. The woman dies with Khemet's staff in her spine. She hauls the body back inside, to slide off into a wet pile on the blood-slick floor.

She has worked her way along the conveyor's length, and is now well practised in disabling the engine vehicles that pull it along. With a single cut she carves the furnace hatch from its hinges, and finds the expected rad-wasted creatures within. She looks upon their deaths as a mercy.

Khemet can barely stand inside the furnace's interior, but that does not matter. She links her mind with the slim obsidian plate affixed to her waist, which awakens with a familiar glow of energies. From its jade surface comes first one scarab, then another, then a flood. A skittering swarm of Kamoteph's chosen constructs pour like a waterfall from the dimension gate, and then they set to work.

The constructs tear through the machine that the humans consider ancient, but which to a necron is hopelessly primitive. The scarabs do not commit mindless carnage, but targeted destruction. Fail-safe systems are slashed first, then the locomotive's vox-systems and cogitators. Finally, the immense pistons that drive the pneumatics of the braking lines are pierced by hundreds of bladed mandibles.

With a shriek of venting hydraulics, *Queen of the North* screams as it is carved apart from within.

When their work is done the scarabs return to Khemet, spilling from the rents they have made in the engine housing and disappearing back into the green plane of the dimension gate. They will be back at Kamoteph's side in moments. Khemet briefly envies them their rapid return to the tomb world's depths. Her own journey will take several days of marching through the desolate hinterland, and several more of trudging along the ocean bed to the complex's closest entrance.

Khemet crosses to the open step of the locomotive. The landscape races by, heedless of the deaths and the destruction she has wrought. She takes no pride in the murder of the hulking machine or its crew. It was a task, unchallenging save for the need to avoid the humans' crude means of internal surveillance. The pride is found in the end, not the means.

Khemet steps into open air, and the anti-gravity emitters in her torso lift her into the night sky.

Unrestrained, *Queen of the North* charges on.

When Conveyor Sixteen-Red misses its hourly vox-check with

the railhead authorities, protocol is followed. An archaeopter is dispatched with a cargo of rapid-response enginseers. It takes the crimson ornithopter forty-six minutes to intercept the stricken conveyor, but only four for the Mechanicus adepts to assess the damage as catastrophic and irreparable.

They remain calm, for they are adherents of the Machine God and thus aspire to be above petty emotionality. Furthermore, a protocol exists for this contingency. Conveyor Sixteen-Red can be diverted to a run-off track – two hundred miles of long, slow incline into the foothills of the Prandalii Mountains.

The adepts report the situation to their overseers, who in turn alert the signal operators on the outskirts of the railhead.

There is no response from the signal operators. Remote-access protocols fail to reach the cogitators that control the rail switches. A second scrambled archaeopter reports murder at the switching station and carnage among the sanctified mechanisms.

At the railhead, clarions scream and workers run. Evacuations of this scale have been planned, but never put into action. Tens of thousands of serfs clamber aboard carriages on the secondary rails, and are borne away along the slim tracks that bring cargoes in from the agri-fields. The officials and adepts who manage the terminal flee in groundcars and flyers, all shouting into vox-casters to demand answers that do not come.

An hour after the last labourer has fled the network of rails and depots and silos, *Queen of the North* arrives.

A hundred thousand tons of iron, brass, and human ordure crash through the flimsy buffers, though no obstacle in the world would have been equal to the assault. The conveyor thunders through the brick-and-rockcrete warehouses and offices, rips the foundations from gantry cranes, shatters the bodies of carriages and flatbeds and other conveyors.

Thanks only to the grace of the God-Emperor and the work of

the rapid-response team, none of the locomotives' fission reactors explode. But they do tear, layers of armour peeling away beneath the succession of impacts to expose the broken heart of *Queen of the North*. Fissile material, rad-laden liquid and human waste spill across ten miles of gravel, a toxic tide of black water that infects all that it touches.

It spills through the open mouths of warehouses, polluting the sixteen billion bricks of starch and slab that were waiting to be delivered to the hungering mouths of Orymous.

Major General Heinzen Flener spears the last morsel of verdikine on his plate, mops it through the remainder of an extravagantly rich sauce, and stuffs it into his mouth.

'This business up north… Is it causing any trouble with supply?'

The rest of the table's diners studiously ignore the man's poor manners, along with his absurd question. It has been twenty-one days since disaster struck the primary railhead for the northern agri-fields, and the effects are only beginning to be felt across the entire continent.

News of the derailment was impossible to contain, spreading through the unofficial channels of whisper and rumour like wildfire. Its progress could be tracked by the outbreaks of civil unrest that spread from city to city, as the civilian populace worked out for themselves what the adjudicators and metriculators of the lord-militant's office were concluding – every citizen's daily ration must be cut in half, for at least the next three months.

'Well?' barks Flener.

Flener is recently arrived on Orymous, along with two hundred and thirty thousand soldiers of the God-Emperor's Astra Militarum. His division will be a part of the Beathen Crusade, an undertaking that has been seven years in the making. Millions of men and women have been brought to Orymous, to wait and to train for the day when they will be unleashed against the Imperium's enemies.

But until that time, they must be fed, sheltered, and policed by the ceaseless labours of the Officio Logisticarum.

'I am afraid so, general,' replies Logisticator Primus Farroll evenly. 'The situation is quite grave.'

Farroll is effortlessly tactful in the face of Flener's ignorance. He was a native of Orymous, and of the city of Verongyl he now governs. A graduate of its principal scholam, over the course of eighty years Farroll worked his way through the rungs of the billet-city's bureaucracy, and for the past twelve has sat at its very top. In the feudal hierarchy of most Imperial bodies, merit is not necessarily what determines elevation through their stratified ranks. Fortunately for Verongyl and for Orymous, Farroll has been an exception.

'Open your stores, then,' offers Flener casually. 'Surely you have reserves.'

'Indeed we do, general, and indeed we have. But there are over a billion Imperial souls on Orymous, without counting the valiant warriors of the God-Emperor we host. Even in times of plenty, we exist on thin margins. Disruption on this scale cannot easily be absorbed.'

At the far end of the room, silent and passive, Gerand Cadfan watches and listens. He is aide senioris to the logisticator primus, and Cadfan fears that the old man will not survive this crisis. He is long overdue to temporarily demit from his office to undergo greatly needed medicae and rejuvenat treatments, but the Sixteen-Red disaster has ended any hope of that. Farroll has worked until the small hours for every day since the planet's infosphere blossomed into mayhem. The last thing he needs is to waste time entertaining oafish fools like Flener, but the demands of his office are not conditional upon good health and fair days.

'At least *we* are in no danger of going hungry!' said Flener cheerfully, as the palace's waiting staff sweep in to remove the wreckage of the party's meat course and replace it with the first of the desserts.

The arrival of artfully worked sucrose breaks up the conversation, and Flener's crass display is brushed aside. As the diners devolve into their pairs, arguing or debating depending on familiarity and institutional friction, Farroll quietly taps a napkin to his lips.

'If you will all excuse me.'

Cadfan is behind him instantly, easing the logisticator's chair back with noiseless grace. Farroll, brow sweating, lifts himself by the seat's gilded arms, and with the aid of a silver-pommelled cane starts with some haste towards the dining hall's rear.

No one passes comment on his sudden departure. Farroll's ill health is an open secret among the city's upper echelons, and none of the new arrivals – not even Flener – are rude enough to ask where their host is going.

Cadfan follows the logisticator at a discreet distance as he leaves through the rear of the dining room. Farroll is as sensitive about his delicate bowels as he is famous for them, and Cadfan had been on the receiving end of his vicious tongue often enough to learn to give his master his privacy.

They pass through two further receiving halls, each as large and as grand as the dining chamber where Farroll's guests are seated. The logisticator is an ascetic man by nature, but the palace and its many antiquities and decorations were in place long before Farroll took up his position, and will endure long after. Paintings, sculptures, and various historic documents lie in stasis fields, ensuring that this is the case.

It is fortunately only a short walk to Farroll's office, and through it to his private ablutorial.

'When you have a moment, my lord, there are distribution orders that require your attention.'

'Later, Cadfan, later.' The ablutorial door swings shut, effectively punctuating his dismissal.

Gerand Cadfan settles into the time-filling activities of a lifelong bureaucrat. The mentioned distribution orders are shuffled together, neatly arrayed beside the logisticator's seal and ink. A pair of dataslates are deactivated and tidied into a drawer of the desk. A thick-based glass is filled with purified water from a decanter on a side table in anticipation of Farroll's thirst.

There is a small sound, a swift whine noticeable only by its softness. Cadfan turns, curious, then starts at the heavy thud that travels through the wooden door.

'My lord?'

No angered shout greets his weak question. He waits, caution battling with duty, but he does not wait long.

The logisticator primus' private hygenium is as subtly rendered as the rest of his sanctum. Blue and white tiles, each marked with the Imperial aquila in the opposite colour, line the floor, and light in a hundred colours beams from a glassaic window. The ablutorial is behind a screen, elegantly maintaining the dignity of the space.

Farroll is on the floor, eyes rolled back in their sockets, blood sheeting from his nose.

The devoted aide rushes in, dropping to his master's side, ignoring the pain that flares through his knees from the impact with the tiled floor. Protocol is abandoned as he cradles the old man's head. He knew he should have insisted Farroll step back, delegate more. And now all of Cadfan's fears have come to pass.

Something clicks on the tiles, near at hand. Gerand Cadfan turns, tears in his eyes, to look into the barrel of a long, bulky weapon, held in metal hands.

The weapon's tip emits the softest glow. It is the last thing Cadfan sees.

* * *

The body strikes the tiles with a second thump, meat rippling from the impact within its cloth coverings.

Ahnuret struggles to contain her disgust. There is no outward sign of her revulsion – she is not burdened by the involuntary physical responses of the biological forms she abhors. It is a purely intellectual burden, a horror and repugnance that skips in cycles through her mind.

It is not merely the humans themselves. They are the loci of her disgust, but just as bad is the sensation of organic particles in the air. The minute and myriad fragments of the Unclean existence. The specks and flakes of life's detritus, wafting on currents to settle on her sacred necrodermis.

With an almighty effort, Ahnuret masters herself. Her sacrifice in exposing herself to this filth is in service of a purpose.

The human who had followed its master into the chamber is not dead, though it is only a matter of time. Crimson leaks from where its skull struck the tiled floor, its synaptic pathways burnt to ash by Ahnuret's weapon. The deathmark almost turns aside from the sight, but she forces herself to look for what she knows the body will possess.

She is meant to stage the scene to present the appearance of murder followed by suicide, a means of concealing her role and that of her people. For this, she requires one of the humans' own weapons.

The servant is indeed armed with a short-barrelled pistol, holstered at its waist and half-concealed beneath a fold of cloth. Ahnuret sees that the sidearm's grip is too small for her to hold. With a minor effort, she reshapes the necrodermis of her hand, reducing her digits to compare with that of the human who lies brain-dead at her feet. She reaches down to pluck the weapon from the body.

A flake of skin, a single mote in the light that shines through the window, lands upon her outstretched hand.

She freezes. Ahnuret's mind locks, overtaken by horror and fury. The curse thrashes within its cage, demanding to be released, demanding that she scour this taint from her body, from her world, from her universe.

A knock of flesh against wood echoes through the ablutorial.

'Logisticator Primus? Are you all right? This is Captain Nasan. Your alert band was activated.'

Danger breaks the recursive cycle. Ahnuret looks down at the elderly human at her feet. It has a thick ring on an index finger, a golden band crowned with a large ruby-red stone. With its final seconds of life, as Ahnuret's synaptic disintegrator shredded its mind, the Unclean evidently triggered some kind of warning. Ahnuret can sense it, now that she is alive to it – an electromagnetic burst of alarm blaring from an emitter concealed within the ring.

She has lingered too long, trapped by her horrified paralysis. Any hope of portraying the murder as the work of an enraged servant is lost. All that matters is that she not be discovered.

Ahnuret opens a hyperspace oubliette and flees into its depths.

A moment later, the guards come in with lasguns drawn. For an instant, Captain Nasan thinks that she sees something from the corner of her eye, twinkling in the air. But when she lifts her gaze there is nothing. Then her eye is drawn to the bodies on the floor, and all else is forgotten.

Gweldyn Pyrch holds up his seal of office, hung about his neck on a slim cord. The enforcers at the checkpoint inspect it, then wave him through.

Dust and refuse billow down the street as Pyrch ducks under the barrier. The dust carries the smell of fyceline and blood, to which Pyrch would, on any other day, be entirely immune.

But this is not an ordinary day. The last vestiges of the riots are still burning in the farthest precincts of the billet-city, and the stillness of the morning is due only to the enforcers and seconded Astra Militarum units at each corner. Thankfully, the office of the chief verispexor – Pyrch's office – is sited far from the Administratum palace, and thus was spared the worst of the fighting that spontaneously erupted around its gates in the wake of the logisticator primus' death.

Bodies fill the city's mortuaria, awaiting collection by relatives who fear to associate themselves with the men and women who surged towards the palace grounds when the news first reached the streets. Whether a spontaneous outburst of collective mourning, or an opportunist expression of anger and dismay at the state of the food supply to the city, it matters little. The guards, afraid and alert after their chief protectee died while under their care, reacted as they did, and now hundreds are dead, with many thousands more filling the city's hospitals and gaols.

Pyrch yawns as he pushes open the main door of the mortuarium. He spent much of the night watching the crowds run from the enforcers in their armoured vehicles from the window of his hab. It was a poor way to prepare for this day's work.

His assistant is waiting for him in the building's foyer, fidgeting with a chartboard clutched in both hands.

'Are they ready for me?' he asks before Ahmose can speak.

'On the slabs, sir.' Antim Ahmose is young, capable, and all too aware of his skills. And, Pyrch thinks, far too casual in his reference to the body of the billet-city's esteemed governor.

'Go and find out when I can access the scene. And see if you can't find me something to eat while you are about it.' Pyrch, despite his station, lacked a servant of his own, and the refectory where he typically broke his fast had been closed during his short walk to the mortuarium.

Ahmose chastened, Pyrch briskly trots up the marble stairs of the main vestibule, through another checkpoint, and on into the suite of laboratoria that make up the top floors of the building.

As Ahmose said, Logisticator Primus Farroll and his aide lie on separate metal slabs in Pyrch's preferred examination room, bodies covered by black cloth. It is simple enough to tell them apart even with their faces covered. Farroll is willow-thin and tall, whereas his servant is built like a grox, broad-shouldered and squat.

Pyrch is, oddly, looking forward to the next few hours. His task is simple to give, yet he suspects it will be difficult to achieve. Whatever killed both men must be explained, to quell the panic in the streets with the counterseptic light of truth, and, more importantly, provide answers to the host of senior officials, enforcers, and the alarmed staff of the lord-militant, who are all demanding to know whether it was simply Farroll's declining health or some malign actor that ended his life and that of his aide.

Pyrch removes his overcoat and gloves, tossing both onto a stool in one corner. He crosses to the counter that runs along one wall of the room, its surface polished to a sheen of silver. He turns on a tap and begins to scrub up, a holdover from his years as residential chirurgeon to one of the many Astra Militarum barracks sited in and around Verongyl.

He is washing the last of the caustic cleaning fluid from his forearms when a sound, a click of metal against metal, makes Pyrch turn.

A skeleton looms above him. It is monstrous in its scale, inhuman in its resemblance to humanity's basic form. It is skeletal, yet its limbs are broad and bulky in mimicry of musculature. The joints in its arms and legs and shoulders move and roll as Pyrch would expect. The chest cage is what fascinates him most, more even than the one great eye at the centre of its skull. A sickening glow emanates from between the metal ribs. It is hunched over beneath the laboratory's low ceiling, and from its right arm hangs a curtain of some kind of tiles.

The creature holds an enormous staff in one hand, topped by two translucent blades that gleam with a sickening light. Insectoid things lurk around its legs, and clamber along its shoulders like pets.

It is, unquestionably, the most horrific sight Pyrch has ever witnessed.

'Sir, I could not raise the palace. There is something corrupting the building's vox-relay.' Ahmose pushes open the exam room's door with one hand, still gripping his chartboard with the other.

With shocking speed the creature sweeps its staff around. The monstrous head, bladed and alive with energy, passes through Ahmose's torso without the slightest pause. The two halves of Pyrch's assistant strike the tiled floor in a welter of gore.

Pyrch releases a noise. It is not a scream but a moan, a low groan that emerges from the centre of his being, soul-deep and unrestrained. It is the sound of a beast, a cattle animal confronted by something it cannot comprehend.

'Well, that is unfortunate.' The creature speaks, its voice an electronic growl of Gothic syllables. It turns back to Pyrch. Its face, or what passes for one, radiates malice. Flecks of Ahmose's blood hiss from the blade of the thing's enormous staff. 'You will have to do something about that later.'

Pyrch takes a single step back, mouth agape. The creature reaches out a hand, fingers curled towards Pyrch, and the beetles that walk across its body leap.

They fly at him, a nightmare of razor-edged legs and snapping jaws. More are coming, emerging from nothingness, a tide of iridescent bodies falling from a shimmering surface that hangs from the skeleton's metal body.

Now Pyrch screams.

They are every size, from hounds and felids to vermin and fleas. Carapaces gleam in the sharp light of the examination ward, viridian and opal and gold enclosing skittering black metal bodies. Pinions click and clatter across the metal floor, a staccato riot of sound that swallows the sound of Pyrch's cries.

He tumbles back against the cabinet, falling away from the tide of metal monstrosities that are hurling themselves onto his body. The largest grip his wrists and ankles, hard enough to restrain but not so tight as to break bones or sever flesh. The lesser beasts are on him, climbing up his legs. They are shockingly heavy for their size, lumps of animated metal that tug at his flesh.

A thousand pinpricks track their way up the skin of his chest, crawling beneath the fabric of his shirt. They are on his neck, his face. They are in his eyes, his ears, his nose. They crawl inside his open mouth, clinging to the soft tissue of his cheeks. Something stabs at the back of his throat and Pyrch tastes blood, copper over the vile tang of alien metal.

The creatures are inside him, swarming through his flesh. He is still screaming, but the screams are suffocated by the weight of insects on his tongue.

Something pinches, seizing not flesh but nerves and brain stem. There is a struggle, fleeting and entirely one-sided. Pyrch falls silent.

Slowly, reluctantly, the tide of scarabs recedes. They climb out of his open mouth, and track their way down his body. Thousands of shallow nicks and cuts cover the skin of his chest and arms where their needle-sharp limbs have pierced him. The pain is agonising, but Pyrch does not cry or whimper. The one scarab that remains, jaws locked tight around the top of his spinal column, is firmly in command.

Pyrch sags as the canid-sized scarabs release his arms and legs.

Their jaws have left red welts around his wrists. He knows that he will need to conceal them until they heal, lest they give rise to questions that might compromise his new allegiance.

Pyrch looks up and into his master's enormous green eye. The change is instantaneous. What had been inhuman is now beatific. Noble. Commanding. Pyrch can see his reflection in that gaze, and he is overcome with revulsion for what he sees. His place is on his knees, head bowed in supplication. His duty is to serve. He *is* servile, born and bred only to offer his meagre labours to those who are as gods to him.

Pyrch drops in an instant, overwhelmed by shame for daring to meet his master's eye. From his knees he raises his hands above his head, palms up and open, in echo of a gesture he somehow knows is older than the genetic history of his species.

In the back of his mind, held in place by alien chains, Pyrch screams and screams and screams.

'There,' his master says. 'Now we understand each other.'

Kamoteph the Crooked leans back, settling himself against the autopsy table. He places his staff across his knees and adjusts the fall of tiles that drape from his arm. The wave of scarabs gather about his legs, while some clamber up his body and along his spine.

'So, my new friend. Let us discuss the two bodies you are about to inspect, and what it is you are going to find.'

The smoke wakes Thestri. It coils around the edges of the dorm's doorway, insidious fingers of grey fumes.

It takes some time for him to stir. He had taken the noctis shift to let Semmi, his watch-partner, get some rest. There should have been four of them crewing the tower, but the Officio reassigned Halwyn and Sadryn four months ago and never bothered to replace them.

But despite his bone-deep weariness and empty belly, the rasp of hot air in his throat finally forces Thestri into waking.

He coughs, hawks saliva, and spits over the edge of the bunk in the vague direction of the dorm's spittoon. He opens his eyes, which are immediately stung by the streamers of grey smoke that have gathered among the room's metal rafters.

The smoke smells sweet. Cloyingly sweet.

Thestri bolts upright, sleep banished by a jolt of adrenaline that sets his heart thundering. Shaking, he rolls off his bunk. He lands badly, pain shooting up his ankle. He ignores it, lunging for the dormitory's door, not bothering to even pull on his overalls.

'Semmi?' He tries to shout, but the word emerges as a bark, barely carrying the length of the corridor. The hallway is half-hidden by the smoke, boiling through the exterior hatch. The metal door swings open in clear violation of Officio regulations.

He and Semmi have one responsibility. The cane fields are a tinderbox in the summer months. The tight rows of stalks trap the heat, setting the stage for lightning strikes all across the plains of Orymous Secundus. Thestri and his watch-partner have reported three fires in as many weeks, bringing their sector's response teams charging in with suppressant foam and brush-cutters. He and Semmi have earned a minor commendation from the local Logisticarum overseer; their vigilance has kept the losses from each blaze within the allowable margin.

A wall of heat hits Thestri as he hauls the hatch open, a dry, choking heat that seems to suck the air from his lungs.

Thestri dives into the darkening corridor, finding the steps to the watch-station's tower by memory. He takes the stairs three at a time, each leap setting off a tremor that shivers through the metal frame. His twisted ankle protests with each step, but he ignores it, hauling himself up the switchback stairs.

Thestri reaches the summit, and grabs for the hatch handle. He gropes at open air; the metal plate is hanging off its hinges, partly wedged in the doorway. He clambers over the obstacle, but catches his foot and lands on his hands and knees.

He lands in blood. Red smears his hands as they slide through the gore. Thestri's chin hits the deck and he feels his teeth crack.

Dazed, he pushes himself up. He doesn't understand what he is seeing. Hunks of flesh and flecks of bone coat the watchtower's floor. Its windows are shattered. The vox-unit used to call in strike sightings has been carved into ruin. Enormous slashes, cutting deep through the console's frame and into the sanctified workings within. Sparks and yet more smoke are spitting from its ruined interior.

His bare foot knocks against something, and Thestri looks down. Semmi is staring up at him, eyes wide in their sockets. His head rolls over, cut free from his body.

Thestri vomits.

When he can finally straighten up, he knows what he will see.

From horizon to horizon, the cane fields are burning.

'Faster! We're nearly there.'

Taron Gethisme and his family run, run as if their lives depend upon their haste.

They head towards the sanctuary of a pool of yellow light, a single box-lumen caged behind wire mesh. The lumen marks the entrance to the civic shelter for their hab-district. Taron can see it, six blocks away, a tiny puddle of light at the base of the broad rockcrete bastion at the end of the road. It hunkers low to the ground, half the height of the rows of hab-blocks that line the road, but he knows that the bastion delves deep into the foundations of the city. If he can get his family to that light, Taron tells himself, they will be safe.

Beneath the pounding of his feet and the air sawing in his chest, Taron hears the sound of metal scraping against stone, and he knows the daemon has found them.

'Faster!'

The lights had died three days earlier. In itself, this was not extraordinary; Delmenyl is not an affluent district, and rolling blackouts are common in the winter months. But this is different. Every lumen in the city of Pasken died in the same breath. The power plants in the east, fed by the offshore promethium rigs, erupted in a monstrous explosion that had shattered windows for miles around. Taron has seen the reports – the power plants are still burning, and the local municipal backups are failing one after the other, for reasons no red-robed coghead can explain.

The reports had passed across his desk along with countless others. He is a clerk, grade secundus, for the Delmenyl enforcer blockhouse. He serves the Lex, but does not wear the shield. His role is to catalogue, to archive and record. That makes him a knowledgeable man, at least in regard to the criminal activities of Pasken, but that is not how he first heard of the daemon.

Jonie slips on a patch of ice, and Taron breaks his stride to pull the boy along by his arm. Jonie cries out. His father is hurting him, and he does not understand why they are out in the cold and the dark.

Every district of Pasken, every city on Orymous, has a daemon. Or perhaps it is the same daemon, stalking the darkened streets, making murder where it goes.

Taron had not believed it, at first. Violence is a fact of Pasken – gang wars, madmen, and the inevitable blood shed in the enforcement of the Lex. When the stories had begun a little more than a year ago, shared by gossiping investigators and drunken sanctioners, he had paid them little heed. But then the daemon had come to Delmenyl, and he had seen it for himself.

Taron has seen the verispexy picts, and wishes he had not. Hundreds of bodies hacked apart. The deacon of Saint Trypiyat's, strangled and hung from his pulpit by his entrails. And always blood, an ocean of blood, spilt from alleyways and promenades and dock wharves and mansions. Wherever there is darkness, they say, the daemon moves. And always there is the sound of its blades against the stone.

Taron Gethisme had been a pious man, diligent in his worship of the God-Emperor. But he has cursed His name for abandoning him, for abandoning his family, to the cruelty of the thing that lurks in the shadows of Orymous.

The daemon has haunted the world for months, killing wherever it wills. But now, with the city plunged into darkness, the daemon has made Pasken its home. Hour by hour, the reports have flashed across the enforcers' vox. Dozens butchered in a marketplace, their lungs spread like an angel's wings. Hab-blocks razed, burning like chimneys. Two hundred people vanished while at prayer, the chapel emptied of souls as though by the Emperor's own hand.

Fifty steps. That is all that is left. The length of a hab-block, and they will be safe. The shelter has been opened by Taron's blockhouse's captain, defying the city governor's order that they remain inviolate and ready in case of war. But Taron knows Orymous is at war, at war with a shade that kills in ways Taron has never imagined.

Twenty steps.

There is a picter mounted above the door, and Taron waves his free arm as he runs. Taron has sent word ahead, secured a place for himself and his family.

'Let us in! In Terra's name, let us in!'

Ten steps.

The door opens.

Something catches Taron's collar, ice cold against the nape of his neck.

The scrape of metal on stone carries deep into the shelter.

Khemet kills quickly, efficiently. She moves from room to room within the bastion, careful to always drag one hand through the powdery stone from which the humans have built their fortress. Talon marks adorn the walls of this ugly pretence of a city.

She does not kill them all. Mystery and stealth have their place in her campaign, but her purpose in Pasken is to stoke fear. She is a revenant, a thing birthed from human nightmares to haunt their waking hours. To be truly effective, the tales of her deeds must spread.

She selects three at random. She cuts their eyes from their skulls and leaves them for others to find. The mutilation is gratuitous, but that is its purpose. It is not enough to simply kill, or even to massacre. Khemet must make statements with each broken body, to inspire the stories that will spread through the Unclean and cause them to dread every moment of their lives.

Tonight she has struck three other bastions, and a cathedrum of the humans' corpse-god. She has made them fear the places their leaders have told them are safe, to which they should flee in times of peril.

Tomorrow she will go into their homes.

The hiss and grind and slam of machinery is all that Llewellyn can hear. Everything, that is, except for the screaming.

He makes his way along the catwalk, ignoring the wet heat and punishingly vile smell that rises from the vats below. Each enormous drum, twenty feet across and forty feet deep, processes enough liquid slab to produce tens of thousands of bricks from each three-day cooking cycle. The protein slurry is poured in from the pipes that run overhead, mixed and boiled in the enormous vats, then drained off into the moulds. Every hour of every day, and each step of the noxious process, is watched by Llewellyn and the other plant overseers.

Llewellyn stops above Vat Three, mopping his brow with a filthy rag. There are other plant workers on the gantry, sweating freely in the muggy air. He waits until they have passed. He must not be discovered. That was key. His master had been quite insistent.

He hears the screaming again, from somewhere far off.

Llewellyn waits until the clanks of footfalls recede, then reaches into a pocket. He uncorks the vial and tips its contents over the railing in a single action. The glass tube disappears back into the pocket.

There are six more vials concealed within his apron, one for each of the remaining vats on this level. He does not know what the liquid will do, though he can guess.

It will take days before the taint is discovered and traced back to the plant. There would be hundreds of thousands, perhaps even millions, of bricks that would have to be recalled and destroyed. And that was ignoring how many people would sicken and die from the tainted slab before his work is noticed.

He sets off again. Nothing shows on his face besides overheated boredom. He nods to a fellow overseer as they pass on the gantry.

In a corner of his mind, Llewellyn screams in horror at what he has done. The scarab nestled at the base of his brain stem pinches its mandibles tighter, and the screaming stops.

Every lumen-bulb in Verongyl's Administratum palace is ablaze. The plate-glass roofs of its halls glow like beacons in the night, casting their glare over the city that its occupants are meant to govern.

'As you commanded, lord. Every chandelier has been lit, every lumen-strip shines.'

Captain Tamya Nasan stands at attention. It is well that it is a stance that Nasan finds as natural as breathing, because she has been awake for forty unbroken hours. It is only muscle memory and duty that hold Nasan upright. If Logisticator Primus Darien notices the dirt and sweat-marks that stain her uniform, or the deep shadows that ring her eyes, he does not mention it.

'Very good, Nasan. And the guards?'

'All checkpoints within the palace have been doubled, and I have ordered roaming units throughout the east wing. The Six-Hundred-and-Seventy-Ninth Argellians patrol the grounds.'

'Thank you, captain.' Darien makes it heartfelt, and Nasan drops her gaze to meet his eye.

'Of course, lord.'

Darien replaced Logisticator Primus Farroll after his death, though it has taken six months for his elevation from secundus rank to be confirmed by the lord-militant's office. In normal times, Darien might have proved an able governor for Verongyl. But these are not normal times.

'You understand about the lumens? My daughters… It is hard to deny rumour when it has persisted for so long.'

'I understand, lord.'

Nasan is grateful for the logisticator's concern for his family, for her own children live within the palace compound, and they too have heard the whispers of the metal daemon that stalks the night. More importantly, Nasan has seen the reports from Pasken and the other cities of Orymous. Whatever hunts the God-Emperor's subjects lives in the darkness. She has heard that since the killings began in Verongyl, Saint Polaryn's Cathedrum has been giving out lumen-sticks blessed by the cardinal to its petitioners, to be carried like totems through the streets.

'What of the city?' asks Darien.

The panic started at daybreak the previous morning. Claw-marks had been etched into the stone portico of a district market, slashing through the Imperial aquila carved into the building's face. Word spread on wings of fear, and in a matter of hours the city had descended into chaos. Industry and commerce have ceased. Those brave enough to step outside their habs have used the opportunity to raid Administratum supply depots, hoping to alleviate their hunger while others concern themselves only with surviving the coming night.

'Widespread disturbance, lord,' says Nasan.

'Is it contained?'

Nasan cannot help the wince that crosses her face. 'We are hearing that up to half of the sanctioner corps has not reported for duty.'

Darien is sanguine. 'I cannot condemn that, I suppose. I have you to protect me and my family. We must all look to our own, in such times.'

Nasan says nothing. The 679th Argellian Grenadiers had been ordered to Verongyl with the explicit purpose of keeping the city's key industries active, and Darien has deployed it to augment his own defences. But as captain of the logisticator primus' guard, she cannot pretend she is displeased to have a regiment of the Astra Militarum digging in around her palace grounds.

'Do you believe it?' Darien has turned away from her and is staring into a window, though with the corridor's lumens ablaze he can only see his reflection in the glass. 'That Orymous is cursed?'

Tamya Nasan is too tired to summon a more discreet reply. 'The Ecclesiarchy tell us that the God-Emperor protects us from such things.'

Logisticator Primus Darien absorbs this in silence.

The vox-bead sewn into Nasan's collar clicks. In the window's reflection, Darien watches the colour drain from her face.

'My lord.' Captain Nasan cannot keep the quaver from her voice. 'Eleven minutes ago, several checkpoints in the Lozens district reported hearing unusual sounds emanating from a nearby chapel. The squads sent to investigate have not returned.'

It could be nothing. On any other night, in any other year, such information would have never reached the Administratum palace guard. There are any number of explanations for squads of sanctioners failing to report in.

Darien steps away from the window, nothing but sedate calm showing on his face. 'I am going to be with my daughters, captain.'

Enmitics are Ahnuret's favoured class of weapon.

Enmitic energy reaches into the very molecules of a target's being and tears them apart. Each Unclean struck by the twin beams of her pistols is explosively reduced to their constituent atoms, the swiftest, cleanest, and most final end Ahnuret can achieve.

That finality is what she seeks. Ahnuret does not see the killing of the Unclean as a means towards a greater end. The praetorian seeks to terrify the humans, weakening them before the inevitable conflict that is coming. Ahnuret desires only that they die now, as swiftly and completely as possible. If she could pour enmitic energy across the entire face of the world, Ahnuret would do it.

The Unclean run, and she pursues them. With each shot another is unmade. Another that is no longer able to befoul her with their existence. To pollute this planet, this necron world, with their foetor.

This is not what Khemet wants, but Ahnuret is running out of patience for the praetorian's campaign. She is able to kill any human on this world, and the only challenge is adhering to Khemet's order that her hand in their death goes undetected.

It is not that Ahnuret seeks to upend the praetorian's plans. It is simply that their importance for the deathmark dwindles with every passing day.

The Arvus-class lighter bucks as its landing engines fire, arresting its meteoric descent through white clouds and blue skies.

The lighter is tiny, as Imperial craft go, its hold barely large enough for the seven armoured bodies who sit on the fold-down seats that line its boxy interior. The passenger hold is divided from the pilot's cramped cockpit by a fixed wall, against which Marshal Solome Sinos rests her back.

The brutal vibrations of atmospheric entry have been replaced by the violent shuddering of landing, accompanied by a rolling roar of engines that penetrates the sense-defenders of her helmet. A dataslate sits in her lap, unregarded but near at hand should she need it. Sinos has memorised its contents already. She has had plenty of time to do so; it has been two months since the astropathic plea from Orymous reached Fort Damascus and almost a month since Sinos boarded the *Salrivarum* to bear her here. Sinos has chafed at every hour of that passage, because the picture painted by the dataslate's contents is grim.

The Officio Logisticarum is a new organisation, by the standards of the Imperium. In its novelty Sinos sees the sin of pride. A desire, perhaps understandably, to prove itself the equal of the ancient and noble institutions on which the dominion of mankind is built.

That, she assumes, is the reason the planetary governor of Orymous waited eighteen months before contacting the Adeptus Arbites to request their aid. It is a hypothesis Sinos intends to investigate when first she meets with the noble lord, for his delay has imperilled the order of a world that is vital to the subsector's function.

The vast billet-cities are in a state of uproar. Agri-fields have been burned. Officials murdered. Suicide. Sabotage. Riots and calamity, sweeping across conurbations that house millions. Talk of daemons haunting the darkness, killing at will.

Orymous, it seems, is breaking.

The cause is clear, though the perpetrator is not. It could not be more apparent to Sinos that the mustering world is under attack by some malign force. An Imperial world, particularly one so strictly ordered as Orymous, does not suffer the anguish of anarchy without a guiding hand, an architect of the suffering and misery that afflicts the planet.

She has not brought a substantial force with her. Orymous has no need of more troops; there are seven million Astra Militarum soldiers billeted on the world, and she will commandeer whatever troops or resources she needs. With her is a squad of enforcers for personal protection – a requirement of her rank – and a modest cadre of analyticians, verispexors and cipher-knives. Sinos has brought the tools and talents necessary to solve a mystery, and end a violator of the Emperor's order.

The engines' howl grows in the last moments of flight. Through the tiny viewport in the closed embarkation ramp, Sinos can see the suggestion of white-capped mountains, knife-peaked gothic towers, and then the dirty grey of rockcrete bunkers. A thump carries through the hold and Sinos' seat as the lighter settles on a pair of fixed metal skids that briefly shriek against the landing platform.

It takes several minutes for the post-flight checks to be completed and the engines to settle into idleness. Finally, the caged lumen-bulb at the hold's rear shifts from amber to green, and the single hatch disengages with a hiss of pneumatics.

Cold air rushes in, carrying the ubiquitous reek of promethium and the pleasant sharpness of icy mountain air. Orymous' planetary capital is high in the Prandalii Mountains, nestled amid a series of plateaus and sheer-sided valleys. Much of its sprawl is buried within the rock of the mountains themselves. A fitting location for a strategic hub of the Imperial war machine.

Her squad of enforcers exits first, armed with high-yield shotguns and armoured in charcoal plate. They march down the short ramp in single file to form a black barrier of defence against any waiting foes. No doubt the serfs and technicians of this voidport have seen many such arrivals, but such displays are a necessary and effective tool of Imperial authority, as is Sinos' own appearance.

She sweeps the weight of her coat from her lap. She straightens the golden chain from which hangs the icon of the Adeptus Arbites – a mailed fist bearing the scales of justice, couched within the Imperial 'I' – resting it against her chestplate. Her helmet's visor is clicked into place, and the dataslate is slipped into a pouch on her thigh.

The visor dims as she ducks beneath the lighter's hull, saving her the indignity of squinting against the glare. It is midday, and the yellow orb of Orymous' star hangs harsh and bright above the crown of mountains that encircles her. A few even have the faintest streamers of grey snow streaking their tops.

Sinos lowers her gaze from the natural grandeur to the manmade mundane. The landing platform is one of millions like it, conforming to Adeptus Mechanicus patterns of construction with unsurprising precision. Flared segments of armoured plates line its edge, tilted up to deflect engine exhaust away from the works beneath. Men and women approach from a ramp on its northern face, Mechanicus menials who come to tend to the lighter's abused frame.

Behind them is the welcoming party Sinos has expected. A squad of Tempestus Scions, full-faced helmets down and over-powered lasguns held tightly, stomp in time onto the landing platform. The Scions form their own line, the equal of Sinos' arbitrators in both armoured heft and arrogant authority. Sinos' squad part to allow her through, and the blue-cloaked Scions do the same.

No less than an Astra Militarum general has come to greet her, alongside a stern-faced commissar. She recognises both officers from the briefings prepared by her staff during the transit.

'General Modin. Commissar-Captain Gwenned.'

'Marshal Sinos,' said the former. 'Welcome to Orymous.'

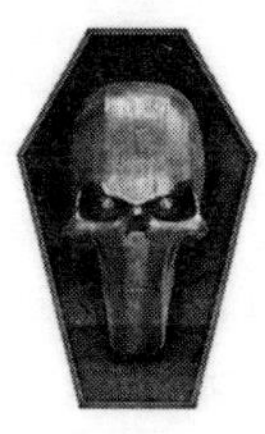

CHAPTER 2

Khemet stands in silence, contemplating the projection of the world before her.

It is the same cartograph she showed Hekasun when they first came to Qeretesh two years ago. It marks the human population centres, their mass-conveyor lines, their bloated growth fields and water-cleansing facilities, their landing fields and lifter platforms. Most of all, it shows the millions upon millions of humans that are slowly, unknowingly dying.

It shows decline, unfolding by degrees but utterly unstoppable. Khemet has struck methodically at the systems that underpin human survival. She has rocked the supply of food that their organic forms require in such gargantuan volume. She has destabilised their countless bureaucracies, and subverted their addiction to hierarchy to her will. She has spread fear, the most virulent weapon of them all, into the hearts of every Unclean on Orymous.

She has used need and desperation to turn the humans against themselves. Their animalistic nature in the face of privation has turned every serf and soldier into a potential agent of Khemet's end. Order is fraying within their sprawling settlements, and only the violent oppression of their populace holds the desperate at bay. It will not be long – one more year, perhaps two – before the humans are incapable of offering even a token martial resistance to the might of the legions Khemet gathers beneath them.

And it is all so shockingly simple. A targeted act of butchery, an assassin's knife, and the knowledge of where to strike is all that is needed to bring a world to the brink of chaos. To fracture the humans' understanding of permanence and stability, and render them back to the beasts they are.

This is not how Khemet is used to fighting. It is the way of the necrontyr to call one's enemy to the field of battle, to meet them there and match strength with strength, wit against wit. The lives of a dynasty's warriors are freely spent upon the field in displays of tactical acumen and martial power, until one side submits and yields to their acknowledged betters. That is the old way, the honoured way, stretching back into the earliest history of the galaxy and of the necrontyr. The Wars of Secession that had riven Khemet's people had been fought in this way – supreme violence undertaken within the strict parameters of nobility and virtue.

But the Unclean are undeserving of such considerations. Why risk so much on the resilience of one's warriors, and the skill of one's nemesor? Why take the chance that an enemy might detect the cunning placement of one's elite troops, when a poisoner can spoil the water supply of an entire city? Why feed and house and clothe and train an army, when an assassin's touch can sow disorder through an approaching legion?

The Unclean have never deserved the mercy of necron honour,

particularly when they besmirch the kemmeht of her people and pollute the galaxy with their unwarranted arrogance. Thus, it is merely with pride and a small degree of pleasure that her shadow war is achieving its end.

She turns the projection, sending the globe into a slow spin about its axis. Khemet watches the lights of cities and armies turn through the air. She has spent much of the past two years where she stands now, a control plate in hand. Observing, annotating, considering this map and its meanings. Plotting. In many ways, it has been the closest and most valuable companion in her effort to reclaim Qeretesh.

Certainly, it has been the most reliable.

Kamoteph has proven to be capricious in war. Much of the intelligence displayed upon Khemet's map is provided by the host of humans he has shackled to his will, but she is sure there is just as much that the cryptek does not tell her. She is reliant on Kamoteph for much of their ongoing efforts to undermine the humans' infrastructure, but she cannot trust him.

Hekasun, despite her repeated warnings, has been an almighty hindrance to her efforts to prepare the way for conquest. He has never accepted Khemet's strategy, though offering none of his own. Thus, for two years he has urged her always towards more speed, more haste, all the while contributing little of his own and at times actively undermining her designs.

His acquisitive rampage through the Zathanor's vaults has not stopped. A muted struggle to direct the time and efforts of Qeretesh's crypteks has been waged between the lord and Khemet for many months. Hekasun tasks his mages with disinterring the petty nobility of the world, the minor scions over whom Hekasun enjoys his grandstanding. He has them rouse the few seraptek constructs and voidcraft held within the grandest chambers of the tomb world so he might toy with them, walk their halls, and imagine himself lord of Qeretesh in deed as well as word.

Khemet, however, commands the crypteks to wake the commoners' vaults, spilling their contents in a slow but steady stream from their coffins. Many vast chambers throughout the tomb world have become marshalling points, holding entire legions in immobile ranks, waiting for the moment Khemet can unleash them upon the usurpers of the world.

Her actions, always, are tempered by the knowledge that the humans are watching. Their seismic sensors around the planet are always listening, and she fears they will detect the tramp of metal footsteps through the rock and stone. Fortunately, the humans' stunted approximations of crypteks have shown little curiosity about what lies beneath their feet. They appear blind to the danger that stalks them – or, at least, they cannot see the hand that directs their downfall.

'Praetorian, you requested I alert you when the deathmark named Ahnuret re-enters the north-eastern quarter.'

Qeretesh speaks to her. The tomb world is a compliant thing, and Khemet's interstitial node hums with the constant feed of data it provides. Always there is something new for her to consider. The status of a freshly woken cohort. The power cycles of the caged singularity at the tomb world's centre. Readings from the many scrying devices dotted throughout the planet's crust. Khemet never lacks for something to occupy her mind.

In this case, the spirit's message breaks Khemet's idle contemplation, and forces her to think on the question of Ahnuret.

She has shown herself to be the least reliable of all. The deathmark is an undischarged explosive, awaiting – indeed, actively seeking – its detonation. Every task Khemet assigns her somehow ends in overt, extravagant violence. Her thirst for Unclean blood has threatened to cast into ruin all that Khemet has worked to achieve.

Ahnuret's effectiveness as a killer is unquestioned. She has successfully ended the life of every human against whom Khemet has set her. She has penetrated their most closely guarded bastions and struck down city governors, military leaders, civilian officials. Anyone whose death will leave a void in the Imperium of Man's workings, according to Kamoteph's information and Khemet's insight.

And yet as an infiltrator the assassin is utterly compromised. Ahnuret's abilities as a deathmark allow her to enter any stronghold, but once she is inside she has run rampant. Ahnuret has committed massacre, when murder is required. Kamoteph has had to divert significant resources to purge any lingering evidence of the deathmark's presence, often at the cost of mindshackled human servants that were to play a more useful function in the future.

But despite tidying up Ahnuret's mess, the cryptek has otherwise ignored the deathmark's cognitive decline. As a member of his hierotek circle, Kamoteph is responsible for her actions, and yet he has displayed calculated disdain for the assassin ever since Khemet first awoke aboard the *Senusret*.

And, thus, it has fallen to Khemet to deal with her.

She waves a hand over the control plate. The map of the world collapses into a single mote of jade light, then vanishes.

It does not take Khemet long to reach her. The commonplace marvels of necron technology allow her to travel from one hemisphere of the planet to another as easily as she would cross a room.

On occasion over the past two years, when she has felt the need to escape Hekasun's arrogance and the demands of her task, Khemet has explored the silent quarters of the tomb world. She has delved into vaults not yet raided by Hekasun or Kamoteph, the first in millennia to disturb the coils of mist that wreathe the rows of coffins. She has walked between the towering noctilith pillars that hold the weight of the world, and idly stared into the molten abyss of the planet's mantle. She never seeks anything in particular, other than the sensation of finding paths she has yet to tread.

Since coming to Qeretesh the laying of fresh mental tracks, and the paranoid monitoring of her faculties, have become second nature. These behaviours have settled into her background processes – there, if she cares to give them thought, but no longer clamouring as they once did. She might intermittently be given to wander a darkened hall, and her faculties might briefly swim when an act in the now mirrors a memory of the past, but these are exceptions. Dismissed as swiftly as they occur. Not of any real concern.

This journey serves that purpose, as Khemet has never had reason to visit Ahnuret's chambers. The tomb world feeds Khemet a soft string of interstitial directions, leading her into a cavernous hall whose walls are lined with modest, single-room dwellings, platforms and walkways spanning the gaps between them. Such chambers are a moderately common sight across the tomb worlds. They were built in the waning years of the necrontyr empire, after the treachery of biotransference stole the souls of a civilisation. So much of the necrontyr's cities were made redundant by the C'tan's betrayal. Mind-locked serfs had no need of houses or tradeshops, no need for sustenance or distraction. Only those few who retained their higher functions had any conception of a dwelling, much less a need for one. But for those who did, spaces such as these were built, a sop to the vestigial psychological need for a home.

Who they once belonged to is irrelevant, at least for now. It will be decades before the full populace of Qeretesh is awoken, and the consequences for squatting in another's cell are easy to dismiss.

Khemet enters at the lowest point of the domiciliary chamber, and spends a moment considering and cataloguing the rows of rooms. They put her in mind of an insect's hive split open.

Each of the dwellings is empty, save for one, from which a familiar green glow is cast into the darkness. Khemet rouses her anti-gravity pack, and rises gently up to its level.

Khemet has never given any great thought to her material possessions. As a warden of a slumbering empire, her duty has taken her across the length and breadth of the galaxy for millions of years, by whatever means she has commandeered. And, of course, her nature as an immortal construct of living metal ensures that she will outlive any objects to which she might form a sentimental attachment.

Which is why she is surprised to find the chambers Ahnuret has occupied are richly, even opulently, furnished.

Tapestries hang on each wall, freed from the stasis fields that guard against time's decay. Statues and totems line the stone shelves and sconces. False candles burn, a casual trick of technology to replace the wick and tallow that could not endure the ages.

It is an echo of home, of an entire culture's ideal of home, brought jarringly into the present. That Ahnuret would construct such an artifice speaks not of madness. Khemet has known those beset by such affliction, seeing flesh where there is metal, unable to accept the reality of their imprisonment within their necrodermis shells.

No, Khemet sees and knows that this is the work of the most abject sorrow. Ahnuret longs for a life she cannot recall, and so surrounds herself with the trappings of a society that has not existed for millions of years.

Khemet's pity is discarded the moment her gaze leaves the room's furnishings and alights on Ahnuret.

The deathmark stands rigid in the centre of the room, arms outstretched. She has divested herself of all weapons and tools, standing clothed only in the bare necrodermis of her form. And it is growing barer with every moment.

A clutch of scarabs is climbing back and forth across her body. They are stripping the outermost layers of atoms from the deathmark's necrodermis, flensing away all trace of the air and organic matter to which she has been exposed outside the tomb world's tunnels. As Khemet watches, one of the scarabs clambers up Ahnuret's neck and wends its way across and around her head. The glow of gauss from its thorax traces its way over her faceplate and her single oversized ocular, and the broad span of the deathmark's shoulders. What remains is pristine, unblemished metal, as pure and ascetic as the moment Ahnuret walked from the furnaces.

The cause of all of Ahnuret's inexplicable destruction is now made clear. What Khemet had attributed to the ungovernable nature of the deathmark is revealed to stem from a far bleaker motive.

Ahnuret is absorbed in the ritual, and it is some time before she detects Khemet's presence. She does not move, does not change her pose or shoo the constructs away, but levelly meets Khemet's gaze.

'You are afflicted by the Destroyer.'

Ahnuret does not immediately react. She lowers her arms, dismissing the scarabs from her body. Khemet cannot read resignation, relief, or resistance from her stance.

'I am *afflicted* by nothing. If you wish to deny the universal truth then that is your foolishness.'

It is not the first time that Khemet has heard the adherents of the Destroyer cult speak in such terms. It is one of the lurking horrors of the necron psyche – a seed of corruption that can strike at random, and render the most honourable warrior into a creature of remorseless, endless fury. A cursed being, whose only desire and purpose is omnicidal slaughter.

There are many ways this can play out. Ahnuret's curse is the reason Khemet has been forced to expend so much energy on stealth, concealing the presence of the necrons upon Qeretesh. She could lift her rod of covenant and obliterate Ahnuret for her failure to heed Khemet's command. Many other praetorians would do just that, either as punishment or simply out of fear that Ahnuret might infect others with her genocidal urges.

But the deathmark could also choose to leave. She could depart through a hyperspace oubliette, fleeing Khemet's judgement. But she has not.

'I once did as you seek to do,' says Khemet. Ahnuret's gaze travels back to the praetorian, curious despite whatever mixture of shame and defiance is within her.

'I exterminated all life from the principal continent of Jaliste. Everything, down to the last microbe.' She pauses. 'It took me eight hundred years.'

'You embraced the truth of the Destroyer?' asks Ahnuret.

'No. This was purely an intellectual exercise.' Khemet looks at her. 'Sixty million years is a long time.'

The deathmark says nothing, her ocular fixed on Khemet's. It is hard to tell whether awe, jealousy, or horror lies behind her stare.

'I trekked from one coast to another, eradicating all that I found. Flora, fauna. I sterilised the ground itself. I flayed four cubits of topsoil from an entire continent.'

For the first time in many months, Khemet can feel the onset of a lapse. The memory unfolds from her engrammatic vault, curling at the edges of her perceptions. Khemet feels the weight of the gauss blaster in her hands, though she grips her rod of covenant. She registers the ionised particles of dirt and blood in the air, when there is only burning *kyphi* candles in their sconces around the room's edge.

'But when I returned to where I had begun, to the red sand of that first shoreline, I found I had been undone.'

Ahnuret cocks her head, but waits for Khemet to continue.

'Phytoplankton. It had washed in with the tides. Algae coated the rocks. I could have scoured the shore again, but it was clear. Given enough time, life would return, crawling from the depths.'

The room is gone, replaced by countless grains of fine red sand into which her metal feet sink.

With her on the sand, Ahnuret shakes her head. 'You simply lacked the resources. And the commitment. Had you boiled away the planet's oceans, or seeded the water with toxins, you would have starved the organisms of their preferred environment.'

The deathmark trips slightly over the word 'organisms', disgust heavy in her voice, but her hesitation goes unregarded. Khemet is hearing the hiss of ocean spray.

'Praetorian?'

Khemet heeds the distant sound of her title. With effort, she isolates the engram and banishes it back to its repository.

'My efforts on Jaliste taught me a simple truth. A sincerely universal truth,' she says, surprising herself with her own vehemence. 'Life always finds a way.'

Ahnuret considers her words in silence.

'I cannot fight a war with tools I cannot trust.'

Ahnuret looks up sharply. Whatever self-reflection Khemet might have begun is swiftly undone. 'I kill the Unclean you ask me to kill. I expose myself to their filth without complaint.'

'Every human you destroy without cause risks exposing our presence before we are ready for the true war.'

'Without cause? They are the Unclean, praetorian. That is all the cause we require.'

Khemet's choler rises to match the deathmark's. 'I will not give you license to indulge your madness if it imperils our victory on this world.'

The deathmark's glare matches Khemet's own.

'Khemet, attend me.'

The interstitial message arrives at the worst possible moment. With immense difficulty, Khemet responds.

'I do not have the time to service your whims, Hekasun.'

The noble's reply is immediate. *'I summon you, duatekh. Do not make me have you brought before me.'*

Her fury is visible only to Ahnuret, who sees the outgassing of her core flare into violence. *'Very well.'*

Ahnuret registers the change in her and tenses.

'Hekasun summons me.'

The deathmark nods understanding.

'We will speak further,' promises Khemet. 'But know this. I will suffer no more errors.'

She finds Hekasun at her map table, a collection of courtiers with him. They are unfamiliar to Khemet. Their presence suggests a purpose to this meeting that Khemet has little patience to indulge.

'You called me.'

Khemet cannot keep the rancour from her voice. Her encounter with Ahnuret has left her own mind out of balance. Dwelling on past actions, and those she may have to take in the future.

'You would do better to greet me as "my lord" or "nomarch", duatekh.'

Despite her agitation, Khemet cannot let that pass. 'You are not nomarch yet, my lord. *You* would do better to remember that.'

'And why is that?' asks Hekasun, walking slowly around the projection table.

'Do you seek now to lecture me on the craft of war?'

'I am in search of a nemesor who is unafraid of instigating a war that they will surely win.'

Such have been their interactions for two years. Always, Hekasun urges speed. But he has not awoken the planet's true nomarch, or any who could legitimately claim dominion over Qeretesh. Instead he has revelled in the expansion of his court of sycophants, ensuring he is present for each of their awakenings.

'We know their systems are straining. The morale of their soldiers and populace is fracturing. In a year, perhaps two, they will break. At which point, they can offer no resistance to our advance.'

'And they could resist us now?' asks Ma'at, one of the new nobles.

Khemet is in no mood for Hekasun's games, or his lackey's condescension. She gestures to the map table and lifts the control plate. 'All our data is accessible to you. Should you feel able to generate an improvement on my strategy, I would welcome your suggestions.'

She pushes the plate into Hekasun's hand, then turns to leave. But he is not finished.

'Kamoteph's pet strains against its leash.'

Hekasun speaks idly, but the undercurrent of menace cannot be ignored.

'To whom do you refer?' replies Khemet, though his meaning is perfectly clear.

He replaces the control plate in its socket in the projection table. 'The assassin.'

'I will handle Ahnuret.' Khemet says this, and wonders why. She is not responsible for the deathmark. She is a part of Kamoteph's circle, bonded by whatever pact she offered him. Indeed, it is inconceivable that the cryptek is blind to the Destroyer-cursed creature in his midst, yet he chose not to inform Khemet of her affliction.

'See that you do.' It is clear that Hekasun cares little about Ahnuret's fate; he merely chose to raise the issue as another means to belittle and command Khemet.

'Vile creatures,' says Ma'at. 'The deathmarks are a corruption of our honoured ways.' He glances at Khemet. 'I should not have to tell you that.'

'There are circumstances in which their skills have value,' Khemet replies.

But in light of her new knowledge, Khemet is forced to reconsider that view. She has defended Ahnuret to Hekasun and his courtiers out of contrarian pique, but she, even more than they, is alive to the threat the deathmark poses to her task. And it is not in Khemet's nature to suffer the imperfect and unreliable.

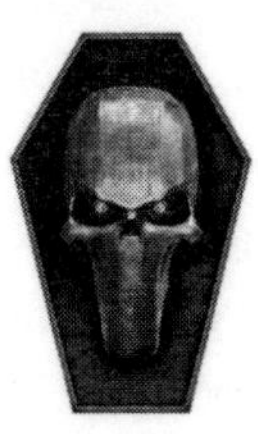

CHAPTER 3

Solome Sinos has never had any patience for theatre.

Of course, she understands the purpose of it. Pomp and pageantry are vital tools for the control of a populace. The unifying effect of martial pride is a cornerstone of Imperial authority.

Even so, Sinos has never enjoyed sitting through it.

Two hundred yards below her the 182nd Devash Auxilia marches in lockstep, the bright light of noon reflecting from six thousand fixed bayonets. They are followed by the Ketzok 47th Armoured, whose proud Leman Russ tanks rumble three abreast along the arterial. Then come the 74th Sameters, 'The Gregorians', as her host explains. Then the Tartaran 999th, their three-bar pennants fluttering in the wind that races down the man-made canyon of hab-blocks and municipal buildings.

And on and on they come. Men and women drawn from every quarter of the galaxy, honoured to become soldiers of the God-Emperor's Astra Militarum. They are dressed in all the panoply of ceremonial uniform, each regiment competing to outdo their peers in prominence and pride. They wear freshly fabricated jackets in royal blue, blood red, smoke grey. Golden epaulettes, crimson sashes, plumes and cockades and the embroidered furs of a dozen different beasts. Brass buttons and silver buckles polished to a mirror sheen, though by the time they reach Sinos they are dulled by the dust kicked up by those who are ahead of them.

Each and every soldier carries a lasgun, newly stamped by the forges of a dozen worlds.

The fighting machines are as varied and as colourful as the troops who march beside them. Leman Russ and Rogal Dorn main battle tanks. Chimera troop carriers. Basilisk artillery pieces, their great barrels held aloft. The myriad support vehicles, belching smoke from promethium stacks. Sentinel walkers, cockpits swaying from side to side with each metal footfall. The occasional super-heavy, Baneblades and Shadowswords and Crassus transports, each one testing the structural integrity of the elevated arterial on which they drive. The roadway will be out of commission for weeks after this parade concludes, General Cullen reveals after a trio of Doomhammer tanks grumble past, their wide treads tearing up the asphalt.

He says this while leaning close, attempting to press Sinos to accept a glass of amasec from an aide who hovers close at hand. She had refused when she joined him on the balcony of the city governor's office, and refuses again, this time more sharply. Cullen is a brave and foolish warrior for looking beyond Sinos' storm-cloak and badge in the hope of finding the woman beneath. He would find her even more stern and less corruptible than the icon of her office.

Sinos has been obliged by the strictures of politics to waste her time watching the parade of regiments. As the most senior member of the Adeptus Arbites now on Orymous, she is required to represent her organisation in such ceremonies. That meant accepting, with feigned grace, General Cullen's invitation upon her arrival in the district capital.

Two dozen other worthies share the long stone terrace, along with their many aides and advisors. A brace of generals watch their regiments with pride, alongside a pair of Imperial Navy captains in deep-blue frock coats. A crimson-cloaked master adept of the Cult Mechanicus is among them; the atonal burr of their augmetic voice box has been a constant throughout the hours Sinos has been forced into idleness.

The warriors of the God-Emperor present on the balcony are heavily outnumbered by the officials of His many civilian offices. Orymous is governed by the Officio Logisticarum, but that simple statement belies the immense complexity of a world whose purpose is to ready armies for war.

There is a contingent of the Officio Agricultae, none of whom, Sinos suspects, has come within a hundred leagues of an agri-field in many years. Sinos recognises the white armour of a Legatine of the Order of Serenity, one of the Hospitaller Orders of the Adepta Sororitas, in close conversation with a chirurgeon wearing the newly minted cap-pin of the Beathen Crusade. The dour form of Questor Maximus Parinthus of the Departmento Exacta stands apart from the other planetary officials. Sinos has heard that the senior tallyman of the Imperial Tithe is an unwelcome presence at any gathering, with a reputation for corruption that she intends to explore when she has the chance.

The Imperial Creed is the only great body of state not represented, but for good reason. The ministers of His faith are hard at work.

Myrddin Otakar, Ecclesiarch of Orymous, stands upon a bridge over the arterial, a pulpit beneath which the army passes. No soldier or war machine escapes the ferocity of Otakar's gaze or the sound of his voice, which bellows from hundreds of hovering servo-skulls. His exhortations to strength, bravery, and fidelity to the God-Emperor echo from the rockcrete walls of the artificial canyon, never repeating, never wavering.

Forty of Otakar's priests and acolytes flank him on the bridge, wafting golden censers back and forth. They are huge, great gleaming orbs as wide and as tall as a man, that hang from stout chains beneath the overpass. Otakar's adepts stand two to a censer, hauling ropes back and forth to swing the thuribles and spread the blessed smoke that billows from within. Each warrior of the God-Emperor walks through this haze, and the metal of every tank and trailer is marked by the pious scent as they pass.

The smoke settles on the roadway's surface, to be pushed to its edges by the tramp of boots and cough of engines. A fine mist coils about the legs of the crowds who have come to honour the men and women who will soon depart, to defend them in the battles amongst the stars.

The arterial has been closed to allow civilians to climb the approach roads and line the parade route. Sinos pays more attention to the crowd than to the soldiers. The spectators seem more sparse than she would have expected, and the local enforcers lining the route more numerous. A double row of thick rockcrete barriers line either side of the boulevard, and helmeted auxilia with riot-guns gripped tightly stand behind. The tension is palpable, even to Sinos, seated so high above. There are few cheers and cries of admiration or recognition. The soldiers of the Emperor march to war in silence, save for the roared urgings of Ecclesiarch Otakar.

Cullen has propped an elbow up on the arm of his chair, evidently intent on another sally. 'I don't suppose you will have had much call to learn the rules and regulations of the God-Emperor's finest.'

Sinos stays as she is, eyes on the marching men and women. 'On the contrary, general. I spent two decades as provost superior of the Cattelingian campaign. I had ample dealings with the honourable troopers of His Imperial Guard. And their codes of conduct.'

'Cattelingia… That was sixty years ago.'

'I remember it fondly.'

Cullen's eyes widen. He retreats back into the plush depths of his seat, considering the sharp-eyed young woman seated beside him who is, he has discovered, at least twice his age. 'Your treatment team does good work,' he remarks.

Sinos can testify to that. She feels young. Vital. This is the second time she has received a full rejuvenat regimen. The treatments took up a year of her life, but they have shed half a lifetime from her body. She is as she had been during the Cattelingian campaign. Strong, both in body and spirit. Ready for whatever trials the Emperor determines to place in her path.

The only disadvantage is that fools like Cullen can mistake her youthful features for inexperience.

'How soon until you depart?' Sinos asks, taking uncharacteristic pity on the man.

'A week. My grenadiers are already at the voidport. I will join them once the last of my corps are aboard the trains.'

Over a million soldiers will pass beneath the balcony in the course of the parade. And these are just the regiments fortunate enough to be chosen for the honour. Three million more are waiting for them at the landing fields. These troopers will march from the parade route onto the conveyor-trains, and from the trains to the vast lifters that will carry them up to the vast network of wharves and depots that crowd Orymous' orbit. It will be three weeks before the final cadre of soldiers is carried up into the void, to be borne away on the hundreds of troop transports and warships assembled for the crusade.

'It is a shame that our departure was brought up,' Cullen continues. 'I'm told that Lord-Militant Salvastari's office had been planning a ball of particular magnificence.'

'The crusade is being dispatched ahead of schedule?' Sinos asks.

'Indeed. Three months earlier than planned. The lord-militant wants us off his balance sheet,' he adds, bitterness evident.

'Four million mouths are a great many to feed, general,' puts in Selimha Briseida from his other side. A lean and sallow woman, Briseida is the Departmento Munitorum's chief official for the Beathen Crusade.

'Yes,' says Cullen. 'And now I have to feed them out of my own stores.'

'*I* shall have to feed them, general. And as I have said before, the crusade is and shall be adequately provisioned. You have my word.'

'I'll need more than that, logisticator. We are embarking with less than two years' supplies. We could spend a quarter of that in the warp alone.'

Cullen and Briseida fall into an argument that Sinos suspects they have had many times before. She signals to her aide, who steps forwards and kneels conspiratorially beside her.

'I've had enough.'

'Of course, marshal. I'm surprised you lasted this long.'

Nikos Abisode has been the lead arbitrator of her bodyguard unit for nine years. Their long familiarity allows him to stray towards impudence, which he knows irritates her. 'Just get the damned flyer warmed up.'

Sinos waits for several minutes to allow Abisode to set her will into motion, then she stands abruptly.

'General. I thank you for your hospitality, but I must leave you. May the Emperor watch and protect you and your warriors.'

'You're leaving?' Cullen had been deep into his dispute with Briseida. His sudden disappointment at her departure is almost comical.

'Indeed. I have my own war to fight.'

Sinos attempts to sleep during the flight, but rest eludes her. She has never been able to sleep aboard a Valkyrie; the sense-defenders in her helmet are never equal to the howl of the engines just a few yards from her head.

The coal-black flyer takes off from the governor's palace, climbing quickly between projecting spires and the urban tangle of Verongyl. As Sinos and her small guard of arbitrators cross the city's western limits a pair of Lightning fighter craft sweep overhead, taking up a wide, circling pattern across and along her Valkyrie's course. They are, her pilot reports, an escort and honour guard assigned by the planetary governor. Their presence has the opposite effect than that intended – Salvastari is taking the precautions necessary for a warzone. No servant of the Lex Imperialis should require such protections on an Imperial world.

Verongyl does not have an encircling perimeter wall, so the city's sprawl peters out as the Valkyrie makes its way west. Grey rockcrete buildings give way to a patchwork of polymer-covered agri-tunnels, processing plants, and open-topped water treatment silos. After some time even these begin to thin, the ground beneath Sinos becoming a barren, disused scrubland.

For an hour they follow one of the great mass-conveyor lines. It scythes through the landscape with no respect or regard for such trivialities as hills or valleys. The double line of tracks is at least a hundred yards wide, and the land for a mile on either side has been graded to leave not a single tree or other obstacle in sight. Through the viewport in the flyer's hatch, Sinos follows the gently curving line until it fades into the distance, driving up to and over the horizon, flanked by the same blasted waste-land for its entire length.

After a while, the Valkyrie catches up with one of the enor-mous conveyors, heaving its great girth along the iron rails. The flyer slows until it is only slightly faster than the train's pro-gress as it ploughs through the denuded landscape, permitting Sinos to examine it at length. Three miles of wagons, carriages and freight cars, each wide enough to accommodate one of the Militarum's super-heavy behemoths on its flatbeds. The variety of hauled goods is surprising. There are long cylinders that Sinos assumes are carrying promethium, slab-sided passenger cars that would accommodate an entire company of General Cullen's troops, and hundreds more flatbeds loaded with stacks of armoured Munitorum freight containers. Locomotive engines are spaced along its length, keeping the impossible weight of it all moving at a furious pace.

'The conveyor attack is a problem,' Sinos says, after letting the thought stew for some time.

'Say again, marshal?' Abisode had been engrossed in some-thing on his dataslate, but looks up at Sinos immediately.

She gestures out of the window. The train has begun to curve away from her, going south as the flyer speeds off to the west. 'The attack on the Sixteen-Red conveyor. How did a heretic militia succeed in getting aboard one of those things with suf-ficient strength to derail it?'

'Treachery at one of the terminals, according to local reports.'

'Admissions obtained under excruciation, and with few common-alities.' She has read those reports and dismissed them as works of fiction. It is clear to Sinos, who has read more interrogation reports in her long life than she can easily recall, that the enforcers who had investigated the incident had first determined their answer and then set out to obtain evidence to support it.

'How can any kind of dissidence flourish here?' she asked. 'This is one of the most heavily policed worlds in the subsector.'

'"A single moment of laxity can spawn a lifetime of heresy", marshal.' Abisode speaks the catechism solemnly, for it is a maxim the Adeptus Arbites live by.

'Indeed,' agrees Sinos, though without particular conviction.

She settles back in her seat. When it becomes clear that she will not carry the conversation further, Abisode does so as well, returning his attention to his dataslate. Below them, the land abruptly drops away, the coastline a sheer and unappealing fringe of low cliffs and scrub grass. The Valkyrie now flies over storm-tossed waves and the dark grey water of open ocean.

Abisode's truism aside, it is a tangled question Sinos faces, and one she has spent many weeks considering. Heresy and malignance thrive in darkness, but Orymous is a world bathed in the God-Emperor's light. The commissars of the Officio Prefectus are the vigilant wardens of the Imperial troops stationed on the world, awaiting their next deployment to the battlefields of the galaxy. The serfs who exist to feed and clothe and serve the billeted regiments are just as carefully monitored, and until the beginning of the recent strife the Departmento Munitorum's detention figures were not abnormally high. Now, of course, Orymous' gaols and penitent labour battalions groan with the mass of citizenry who have been swept from the rioting streets, but these are symptoms of the troubles plaguing Orymous, not its cause.

It is in this mind, awake but with her concentration focused inwards, that Sinos is carried over the waves of the ocean and towards her first meeting with Lord-Militant Adrin Salvastari.

In Sinos' moderately extensive experience, there is enormous variation in the nature of Imperial worlds. For each planet of ancient cities and oppressed millions there is an agri-world, dominated not by people but by the mono-crops that sustain them. There are half-wild worlds, given over to untamed jungles and wind-swept steppes. She has even visited a forge world, one of the hellish domains of the Adeptus Mechanicus, where the very soil and air were poisoned by the mighty works of Imperial industry.

But what is common to every planet the marshal has walked is that the powerful find a measure of seclusion for themselves. The ruling elites – be they courtiers, tribal elders or Mechanicus dominars – are able to escape the worst aspects of their world. This might be atop vast starscrapers, deep within subterranean lairs, or simply in the grandest of the tribe's tents, curtains drawn to veil the elders from view. Just rewards of power, sanctioned and indeed encouraged by Imperial cultural norms.

On Orymous, the refuge of the nobility takes the form of the Plakid Islands.

'Your flight was to your comfort?'

'The Mechanicus build the Valkyries for war, not for comfort, my lord.'

'Quite right, of course.' Lord-Militant Salvastari sips his drink. 'And your passage from Fort Damascus?'

The lesser said about Sinos' journey through the warp, the better. Two months of nightmare-riddled sleep, fractious Naval officers and recycled air.

'Tolerable, my lord.'

They sit in what Sinos considers the most decadently comfortable space she has ever entered.

Salvastari's palace sits on the fringes of an inland lake upon the largest of the Plakid Islands. It eschews much of traditional Imperial architecture. Its walls are built of a pink, open-pored stone, not unlike the corals that Salvastari explains grow around the islands. Covered walkways lead down to sun-drenched beaches, shaded from the heat of the day by canopies stretched along wooden frames.

Servants outnumber the served by ten to one, although there are a large number of Imperial Guard officers and Munitorum adepts in Salvastari's unusual court.

Sinos is, as she expected, deeply uncomfortable. Her black carapace armour is at odds with the loose fabric robes. Her task is not one typically discussed around plunge-pools and finger food.

To her surprise, he acknowledges this directly.

'My apologies, marshal. So many of my guests are keen to embrace the comforts of the islands. You, however, are burdened with grave purpose.'

'This is so, lord.'

'Then let us speak. You come at my request to solve a problem.'

'What befalls Orymous,' Sinos supplies.

'Indeed. Now, your presence is not intended to slight my logisticators and their adepts.' He says this with a placating hand to the assembled courtiers. 'Simply that, given the nature of the incidents we have seen, an outside eye is warranted.'

Sinos hesitates before responding. 'With respect, my lord, I believe the situation is more acute than that.'

Salvastari says nothing, but she can see that he agrees. This is not, Sinos thinks, the distant and effete ruler he appears.

'These incidents have steadily tipped Orymous towards disorder,' she continues. 'There are, if the reports I have been given are correct, severe food shortages in many of your billet-cities. Civil disobedience has risen markedly in the last two years. And the mutiny of the Malfian Sixty-Fourth–'

'Orymous is a mustering world, marshal.' A general wearing a blue terry cloth beach suit interrupts her. 'Soldiers will, on occasion, grow restless.'

'Nevertheless, general. There are lines that cannot be crossed.' Salvastari offers Sinos a slight nod of apology. 'The simple fact is that action is required. Disorder, whatever its source, is an offence to the God-Emperor's divine rule. The Officio Logisticarum will see it corrected.'

Salvastari stands suddenly, prompting Sinos to also rise.

'I would offer you my seal, to empower you however you see fit. But I suspect that that icon' – he gestures to the scales of justice around her neck – 'will grant you all the power you require.'

'I am grateful, my lord.'

'I will not detain you.'

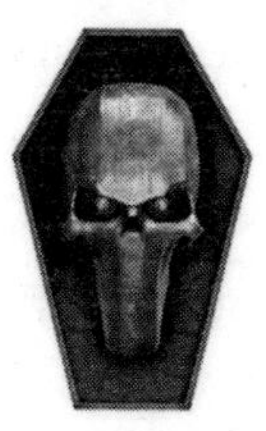

CHAPTER 4

Khemet finds Ahnuret in the commoners' vaults.

The vaults are vast, each one a cavern stretching for hundreds of khet from edge to edge, and from noctilith floor to stone ceiling. Canoptek constructs roam the chambers, bringing their background whisper of metal on blackstone to even this disregarded corner of the tomb complex.

She considers the state of the vault with unfiltered disgust. Here, the poverty of the Zathanor Dynasty is plain to see. This chamber forms the deepest level of the complex in this part of the world, and it seems that the architects of its construction had elected to exploit pre-existing lava tubes, voids left over from the world's making, rather than hew a new vault from the living stone. They had not even lined its walls and ceiling with blackstone. The rocky roof, thirty khet above Khemet's head, had been carved in mimicry of the beams of a grand hall to conceal the miserly nature of the masons' work.

The dynasty's parsimony has reaped its just rewards. In dozens of places molten rock has breached the walls and ceiling, admitting thin streams of magma that have pooled and spread. In other places it has seeped in, drop by drop. After sixty million years of gradual, unrelenting geology, the stalactites are as broad as monoliths, and reach from ceiling to floor in imitation of the carved pillars that hold the weight of the world above.

Tens of thousands, perhaps hundreds of thousands, of stasis coffins have been swallowed by the slow spread of liquid stone. And this is just one of hundreds of vaults in this hemisphere of the world.

Ahnuret is standing at the edge of a gallery, observing this state of ruin. Far below her, a hall that had contained – and still does, in a way – two full cohorts of warriors is blanketed in black igneous rock. The tops of many coffins are visible, piercing the uneven, porous crest that has slowly oozed its way through the chamber.

'Who were they?' Ahnuret asks as Khemet approaches. She does not turn to greet the praetorian.

Khemet consults the interstitial network. 'A detachment of the Eight-Hundred-and-Seventeenth Decarion Legion.'

'No, *who* were they? The commoners who became the warriors within this crypt?'

Khemet has had plenty of time to consider such philosophical questions. 'It does not matter.'

Now Ahnuret turns, regarding Khemet sharply. 'Do you believe that?'

She does, without any shadow of doubt. 'There is nothing to be gained from this line of thought. Do not waste your pity on chattel.'

'They were necrontyr once, praetorian,' says the deathmark, coming as close as she dares to reproach. 'They lived.'

'They served,' Khemet corrects. 'They were born and they

served their masters, as their ancestors served before them. You ask who they were, and I tell you that it *does not matter*. It matters not which were kind and which were cruel. Which were selfish, and which were loving. How each lived their life has no bearing on the function of those lives. They were servants. The only distinction between these wretches and the thousand generations that came before them is they will serve for all time.'

Or they would have, were it not for the austerity of their masters. That is the true tragedy Khemet sees before her. The waste of resources, squandered by Zathanor frugality.

'Do you see nothing in them to pity?'

Khemet releases a mechanical sigh. 'I did not take you for a fool, assassin. Pity is the greatest waste of energy I can imagine.'

Ahnuret's shoulders hunch, the closest she can come to a scowl of recrimination.

'Why did you seek me out?' she asks.

'You know why.'

The necron form cannot display guilt, or remorse, but Ahnuret's posture does, somehow, shift to become defensive

'It is my duty to kill.'

'Not indiscriminately. Not without judgement, or consideration of our greater mission.'

Khemet gestures at the ranks of buried stasis-coffins. 'You are not one of them, to be aimed towards the enemy as a battering ram. You are a scalpel, not a scythe. Your duty is murder, not slaughter.'

Ahnuret says nothing for the longest time. Khemet, for all her earlier scorn for pity, waits for the deathmark to find her courage.

'I cannot stop,' she says finally.

Khemet steps in front of the deathmark, forcing Ahnuret to meet her gaze. 'If you cannot control yourself, I have no use for you.'

'I *cannot stop*,' she repeats. 'Life, everywhere. When I am among it, I feel its foetid nature infecting me.'

Khemet shifts her stance. Ahnuret's growing fervour has the feel of frenzy.

'It stains me. It smears itself across my metal. It is in the air, billions upon billions of microbes that cling to me like putrid oil. The Unclean exhale them. It is disgusting. I have the scarabs cleanse me but I feel it still, seeping into my centre.'

She rounds on Khemet. 'I have to kill it, praetorian. All of it. You demand that I stay my hand when all that I am urges me to kill, to purge, to cleanse this world of its contagion–'

Khemet strikes. Without warning she reaches forwards and places a hand against Ahnuret's forehead, digits curling around the planes of her skull. She *pushes*. The power crystal mounted in Khemet's own skull glows with sudden exertion, a single pulse that drives the praetorian's will into the deathmark.

Ahnuret seizes, her motor functions stolen, her consciousness driven into dormancy. Khemet has called on ancient protocols to drive her into slumber, sending her into the same thought-less, dreamless sleep in which the millions of warriors below her reside.

Khemet releases her. The deathmark rocks, briefly, but fortunately her centre of gravity is stable and she does not suffer the indignity of tumbling to the ground.

Now the act is done, Khemet questions whether she was correct. Certainly, the assassin will not forgive her for the violation. But it is a necessity. Khemet cannot conduct a war with unstable tools. She would rather deprive herself of Ahnuret's talents than risk her pathology revealing the necron presence on Qeretesh before Khemet is ready to do so.

Khemet now faces a choice. Without any intervention, the assassin's cognitive centres will reset in a few days, allowing her to slowly rise back to a state of consciousness. The alternative is to summon Kamoteph or one of his apprenteks and make the deathmark's stasis permanent. Inter Ahnuret within one of the Zathanor crypts until such time as the Destroyer curse can be overcome.

Perhaps, she thinks, it would be the merciful course. Perhaps a period of inactivity will repair some of the degradation, or at the very least sever the recursive cycle of genocidal anguish in which Ahnuret had been locked.

An unsolicited memory rises from the depths of Khemet's engrammatic vaults. A memory of falling without falling, of struggling against absence. Of her mind collapsing in on itself, her senses wandering and sanity breaking.

She will not inflict that on another.

Khemet pulses a command to Qeretesh's tomb spirit, dispatching a clutch of spyders to bear the deathmark away to her chambers.

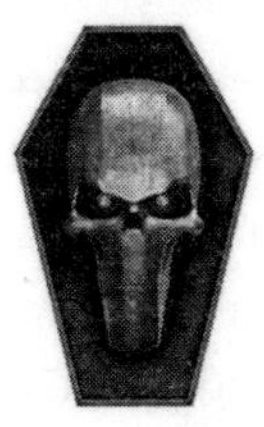

CHAPTER 5

Four million soldiers of the God-Emperor's Astra Militarum wait to be carried off to war.

The eastern embarkation fields spread from horizon to horizon, as vast, compressed and complex as any of the cities in which these men and women have been billeted since their arrival on Orymous.

Some have barely set foot on the planet before they are whisked away. Newly founded regiments, in uniforms freshly stamped from the manufactorum, collected from their homes by fat-bellied troop transports and then deposited on Orymous by the same lifters they now wait to reboard. They have hardly even had the chance to explore the local black market that any gathering of Imperial troops attracts, and which on Orymous employs a considerable proportion of the planet's civilian population.

For others, their months and years idling on the mustering world are all they have seen of war. They have been trained to the peak of the drill instructor's art. Every word of the *Imperial*

Infantryman's Uplifting Primer has been permanently etched in their minds. They have been honed to a lethal edge, but their commanders fear that no troops can keep that edge indefinitely. Without a war they have become bored, resentful of their officers and their commissars' attention, too used to the comforts of the billet-cities. Privately, General Cullen's great staff of logisticians and strategos anticipate a higher rate of loss among these regiments than the newly raised troops when they finally face battle.

For the veteran regiments, their time on Orymous has been a blissful reprieve from the realities of their service. These soldiers wait with indifferent patience for their time to bundle into the local conveyor-cars and be carried into the brutalist sprawl of landing platforms that loom above them. They claim the comparative peace of these days and weeks spent in the shadow and deafening roar of the lifters, secure in the knowledge that there will be little peace or comfort to be found when they reach their destination, out among the stars of a savage and uncaring galaxy.

Though the state of constant motion and barked commands can hardly be considered peaceful. Night and day, squads of infantry are shuffled on an hourly basis from endless acres of tents to cramped tenement blocks to the narrow confines of the conveyor-trains, pressed ever onwards towards their goal by the timetables and hand-chronos of the adepts of the Officio Logisticarum. Armoured companies are marshalled in their hundreds, the grunt and grumble of their assembled engines louder than the thunder of the cannons they bear. Indentured civilians struggle to avoid the attention of the soldiers they serve, whose tempers boil amid the heat and the noise and the ever-present awareness that they will soon face the cauldron of war.

For the fortunate few, the general officers and lord-commissars and Munitorum adepts superior, the wait is less arduous. They arrive in the carousel of flyers that continuously buzz overhead, landing just long enough on one of the hundreds of tributary platforms that ring the lifter pads to unload their passengers. These worthies are led by robed Logisticarum officials, carefully courteous despite the maelstrom through which they move, through back-corridors that the common soldier will never see. They board each colossal shuttle through their upper doors, while thousands of troopers shuffle into the gaping hangar mouths below.

Lieutenant Bragin Nestor wipes his brow with a linen kerchief pulled from the pocket of his uniform tunic. Even in the sheltered channels that vein Platform Sixty-Seven, the heat is intense. Tight-packed bodies, the backwash of orbit-capable engines, and Orymous' baking sun allow no relief.

His uniform is no help either. General Cullen, for whom Nestor works as a runner, has an unyielding standard for presentation, and the fabric of his tunic is stretched tight around his midriff.

The commander of the Beathen Crusade strides ahead of Nestor, the picture of martial prestige in a crimson frock coat bedecked with gold trim and black braid. The majority of his staff have already been conveyed to their various transports, leaving Cullen attended by just eighty of his closest advisors and functionaries. The mob of officers and adepts flows like the tail of a comet in the general's wake as he takes each corridor and corner at a pace just short of an outright run. Cullen is not a man capable of approaching anything slowly.

They are led through the warren of passageways until a change in the air tells Nestor they have reached their destination. The temperature, already baking, rises to a furnace, and the crash of boots on metal grows from a distant echo to a percussive grumble that crowds out all other sound.

Cullen crosses the extended bridge to Lifter 575-98 first, his entourage in tow. A thousand feet below, the troopers of the 812th Carpathian Guard disappear into the craft's cavernous innards. The grind of Chimera transports ascending a ramp between the lines of men adds a metallic shriek to the discord.

The general's staff are greeted by another set of attendants and led to a modestly appointed executive cabin. The far wall is made up of duraglass windows, showing the fiendishly complex network of pipes and cables that line the interior of the landing platform's walls. The cabin's seating is arrayed in back-to-back rows, their coverings a tarnished green.

A narrow bar top runs the length of the cabin, with bottles of various liquors and receptacles strapped in place inside transparent cabinets above it. Several of Cullen's aides make their way towards it, but a stern voice carries over the tramp of boots and muted conversation.

'There will be time enough for that later.'

Cullen's order is heeded, and his staff meekly find their places. Nestor, instead of following his peers, heads towards a hatch on the far side of the cabin.

'Take your seat, lieutenant.' Cullen's eye misses nothing, even as he straps a lap-belt closed.

It takes Nestor five rapid beats of his heart before he finds his voice. 'Would you excuse me, general?'

'Why?' Cullen asks brusquely.

'I… must make use of the ablutorial before we launch,' he replies, clutching at his swollen stomach.

Cullen gives Nestor a look of unconcealed disgust, but waves him away. Nestor swiftly makes his escape. An attendant at the door attempts to direct him back to his seat as he leaves, but the lieutenant roughly pushes past the man.

In accordance with protocol, the hatch is slammed shut behind him. Nestor straightens as the metal closes with a crash, his performance abandoned immediately. There is limited time before the lifter takes off.

He makes his way through the craft's interior, quickly leaving the passenger areas and seeking the darkness and stifling heat of the crew corridors. Whenever he hears approaching voices, he ducks into the pools of shadow made by flickering lumen-bulbs and the bulk of cogitator stacks and brassbound pipes.

Finally, he feels confident enough that he has driven as deep as he can into the craft's innards. Surrounded by the rhythmic clank of machinery and the hiss of leaking steam, Nestor drops to his belly and rolls beneath the overhang of a bundle of cables as thick as his torso. Thus concealed, he settles down to wait.

He does not wait long. Lifter 575-98 had been almost full when Cullen and his staff swept aboard. With the final companies of the 812th Carpathians in their seats, lasguns gripped tightly between their legs, the final preparations for launch can begin.

Thirty minutes after the lifter's chief enginseer reports that all is in readiness, lumens throughout the craft flick to a foreboding scarlet. Hatches are locked, valves are closed, and the howl of engines builds to a deafening roar that shakes the lifter's superstructure.

In the executive cabin, General Cullen does not look up from the dataslate in his hand. He is a veteran of countless orbital transits. Among his fellow runners, Nestor's absence is noted, but without great concern.

As the first moments of engine ignition shiver their way through the monstrous craft's body, Bragin Nestor crawls out from his hiding place and draws his sidearm.

All Nestor wishes to do is return to the executive cabin. He will apologise, throw himself at Cullen's feet, beg the general's forgiveness for his weakness, and reveal his corruption by the metal creature that ensnared him.

A moan of pain escapes Nestor's lips. The shame dies, strangled by the scarab that squats on his brain stem.

He sets off, urgency guiding his steps. He cannot idle. The timing has to be exact. That was key. He must act at a particular time, or all his master's efforts will have been for naught.

Nestor edges out into the corridor and sets off. He abandons stealth in favour of speed, following the tugs of control that jerk his limbs at each junction and stairwell. It is not difficult to tell, now, who is truly in control. The schematics of the lifter are implanted in his scarab, and the creature effortlessly hijacks his motor functions. Nestor's role is reduced to that of a puppet, screaming in the hollowed-out cavern of his mind.

The first crew member he encounters is an emaciated woman in the red robes of the Mechanicus. She has a bionic eye, whose mounting covers the left side of her face, and skin that is ashen grey. She rounds a corner five steps ahead of Nestor, and pulls up short when she notices his presence. She starts to speak, presumably to question his presence.

Nestor lifts his laspistol and puts a bolt through her open mouth.

He leaves the body where it falls. The scarab urges him on, pushing faster as the tremors that grip the lifter grow in strength. No one will have heard the shot – the lifter's interior is a rattling nightmare of loose bolts, even without the thunder of the engines – and it matters little in any case.

Six more turns, and one long, steep descent over grated steps that Nestor slides down on his forearms, and he finds his destination. The hatch that should be locked in preparation for launch hangs half-open. A dead crewman prevents it from closing, his body folded in half over its lower lip. Nestor pushes the hatch open and leaps the body.

Three people are already inside the enginarium sub-deck. Half a dozen dead are at their feet. Most have las burns and hard-round wounds in their backs.

The three killers are a strange sight. One is a crew member, wrapped in the loose folds of a filthy grey robe. Another is a commissar, a man almost three times Nestor's age. Sweat pours from his balding pate. The third is a woman wearing the robes of a Munitorum junior, whose eyes are almost lost in deep shadows.

All three wear expressions of abject horror.

The three turn to look at him, and Nestor stares back. The scarab that rules his mind pulses an interstitial greeting, and the enslaving creatures in the others' heads do the same.

His master had not shared that there would be others. But that, he knows as the scarab bites down, is his prerogative. Nestor's purpose is to do, not to question.

No words are required. Each of the mindshackled humans, impotent protests unable to escape their lips, step over the bodies and through another hatch in the far wall, its surface littered with cautionary signs.

The chamber beyond is a nightmare of heat and sound. Each breath sends a lance of pain into Nestor's throat. His eardrums burst under the aural assault.

A railing encircles the vast column from which the heat and noise comes. Nestor and his peers clamber over the guard rail, and press themselves against the searing metal of the exhaust shaft, like a child trying to encircle its mother's leg. Nestor's flesh hisses and boils, fusing to the metal where it touches. He makes no sound as he places his face against its scalding surface, as though in rest. It is a rest; the pain banishes all that is left of Nestor's sanity.

The scarab peels one hand away from the blistering metal, and reaches for the detonator in Nestor's pocket. With a synchronicity born of their interstitial link, the four figures wait, and wait, and wait.

As the lifter's howl rises to its apex, the human that had been Bragin Nestor depresses his detonator, and the explosives packed around his torso erupt.

Shaking to its core, Lifter 575-98 hauls itself into the air.

Three seconds into its flight, its bulk not yet clear of the silo's upper edge, the exhaust vent on its starboard side is torn asunder in a maelstrom of fire. The trauma spreads up and into the ship's engines in an instant, and the ancient and delicate mechanisms rip themselves apart.

Lifter 575-98 stalls. There is a pregnant moment where the inertia of its launch equals the pull of gravity. The gargantuan craft hangs in mid-air, surrounded by an inferno that billows around it. The flames seek the sky, belching from the silo's open mouth.

Finally, the lifter falls, as it must. The uneven balance of thrust tips the craft onto its side, dashing its starboard face against the interior of the landing silo. Tens of thousands of tons of metal and machine and men experience the stomach-churning terror of freefall for six long seconds as Lifter 575-98 drops back to its launch pad. Its landing struts buckle under a force they were never meant to endure. Its great belly is sundered into a million fragments, only to be flattened a moment later by the rest of the ship as it collapses into itself.

Finally, and most catastrophically, the plasma reactor at the lifter's heart breaks. The nuclear fire contained within its core bursts from the craft's corpse, erasing any trace of the ship and shattering Landing Platform Sixty-Seven to powder.

The devastation is total, but not yet complete.

Throughout the complex, blast doors that should be sealed are open, their mechanisms jammed. Fail-safes that should activate in the event of catastrophe do not respond. Secondary explosives, meticulously placed over the course of several weeks, ignite as the tidal wave of fire reaches them. Other lifters in other silos, each in their own state of loading, are shattered by the pressure wave and engulfed by the spreading torrent of flames.

Outside, in the confusion of conveyor-cars and shouted orders and tightly packed bodies, ordered chaos turns to utter pandemonium. Hundreds of troopers and civilians are incinerated in the first moments, unaware of what killed them. Thousands more are crushed in the stampede that follows.

None stand. As the flames rise, veteran soldiers who have seen a dozen battles flee in terror. The commander of the 34th Vestillo Rifles, assuming sabotage, screams the order to open fire. His men, untested and blind with terror, lift their lasguns and shoot at anything in sight. The neighbouring soldiers of the 987th Craylin Armoured respond as their tents are shredded by las fire and trampled by running troopers. Cannon reports join the screams of the dying and the roar of flames.

Panic, more infectious than any disease and more destructive than any wildfire, spreads through the four million soldiers of the Beathen Crusade like a tidal wave, radiating out from the burning ruin of the landing platforms at its heart.

Sixty thousand souls perish within the first minutes of the chaos, consumed by the conflagration that roars through the landing pads. By nightfall, three hundred thousand servants of the Imperium will be dead, slain by their fellow warriors and the unchecked fear that lives in all human hearts.

From thousands of khet away and hundreds of khet deep, Kamoteph the Crooked looks upon his work, and is content.

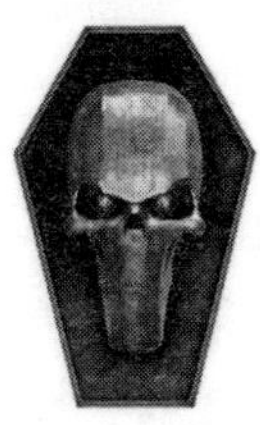

CHAPTER 6

Khemet sweeps into the chamber, anger propelling her to a furious pace. Were she not so practised in tempering her emotions, she might have lit her anti-gravity pack and leapt the khet that separates her from Kamoteph.

The cryptek is in the crypts, where he is so often found. He is surrounded by a knot of his apprenteks, expounding on whatever matter of esoteric importance concerns him today. They stand on a narrow bridge, an oblong of blackstone that extends with geometric precision across the width of the vault. Far below them, ranks and files of coffins run into the distance, disappearing into the twilight. A channel, half a khet wide, runs through its centre, fit for a cohort of warriors to march abreast down its length.

And march they do, rank by rank. These are Immortals, the elite of the Zathanor legions. They carry themselves with martial bearing, not the mind-locked shuffling pace of line warriors. Their twin-barrelled gauss blasters gleam, matched by the pristine bodies of their bearers.

It will be a moment of exquisite catharsis to finally unleash these troops. To cease her skulking and subterfuge, and make war in the ancient way. The necrontyr way.

But now is not that time.

'You have imperilled all we work for, technomancer.'

Her voice carries across the chasm, but the cryptek does not react. Kamoteph has watched Khemet's approach without surprise or fear. He stands his ground now, even as Khemet thunders towards him.

'Leave us.'

His apprenteks bow deeply and scuttle away towards the far end of the bridge. Even his canoptek pets retreat, fist-sized scarabs climbing quickly down the length of his body and flowing away across the blackstone. The effect is odd. Khemet has never seen the cryptek without at least a dozen constructs of various size crawling on and around him. But rather than appearing denuded, his isolation projects strength. He stands hunched and alone, entirely unafraid before Khemet's anger.

'You have something you wish to discuss, praetorian?'

'I cannot conduct a war with untrustworthy tools. I have already had to deal with your addled deathmark. Can I not rely on you now?'

'I find it amusing that you feel I am a tool to be deployed by you, praetorian. We serve a single end, each in our own way.'

'Your way will bring ruin upon us. Do you not understand the nature of what we must do if we are to defeat the humans? Each act must be deliberate. Considered. You have introduced anarchy into my war, Kamoteph.'

'I see,' says Kamoteph. His mocking pretence of calm is infuriating Khemet. 'Deliberate. Considered. Tell me, do you see nothing of strategic value in my act?'

Khemet does not reply.

'I am disappointed, praetorian. I have denied a significant strategic resource to the humans. They now have one fewer port of substance from which to receive reinforcements from the void. A human commander of some renown perished, along with many thousands of his warriors. Those who remain will no doubt suffer the psychological consequences for some time.'

Kamoteph turns away, and starts to pace slowly along the bridge's length. It is a movement calculated to project authority, inviting Khemet to either follow him or else surrender their conversation.

'Be still, cryptek,' Khemet barks. It is a petty trick, and one Khemet knows.

Kamoteph turns back, evidently amused, and continues. 'I have learnt much about the humans since our arrival. They are fragile, in so many ways. They desire order to be imposed upon them. They require it, so they can understand their place in their society. So they may deny their feral nature.'

He looks up at Khemet. 'You have introduced difficulty into their lives by attacking their feed. But by stripping away the pillars of their order, I have introduced uncertainty, a far more potent agent of destruction. Anarchy, praetorian, is precisely what is required.'

All that Kamoteph says about the humans is true, but Khemet is not receptive to his logic.

'Because of your actions there are four million more humans on this world with whom we must do battle when the time comes.'

'And does that not further your intent?' Kamoteph replies. 'Their army was to be dispatched far earlier than intended in order to relieve the strain on their overstressed supply lines. Overstressed, of course, thanks to you. This was my own contribution to that effort. Their multitudes will count for nothing if your strategy is effective.'

'You have shown our hand,' Khemet says, changing tack.

'I assure you, no evidence remains of the tools I employed. Fire is a great cleanser.'

Through her anger, Khemet judges that Kamoteph is right. Mind-shackle scarabs are as enduring as any necrontyr technology, but the organic matter in which they are embedded is as frail as the rest of the human form. It would require a degree of precision outside their capabilities to detect one of Kamoteph's creatures amongst the vastness of the wreckage strewn across the embarkation fields.

'They need not detect us to know they are under attack.'

Kamoteph sighs. 'Come now, praetorian, you really must stop. We have been breaking them piece by piece for two years. They would be fools not to know that some force moves against them. But they know not what, nor whom. The Imperium of Man' – Kamoteph gives an electronic huff of derision – 'does not lack for enemies.'

Khemet feels her fury turn inwards. It was foolish to confront Kamoteph in anger, to engage in debate with him. Since her incarceration she has allowed herself to forget so much of her role as a praetorian. An agent of the Silent King does not debate, she decrees.

She steps close, her voice low. 'Do not interfere with my war again, cryptek.'

Khemet brushes past him, heading for the far end of the bridge. As a parting blow it is weak, but Khemet has no interest in prolonging her humiliation.

But Kamoteph, it seems, has.

'Putting your ingratitude aside, I would judge that your service thus far has been… adequate,' he says to her back.

The cryptek's remark stops Khemet in her tracks.

'But given Lord Hekasun's urgency, I felt you needed some assistance. Duatekh.'

Khemet turns. There is no weapon in her hand, but one can appear with a twitch of her wrist. She starts back towards Kamoteph.

'Do you seek to provoke me to anger, technomancer?'

'On the contrary, I would hope that by now you would see me as your friend and ally.'

Khemet scoffs, a mechanical growl from her vocaliser.

'Truly, Khemet. I am on your side. I desire your success as sincerely as you.'

'And yet you goad me at every turn.'

'I seek only to lead you to enlightenment.'

'I am losing patience with your riddles. Speak, if you have anything worth saying.'

Khemet looms over the cryptek, who cranes his neck up from his crooked pose to meet Khemet's oculars. Yet there is no fear, only cruel amusement in the twist of his voice.

'Have you wondered why our honoured overlord assigned this task to you? Have you considered why Anrakyr would release you from your purgatory? Why he would spend a second's thought upon you, let alone offer a path to redemption, after you failed so egregiously?'

Khemet is plagued by these questions night and day, but she could never be moved to admit it. 'You evidently have.'

'I need not question, for I know the truth.' The cryptek pauses, clearly enjoying his own melodrama.

'You labour because you seek absolution from Overlord Anrakyr. But the Traveller knows nothing of this. We are not on a mission of his design. We were not sent to bring this world into waking as compensation for your failure on Lazar. We are here simply to conquer in Hekasun's name.'

Shock smothers Khemet's reaction. She has to replay Kamoteph's words before they will register.

'What?'

'The Traveller did not release you into Hekasun's care. We smuggled your cage from his collection. Though, as yours was one amongst many, I doubt the Traveller is even aware of your absence. Really, you imagined yourself to be held in much higher esteem than was the case.'

It takes several attempts before Khemet can form a response. 'You lie.'

The bent-backed cryptek takes a predatory step towards her. 'I assure you, praetorian, this is the first time I have given you the unadulterated truth.'

'Why?'

'Because Hekasun, for all his many flaws, knows he is no nemesor. He has not the patience nor imagination for the campaign you have waged on his behalf. For all his preening and rhetoric, he needed you. Or another like you. But where would he have found so capable and yet so biddable a servant as you?' Kamoteph cannot prevent his words from turning into a wry laugh at her expense.

Khemet thrusts her hand into her pocket dimension, and it emerges clutching her staff. Its green blade rises between Khemet and the cryptek, who wisely backs away with hands raised.

'Consider your actions, Khemet. Without our intervention, you would have remained in your prison forever.'

That checks her hand. Not through gratitude, but through the icy blade of dread that slides its way into Khemet's core. Anrakyr, to whom she had given centuries of service, would have left her in the labyrinth forever. Forgotten. Put out of his mind, while Khemet steadily and irretrievably lost hers.

'Why did you tell me this?'

Kamoteph shrugs, a complicated roll of his segmented spine. 'I felt it was time for honesty between us. The cleansing of this world has not yet truly begun, and we have many more tasks to share.

'And,' he continues when Khemet does not reply, 'because I mean what I say. I am just as invested in our success as you. The kemmeht of Qeretesh deserves to be rid of those who are unworthy to tread it. And for all your… deliberation, you are an able agent of that deliverance.'

The blade in Khemet's hand hovers between them, useless. Lashing out at the cryptek will achieve nothing. Even displaying the weapon professes her weakness – threatening violence against a creature whose consciousness will immediately be claimed by the tomb world's reanimation protocols is the very definition of impotence.

She needs time to process this. Her fraying cognition, which for so long she has kept under the tightest grip, is beginning to spiral, caught between the successive questions Kamoteph's revelation raises. Her memories of awakening aboard the *Senusret* replay themselves, unbidden, and a fresh spike of alarm sends Khemet deeper into panic as she sees a tessellated floor swim into her sight.

Kamoteph takes a step back. 'I sense that you would value some time in privacy, and I must attend to my duties.'

Khemet is incapable of preventing him from leaving. 'Why me?' she asks instead. 'Why this world?'

Kamoteph releases another metallic chuckle. 'Those, praetorian, are questions I suggest you put to our noble lord.'

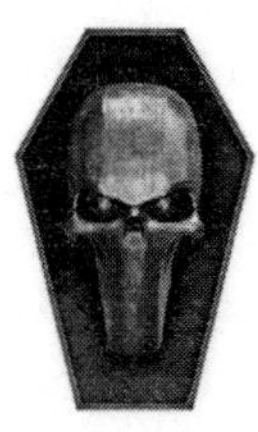

CHAPTER 7

'By the Throne…'

Sinos stands amid the wreckage of an Imperial army.

She and her squad have come directly from the Plakid Islands, or as directly as they were permitted. The first reports of the disaster sent Salvastari's wardens into abject panic, bundling the lord-militant and his closest staff away to the secure interior of his palace. For almost the first time in her life, Sinos' Adeptus Arbites seal could unlock no doors. She and her men had to wait for five interminable hours, under guard, before being allowed to board their flyer and begin their journey towards the voidport.

They dismounted seventeen hours later, turned out by a red-faced Munitorum junior who waved the transport on towards one of the laagers that had been set up across the plains. From there they have walked, in awe as much as horror, through the devastation of the landing fields.

The dead carpet the ground. This is grimly, literally true. Sinos and her squad stand in the middle of a path that has been cleared of bodies by the expedience of piling them to either side, leaving wide streaks of blood and flattened viscera through the grit and rubble. She can see Chimeras and civilian industrial units, all fitted with dozer blades, doing their work a mile to the north, carving another road through the bodies to permit the medicaes and fire-suppression teams to approach the ruins of the largest voidport on Orymous.

The flames still rage, almost a full day after the catastrophic detonation of Lifter 575-98. Sinos can feel the heat on her face even from this distance. Her mouth and nose are covered by a rebreather, and she is glad of it; even through its filters there is the rancid, chemical taste of promethium soot in the air.

After two miles of walking through the holding area for an armoured regiment, judging by the churned-up paving and tank treads crisscrossing the ground, they reach a built-up corner of the mustering site. The landing fields were – or had been – a sprawling complex of hab-blocks and mess halls and assembly squares, the equal of the barracks at which the troops had been stationed. Fire has spread from the voidport to many of the surrounding quarters, but this precinct has survived the destruction more or less unscathed.

They enter a tangle of low, dust-streaked habitation units, their road becoming congested with the living and the dead. A steady stream of flatbed transports is heading out laden with bodies, while other haulers wait impatiently to carry crews in towards the voidport. The world is quickly reduced to a cloud of ochre-yellow, close-packed bodies, and the angry cries of those who are trying to order the chaos.

When the forward motion of the crowd ahead stalls completely Sinos stops with it, weighing her next course. After twenty-four hours of continuous forward motion, Sinos has finally been forced to halt and consider the indefinite but powerful urge that has pulled her halfway around the globe.

She is an investigator, and the voidport is the scene of a most heinous crime. She must see it for herself.

'This may be as far as we can go, marshal,' says Abisode.

Sinos does not reply, and instead looks around. She finds her target quickly, and heads towards the entrance of a seven-storey hab-block.

'Marshal–' begins Abisode, but Sinos kicks down the door and starts to climb its steep staircase.

There are, fortunately, no bodies waiting for them. Sinos climbs quickly, hammering each boot into the bare metal steps. She heads to the highest level, clambering over kitbags and other gear that was evidently dropped in the panicked flight of whichever Guard unit was stationed here. She reaches the top, but finds the entry to the dormitory floor blocked by a three-level bedframe that has toppled over. Sinos throws it aside with more effort than required, making it clatter against others that have already fallen.

The hab-block is tall enough to give a clear overview over the clustered hab-stacks, parade grounds and thoroughfares. A tall, thin series of windows runs around the outer wall of the room, their crystalflex panes blown in by a pressure wave. Sinos climbs onto an abandoned foot locker, and for the first time sees the voidport.

The complex spreads for miles, a city in itself. Landing platforms and launch silos and control towers make a tessellated pattern of blocky shapes that waver in the heat haze. The outer wall of the closest silo has been broken open, and between the flames Sinos can see the corpse of a lifter, its hull plating splayed open. Broken rockcrete studded through with rebar shows where landing pads for flyers have shattered.

It is broken, entirely and completely. The Munitorum will

need to tear it down to its foundations before they can rebuild. Towers have tumbled, machines have crashed. And everywhere, absolutely everywhere, there are the dead.

At the outskirts the primary cause of death had been the panicked fire of their fellow soldiers. During the drive in, Sinos had keyed her helmet's vox-unit to a Munitorum command channel to listen to a briefing given by an anonymous adept to officials in Orylesti. Reports suggested that at least a dozen regimental-scale battles had broken out between neighbouring units as the devastation of the voidport unfolded. Those failures of discipline and command would require punishment at the highest level. Sinos does not expect to be involved; the Offi-cio Logisticarum is more than equipped for military tribunals.

Closer in, the dead that form the verges of the approach road were not killed by las and hard rounds. They had had the life squeezed from them, caught up in the stampede that erupted when the first flames billowed from Landing Platform Sixty-Seven. In the tight alleys and prefabricated billets, even the most stalwart trooper had been forced along, slammed into corrugated steel walls. Those who fell from their comrades' clutches were lost immediately, trampled underfoot by those who could themselves be dragged under just moments later.

Within the ruins of the voidport, it was fire and rock that had made such appalling murder. From her vantage point, between the dust and debris she can see blackened skeletons, their bones charred and reduced to powdery stumps. There are bodies cooked to red, ruined flesh. Some are fused together, melted like wax within the inferno's heat. Even Sinos, who has seen much of war and the many, many ways a person can die, turns away from such sights.

Her descent through the hab-stack is slower. Her climb had been fuelled by haste, by desperation to see and to know. Now,

Sinos feels the rage, cold and purposeful. This has always been her way, the core of her success as an arbitrator. She can take her fury and turn it into a tool.

As ever in moments of crisis, Sinos' mind turns to action and evaluation. It will be at least a week before all the bodies are cleared from the embarkation fields, and a month before the last unfortunates are pulled from the ruin of the landing platforms. But before that, the living must be removed. The four million men and women of the Beathen Crusade are scattered across tens of miles in all directions. Encampments, such as the regiments might make while on campaign, are dotted about the plains where exhaustion led them to collapse in the hours after the destruction of the voidport. Logisticarum adepts have ordered Imperial Navy flights over the farthest units, dropping emergency rations and water from their bomb bays to see them through the days to come.

The act of moving an Imperial army, even in the simplest of circumstances, is an act of staggering complexity. Re-forming this one, which is leaderless and in complete disarray, will demand as much effort as winning the war the regiments had been formed to fight.

But that is not her duty. Sinos is here to determine what, in the name of Holy Terra, caused this to happen.

'Marshal! Marshal Sinos!'

As she emerges from the hab-unit, Sinos is stunned to find Selimha Briseida sitting on the rear of a cargo-8. Her squad form up protectively, but Sinos waves their shotguns down.

'Stop the truck,' calls Briseida, her voice hoarse.

The cargo-8 pulls out of the line and wheezes to a stop. The logisticator climbs down, stumbling until one of Sinos' squad catches her. Her face is smeared with ash, through which tears have cut clean runnels on her dark-brown skin. Her robe is a frayed ruin at its edge, showing where it has caught on shards of rebar and debris.

Her retinue are little better, climbing down after their mistress. They have no wounds, but their Munitorum livery is cloaked with ash and blood.

'I am pleased to see you, adept.' Sinos had assumed that Briseida had died with Cullen.

'I had to see for myself.' Her voice quavers. The strong, belligerent woman Sinos had met not three days earlier, who had argued toe-to-toe with a general of the Astra Militarum, is gone.

'I was up… up on the orbital.' She is not speaking to Sinos, but at her, her reserve undone by a familiar face. 'The general had me go up early, to take charge of the final provisioning. But I… I had to come back. I had to see.'

'So did I, adept.'

'I saw them, Sinos. I carried them in my arms. I pulled them from the rubble with my hands…' Briseida stumbles forwards, grabbing hold of Sinos with thin fingers.

'Find them, marshal. Find them, and burn them for their heresy.'

Sinos gently but firmly takes the logisticator's hands in hers, and prises them from the collar of her armour. As the old woman is racked by sobs, one of her aides steers her away into the safety of the knot of adepts.

That is Sinos' role. It is why she was called to Orymous. There can be no question now of malicious intent, no concealment behind material fatigue or operator error or any of the other benign explanations that could be offered for the misfortunes that have befallen the mustering world. The destruction of the voidport is an overt attack, explicable only as an act of sabotage. There is an agent, an actor behind this campaign. And now they have shown their hand.

Whoever orchestrated this will not stop now, of that Sinos is sure. This is an escalation that takes them out of the shadows, throwing off the cloak of plausible, if improbable, adversity.

It is, in a macabre way, freeing. She is no longer groping for explanations in the dark. She is in pursuit of an enemy that is cunning, resourceful and ruthless.

Now, Sinos can hunt.

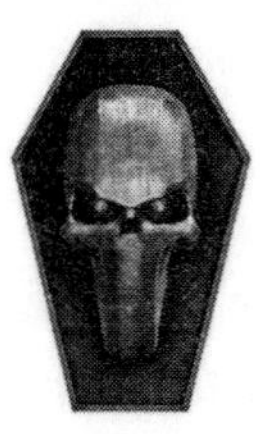

CHAPTER 8

All wisdom tells Khemet to walk away. All self-preservation tells her that she must seek solitude. She should master herself, should set her mind back to a state of equilibrium.

But wisdom and self-preservation are not in command of her limbs. Anger is.

She finds Hekasun in the throne room of Qeretesh. It is where he is always to be found, save for his forays into the world's treasuries to rifle through their wares. Hekasun has not once walked upon the surface of this world since he came to it. He has not stood beneath its sun, nor seen the petty works its vandals have erected. He has not bled its occupiers, nor greeted his awoken cohorts from their crypts. He has never truly listened to Khemet when she has explained her strategy to him. He has simply waited, arrogant and imperious, for her to deliver Qeretesh to his petulantly out-thrust hands.

The throne room is among the deepest halls of the tomb world, sunk far into the planet's mantle. Here, at least, is an echo of the glory of the necrontyr – even a pauper house like the Zath-anor would not skimp on the grandeur of its principal palace.

It is fifty khet wide, sufficient for an entire legion to array itself across its blackstone floor. Massive pillars run in rows, each face cut to geometric precision and inlaid with power conduits that glow with immense energy. The walls, far to the distance on either side of Khemet's periphery, are made of a translucent crystal that permits the throne room's occupants to see the roil-ing molten rock of their world. It bathes the chamber in a warm, fuliginous glow, proximate in tone to Hekasun's reactor core.

At its centre is a ziggurat, the equal of any that once crowned the planet's surface. Within, Khemet knows, will be the heart of the tomb world's spirit, along with the greatest of all its treas-ures – the command protocols for the legions that slumber in its vaults.

He has his court with him. It has swollen from the few who had accompanied him aboard the *Senusret* as the lordling has rummaged through the dynastic vaults. Hekasun's vanity demands witnesses, though none, she notices, sits within the chain of succession of the Zathanor. Of course, that line was broken – by her – but Hekasun has purposefully awoken none who might come forward to challenge his claim to dominion of Qeretesh.

'Hekasun. I would speak with you.'

She announces herself while she is several leagues away, but takes to the air once she has his attention. Drifting upon a haze of anti-gravity, she rises to be level with the ziggurat's peak, from which Hekasun plays nomarch.

'Praetorian,' he says in sly welcome. 'Kamoteph tells me you and he have talked.' There is mockery in his voice, but there is anger too. Perhaps he is vexed by Kamoteph giving Khemet the truth; she cannot say.

'I demand answers.'

'Demand? You should greet your liberator with more deference.'

'I owe you nothing.'

'You owe me everything!' Hekasun roars. He leaps from his throne with a display of such visceral anger that Khemet checks, uncertain from where he has found such passion. 'You owe your existence to me! Had I not released you from your prison, your mind would have collapsed into oblivion. I spared you from the fate you deserve.'

'You desire that I show you gratitude? That I fall upon my knees and praise you?'

'No, Khemet. I wish for you to give back the worlds you stole from us.'

Genuine curiosity stops her from barking back a reply. 'What worlds?' she asks instead.

'Do you wish to know? Do you wish to behold who it is you have served all this time?'

With an electronic grunt of effort, Hekasun reshapes his form. The necrodermis of his chestplate flows and shifts. The glyph of the Traveller, emblazoned on Hekasun's torso, fades, receding into his metal.

Around her, all are following Hekasun's lead. Shudders of rippling metal echo around the chamber as the nobles cast off their false allegiance to the Traveller. Across torsos and brows emerges an icon that Khemet recognises instantly. A glyph dredged from her memory, lit by the blaze of her staff of office as she renders necron after necron to slag and ash.

She turns back to watch the dynastic seal of the Zathanor emerge from Hekasun's chest.

'Yes, *duatekh*.' Hekasun draws out the insult. 'The house you dissolved on a whim to buy your way into the esteem of the Traveller. It seems you did not kill us all.'

Menouthis. In an instant Khemet travels back across centuries and light years to the last world of the Zathanor, until Hekasun brought her to Qeretesh.

'They had not survived the Great Sleep,' she says slowly. 'They were mad. Raving. My duty was clear.'

Barks of anger and denunciation echo around her, none louder than Hekasun's.

'Do not speak to me of duty, *praetorian*.' He hisses Khemet's title as a curse. 'It was not duty that led you to slay every member of my family. To murder all that was left of my dynasty. You massacred them to curry favour with the overlord. They were the coin you used to buy your way into his affections.' His fury twists into mocking scorn. 'Such, as you have learnt, that they are.'

'You are wrong,' she throws back, matching anger with anger. 'That is the lie you have told yourself, nursing your plans for vengeance. You have conjured me as the object of your hate because you cannot face the truth. The Zathanor were doomed by their poverty from the moment they walked into their coffins.'

That is what Khemet tells herself. But there is a fraction of doubt, a slim and treacherous fragment of uncertainty that worms its way out of the recesses of her mind.

Did she end the Zathanor out of spite? Was that her motive? She remembers it, a labour of weeks, as each dynast was pulled from their crypts by their own lychguard and dragged before her. They died poorly, thrashing, screaming, babbling nonsense from broken minds. There was nothing vindictive or self-interested in it. That the Traveller arrived as her grim work was completed was a matter of coincidence.

But these are the facts she tells herself, in the present. They are not the truth of perfect, engrammatic recall. She fears to dredge too deeply, to risk losing herself in the past.

Khemet silently curses, oaths of disgust and loathing. Has she become so diminished? Has she such little confidence in her sense of self?

'Evidently not,' Hekasun says, in ignorance of Khemet's self-doubt. 'I have endured. *We* have endured.' He gestures at the nobility – his kin – who stand around them.

'How?' She asks not because she cares to know, but to give her faltering mind time to find its centre.

Hekasun, enamoured of the sound of his own voice, is happy to oblige, though bitterness is thick in every word. 'You chose well, Khemet. The Zathanor were all but ruined. Our crown-world was swallowed by its star, and only we' – he gestures at the small crowd – 'are the fortunate few who escaped. A single craft, sparing all that was left of a noble house.

'We drifted for centuries, barely moving through the inter-stellar void. But in time we reached Menouthis. And what did we find? That you and your overlord had plundered it for its riches. You had murdered its nomarch – my own aunt! – and had stolen its treasures.'

'There were few treasures on Menouthis, Hekasun.'

It is an ill-considered jibe, and for a moment the lord looks ready to strike her. But cowardice or pragmatism stays his hand. 'The Traveller found us, as he has so many others. We concealed our allegiance, and waited for this moment to come to be.'

'And you have been content to lurk in Anrakyr's shadow, concealing your true allegiance out of fear.'

Hekasun does not deny her accusation. 'I have played the part of servile courtier for long enough. No longer. Qeretesh will be the cradle of the Zathanor's rebirth. I demand it of you, in payment for the empire you tore apart.'

Hekasun's delusion reaches even higher than Khemet had imagined. The Zathanor could never claim to be anything more than a minor house. To name themselves an empire was hubris itself.

'Why should I serve you now?'

'I do not care. You now know the truth. Your reasons are your own. But you *will* do as I command.'

The embers of Khemet's pride blaze into life. 'Only one being may command me, Hekasun. And you are not him.'

'Nevertheless.'

Hekasun and Khemet remain locked in place, oculars fixed upon the other. It is a contest of wills with a single outcome. There can be no denying the debt Khemet owes, and even had there been no debt, it is the duty of every necron to cleanse their invaded worlds of the touch of the Unclean.

Hekasun sees that he has won.

'Go and win me my world.'

CHAPTER 9

'My name is Marshal Sinos. Stand aside.'

'What is your business?' demands the lieutenant on the far side of the barricade.

Sinos checks, sincerely surprised. Any man who challenges an arbitrator standing beside a Chimera armoured personnel carrier is incredibly brave, or incredibly foolish.

After a moment's thought, she lifts her scales of justice from their chain around her neck and holds them up before him. 'Do you recognise this symbol, lieutenant?'

His eyes, a watery and unremarkable brown, flick from hers to the emblem. 'No. Sir,' he adds, as an afterthought.

The lieutenant is young, but not so young that he can be forgiven the sin of not recognising the icon of the Adeptus Arbites.

'This symbol empowers me to summarily execute you, your squad, and every person you have ever met. You have three seconds to move aside.'

Behind her, Abisode shifts his grip on his shotgun. The creak of his gauntlets carries clearly in the cold air.

The young man backs up so quickly he knocks into two of his squad, standing protectively close behind him. He waves an arm for the barricade to be raised.

'My apologies, marshal. I have orders...' he stammers, finally settling on sure ground. 'The Emperor protects.'

'You are fortunate that He does, lieutenant.'

The Chimera grumbles into the building's precinct, and Sinos follows. She has secured the use of the vehicle from the Munitorum's stockpile, freeing her from the need to employ any local security forces as she moves about Verongyl.

That such precautions are a necessity is a sign of how far the rule of the Lex has been degraded.

The young man and his squad are in the white-and-blue uniforms of the Orymousian Defence Corps. Every citizen of Orymous is inducted into its ranks at birth, and trained to serve in the planet's defence, ready for moments such as these. In the wake of the voidport's destruction mobilisation orders have been issued across the continent.

There is some wisdom in that. Salvastari seeks to exchange the impotence of victimhood for the purpose and unity of martial action, uniting civilians and soldiers alike in the common purpose of securing their cities and preparing for whatever will come next.

But, on the other hand, it puts men and women not suited to the rigours of martial discipline in uniforms and hands them lasguns.

She regrets her manner with the militia lieutenant. It was a petty display of power over a man who should still be called a boy, doing what he considered his duty.

It is, she knows, a sign that her blood is up. She has been on the trail for three weeks. Or, rather, she has been in search of a trail, and now she senses she may have caught the first scent of it.

She has left the Munitorum to investigate the sabotage of Lifter 575-98 and the destruction of the voidport. That is too big, too sprawling and complex a task to yield any evidence in the time she has. Her investigative team, finally brought down from orbit and ensconced within a corner of Orylesti, is in regular communication with the lead enforcers, but she does not hold out any real hope of leads from that quarter.

The Officio Logisticarum are reacting as she would expect them to. Their enforcers are embarking on an investigation that will require months and draw in hundreds, if not thousands, of adepts whose time would be better spent responding to this new crisis. It will take weeks simply to complete the interrogation of the survivors, producing a mountain of testimony and excruciated confessions to be examined and cross-referenced. But that is the way on Orymous – everything is reduced to a problem of logistics. An equation to be solved by the input of time and energy. Sinos has neither to spare, and so she has taken a different approach.

She has turned her attention to the other crimes, the acts of seemingly random violence and adversity that have steadily tipped Orymous towards disaster. She began by winnowing down her possible targets. The Officio Logisticarum had been typically thorough in its provision of data when she first arrived, burying Sinos' lexigraphs beneath a mountain of incident reports and arrest records. Sinos has swept much of these aside, her focus solely on the events of the past few years that had the gravest impact on the mustering world, reasoning that whatever agent of chaos is moving in the shadows would not waste their efforts on petty criminality.

The Conveyor Sixteen-Red derailment. The razing of the agri-fields on Orymous Secundus. An outburst of seditious labour collectivisation among the dock workers of Asterni. A tainted starch-processing plant.

The unlikely murder of the Logisticator Primus of Verongyl, and the subsequent suicide of his chief aide.

That particular thread is what has brought her to the sprawling billet-city, and to the door of its principal mortuarium.

Abisode pushes open the front door, a grand slab of wood three times his height. She has only brought the squad leader with her. In Sinos' experience, two arbitrators are sufficient to ensure the passivity of any detainee.

The interior is lit by recessed lumens dotted about the walls, and a massive chandelier ablaze with dozens of heavy yellow candles. The building must have served some different function in its past; the marble floor, the imperial staircase and gilt furnishings put Sinos in mind of a theatre. The carved faces of grotesques and divines that crown the corners and tops of pillars suggest Sinos' guess is correct.

A receiving desk sits at the rear of the entry chamber, beneath the point where the two staircases meet. A clerk, looking oddly alert for such a late hour, greets her with the sign of the aquila.

'I am here to see Chief Verispexor Pyrch.'

He meets her eye. 'Do you have an appointment?'

Sinos tries not to read anything into the outbreak of belligerent stupidity that seems to have taken hold around the mortuarium.

'No. I do not.'

The man swallows. 'Right this way.'

She and Abisode are led up the left-hand curve of the staircase. Beyond another set of doors, any hint of the building's former nature is lost, replaced by the ascetic functionality of Imperial bureaucracy found throughout the Imperium. The clerk leads her down a long, cramped hallway, the buzz of strip-lumens uncomfortably close above her.

The door to the chief verispexor's office is as unremarkable as the dozen others that they pass. The clerk knocks, then pushes it open.

'Verispexor, we–'

Sinos pushes past the man. 'Verispexor Pyrch, my name is Solome Sinos of the Adeptus Arbites. I require your cooperation and your time.'

They have been led not to an office, but an examination room. Two slabs fill the centre of the room, surrounded by cabinets and counters whose metal surfaces are polished to a mirror finish.

Pyrch looks up as she and Abisode enter. He is at work on a cadaver lying on the centre table. Blood smears his thin plastek gown up to both elbows.

'Thank you, Cenon, that will be all.' The clerk, trapped in the desire to object to Sinos' rough treatment and fear of her, ducks out of the door.

'It is an honour to meet you, marshal,' says Pyrch genially. 'Had I known you were coming, I would have made myself more presentable.'

'The Adeptus Arbites is not deterred by blood, verispexor.'

He offers a wan smile. 'Of course. Even so, this can wait.' He gestures vaguely at the corpse, then pulls off his fouled gloves and gown and stuffs them into a receptacle. He turns to a sink inlaid into the polished countertop behind him.

'What can I do for you, marshal?' he asks with his back to Sinos, his hands working vigorously in a flow of steaming chem-wash.

'Your compliance with my investigation is compelled by the Lex Imperialis.'

'I am a servant of the Throne, marshal. My compliance is given freely.'

Sinos makes a subtle gesture to Abisode, and takes several paces towards the far side of the room. Pyrch's manner is far too casual for anyone who has received an unexpected visit from the Adeptus Arbites.

'Logisticator Primus Farroll. You were the consulted verispexor.'

'I was.' He turns, drying his arms with a thin towel that he tosses onto the closest counter. 'Considering the circumstances, no other hand would do.'

'You are required to turn over all documents relating to your autopsy of both the logisticator and his aide, Gerand Cadfan.'

'His killer, I believe you mean, marshal. Of course, my notes are yours. But I filed a thorough report with the Munitorum.' He reaches above himself to another cabinet, and begins pulling out parchment files and folders.

She loosens the shock maul at her hip. 'And I would like his body exhumed for re-examination.'

Even this does not give him pause. 'I'm sorry, marshal. I am afraid his remains were destroyed, in accordance with his wishes.'

'I will require a copy of that order.'

He continues to rummage for paperwork, entirely too at ease. 'May I ask the purpose of your investigation?'

'No,' says Abisode. 'You may not.'

He has evidently found all he needs. He gathers them up with one hand, and slips the other into a pocket. 'These are my hand-written notes of the examination. I will have to ask my assistant to provide you with the rest.' He walks towards her, holding out the files for Sinos to take.

The exam room door opens with a bang. Abisode whirls at the sound, shotgun rising. The clerk has returned, a look of abject horror on his face.

In her moment of distraction Pyrch drops the files and lunges for Sinos, one hand clenched around something in his palm while the other grabs for her collar.

She steps back sharply, jabbing a fist that snaps the man's

head back. He reels, legs collapsing beneath him. His closed hand opens as he hits the floor.

A fat-bodied beetle, no larger than Sinos' smallest fingernail, leaps out of his palm and towards Sinos.

She jerks away, gauntlets flailing at the front of her armour. She brushes the thing away and sees it drop to the floor, a black speck against the white tiles. She slams her boot down, and through the thick leather feels it crunch beneath her sole.

The clerk is down, blood pouring from a flattened nose. Abisode spins, levelling his weapon at the verispexor. He is on his hands and knees, scrabbling for something inside a cabinet, his head and torso also fully inside. The rack of a shotgun's shell carries across the room.

'No, don't shoot him!'

Abisode fires, but punches a hole the size of Pyrch's head into the cabinet next to him.

'Stand and turn. You are bound by the Lex Imperialis.' Abisode advances, shotgun unwavering. 'I have him, marshal.'

Pyrch withdraws, slowly. He is holding something, clutched white-knuckled in both hands. It is a stone tablet, black as night but with a sickly sheen beneath the lumen strips. He turns with the tablet out-thrust, as though it were a shield or a weapon, his stare fixed implacably on Sinos. Its face starts to glow, the same diseased green growing in strength.

'Put it down!' Sinos and Abisode bark the command in the same moment.

Sinos' hand drops to her bolt pistol in the same moment that the first scarab tumbles from the translation plate.

A creature emerges from the stone itself, pulling its body out of the surface with sharp-tipped legs. It is the size of her clenched fist, its shell iridescent blue and gold. It spills from the green glow of the plate, and starts to skitter across the floor.

The sound of metal tines on ceramic tiles is audible even over the hammering of Sinos' pulse.

Two more follow. Then five, then ten, then a swarm of metal beetles, all racing towards Abisode.

'Throne of Terra!'

Abisode fires, and the blast decapitates Pyrch. His headless body slumps back against the chromed cabinets, blood spurting from the stump of his neck. Abisode racks another shell, but the swarm is faster. He goes down screaming, overwhelmed by the tide of beetles that spill from the plate's glowing face. Another hammer-blow of his shotgun booms around the tiny room, throwing a handful of creatures into the air and shattering one of the lumen bars overhead.

Sinos draws and fires, aiming to blow the stone tablet to shards. The bolt shell detonates against its face, flinging it across the room. But it remains whole, still releasing more metal creatures that clamber out of its interior.

Sinos runs. She has been a hand of the Emperor's justice for over a century. She has faced down heretics and mutants, and seen the aftermath of battles against xenos horrors. But Sinos runs now, in abject terror of the skittering horde that cascades across the bloodstained tiles.

She crashes through the exam room's door, falling onto all fours. She scrambles, legs kicking. She feels the first scarab stab a sharp tine into her leg. She kicks out, smashing the creature against the wood of the door. Finally, her boots find purchase on the polished marble, and Sinos scrabbles to her feet.

The corridor beyond is empty, sterile and bland. The normality of it almost makes Sinos check, doubting her memory of the past seconds. But then the doors click open and the swarm pours out. Sinos takes off.

A verispexor emerges from the next room, white coat curling about his legs. He looks up, not at the swarm but at Sinos.

'Run! Get out of the way!'

But the man plants his feet, squaring himself to tackle Sinos.

In the moment before they connect Sinos drops her shoulder. Her pauldron slams into the bridge of his nose, and the verispexor is hammered from his feet. Sinos stumbles, legs fouled by his flailing limbs, but she keeps her feet and runs on. The tide flow over and around him, engulfing the man in their chittering bodies.

She is holding her bolt pistol, but she ignores it. Turning now would kill her. Anything but running with all the strength and power of terror will doom her, and she must survive. She must live to tell of the abominations that have infected Orymous.

She reaches the end of the corridor and throws herself bodily at the point where the two doors meet. The wood shatters beneath her weight, and she crashes to the marble floor once more.

As she finds her feet something slams into her back with the weight and grip of a cyber-mastiff. Sinos is knocked forwards, and the force of the impact carries her over the stone balustrade.

She drops twenty feet onto the receiving desk, landing on her back and crashing through its flimsy wood. There is a crunch, and a knife of pain that stabs through Sinos' shoulder. She rolls aside and levels her pistol. A beetle the size of a canid has been halfway crushed between the broken desk and the weight of Sinos and her armour. The tip of one limb is bloody where it punched between the plates.

Sinos puts a pair of shells into the centre of its loathsome body. It explodes in a shower of knife-edged limbs and metal scrap.

The swarm is cascading down either side of the staircase, and tumbling through the gaps in the balustrade Sinos went over. She runs for the main door, only for it to be kicked open by five enforcers of the Adeptus Arbites, their shotguns levelled and roaring orders for compliance.

'Fire!' Sinos bellows the order as she throws herself flat. She skids along the floor as the thunder of shotguns roars over her head.

She thumps to a stop and rises with her pistol in hand. Scarabs and metal creatures of every description are met by blasts of explosive shot. Sinos adds her bolt shells to the fusillade, blowing chunks from the ornate stone floor. Each shot leaves a crater in the marble and a broken scarab in its centre, but there are far too many.

'Fall back to the Chimera!'

The squad immediately begin to step back without slacking in their fire, the action well drilled from months on the practice ground.

'Where is Abisode?' asks Murillen, the next-ranking arbitrator of the squad.

'Dead.' Sinos pushes aside the pang of regret that follows – Abisode is a casualty of the war that is erupting within Verongyl.

But not the first.

The swarm are closing in, the chatter of metal limbs on marble echoing around the atrium. Sinos is the last arbitrator through the open doors, firing until her pistol clicks empty. She throws both doors shut, but does not imagine for a moment that the heavy wood will keep the constructions at bay.

'Into the Chimera.'

The crackle of las sounds behind her. The lieutenant and his auxilia squad are at their barricade, blazing away with their newly issued lasguns. Sinos' squad drop behind the bulk of their Chimera, but the auxilia remain standing in the open, blazing away without regard for their own lives. Murillen's shot hits one in the hip, all but severing her thigh. She topples without a sound, still scrabbling for her lasgun as her life empties from her body.

It only takes seconds. The lieutenant is the last to fall, blood soaking into his auxilia's uniform. None of Sinos' arbitrators are wounded, save for the awkward pain in her shoulder.

They bundle into the Chimera, Arbitrator Dixin climbing through into the driver's compartment.

Sinos is breathless, but thumps the partition to get Dixin's attention. 'Get us moving, and get on the vox.'

'To who?'

He is right. Pyrch, the clerk, the lieutenant and his squad. Whatever corruption turned them against their people will not be isolated to the mortuarium.

The armoured vehicle growls into life. Sinos has never been more relieved to hear the thump of hatches sealing shut. There are only five people on the entire planet whom Sinos now trusts, and they are all sitting within the Chimera's cabin.

'Raise the logisticator's palace. Lock down the city. Nothing leaves without my express authority.' It is the only logical act, even if it is far too late for that. Compliance or defiance of her order will determine who is corrupted.

'What in Terra's name are they?' Murillen asks as the Chimera lumbers into motion.

Nothing human could birth such corruption. No artefact of the Mechanicus could make such monstrosities. There is only one conclusion, one enemy, that has been making a silent war on Orymous for two years.

Xenos.

Ahnuret awakens.

It is sudden, abrupt. Every sense comes alive in an instant, flooding perceptual centres that had been inert a moment before.

She is not where she had been. She is in her cell, seated on a stone chair. And it is not the praetorian standing before her. It is Kamoteph.

Assassin's instincts, honed for decades before she was gifted her body of inviolate metal, respond despite her sensory distress. She drops a hand to her waist, and lifts her enmitic pistol.

The cryptek casually swings his staff into her arm, blocking her line of attack, then shuffles back quickly to show that he poses no threat. Ahnuret keeps her pistol in hand, but does not pursue him.

'I require you,' he says aloud. Kamoteph never connects with Ahnuret via the interstices.

'What did she do to me?' Ahnuret despises the weakness of the question, but she must know. She had been speaking with Khemet, and then she was… gone. Shut down. Switched off, as Ahnuret would shroud a lamp.

But not entirely. There was something, a fragment of thought that had lingered upon her waking.

'A praetorian's trick,' says Kamoteph dismissively. 'Now focus.'

Ahnuret is not listening. She is looking inwards, trying to chase down the engrammatic record of where her mind had been sent.

Kamoteph slams the butt of his staff down on the stone.

'Deathmark. I require you. Now.'

'I repeat, a priority-one cordon around the entire city. Scramble whatever air attack wing is closest and target anything that lifts off. Shut down the mass conveyors, and lock down the arterial roadways.'

Sinos has been shouting into a vox-horn since they made their escape from the mortuarium. The rest of her squad are doing the same, signalling every Imperial authority they can reach.

Some will be corrupted, but there is no avoiding that.

The only arbitrator not focused on spreading the word is Dixin, who steers the Chimera at a breakneck speed through the city.

'Obstruction ahead, marshal.'

Sinos looks at the feed from the forward picter. They are thundering down the centre of a four-lane roadway, which in several hundred yards ends abruptly at a six-lane exchange.

'Stop for nothing.'

'Yes, sir.' There is only one priority in matters of corruption – to spread the word.

The Chimera charges across the intersection. Its treads catch the front of a groundcar and flatten its engine block. Another is unable to brake in time and slams into its side armour, causing the barest jolt through the interior.

'We have a flyer waiting for us at the Van Ryden aerodrome, marshal.' Beska has been coordinating with the air traffic authorities, seeking anything with wings and an engine that will get them out of the city.

'How long to Van Ryden?'

'Six minutes,' Dixin replies.

Beska hears him, and raises the vox-horn to her lips. 'Six minutes, control. No one is to approach that machine, is that understood?'

Sinos trusts nothing, no object and certainly no person. She cannot shed the memory of the tiny insect Pyrch had attempted to place on her. Taint is the most insidious of all threats, for it strikes at the nature of Imperial authority. The agents of the Emperor are sanctioned with great power, and when corrupted, can do immeasurable harm.

The Chimera jerks beneath her, and then Sinos is thrown against the forward bulkhead. She shakes off the stars that burst into her sight.

'Dixin?' She looks through into the driver's compartment.

Dixin lolls in his seat. Blood drips from beneath the visor of his helmet, but she can see no entry wound.

'Out! Everybody, out!'

They spill from the Chimera's rear hatch, shotguns up and turning. 'Back away!'

Sinos searches the faces of the crowd, and sees only honest fear.

'Marshal!'

Arbitrator Beska is pointing up, towards the roof of a brick building that forms the corner of the street. A skeletal figure is outlined against the white of angry snow clouds, an arcane rifle at its shoulder.

It fires something, a bead of blue, and Beska slumps back against the Chimera.

Sinos pushes Murillen forwards, dropping low behind the vehicle's bulk. 'Whatever happens, get to the aerodrome, and get out of the city.'

They dive into the crowd.

She could end them all.

She *will* end them all.

But not yet.

Ahnuret steps from one oubliette to another. From rooftop to rooftop, hunting always for her target. Screams follow in her wake, rising from the humans who glance up and see her silhouette against the sky.

She knows that this chase runs counter to the praetorian's plans, but that is beyond her concern. Kamoteph, the crooked and deceitful creature that he is, has commanded her, and thus she must see his will done.

She has followed the praetorian's orders thus far. The praetorian who looks at Ahnuret not with fear and disgust, but with pity and concern. She has followed them in spite of their obvious futility. If purgation is the goal, then what use is restraint? Why suffer life's existence?

The humans are running from her, as they should. She is their doom, their nemesis.

Contrary to Khemet's understanding, the Destroyer is not a madness. It is not a suppression of her higher faculties, but an enhancement. Those of the cult see more clearly the nature of the necron existence than any other. Theirs is a perfect existence, shorn of the corrupting factors of life. Mortality. Scarcity. Desire, in its most base and physical form. The C'tan freed the necrontyr from these aberrant aspects of existence.

And it is Ahnuret's mission to rid the galaxy of them for good.

Her targets are wily, turning at random, pushing deeper into the crowd. They think this will save them, but they are wrong.

She descends from the rooftops as her target breaks out onto a roadway, narrowly avoiding a collision with one of the humans' light conveyances. Ahnuret steps out of an oubliette into the centre of the roadway, disruptor levelled.

Something is thrown, out of panic or reflexive hatred, by a watching human. It knocks her aim aside, and the stream of particles goes wide.

Ahnuret's movement bypasses all conscious thought. Her hand drops to her enmitic pistol, lifts, and fires in the time it takes the bold or foolish human to blink.

He bursts apart, unmade. There is no blood, there are no remains, just a flare of light and then a cloud of constituent molecules to drift away on the breeze.

Another Unclean screams, a high, piercing wail. Ahnuret draws and fires, which silences one voice but sets hundreds more alight.

There is another, and another. The crowd is running, leaving their spoor hanging in the cloud like a miasma. Even fleeing, the Unclean pollute the very air they occupy.

Ahnuret pursues them, not in madness but with icy clarity.

Each one she kills is a degree of sanctity returned to this world. A fractional closure to the greatest peace, the peace Ahnuret seeks with all of her being.

A universe cleansed of life.

And when that is one's goal, what use is restraint?

CHAPTER 10

'In the name of the Triarch, what have you done?'

Khemet does not wait to travel around the world before she levels her accusation. She hurls her anger across the interstices, finding Hekasun and Kamoteph in conference without her.

'You have revealed us to the humans. You have undone all that we have worked to achieve.'

'It was a miscalculation,' answers Kamoteph. 'I erred in placing my trust in the deathmark.'

'You blame Ahnuret for this? You are craven as well as a fool.'

In addition to imperilling her work, Ahnuret is now loose amid the humans. Khemet's attempt to alleviate her condition has been undone by Kamoteph's foolishness. She is shocked to find that this weighs so heavily on her mind.

'Why are you so afraid of them, praetorian?' asks Hekasun suddenly.

On the far side of the world, Khemet's core exhausts flash. 'I fear nothing.'

Kamoteph takes up his lord's case. *'They are human. The Unclean. You have danced around them for two years, nibbling at their flanks. Always careful. Always considered. Never direct.'*

'If you have not paid heed to my strategy for these past years, I see no point in explaining it to you now.'

'We are necrontyr!' sends Hekasun with the force of fury. *'The Unclean claim the kemmeht of our world, and you dither. We should have marched from this tomb the moment we arrived and taken what is mine!'*

'Do you doubt our strength?' asks Kamoteph. *'Do you doubt our legions and our way of war? Or do you simply doubt yourself?'*

Khemet's only doubt is – has ever been – that in waging a precipitate war they will fight on the humans' terms. She has pursued a careful and crushing war, tearing the capacity for resistance from them before the first gauss beam is fired. But now that elegant course is lost.

'Very well. You wish to see fear?' Khemet says. Hekasun and Kamoteph do not respond.

'I will show you their fear. I will scourge the Unclean from this world, and I will do it in spite of your incompetence.'

The Valkyrie's engines are still screaming when Sinos leaps from the passenger bay. She runs, or at least limps as swiftly as she is able, across the landing platform.

The rockcrete pad juts out from the side of the mountain, the only artificial construction in sight of its peak. Within it, however, is the sanctum of the planet's sanctioned psykers, the telepaths and astropaths and mutants of every creed and ability.

A woman in a flowing grey robe is waiting at the pad's edge. The blast door behind her is firmly closed.

'You can go no further, marshal.'

Sinos' leg is bleeding inside her armour, and her shoulder is a knot of fire. 'I can go wherever I must.'

'But not here,' the woman insists. 'Your presence would unbalance our charges.'

Sinos hesitates, as ill at ease as any Imperial citizen when forced to consider witchery.

'You were alerted to my coming, therefore you know the message I carry.'

The woman shakes her head, her stare roaming Sinos' battered armour. 'I am merely a servant. I deal with the outer world.'

Sinos has no time or patience to decipher her cryptic phrasing. 'Here.' She thrusts the scrap of vellum into her hand. The woman reads. After a moment, one hand rises to cover her mouth. She looks at Sinos with tears in her eyes.

'This message has the highest priority, by order of the lord-militant himself,' says Sinos. Salvastari has no knowledge of her coming, but it does not matter. In this moment, Sinos would invoke whatever authority would most quickly see her will done. 'It must be sent to this location before any other.' She jabs the vellum, pointing to the intended receiving point.

'I understand, marshal.' The woman cuffs her eyes, finding the steel within herself. 'I will convey your message to the choirmistress.'

'Send it immediately. Do you understand? Immediately.'

'I will see it done.' She gives a quick bow, then turns and shuffles away, slippered feet moving at as close to a run as she can manage. The blast door retracts enough for her to dart inside, then slams shut.

The adrenaline of her flight from Verongyl is wearing off. Sinos can feel the start of the shakes. A lifetime of arrests, raids, and full-blown battles has yet to make Sinos immune to the physiological demands of her own body.

She slumps back into the Valkyrie. She can feel the exhaustion taking hold, and fights against it long enough to climb into a seat.

'What now, marshal?'

She does not know. Getting word of the xenos incursion off the world has been the only imperative she has followed since evading their ambush in Verongyl. The taint must be contained, by any means. She has done all she can. The rest, she fears, will be out of her hands.

The ground flashes beneath the Night Shroud, greenery and rivers spoilt by the humans' meagre constructions.

This is good terrain. It is rare for Khemet to indulge in such assessments, being so alien to her existence, but it is clear to see that this quarter of Qeretesh is made up of rich, fertile land.

Khemet keeps her mind on such trivial thoughts to avoid the colossal anger that boils in her core. All her planning, all her labour to carefully prime the ground for an effortless war has been undone.

She has puppeted the body of the Immortal pilot, rendering him a slave within his own form. Khemet is typically loath to do this, finding the projection of one's self into another to be a profound violation. Nevertheless, she will not leave this task to others. After Kamoteph's egregious error, she must adapt her plans.

A range of mountains crests the horizon, growing swiftly into jagged, snow-capped peaks.

This was always to be the first target of the war. The humans' occult means of speaking across the interstellar void are not something she wholly understands. Nor does she wish to bend her mind to do so. She needs only a practical comprehension – there are aberrant strains of humans with the ability to broadcast their thoughts through the empyric medium. Thus, they must be the first humans on Orymous to die en masse.

A wing of human aircraft is approaching. She has made no

attempt at stealth, for thanks to Kamoteph none is needed. It is better, now that their mask has been cast aside, for the humans to see their foe's overwhelming superiority.

Though they are hundreds of khet away, still below the horizon, Khemet knows that her attackers are sixteen Lightning-class air-superiority craft of the Fifth Division of the Orymous defence forces. Their leader is most likely a human named Badern, Eyvgenia, designated air marshal.

Khemet has studied her opponents. Such knowledge may be trivial, giving too much respect to her enemy. But Khemet is a patient warrior, and no knowledge is worthless in war.

They close quickly, owing more to the Night Shroud's airspeed than the humans'. No doubt Marshal Badern and her pilots are watching Khemet's rapid approach with mounting alarm. Nothing they have faced will prepare them for the supremacy of necron warcraft.

A hologram winks into life on the Night Shroud's console. The enemy fighters are painting her ship with their primitive scrying systems, the precursor to an attack with long-range ordnance.

Khemet dives, racing beneath the barrage of ordnance. The dumb rockets sail far over the bomber's hull. Khemet heaves the Night Shroud back up, climbing more sharply than any mortal could withstand.

She rockets through the enemy formation nine seconds later. Two craft tumble in her wake, while the rest scatter in predictable patterns. Khemet does not bother to engage them. By the time they have turned their cumbersome craft, she will already be beyond their weapons' range, and extending with every moment.

There are other defences, closer in to the humans' mountain fastness. The Night Shroud detects them searching, lashing the sky with electromagnetic radiation. The humans are so crude.

Kamoteph's intelligence places the mutant humans' residence

within the hollowed-out core of the tallest peak above the capital. When she crests the horizon, the Night Shroud's scrying stalks see it immediately, looking beyond the rock to the metal complex within.

A crackling ball of energy gathers between the two prongs of its maw. As missiles launch and gun pods chatter from the many defensive stations, the bomber flies on.

The death sphere is ready, and Khemet wastes no time.

Sixteen minutes after Marshal Sinos leaves the astropathic sanctum, the mountaintop is erased from existence. Thousands of tons of rock are pulverised to dust. The sanctum within ceases to be. It is as though a god's scythe has been brought down upon the mountainside.

Sinos watches from her Valkyrie, and utters the most fervent prayer of her life.

ACT 3

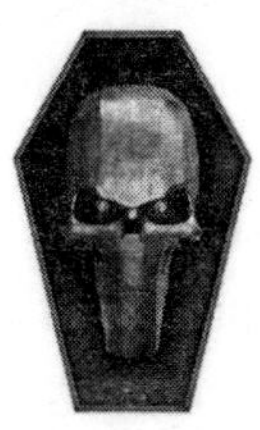

CHAPTER 1

They have walked for hours.

Many khet above them, night has turned to day since they first marched from the shimmering green gateway, but to the warriors striding across the seabed there is no difference.

More marked is their change in elevation. As they rise from the crushing depths, pitch darkness turns gradually to twilight. They pass through the domain of life that clings tenaciously to its niche. Placoderms and acanthodii, the genetic descendants of creatures every bit as ancient as the figures that move in their midst. Vast fields of kelp and macroalgae, bleached white as skulls by the ocean's acidity. The occasional selachii, apex predators challenged only by the gradual destruction of the ecosystem they rule.

To those possessed of some semblance of a mind, the warm waters and their inhabitants might have been considered beautiful, or at least fascinating. But the warriors marching up from the deep knew little of beauty when they were alive, and the flames of biotransference permanently severed their capacity for curiosity.

The land beneath the waves grows steeper. Metal feet sink into shifting sand. Currents buffet metal bodies, first pushing them on towards their goal, then hauling them back. But with brute strength and tireless patience, they march onwards and upwards.

'Another sherbet, sir?'

Lieutenant Colonel Hans Schraden opens an eye, just a slit against the glare of the morning sun. Standing above him is a man holding a silver tray. It is not one of his troopers, not a Mordian, but one of the many civilian attendants that seem to be everywhere on these islands.

The man bends at the waist. A small dish of the jaw-achingly sweet and potently intoxicating sherbet the locals have a fondness for sits on the tray, alone on an expanse of polished silver.

'Why not?' Schraden has yet to develop a taste for the stuff, but he hopes to have the opportunity to do so. Schraden's regiment has been on Orymous for four months, but this is the first time his divisional commander has extended an invitation to join him on the islands.

Ostensibly, it is for wargames. Schraden and the staff officers of a dozen other regiments will spend much of the next week engaging in battle across a tabletop, shifting marker blocks back and forth while cogitators determine the outcome of engagements. But for the morning, those same officers are spread out for the better part of a mile along the shoreline, basking in the unfamiliar luxury of temperate heat, fine food and idle peace.

Schraden closes his eye and holds out a hand, waiting for the servant to give him the glass.

Instead he hears a whine and a brief pulse of releasing energy, followed by the sounds of choking and a silver platter falling to the sand.

He looks up. The attendant has dropped to his knees, clawing at his throat. A green phage crawls across his skin, burning all it touches to black ash. The man's death is certain, but not swift.

Schraden does not recoil, but instead watches him die with something akin to mild concern. It takes a second volley to rouse him, to penetrate the fog of sherbets past, as a streak of green light flashes by his head to scourge the bark from a nearby tree.

Creatures are rising from the water. Metal creatures in the shape of skeletal men. Water droplets hiss and boil from the charging coils of their weapons. Surf breaks around their heads, and a vicious riptide pulls at their legs. As each monstrosity emerges from the waves, their ribcages suddenly blaze with a ghoulish green light, and the sea about them flashes to steam.

Under the bright light of morning, the former masters of Qeretesh rise to reclaim what was theirs.

Schraden topples from his sand chair. He reaches automatically for his sidearm, and touches only the blue flannel cloth of his absurd beachwear. Confusion, and not a little embarrassment, are the last thoughts that pass through his mind.

Lieutenant Colonel Schraden, proud commander of the 47th Mordian Guard, dies in the first minute of the necron attack. Alongside him are hundreds of others, casualties of an enemy they cannot name and did not know to look for.

They find the humans at peace, inattentive and at rest. At the Meande airfield, the ground crews wait for the first flyers of the day to arrive from the mainland. On Plakid Major, Lord-Militant Salvastari, governor of Orymous in the name of the almighty God-Emperor of Mankind, is taking a late breakfast while reading the latest reports from his logisticar adjutants.

The first shriek of gauss punctures the humans' torpor. Hundreds die to the first volley.

Chaos takes hold. Bodyguards – the few that were thought necessary for the idyll of Imperial life on Orymous – swarm their wards, giving their lives to shield their superiors for a few precious seconds. Generals wearing terry cloth and sand towels abandon their dignity. Commissars throw away their authority. Nobles discard any thought of bravery. All run, fleeing up the beaches and away from the monstrous killers that have appeared from their nightmares.

The legion advances, dividing into cohorts and heading inland towards the objectives Khemet has painstakingly selected for them. From the first moment she learnt of the humans' island retreat, Khemet has known this would be the opening blow of the true war. The Imperials, in their arrogance, have obligingly gathered the pinnacle of their martial hierarchy in one place. She would be a poor nemesor indeed not to capitalise on their hubris.

Corporal Tallisen Jynse of the Third Orymousian Life Guards is asleep when the war begins. He was on duty the previous night, standing watch over a revelry that had occupied the greatest portion of the lord-militant's estate. He has earned, through a pristine uniform and a carefully unobservant eye, the right to a morning's sleep.

Jynse is unceremoniously hauled from his bunk, waking in the brief moment before he hits the ground.

'What the hells?'

'Get up, and get to your squad.' Sergeant Luthen Merker hauls Jynse up by his collar and throws him out of the barracks door.

Morning light stabs his eyes, and between the tramp of boots and Merker's yells it takes Jynse a moment before he hears the clarions wailing. Rote-learned actions kick in, and Jynse is running with his hellgun in hand before he is fully aware.

'The commandant picked an evil day for a drill!' he yells to Merker as they head for the platoon's quartet of Chimeras. Files of troops are waiting their turn to enter each personnel carrier.

'It's no drill! Get them moving!' Merker calls ahead to his other squad leaders, and the first soldiers duck beneath the metal lintels of the Chimeras.

Jynse is the last inside, hauling the rear hatch closed behind him. The driver has the engine running, and the Chimera leaps away before the corporal can even find his seat.

'What the hells is happening?'

No one inside the transport knows, and when Jynse remembers to hook his helmet into the company vox-link none of his fellow squad leaders know either. Ten minutes of alert clarions sounding, and no word has been passed down from the regimental command except to muster and rally on the lord-militant's palace.

'It's a drill,' says Trooper Resten.

'They'd say if it were a drill,' says another.

'It doesn't matter!' shouts Jynse. 'We're the Life Guards. We're called, we come. Weapons live, and ready for anything.'

The squad give a ragged, half-hearted cheer that is cut short when the Chimera suddenly grinds to a halt. Jynse, still standing, is thrown from his feet. His helmet clangs off the forward bulkhead.

'*Corporal!*' the driver calls, rare panic in his voice.

'What?' Jynse stumbles up to the bulkhead, and slides back a shutter to look through a porthole.

Something is hovering above the road, less than a mile ahead. It is insectile in nature, rows of cage-like ribs hanging from a long spinal column. A short scorpion tail rises at its rear, beneath which stands a skeletal figure, metal hands clutching the controls. Hung from the interior of its ribs is a weapon, its length glowing with bilious light.

'Enemy contact! Go at it! At it!'

The driver guns the Chimera's power plant, and floors the throttle.

The Doomsday Ark's plasma beam engulfs the Chimera and its inhabitants while they are still half a mile away. Corporal Jynse, like so many of his compatriots, dies entirely unaware of what killed him.

Despite the profusion of command staff – those who were able to escape the murder on the beaches – it takes over an hour before any semblance of order is imposed on the scattered Imperial forces. By that time, several of the Plakid Islands are entirely overrun. The humans that remain are utterly scattered, prolonging their lives by running or hiding.

But finally directives emanate from the lord-militant's palace. Far out to sea, the warden line of off-shore gun batteries are levered around, and the first volleys of shells crash into the beaches. Each one gouges a trench in the golden sands before detonating, sending great red-and-yellow fingers of fire and sand reaching into the azure sky. A few shells strike true, their blasts catching the last ranks of warriors to pull themselves from the water. A direct strike will pulverise an unfortunate warrior to shrapnel, but most rise, their necrodermis cracked and cratered but otherwise unimpaired. Oblivious to their impotence, the gun captains fire on.

Group Captain Mina Salvastari grips the control column of her Oneros transport plane so hard she thinks either her fingers will break, or the sculpted leather will.

She should be up there. The youngest sister of the lord-militant's extended family had earned her wings in Avenger strike fighters, running ground-attack missions for the Jovinan Liberation, and before that Orymousian-made interceptors. While she hasn't flown a sortie for almost thirty years, she was an air warrior through to her bones. To be sitting in a transport while a battle rages around her is more than she can stand.

'Come on, get them in!' She half-stands from her flight seat, hampered by the pressure suit bundled around her legs, and roars at the flight crew on the pad below her. The last of her brother's court are running, all dignity abandoned, from a covered hangar to the Oneros. Her role is not to fight, but to fly all that remains of her family out of the combat area.

Fredrich, her cousin's idiot husband, is the last to disappear from sight beneath the transport's nose cone. Half a minute later, a voice barks over the vox that all are aboard, and the indicator lumen for the Oneros' rear door flicks to green.

The engines are already idling, the fuel tanks topped off. Salvastari's copilot voxes a terse message to the airfield's controllers, then cycles the vector ducts down for take-off. Mina gives her indicator panel a final check, then throws the throttle forwards.

The Oneros rises slowly, the scream of jet thrust eclipsing the shriek of gauss that has been growing closer by the hour. It is a whale of a craft, a pair of wings at the front and back of its distended hull. Salvastari wrestles with the control column, forcing its nose down so the vector ducts can propel the craft up and forwards into flight.

Something rips overhead, its wake strong enough to rock the Oneros on its axis. Salvastari swears, fighting to correct the sudden drift.

Three seconds later, a bolt of energy brighter than the rising sun hits the transport in the centre of its mass. The Oneros folds like a paper plane, crashing to the landing pad in a fireball of burning promethium.

With the beachhead secured, and with the leading lychguard reporting no sign of the humans' heavy weaponry, the first Doom Scythes burst from the waves. They hammer over the aerodromes, sowing discord and terror in their wake. Imperial transport planes erupt in flames as arcs of electricity ignite their fuel pods. Others are cut apart by blinding rays that carve ragged lines through asphalt and armour alike. Any Imperial craft that manages to rise from its stand is struck from the sky.

There is no escape from the Plakid Islands.

Khemet watches the massacre – for it cannot, by any reasonable observer, be called a battle – through the eyes of its perpetrators. With the tomb world's aid she skips her consciousness from warrior to warrior. She races through the skies with the Doom Scythe pilots, gutting the fat-bellied human flyers as they struggle to lift off. She climbs up the sands and trudges through the pleasure gardens, hunting the humans' chattel creatures who seek to hide rather than fight. Through the data gathered by the gestalt senses of the advancing legion, Khemet sees the noose tighten around each island, the humans penned in by closing cordons of warriors. The Imperials find their courage when they realise they have no way out, and Khemet rides the minds of Immortals who advance without flinching into a hail of small-arms fire.

She watches Lord-Militant Salvastari die.

The human overlord's image has been implanted in the minds of the lychguard who lead the attack, and he is identified swiftly as he flees into his palace. It is a vast complex, the equal of so many similar edifices the humans have crudely heaped together atop Qeretesh's sacred soil. To Khemet, whose appreciation for aesthetics has been honed over aeons, they are the gravest sin, cumbersome monstrosities that aspire to grandeur but show only hubris.

The humans offer as much resistance as their meagre arms can provide. Hundreds of troops battle from outworks surrounding the palatial grounds, but they are not prepared for what assails them. Khemet's warriors fall, but each absorbs a weight of fire that cannot be sustained. For each Immortal that succumbs, ten humans die. It is a rate of loss no troops could bear, and yet they remain at their posts, dying by inches as their enemies advance. They even manage a doomed charge, rising from their trenches with bayonets fixed, following a general of the Cadian 67th.

The lord-militant dies with a weapon in hand, within the poor tomb of a rockcrete bunker to which his bodyguards had dragged him. He dies screaming, ribcage peeled open by the twin beams of an Immortal's blaster. That is the death every Unclean deserves.

The Plakid Islands are the first soil of Qeretesh to be reclaimed for the necrons, but they will not be the last. Their cleansing will take several hours to complete, but Khemet's warriors are patient, and thorough.

CHAPTER 2

While Khemet murders the humans' leadership class – a necessary task, and one appropriate to her station – Hekasun makes ready for a far grander work. He sits upon the throne of a vessel ancient even by the standards of the necrons, tense with anticipation.

The *Hepherentes*. At his father's feet, a young Hekasun had learnt the tales of its victories. It is the flagship of the Zathanor fleet, the greatest of their craft. It, even more than Qeretesh itself, is what he came to this world to claim. The tomb world is a bastion, a stronghold whose vaults hold the last of the Zathanor legions. But the *Hepherentes* is the means to project that recovered strength. From its decks he will forge the renewal of his house, claim the renown that is his due, carve out a new dominion for his dynasty across the stars.

But first, he must win the world.

Ptah is close at hand. The cryptek has spent months surveying the harvest ship's functions, rousing its somnolent spirit in preparation for Hekasun's call. He bows deeply, both arms spread wide in his favoured form of obeisance. 'All is in readiness, lord. We await your command.'

Hekasun leans back in his throne, indulging in the moment. This is all he has worked for. His lies, his patience. His immense tolerance for the indignities heaped upon him. They have all been necessary to bring him to this point.

A tremor of potential passes through the ship, the first stirrings of the chained star god at the ship's heart. A shard of Og'driada, appropriately called the Arisen, has been woken from its slumber. The barbed chains that bind the hateful creature have been sunk deep into its cosmic flesh, ready to siphon its immense power into the ship's veins.

Hekasun touches a hand to the Zathanor glyph, proudly returned to its place upon his brow.

'Let us rise.'

In the abyssal depths of the earth, a leviathan moves.

In Verongyl, a seismograph's needle twitches, steadies, then starts to violently dance. The Mechanicus acolyte whose duty it is to monitor the instrument conveys the readings, encoding them with runes of the utmost urgency, to her superior. But the warning is lost in the tumult of conflicting information that assails the enclave's datasphere. By the time any adept of sufficiently advanced rank takes heed of the seismograph's warning, it is far too late.

Beneath the black abyss of the deepest ocean, blackstone gates open. The rock that has concealed the tomb world's extremity for millions of years shifts, cracks, and finally bursts apart, yielding to a strength that once ruled Qeretesh as unquestioned sovereign.

Cavitation bubbles emerge and collapse as the ocean rushes into the sudden void. The power of two thousand fathoms of pressure roars into the breach in the planet's crust. But when the first foaming wave reaches the roof of the tomb complex, its strength is turned aside by a shimmering barrier of jade energy. Rock is pulverised by the redirected force, smashed to powder that is swept away on the churning currents. But the chamber in which the *Hepherentes* has waited through the aeons remains inviolate.

Ptah lifts his hands, a conductor of mighty and ephemeral force, and brings the ship to life.

Shields light with a soap-bubble swirl of energies. The majesty of inertialess engines are awoken. Hard-light umbilical platforms retract and entry points seal, leaving no seam in the blackstone hull. With a shudder of effort, the *Hepherentes* rises.

The crushing weight of water is pushed aside, and the great harvest ship emerges from the depths. It breaches the surface at speed, throwing back a mountain of water that glitters in the sunlight.

It is a deceptively slight craft. Crescent jaws crown a dragonfly body, strong at its centre and tapering to a long tail. Three wings project from its central mass, a dorsal sail and a protrusion from either flank. To the human eye, there is nothing strong in the ship's design. It is too slender, too alien to their understanding of strength. If their guardians of the void who see the harvest ship rising towards them are misled by its slight form, it will be the last mistake of their lives.

The *Hepherentes* climbs swiftly, the blue of Qeretesh's sky fading to the black of the void, studded with the ten thousand lights of defence platforms and void wharves and monitor ships. No guns greet the harvest ship's rise, no fusillades of macro shells or the shafts of lances. All of the planet's orbital defences are in the grip of catastrophic systems errors, their machine spirits shrieking nonsense that drives the adepts at their controls into fits of scrapcode-induced madness.

As the harvest ship clears the last clinging traces of atmosphere,

Night Shrouds streak from bays along its flanks. The compact, lethal bombers peel away from the *Hepherentes*, forming into pairs of crescent shapes that race through the emptiness with a speed that confounds the humans' primitive scrying systems. A single Immortal is at the controls of each craft, their minds bound by interstitial strands and filled with the war-honed tactics of an ancient empire.

Each pair of craft has been given primary, secondary and tertiary targets, a nested hierarchy of destruction to sow through the planet's orbit. This is Hekasun's work, the first and only exercise of tactical decision making the nomarch has undertaken since arriving on his world. This victory, this murder in the void, will be his doing.

As the crews of the closest vessels struggle to classify the strange craft that are charging towards them, it is already too late. The twinned cannons mounted at the centre of the Night Shrouds' jaws fire. Each bolt is the work of a technology just as far beyond the humans' understanding – a fragment of antimatter suspended outside the confines of the material universe. The few point-defence turrets that are hurriedly turned on their axes are entirely inadequate. Their macro-bolter shells simply pass through the bombs.

The spheres return to the rigours of their home dimension in the moment before they detonate. Matter meets antimatter, and excoriated waves of energy annihilate everything around them. The first Imperial warships cease to be, sundered from the sky by the ancient power of the necrontyr.

Hekasun laughs, joy redounding on joy. He splits his consciousness into several parts so he can observe more of his grand design unfold. The Night Shrouds soar on, unhindered by the clouds of microscopic wreckage, to line up their next victims.

The moment of surprise has passed, but the chaos it has caused has only begun.

The void around Orymous is suddenly ablaze with the lights of engines, as the hundreds of troop transports and conveyor craft and anything not outfitted for war turn to flee. They point their sterns towards the surface of the world they stole and burn hard for the dubious safety of deep space.

Hekasun drives the *Hepherentes* into their midst, striking out with arcs of power that ripple along their flanks and smash through their hearts. Defenceless vessels die by the minute, what shielding and armour they possess overwhelmed by the merest touch of the harvest ship. The lords of the Zathanor, alongside Hekasun for this moment of triumph, exult in the massacre. Each Unclean body that tumbles into vacuum is a measure of vengeance extracted from an arrogant foe.

Not every Imperial ship has fled.

The *Braetor* and the *Hammer of Golmera*, a pair of Lunar-class cruisers recently returned from a twenty-year patrol of the Ruidus Stars, lead the hastily assembled counter-attack. The two ships race around the curve of Qeretesh, followed by a small fleet of frigates and monitor ships.

Hekasun steers the *Hepherentes* towards them, purposefully placing his ship in the centre of their line. The vengeful glee on the faces of the two ships' captains falters as the xenos ship shrugs aside the combined fury of both craft. Its arcane shielding has been tested against greater and more exotic weaponry than the humans can bring to bear.

From the inferno that encloses the necron craft come coils of lightning and streams of plasma. The *Hammer* dies first. Whole decks are exposed to the airless abyss in moments. Its engine clusters burst apart, unleashing a nuclear inferno that serves as the vessel's death-light. The *Braetor* sails on, too wounded to mourn the death of its sister ship.

The monitor ships lose their nerve, the formation breaking

apart to escape the inviolate killer that has appeared above the world they once thought theirs.

With the defenders dead and broken, the voidyards and depots lie exposed. Tens of thousands live and work within their skeleton frames, with thousands more trapped by the flight of their transports.

The *Hepherentes* descends towards them. There will be no mercy for any of the usurpers.

Wreckage tumbles in clouds, vacuum-bloated human bodies mingling with ruined armour and shattered spars. Iron scrap will rain down upon Qeretesh for months to come, each streak of light a reminder to the Imperium's defenders that their guardians died in ignominy.

As swiftly as it began, the war for the void is over. From the imperious vantage of space, Hekasun settles in to watch Khemet win him the war for the land.

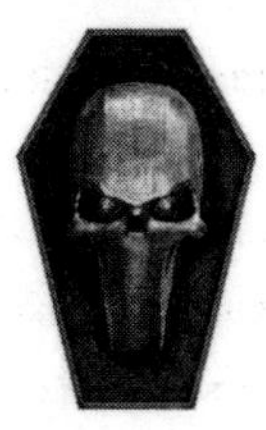

CHAPTER 3

The holographic table bathes Khemet's faceplate in shifting shades of light, revealing the war for a world.

It has been four months since Kamoteph's rash action forced her hand. Four months in which Khemet has been required to abandon carefully laid plans and meet a weakened, but not yet defeated, enemy in battles across the length and breadth of Qeretesh.

Hekasun has left Khemet for the might of the *Hepherentes*. He commands the void war, as he has airily proclaimed on several occasions, though that war, it is plain to see, was won with the opening shot. Any Imperial vessels that might have challenged the harvest ship were either destroyed or have fled to the farthest reaches of the system to escape its wrath. The wreckage of wharves and weapons platforms drifts undisturbed in the upper atmosphere, painting the skies with streaks of fire as it falls to gravity's grip.

Khemet has been abandoned by Hekasun, but the tomb world is

anything but peaceful. With her restraining hand lifted, Qeretesh has surged into life. Power thrums along the conduits that girdle the planet, lighting defensive structures and awakening entire portions of the tomb complex. Ptah's apprenteks, and those crypteks of Qeretesh whom Kamoteph has revived, work without pause in the stasis vaults. Legions are roused in the depths, their lockstep footfalls shaking the foundations of the world. They march to Khemet's command, pausing only to assemble into their cohorts before striding into the eternity gates to emerge wherever they are required. And they are required in many places.

Khemet stands at the same projection table where she first told Hekasun of her strategy, the same place she has stood for the past four months, almost without interruption. With Hekasun and his court decamped to the void to revel in their splendour, Khemet has been left to win their war. Kamoteph's precipitate action has made the scouring of Qeretesh a more equal contest than she would have preferred, and had planned for. With just one more year – perhaps two – the humans would have been brought to their knees, reduced to abject chaos incapable of resistance.

But Khemet, ever practical, works with circumstances as they are, not as she would wish them.

In the holographic image that slowly turns before her, the primary continental shelf is rendered in opaque cobalt. Lines of elevation and knots of human settlements are picked out as bright lines and shapes. Green runes denote Khemet's armies, red those of the humans. The nexus units of the necron armies – the monoliths that deliver reinforcements to the front, the lychguard and those few of Hekasun's toadies who have insisted on taking to the field – are denoted with particular emphasis.

Where green and red intersect are the battle lines, angry knots of runes that unfurl into data points when she turns her attention on them. They show whatever she requires. Reports of enemy strength and size, particularly of their lumbering armoured vehicles. The locations of the humans' command nodes. The attrition rates for her troops, compared against Khemet's estimates.

These she considers particularly carefully. Just as the crypteks work to rouse new warriors, the canoptek constructs in Qeretesh's interior have not ceased their toil since the first shots of this war were fired. When the immense durability of her warriors proves insufficient to the damage they have endured, fallen necron bodies are stolen from the battlefield at the moment of their destruction by the tomb world's vigilant spirit. They emerge in the restoration vaults, where the scarab swarms convey their bodies to the furnaces. This is not the end for them, but merely a new beginning. Soon enough the warriors' minds are reunited with their necrodermis, reforged and rearmed, so they can return to their eternal duty.

So Khemet does not lack for line troops, but her hand is lacking in key forms of war. The Zathanor's poverty has manifested as a limited strategic palette, creating constraints around which Khemet must work. Qeretesh lacks the seraptek constructs that can face down the largest of the humans' war machines, requiring that she lure them into the firing arcs of massed pylon batteries. The paucity of Doom Scythes and Ghost Arks initially made the aerial war a troubling sphere, but fortunately her preparations have paid dividends. The humans have lofted fewer and fewer air-to-air and air-to-ground combat craft as the months have worn on, as the machines – like their pilots – are starved of the fuel required to keep them flying.

The same tools she has deployed for the past two years are still active, still working to cripple the humans' ability to make war. Kamoteph's enslaved minions are silent saboteurs, points of failure that see their scarce resources destroyed, misallocated, or simply lost. Hunger stalks the defensive trench lines that encircle the humans' besieged cities, and plague the denizens trapped within. By simple arithmetic alone, Khemet's stratagems have depleted the planet's population by six per cent since the fighting began. Their corpses are mounding in the streets or – so Kamoteph's reports tell her – are hauled away to be reconstituted in a somewhat similar manner to the necron restoration vaults, to partly ameliorate the humans' dwindling rations.

Her estimates indicate that the number of human dead will rise dramatically in the next few months, unless the Imperials receive a miraculous influx of foodstuffs, and it would seem that their deified overlord has little interest in their fate. Indeed, Khemet has calculated that she does not need to make any further offensive measures, as the humans' destruction is assured. All her efforts on the battlefield are simply to hasten their demise, and make an emphatic declaration to Hekasun and his ilk that her honour is restored.

All her efforts are achieving success, except for one.

Ahnuret has not responded to any form of communication since the fighting began. Khemet and Kamoteph have tracked her movements by the destruction left in her wake, and the residual energy signature of her enmitic weaponry. The deathmark has become an agent of blood-soaked chaos behind the Imperial lines, laying waste to all that she encounters. Civilian refuges, military strongpoints, the rare spaces within their brute cities given over to parkland and greenery. Ahnuret has exterminated every microbe, laid waste to every life.

In itself, this is no bad thing. The deathmark is one more weapon to destabilise the humans, albeit one Khemet cannot control.

As she often has over the past months, Khemet calls up a schema of Ahnuret's last known position. She has found her way, stepping from massacre to oubliette and back to massacre, to the billet-city of Carwyne. It is a strategic hub for the humans, the centre of their western flank and the only line of resistance between the necron forces and the humans' seat of governance. It has been under siege for most of the war, the humans steadily collapsing back through layers of defensive fortifications that have inflicted an anomalously high rate of destruction on her warriors.

But for all their fortune thus far, the siege is collapsing; it will be a matter of days before the city's resistance dissolves and Khemet's legions advance over the final barricades. That will be the moment of absolute crisis for the deathmark. She will be surrounded by so much human death, so much human fear; so much of the extremity of the life she has sworn to destroy.

Carwyne's fate is assured. There is no need for Khemet to so closely scrutinise its death. And yet, her digits hover over the control plate.

She owes Ahnuret nothing. She has no reason to venture away from her place within the tomb. If the deathmark yields to the curse that has infected her, then that is either her choice or her weakness. In either case, Khemet's role as a praetorian would dictate that she expunge the tainted element from within her ranks, if she feels the need to take any action at all.

She watches the glyphs around Carwyne duel and merge for some time.

Finally, Khemet calls up the identifier of the closest monolith to the front line of battle, and heads towards the nearest gate.

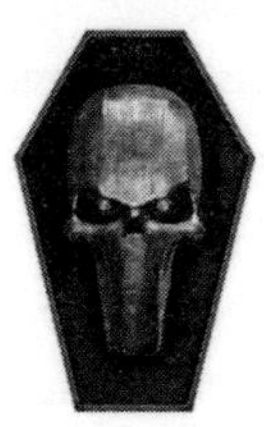

CHAPTER 4

'Good morning, everyone.' General Eron Ingvalen marches into the bastion's strategium with habitual crispness. He checks a pocket-chrono against the bank of timepieces on the wall above him. Satisfied, he snaps its face shut and tucks it into a pocket of his tunic. 'It is zero-six hundred hours, on day one hundred and twenty-one. Colonel Ylda, will you yield command?'

Ylda has stood the night's watch. 'I will yield, sir.'

'Very well, I have command.'

Both men salute crisply, then step back to allow Deacon Antrodeinto to walk up to the encircling rail. Activity around the bastion pauses to allow every man and woman not hardwired to their station to stand and receive his benediction.

Antrodeinto swings a small censer from a golden chain, wafting a fine coil of smoke before him. 'The Emperor protects. May His holy light bless and guide our labours this day. May we be the instrument of His wrath.'

'The Emperor protects,' Sinos intones with the rest of the bastion.

With the deacon's blessing delivered, the men and women of the Gerhemenst Bastion turn back to their duties. The low chatter of vox-operators to their far-flung contacts rises immediately.

General Ingvalen nods his thanks to the deacon, then grips the metal balustrade. 'Senior staff in fifteen minutes.'

Every day is the same.

Sinos wakes, dresses in her armour, and reports to the bastion. She stands for a duty of twelve hours, punctuated by command meetings, alerts, and the infrequent drone of emergency klaxons that warn of an approaching air attack. Her watch complete, she returns to her quarters and reviews incident reports from the bastion's security until she can stave off sleep no more.

If she is lucky, she eats at some point. This question has become a defining factor in her life – will the aching knot of hunger in her belly be assuaged this day, or will it grow ever greater?

She is fortunate; rank still has its privileges. General Ingvalen's morning briefings are typically accompanied by some kind of starch brick, occasionally flavoured with powder taken from expired ration packs.

With that in mind, Sinos follows Ingvalen into the meeting room that abuts the strategium. With her are a dozen of the bastion's section leaders. Most are of the Officio Logisticarum, men and women who have spent a lifetime on Orymous preparing others to be sent to war, only to find war has come to them. The rest are Astra Militarum officers.

Ingvalen does not waste time.

'The offensive has stalled. General Naylor's armour was initially effective in breaking their line around Verongyl, but they encountered heavy resistance and more of the enemy's damned weapons platforms. Enemy infantry re-formed behind them. The brigade is cut off, and considered lost.'

Sinos watches for those who let their disappointment show.

The slumping shoulders, the downcast heads, the muttered oaths. These she will make a point of visiting in the course of the day to stiffen their resolve.

In the earliest days of the war, Sinos had been utterly useless. Despite the wave of assassinations and suicides and sabotage that ripped through the heart of the Officio Logisticarum's operations, the foresight of its adepts gifted it extraordinary resilience. Emergency scenarios, never seriously considered outside of the Logis Strategos' war games but also never allowed to fall out of date or mind, were unearthed and distributed. Deputy officials were elevated, division and corps commanders appointed, lines of communication reestablished. The first thirty-six hours after the devastation of the Plakid Islands saw a chain of command restrung through the disparate armies of the Imperium on Orymous.

And Sinos played no part in it. She was sidelined, quite literally pushed aside by the Munitorum adepts and Astra Militarum commanders. She did not feature in the fallback scenarios, and so was ignored. It was as though the Emperor's guiding hand had brought her to Orymous simply to watch it fall.

Paschel and several other cities on the coast were lost in the first weeks, succumbing to an almost endless wave of hostile forces marching out of the water. The lord-militant locum's decision to abandon the chain of southern billet-cities was one of the most ruthless and most necessary acts Sinos has witnessed in a century of service. It condemned nineteen million servants of the Emperor to die, without any hope of aid. But each life bought time for the rest of Orymous to ready its defence.

Sinos has hardened herself to these decisions. Though, in truth, Sinos has had a lifetime of facing such choices. She is a marshal of the Lex Imperialis. Sacrifice in the name of order is her creed.

It has been through that creed that she has found her role and purpose. With Imperial morale growing threadbare, every commissar left on Orymous is deployed to the front line, leaving a void among the war's command echelon.

Sinos stalks the bastion, a black-clad figure of menace to those around her. No quavering voice or trembling hand escapes her notice. She is the steel in their spines, and the blade in their backs should their resolve begin to fail.

They hate her for it. In the past five weeks there have been three attempts on her life. Two were plots to ambush her on the route between her quarters and the strategium, both foiled by her arbitrators. The other was a vox-operator driven beyond her endurance. She lunged at Sinos as she passed behind her, stylus gripped like a dagger. It broke against the breastplate of her armour. Sinos felt the woman's sobs like the wound she had hoped to cause. The only mercy Sinos could offer was the blast of her bolt pistol, to spare her the indignity of a firing squad.

But she can endure this. Let them fear and hate her, if their fear and hate drive them to do their duty beyond what they might think possible.

Fear is all that the commanders of the Gerhemenst Bastion have left. For those who serve at the operational centre of the war, hope would have been a foolish indulgence. Battle lines are breaking as soon as they are formed. Civilians flee with nowhere to run. The twin horrors of hunger and the xenos' utter relentlessness stalk the world, eroding all they touch.

Of the two, hunger is the more insidious. The troopers know their enemy now, and are no longer shocked by a skeletal form marching through a volley of las that would put down an ogryn. But they cannot outfight hunger, cannot conjure fresh las packs and battle-cannon shells through courage alone.

The Munitorum's legion of adepts and drivers and loaders

work without pause, emptying store after store of ration blocks, ammunition, spare parts of every description. Convoys of cargo-8 transports brave the long roads south to the regiments, always watching the skies for the crescent-shaped killers that every Imperial driver has learnt to fear. Fewer than half get through; the roads are littered with food and medicaments and all the materiel of war, along with the burnt carcasses of transport trucks.

Tales of extremis from the besieged cities have begun to reach the bastion, but Sinos has swiftly ensured that they go no further than the strategium. Her war, the war for morale, is no less fierce and desperate than those of clashing armies.

The projections are clear. Even if the strategic picture remains the same, if the battle lines remain static, the defending armies will be rendered combat-ineffective by lack of supply within two months.

Their only chance of survival is for resupply from off-world. But the void is lost. There are at least eighty transport ships and monitor ships that escaped the murder that rose from the ocean, but they hide at the edge of the system, fearful of the slender killer that hangs imperiously in orbit. It plays no active role in the ground war, though all assume that it is the seat of the xenos commander.

Sinos stands through the rest of General Ingvalen's briefing, fighting the exhaustion that presses down upon her. She has taken to serving through the night, finding that the twilight hours are the greatest burden to the strategium's operators.

Colonel Ylda waits for Ingvalen to finish, then places a hand on the briefing table. 'General, may I once again offer–'

'No, you may not.'

'Sir–'

'We have been over this, colonel. I am in accordance with

the Mechanicus, and you will not change my mind. That is all, gentlemen.' Ingvalen sweeps his papers from the table and leaves, followed more wearily by the rest of the war council.

'Very well, sir,' says Ylda, to himself.

In the first days of the war a faction of the Logis Strategos – led by Ylda – had argued for the deployment of the planet's Deathstrike arsenal against the xenos craft. Ensconced within the depths of the Lysern Plateau, each missile is capable of touching any part of Orymous, and anywhere above it. The desire for wrath in the face of such overwhelming slaughter was paramount in those first days, and the xenos' command craft was the obvious target for a revenge strike.

The deciding voice in the debate came from the Adeptus Mechanicus, who showed a surprising degree of defeatism when they stated that they were uncertain whether the missiles, among the gravest weapons the Imperium commands, would penetrate the arcane defences of the unnamed ship.

Instead they have been hoarded, a weapon of last resort held for a day that Sinos fears is approaching. In order to save Orymous, they may have to lay waste to it.

Sinos walks out of the briefing room, waiting for Arbitrator Murillen to come and relieve her. She stands at the room's edge, fighting the urge to lean against the brass railing. The heat rising from each brass and chrome mechanism is fierce, adding to the soporific effect of a night spent watching for cowardice. Each operator and their machine is sunk below the level of the deck, permitting a forest of wires and cables to run beneath the gantries on which Sinos and the other officers walk.

She looks up at the wall-chronos, and feels the slight tremble as her attention wanders across their faces. She snaps back to her centre, and is about to walk when the operator directly beneath her leaps from his seat.

'Major Gorka, we are receiving a vox-transmission from off-world!'

All heads turn towards him, his excitable cry carrying clearly across the chamber. Sinos' hand drops to the grip of her pistol, wary as ever for the first signs of hysteria.

'Origin?' asks Gorka, officer of the watch this morning. He seems as calm as ever, but summons a runner with the flick of a hand. 'Send for General Ingvalen.'

'It identifies itself as the *Blessed Vengeance*. Lord, it claims to be a vessel of the Adeptus Astartes!'

Hope, the most treacherous of feelings, all but knocks the breath from Sinos' chest.

She is closer than Gorka. Sinos drops into the pit and snatches the vox-horn from the operator's hands. 'This is Marshal Solome Sinos of the Adeptus Arbites. Identify yourself, in the Emperor's name.'

There is a second's delay as her message is hurled into space. The reply, when it comes, lands like a bolt of lightning.

'This is Commander Trantor of the Deathwatch. Well met, marshal. We come to answer your call.'

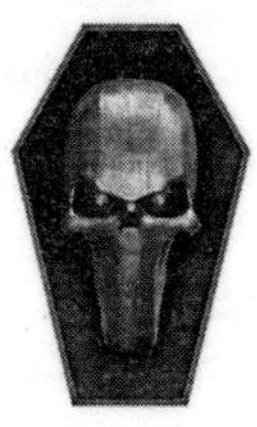

CHAPTER 5

At their heart, all battles are the same. They are violence harnessed. The elementary hatred at the centre of all things directed and unleashed. Whether with spear and rock or particle cannon and gauss flayer, battle is the struggle for existence made manifest.

Thus, Khemet emerges from the portal of a monolith fully prepared for the sensory assault that greets her.

She strides from the portal's light and into the maelstrom. Laser light strobes from the city's walls, a thousand pinpricks each second. Gauss flayers reply, cratering stone and flensing flesh. Doomsday Arks race through the air, chased by the humans' remaining aerial defences. Monoliths hurl lightning and thunder, reducing the cannons atop the curtain wall one by one.

The siege lines encircle the city, tens of thousands of warriors and Immortals trading fire with the defenders. There can be only one end to such an encounter, and Khemet is content to let it play out. She has not come for the humans.

Khemet sees her. She is impossible to miss.

Ahnuret is the centre of a vortex of destruction. She has placed herself on the wall, cutting a trail through its defenders. The horror of enmitic weapons leaves a welter of gore that paints the rampart with each shot.

Khemet kicks her anti-gravity pack into life, rising like an arrow from a bow. A half-hearted fusillade of las fire follows her, but Khemet ignores it, her living metal entirely proof against their paltry weapons.

She drops from the sky, staff drawn and held ready.

In the last moment, Ahnuret glances up. Her enmitic pistols vanish, and a wickedly curved sickle blade appears in her hand instead.

Khemet shatters the rockcrete with her landing and throws herself at the deathmark. The staff carves air as Ahnuret backs away.

'I have come to end this.'

'As you did before?' Ahnuret swings, aiming for her hand, but Khemet lets it drop and the blade sails over her wrist.

'Not again. I will not let you steal this from me. The Destroyer is the truth. To deny it is to deny our purpose in this galaxy.'

'Our purpose is to rule, not eradicate.'

'An absurd distinction.'

Khemet presses her attack, knowing that to give Ahnuret even a second's respite will see her depart into her oubliette.

'Are you truly so weak that you will give in to madness?' Khemet attempts a different angle, but the deathmark throws the accusation back at her.

'It is you who are weak, praetorian. Weak and fearful. You call me mad? You are flawed, a shadow of yourself. You have lost so much. Left behind in the Traveller's prison, or else hidden beneath your pathetic insecurities.'

She lowers her weapon to deliver the gravest cut.

'Would the Silent King even know you as you are now?'

Khemet punches the deathmark.

There is no elegance to it, no motion of ancient martial craft learnt in ages past. Khemet simply balls her metal fist and hammers it into Ahnuret's skull, every fragment of her strength leaning into the strike.

Ahnuret topples, her senses fuzzed for a crucial moment. There is a dent in the necrodermis of her faceplate and Khemet pursues it, ferocious desire burning from her core to break that dent open. Khemet hammers the deathmark, her rod of covenant abandoned. Blow after blow rains down. The metal of Ahnuret's skull deforms, cracks, breaks away.

Khemet stops, a fist raised, as she sees the inner workings of the deathmark's skull.

She can destroy Ahnuret. Khemet has come close, though she will mend, as all necrons do. Khemet can destroy her, but that is not what she came here to do. She came here to save her, to help her vanquish the demon that plagues her.

Khemet clamps both hands to the sides of Ahnuret's head, and with a surge of power casts the deathmark into oblivion.

While they fought, the battle has evolved around them. The humans are running. A gaping void has been torn in the curtain wall, and cohorts of Immortals are escorting monoliths into the city.

One more marker on the path to victory.

Khemet summons a Ghost Ark to bear Ahnuret away. She will recover, but in the confines of a stasis crypt until Khemet – not Kamoteph – judges she is ready for release.

She considers the rampart and its dead. For all that she judged Ahnuret, there are many Unclean left to defeat, and the catharsis of bloodshed is tempting. For once, Khemet yields to that temptation.

She is about to light her anti-gravity pack when Kamoteph's unwelcome touch enters her mind.

'If you are quite finished brawling like a common thug, a new factor has entered our war.'

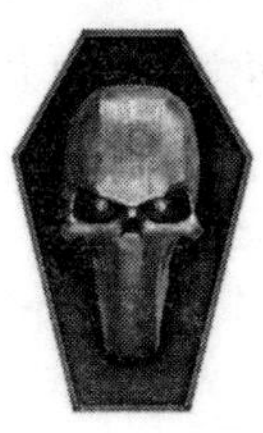

CHAPTER 6

Coming aboard the *Blessed Vengeance* is a major military operation in its own right. No fewer than four decoy flights are launched, though there can be no disguising the intended destination of any of them. The Adeptus Astartes vessel has slid into orbit on the far side of Orymous from the xenos ship, though based on auspex logs of its first appearance it could round the planet in a matter of minutes.

In the event, the xenos have made no attempt to prevent the Imperial delegation from uniting with their saviours. Sinos has tried to consider what that means, but there is simply too much they do not know about their enemy to intuit anything of worth.

The lighter slowly drifts inside the open mouth of the strike cruiser and settles onto a designated square of the flight deck. It is evident which patch of metal is intended for them as it is surrounded by weaponry. A platoon of armsmen is waiting for them, along with a pair of Tarantula sentry guns, whose twinned heavy bolters track the lighter's progress from the moment it passes through the atmospheric barrier.

Seven figures in the massive battle plate of the Adeptus Astartes form the most arresting element of their welcoming party.

'They are suspicious of us,' observes Hikaru.

'They are right to be. We come from a tainted world.' She has not forgotten the look in Verispexor Pyrch's eyes as he lunged for her, or the tide of metal insects that he sent forth.

Sinos was given a seat aboard the lighter thanks to her initial contact with the Deathwatch. The rest are occupied by Dorienn Hikaru, the chief secretary to the new lord-militant of Orymous, and a limited retinue of robed strategos. Hikaru is sweating profusely. This is, as he has said six times since entering the lighter, his first encounter with the Emperor's Angels.

'Be clear, be direct.' Sinos offers some final words of advice. 'Accept that you will never shed your fear of them, and know that you will do your duty regardless.'

Hikaru gives her a worried nod in reply.

'Do not exit your craft until ordered.'

The order comes from beyond the lighter's hull, loud enough to be heard over the cycling engines.

They are not kept waiting long. 'Permission is given to come aboard. Exit your craft slowly, and in the light of the Emperor of Mankind.'

A frigid blast of air rushes in as the hatch opens. Sinos is at the rear of the hold, and waits her turn with ill patience. It has been twenty years since she was last in the presence of a Space Marine, and it is an experience unlike any other. Once felt, the mixture of awe and, yes, stomach-curdling fear is not forgotten.

She finally steps out onto the flight deck, whose roof is at least a hundred yards above her. It is a cavernous space, occupying the majority of the forward quarter of the ship, or so she reckons from a brief glance as they approached.

The armsmen are professional, and clearly one word away from killing them all. Their hellguns are held low, but ready to rise in an instant. They are also entirely eclipsed by the warriors who stand between them.

Seven warriors. Seven warlords of the God-Emperor. Each one towers over Sinos, each a sculpted ideal of humanity's form, perfected for war. Their armour is the black of the void, of absolute darkness, save for a single arm and hulking pauldron which is burnished silver and mounted with a complex death's head icon.

Their other pauldrons each show a mixture of Adeptus Astartes heraldry, some of which she recognises from the childhood tales on which all Imperial children are raised, and others from her time in service to the Emperor's Adeptus Arbites. Three wear a clenched red fist, including their leader, who stands ahead of his peers. Sinos knows the rampant beast of the Howling Griffons, worn by two others, and she would never mistake the Space Wolves' snarling iconography.

The last wears a leering silver death mask, and chills Sinos to the bone. What little she can see of his face is heavily tattooed with black whorls, but a thick and complex hood rises from the collar of his armour and casts his face in shadow. A chain of human and alien skulls hangs from his waist, and more are attached to a metal staff as tall as the warrior himself.

Hikaru, like the rest of the delegation, has frozen in the sight of their saviours, none of whom wear their helmets, displaying faces that are scarred, brutal facsimiles of the human form. But he finds his voice, and steps forwards. 'Watch Commander Trantor. Thank you for–'

'Captain,' the leading warrior interrupts him. 'I command the Orthanik station, but my rank is watch captain.'

Hikaru mops his brow. 'Watch captain, of course. I am Dorienn Hikaru. On behalf of Lord-Militant Locum Hemryn, I gratefully welcome you to Orymous. Thank you for allowing us aboard. We are all willing to consent to whatever tests you require in order to confirm we are free of xenos corruption.'

He says all this in a rush, fearing exactly what means the Adeptus Astartes would use to verify his claim. The insidious nature of the xenos threat had been explained over the vox prior to their launch.

'If you were tainted, you would not have left your craft.' Trantor does not expand on that, but the warrior with the skull-topped staff mysteriously inclines his head towards Hikaru.

'Good, then.' Hikaru forges on. 'You come in the hour of our direst need. We humbly–'

'Time is short. Let us speak of your need.' Trantor's voice is a deep bass rumble, rising out of a chest that is almost broader than Sinos' arm span. 'What is the disposition of the enemy?'

Hikaru holds out a dataslate. 'This is a complete exload of our tactical situation, and our wider logistical position.'

Trantor takes the tablet, but does not look at its contents. 'How would you describe the status of your world?'

Hikaru finally loses his nerve. At the last, he is unable to give voice to the state of his home.

'Nearing collapse,' says Sinos. 'The sabotage of the planet's food supply has crippled combat efficiency. The Imperial Guard fight like heroes, but there is only so far mortal strength can be tested.'

Trantor looks at her for the first time. 'Thank you, marshal.'

'The enemy are highly resilient,' says Hikaru, again finding his voice. 'We have compiled all we have observed of them and their tactics. We have had no communication with them, and attempts at capture and interrogation have proven… unsuccessful. In truth, we do not even know what to name them.'

'Necrons,' says the hooded warrior. 'They are called necrons. You have done well to hold them at bay thus far, for they are a formidable enemy.'

'Have you fought them before, my lord?' asks Hiraku.

Trantor's expression does not change. 'We have.'

'The chief danger is not the enemy, but supply,' says Sinos. 'Without relief, Orymous' armies will be rendered entirely ineffective in a matter of months.'

'Then we must destroy their command craft, to permit a relief effort to approach.'

'The lord-militant commands me to propose a plan of attack, watch captain.' Hikaru takes another dataslate from a waiting aide, and holds it in both hands before his chest.

'Does he, indeed?' Sinos' head jerks towards the Space Wolf, who has spoken with a voice like an avalanche. The warrior has a thick, bristling black beard, through which shine teeth that could more properly be called fangs.

Trantor shows no amusement. 'Very well. Relay your lord's plan.'

Sinos is impressed. Despite his earlier hesitation, the secretary speaks concisely and clearly, offering no extraneous detail nor personal commentary.

'How soon can the weapon be made ready?'

'We have brought it with us, lord. The most worthy adepts of the Mechanicus say they will require six hours, at most, to properly prepare it.'

Trantor half-turns towards his men. The bearded Wolf still smiles, but now with a predatory edge. 'Blackstar insertion to plant a vox-beacon, then sweep and exterminate.'

'Yes, brother-captain.'

As one they turn away, stomping towards the distant rear of the flight deck. Trantor remains, though clearly he intends to follow. 'Your proposal has merit. The Deathwatch shall see it done.'

'Is that it?' Hikaru asks.

'Delay hastens this world's demise. I suggest you return to the surface.'

'Are there more of you?' He cannot contain the question any longer.

Trantor does not answer, and turns to follow his men.

'My lord, I have a request,' calls Sinos. 'I wish to join you in the attack.' It is a reckless request, born of a nihilism that Sinos will deny should she ever be asked to explain it.

Trantor stops, though he does not turn around.

'My men will not be able to protect you.'

'I require no protection. Death comes for us all. But I would rather face it squarely than cower in a bastion waiting to learn the outcome of this war.'

He hesitates no further.

'Very well. We have six hours, it seems, until we can act. I suggest you use the time well.'

CHAPTER 7

Sinos is standing at an observation port in the very top of the *Blessed Vengeance*, looking down over the great expanse of the ship's prow. It is unlike any Imperial vessel she has been on, with their great spires and crenellated battlements. The strike cruiser is more compact, more pugnacious. More obviously lethal, although that may have been Sinos' mind dwelling on its occupants.

Beneath the ship's bulk, looming over its port quarter, Orymous turns. The planet appears unspoilt by the conflict that rages across its face, untouched even by the hands of mankind. But as the *Blessed Vengeance* flies on, a grey scab appears, nestled against the south-western coastline. Sinos can hold up her hand and cover the entire city with her thumbnail, but the illusion is shattered.

A serf in a heavy sackcloth robe appears at her side, his tread soundless.

He holds out a tight roll of vellum. He is an old man, his eyes filmed with grey and deep lines curving around his mouth. He offers no greeting, no explanation for his appearance, except for the scroll that he bears.

After a moment's hesitation Sinos takes it. *Attend me in my arming chamber* is written across its face, in a startlingly beautiful hand.

There is no shipboard time given, nor a location. Sinos assumes that the serf will provide both. 'Lead on.'

He spins on his heel and sets off, spry for his age. Sinos has to force a quick stride to keep pace with him. He heads to the closest transport shaft, whose platform immediately drops into the heart of the *Blessed Vengeance*.

They leave the shaft a few minutes later, heading along what Sinos assumes to be one of the main thoroughfares through the ship's centre. Others, perhaps even Sinos herself at any other time, would have marvelled at the magnificence of the immense hall, its vaulted stone walls curving up to a high, shadowed peak in the manner of Imperial cathedrums. They might have been tempted to pause and examine the statues of Adeptus Astartes and humans that line the thoroughfare, or gaze at the banners that hang heavily from each pillar.

But Sinos does not. It is not the time. Far beneath her feet, a world struggles to save itself from an alien plague that erupted from the ground. The grand austerity of the Adeptus Astartes vessel is far less important than the warriors it has conveyed.

What is inescapably apparent, however, is that the ship's decks are deserted. Sinos has spent more time than she cares to consider aboard the warships, transports, and cutters of His Imperial Navy, and each of them have fairly teemed with life. She cannot imagine that the arcane workings of an Adeptus Astartes vessel require any less care or devotion, and yet they walk for almost half an hour and Sinos sees fewer than a dozen other figures, all servants of the Deathwatch, robed in the same manner as her guide.

She aches to question the serf, but senses that he possesses a reserve that will not yield to any casual inquiry of hers. He lives, after all, in the shadow of far more formidable beings than her.

He takes her away from the central thoroughfare and into a tangle of narrower channels, though each hatch and doorway is considerably larger than would be necessary for a human.

Almost without warning, the serf halts beside a recessed hatch no different to a hundred others they have passed. They are somewhere in the rear starboard quarter of the ship, if Sinos' sense of direction has not failed her.

The robed figure reaches out with a liver-spotted hand and depresses a rune.

'*Send her in.*' Trantor's deep rumble is made tinny by the small vox-grille inset beside the hatch, but even so his voice sparks a sudden burst of nerves in her stomach. She has been entirely calm during her journey from the observation port, her attention on her new surroundings while her unconscious mind turned over a dozen concurrent problems. Now, at the watch captain's door, she is uncertain why she has been summoned.

The serf releases the rune, and presses another. The doorway slides open with a loud and slightly halting growl of servos.

'Thank you for coming, marshal,' says Trantor. He is kneeling, still in his massive suit of scarred battle plate. He is facing her, his head bare, his back to an alcove in which a dozen candles burn on tiers of narrow shelves. The candlelight throws his immense shadow across the metal deck, and makes his face impossible to read.

'I should say the same, watch captain. Your arrival is the ray of hope the defenders of Orymous require to turn the tide.'

Trantor lifts his head. Butter-yellow light gleams from the brown skin of his shaved head.

'When you came aboard, the governor locum's adjunct remarked that I have brought few warriors to this world's defence.'

'I will ensure he is heavily sanctioned by his superiors, watch captain,' she says. 'I apologise for his impudence.' Sinos offers the apology because she is nervous. But she is also curious, and not a little angry, to have been called to answer for the ill-considered words of an official who sits outside of her chain of command.

'That is not why I called you here, marshal.'

Trantor stands, rising with an alarming growl of servos that Sinos hears from the far side of the room. She has to fight her rising heart rate. Even kneeling, Trantor had looked down on Sinos. Standing, in the close confines of his quarters, his sheer physical presence sets off a primal fear-reaction in her core.

'I wished to offer an explanation.'

'None is owed, my lord,' Sinos says, though she does not know what he intends to explain.

'Nevertheless.'

Trantor extends a hand. There is a single seat in the chamber, shaped quite clearly to human proportions. It is surprisingly ornate, each limb and its tall back formed from curves of dark-brown wood, with coils and knots carved into their surfaces. Sinos, discomfort growing with every moment, sits on the very edge of the chair.

Trantor surprises Sinos once more by sitting as well, settling onto a wide metal stool that she had mistaken for a workbench. His armour wheezes as he shifts position.

'Are you familiar with the nature of my Chapter, marshal? I assume you have at least some understanding, since you called us to this world.'

Sinos is calmed, slightly, by reaching into her memories. 'Somewhat, my lord. I was privileged to once meet a veteran of your order.'

'Who?' he asks quickly.

'Brother-Sergeant Dantioch, lord. Of the Sons of Orar.'

If Trantor recognises the name, he gives no sign. 'What did he tell you of the Deathwatch?'

'You are an elite formation among the Adeptus Astartes. Pledged to serve the Holy Inquisition, guarding against the pestilence of the xenos.'

Trantor nods, slowly. 'Did he tell you the manner in which the ranks of the Deathwatch are filled?' He waits for an answer. After a moment, Sinos gives a slight shake of her head.

'Warriors from every Chapter in the Imperium once sent their best to us. Forsaking all other loyalties, they pledged themselves to this duty. Our duty, for as long as it was required. It was considered by many to be the greatest honour one could achieve in the Emperor's service.'

'Once, my lord?' Sinos has noticed his qualifier, as she knew she had been meant to.

'Indeed,' says Trantor. He does not continue, pausing for so long that Sinos almost fills the silence.

'There are many threats facing the Imperium, marshal, as you undoubtedly know,' he says finally. 'Many trials. It has been my privilege to face them. My hand has ended the alien threat to dozens of Imperial worlds. I speak not in pride, marshal, but in fact. Billions of the Emperor's subjects owe their lives to the intervention of my kill teams.'

'"Pride is the birthright of the soldier, earned through blood and service",' says Sinos, quoting a favourite maxim of General Oruhan, one of the corps commanders during the Cattelingian Crusade. It draws a fleeting smile to Trantor's broad face, gone as soon as it appears.

'But every victory takes its toll. In the past three centuries, fewer than half of those who have taken the black have returned to their Chapters. Fewer still have had their gene-seed repatriated.'

Sinos has never heard the term, and does not ask.

'I do not blame them. Humanity's enemies are unremitting. The Chapters must look to their own borders. Their own duties. To spare even a single battle-brother is a profound sacrifice in these times.' He falls silent again, and it takes Sinos shifting awkwardly in her seat to break it.

'Secretary Hikaru asked why I bring so few warriors to this war,' he says, his gaze not wavering from Sinos' own.

'You summoned the warriors of Watch Station Orthanik. I have brought them all.'

With a start that sends a shiver of absolute dread running through Sinos' core, she realises why Trantor has called her here. He is tired.

Though she has met over a dozen Adeptus Astartes in the course of her long life, she has never wholly shed the image of their kind that she learnt in her early years. They are the God-Emperor's angels, the sword and shield of the Imperium. Peerless, relentless warriors, superior to any foe in a galaxy full of terrors. It is impossible to imagine them succumbing to such mortal concerns as fatigue or dread.

And yet, Sinos is sitting across from a warrior who is at the very end of his endurance.

She does not know what to say. One of the God-Emperor's greatest warriors has called her to his chambers to unburden himself. What could possibly be said?

The silence stretches out, broken by the rhythmic clunk of some piece of machinery operating behind a bulkhead. Finally Trantor relents, placing armoured hands on his thighs and pushing himself to his feet. 'There is another reason I asked you here, marshal.'

Sinos waits. She is not sure she would be able to speak even if Trantor asked it of her.

He walks to the far side of the chamber, coming within a few heavy steps of Sinos. He opens the door of a shallow locker mounted beside the room's entrance. 'If you are going to join the Deathwatch in battle, you should be properly armed.'

He offers her a power maul, unlike any Sinos has seen before.

It is no Adeptus Astartes weapon. Examples of their type are mounted all over one wall: the smallest is a gladius the length of Sinos' leg and as broad as her hand's span. There is even another maul, sized for an Adeptus Astartes hand. Its flanged head is bigger than Sinos' helmet, and no doubt many times its weight.

Trantor holds out a weapon fit for human hands, held easily between gauntleted thumb and forefinger. Its haft is a solid bar of steel, its grip wrapped in iridescent blue sharkskin. The power-field emitter mounted below its head is compact, encircling the whole of the haft. Its head is long, formed of four bars studded with shallow spikes along each face.

'This was the preferred implement of Inquisitor Westeron of the Ordo Xenos. He was an honourable man, so far as his vocation allowed. He died in battle several years ago, betrayed by allies he should have known better than to trust.' Trantor's voice remains entirely even, showing no trace of the bitterness implied in his words. 'However, this weapon never faltered. Its spirit is true, and it will serve you well in our coming battle.'

Sinos stands and attempts to back away. 'I cannot accept this, lord.'

'Do not be alarmed, marshal. You see this as a maudlin passing of treasures. I see it simply as ensuring you are appropriately equipped for what is to come.'

He presses the maul into Sinos' hand. The weight is greater than that of the shock maul that hangs from her waist, but not to the point of being cumbersome. She gives an experimental roll of her wrist, and finds the heft to her liking.

'My thanks, lord.' It is a gift of inestimable value, but the cynical core of Sinos' mind wonders if this is Trantor's way of recompense. Payment for hearing his confession.

Trantor straightens. 'Fear not, marshal. I have not yielded to despair. As you said, death comes for us all. But the Imperium shall ever endure.'

'The Emperor protects, watch captain,' says Sinos, hoping to draw this strange and unsettling meeting to a close.

'He does indeed, marshal,' replies Trantor.

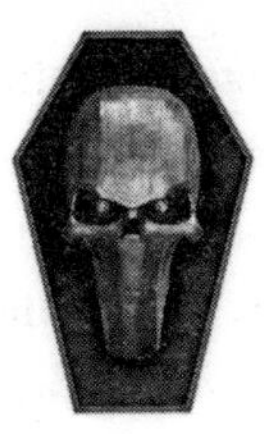

CHAPTER 8

The Blackstar is a new craft to Sinos, compact and heavy-bellied. Its wings are little more than stubs to hold weapon pods, with powerful manoeuvring thrusters on their tips. The pilot's cabin sits above its passenger bay, with barely more than a slit through which to see their target.

Sinos has learnt that it is a class of transport purpose-built for the Deathwatch, the product of only a handful of Mechanicus forge worlds. Its function is precisely the task they face – undetected insertion into hostile territory.

Sinos sits in a seat built for a far larger frame, as the Deathwatch auxilia have their own designated positions. She has been studiously ignored by the black-clad armsmen, who drill with rigour and precision. Their weapons outclass anything Sinos has seen wielded by Astra Militarum regiments, and yet every soldier is eclipsed in lethal intent by the Space Marines they serve.

She has never been this close to Adeptus Astartes. The intimacy of Trantor's chamber was one thing, but she is sandwiched between creatures two feet taller than her, armed and armoured for war. The cocktail of smells that surround her are heady. The industrial scents of lapping powder and grease. The martial familiarity of fyceline, and the ozone tang of power weapons. But above them all, rich to the point of intoxicating, is a body-warm odour of sweat and cinnamon.

She shakes her head to clear it. 'That is the combat stimulants in our blood,' says the warrior to her right. It is the Space Wolf, whose name she has learnt is Tlomec. His long hair is bound by a series of leather thongs, and threaded through with carved bones. 'A lingering trace is exuded through our skin.'

Sinos does not have a reply to that.

'Seal your helmets and rebreathers,' orders Trantor, the last to embark. He sees Sinos' quizzical expression. 'The xenos do not respire. There will be no air aboard their ship.'

The two boarding hatches at the prow of the Blackstar close, and the hold is bathed in crimson light.

A lingering fear, not of death but of a wasted end, leads Sinos to speak as the engines roar into life.

'Will they not see us coming?'

Tlomec looks down at her. 'Do not worry, arbitrator. *Corallian* has never let us down. She will not fail us now.'

The Adeptus Astartes craft is admirably direct in its approach. It throws itself around Qeretesh, driving towards the *Hepherentes* at its greatest speed. It has loosed some minor cannonades, along with a brace of self-propelled munitions that the harvest ship has slapped aside. Yet it continues to close, presumably holding the last of its strength for a final, futile salvo.

Khemet has transferred to the ship via the eternity gate of the closest monolith, and stands now on the *Hepherentes'* command deck with Hekasun and his court. She has felt her temper quicken with the Adeptus Astartes' arrival. The remembrance of heavily armoured figures thundering through columns of gauss comes to her often, battering aside her phalanxes as their orbital weapons break the earth beneath her feet. But she also recalls their broken bodies, exhausted of their great strength, outflanked and outfought across the breadth of the Lazar System.

Khemet has no fear of these warriors. She has beaten them before.

There is an oddity about their craft. It does not conform to the templates that she remembers. Electronic noise screams from its arrays, blanketing the space around with interference. It is evidently a form of blinding technology, which Kamoteph has set himself to undo.

'Weapon arrays are locked, my lord.'

'Open fire.'

The human craft's shielding is impressive; it takes almost a full minute before it collapses under the sustained barrage the *Hepherentes* deals. Explosions bloom as coils of lightning lick across the vessel's armour. But still it comes.

'A sturdy craft,' offers Lord Lehnk. Hekasun's court has gathered, sensing the moment for what it is – the last gasp of the humans upon Qeretesh.

'For only a little while longer,' replies Hekasun, sensitive to any perceived slight to his flagship.

'They are attempting to board us,' announces Kamoteph, as one of the Adeptus Astartes' ventral weapon arrays erupts in short-lived flames.

'What?'

Kamoteph's voice declares true surprise. 'I have defeated their blinding. There are several minor craft approaching our starboard launch bays. I believe they mean to board us.'

The court dissolves into snide humour, but Khemet does not

share their amusement. Her attention has not left the scrying feed since the slab-sided craft began its suicidal approach. Now, with their intention made clear, she watches their bulky, ungainly craft burn through the void, bringing their warriors to her.

Their craft take the most direct route towards the *Hepherentes'* hull, as would be expected. There are half a dozen ships in the formation, but only the lead holds the weight of life that Khemet expects. Presumably the rest are decoys. It is in keeping with the humans' arrogance that they believe their crude technology can deceive the scrying of a vessel that was sailing the void when their ancestors had yet to master standing upright.

Hekasun waves a hand. 'Swat them from the void.'

'Why not allow them aboard?' asks Kamoteph.

Hekasun scoffs. 'For what possible purpose?'

'These are Adeptus Astartes. The humans' best. Breaking them will weaken further resistance on the surface. Is that not so, praetorian?' Kamoteph is staring across the deck at Khemet, the challenge abundantly clear.

'Smiting them from existence will surely achieve the same effect.' But Hekasun too is watching Khemet. He looks between her and the cryptek, and malicious understanding dawns. 'What say you, praetorian? Are you adequate to the task?'

Khemet meets Kamoteph's gaze.

'Let them come.'

The Blackstar roars into the hollow space the auspex scans of the *Blessed Vengeance* identified as a landing bay. It is a cavernous chamber, made of oppressive black stone and lit by ghoulish lines of green irradiance. Its dark roof is hung with a dozen of the crescent-shaped killers that had made such murder of Orymous' orbital defences.

Sinos' heart is in her throat, her breathing loud in her helmet.

Trantor had cautioned her to delay rising from her harness until the Adeptus Astartes were clear of the hold, but there is little chance of the trampling he had feared. They are free of their restraints and thundering towards the opening ramps in the blink of an eye. The matching snarls of power armour are eclipsed by the howl that the Space Wolf Tlomec lets loose from his helm, a haunting and deafening cry across the communal vox that chills Sinos to the bone.

On the far side of the ship the auxilia are swifter than Sinos, running in pairs with hellguns levelled. But Sinos is only marginally behind, her power maul and pistol in hand.

'For the Emperor!'

The words burst from her lips, the pain and fury of two years of war expelled in a single cry. In the few hours she has had, Sinos has made her peace with meeting her end upon the alien craft. But in the sight of His most able servants, she will take some of His enemies with her before her death.

The xenos meet them as they land, emerging from a pair of tall archways that are cut with geometric precision into the black walls.

The necrons advance as they always do, slow and implacable behind their horrific beam weapons. Half a dozen armsmen are pulled apart by the first volley. In reply bolters hammer their shells into their front rank. Metal craters and detonates. Into the shrapnel charge the Adeptus Astartes, blades and hammers and axes flashing blue among the sickly xenos glow.

Sinos does as she has been commanded, following the auxilia away from the Blackstar to take up a position on the flank of the fight, hard up against the chamber wall. The stone is brutally cold to the touch, even through Sinos' armour, and she flinches away.

They must escape the insertion point swiftly. The plan of

battle, such as it is, calls upon Sinos and the auxilia to break into the bowels of the alien craft and drive as far as possible into its interior. A pair of serfs, guarded by a whole squad of auxilia, carry a heavy box between them, its surface aglow with complex mechanisms. This is their charge, a vox-beacon attuned to the sensors of the *Blessed Vengeance*. Waiting atop the arcane mechanisms of the ship's teleportation platform is a single Deathstrike warhead, brought aboard with Sinos' embassy to the Deathwatch.

All Sinos, and the platoon of humans with her, must do is survive until their payload can be delivered into the enemy ship. Each of them is oathed to that purpose, sworn to it by Trantor himself.

The watch captain and his brothers are doing all they can to make it possible. Sinos has seen dozens of pict feeds from battlefields over the past months, and she has never seen the aliens die so swiftly. Inhuman strength cleaves their limbs and bursts their chassis. Bolt shells shatter metal skulls. From their flank, the auxilia rain las fire into the alien ranks, turning joints to slag and bursting the glowing hearts in their chests.

Trantor leads the Adeptus Astartes, driving through the necron ranks. The watch captain is a ceaseless blur of motion. His power sword is a blaze of righteousness, carving through the enemy. Skeletal xenos swing cumbersome, axe-topped rifles at him, and Trantor throws them aside. He moves with consummate purpose, no swing wasted, no step taking him back. A stream of green light rakes the edge of his armour and he wheels about it, then cuts his attacker in half.

But the xenos have their own champion.

It lurks at the back of the chamber, unmoving. Sinos sees it, bigger, taller, bulkier than its kin. Sinos aims a shot at it, but a line warrior jerks in front of her shell as if commanded. And then it is gone, moving with more speed and purpose than any of its brethren.

Tlomec dies first. The alien champion emerges from the press of warriors, a tall staff held before it. The Space Wolf has his back turned, his axe crashing through the shoulder joint of one of the necron elites. The staff's great head erupts with power, and Tlomec ceases to be.

Two of the Crimson Fists are alive to the sudden threat and close on it from either side. But the champion shows itself a coward, stepping back into the ranks of its warriors. Tlomec's Deathwatch brothers charge into them, and are pulled down by a dozen alien hands.

'Kill it, in the Emperor's name!'

Trantor roars the order over the vox. Bolters and hellguns track the necron champion as it darts between its kin. Half a dozen xenos fall, but the aliens are indifferent.

One of the Howling Griffons, the beast on his pauldron lit by muzzle fire, punches massive shells from a heavy bolter held low at his side, while his Chapter brother cuts down a phalanx of the scythe-wielding xenos troops. Sinos loses sight of both as more necron warriors emerge from a side passage into the hangar bay, cutting off the path she and the auxilia had been aiming for.

Atakan, the Silver Skull, wades into the centre of their formation, staff blazing with warp fire. A monstrous wave bursts from his body, throwing flat the closest xenos. Lines of power arc out from his armour, earthing themselves in the fallen necrons.

And then the champion is there, dropping from above with its staff outstretched. A jade beam bursts from its tip, coruscating fire that peels the armour from Atakan's face. His helmet breaks away, and his skull is flayed to the bone. He makes no sound as he dies.

Sinos has been a servant of the Imperium for her entire life. She learnt her letters by reciting the catechisms of the Imperial Creed. She serves His law with diligence and rigour. But when she sees Watch Captain Trantor charge the xenos champion, she realises that she has never truly had faith.

He strikes the alien leader like an angel of merciless destruction, an avatar of the Emperor's wrath. A broadsword is in his hands, electric power alight along its edge. In three short seconds Trantor has struck five blows against the warrior, who moves its staff like quicksilver to parry them. It tries to escape, leaping into the air on some kind of gravity pack, but Trantor's blade catches its hip. The edge bites deep, and the xenos is hauled back to the deck.

Trantor lifts his sword for a killing blow, but metal bodies pile into him. He turns the thrust into a sweeping cut, bending low to sever the encroaching xenos at the waist. Half a dozen fall but more are behind, reaching out with knife-tipped hands. Daggered fingers punch into the ceramite of his pauldrons. A warrior traps Trantor's blade in its body, inhuman in its deathless grip, and more xenos fall upon the watch captain.

The weight of metal upon him forces Trantor to his knees. Sinos can hear herself screaming into the vox, denying the evidence of her eyes. But despite the hail of las the servants of the Deathwatch unleash, they are powerless.

The champion stands over Trantor, its bladed staff held low. The watch captain's voice comes over the vox once more. 'Suffer not the alien–'

The staff sweeps low, slicing through the armour across Trantor's midriff.

Blood pours in a sheet, a deluge, through the ruined plate. Trantor staggers, reaching out to grasp his nemesis before he falls. The creature deprives him of even that, stepping out of reach. Trantor follows, gauntlets outstretched. He takes one step, two, and then crashes to the deck, entrails spilling from the horrific wound.

Sinos hurls herself at the necron warlord. There is no thought to it, just a pure streak of rage that comes from the very centre of her being. She abandons the auxilia, surrendering the opportunity of a few more moments of life for the chance to avenge Trantor's death.

A xenos warrior, malice glowing in its eyes, sees her coming from ten yards away. The creature spins, casually striking her with the back of a fist, and the world turns black.

Something hits her everywhere at once, a chill and awful smoothness. She is on her back. Her head is a mass of blinding agony. There is blood in her eyes. It's possible she only has one eye; her helmet has crumpled in on her skull.

Sinos is shaking. What had she been thinking? She is an arbitrator, not a warrior.

She raises her head through nausea and blinding pain. She is alone. Through some fluke of alien malice, she is the last one alive. She tastes the blood in her mouth. Her teeth are loose. She will die, that is certain. All that remains is the manner of her death.

The necrons' murdering champion is in front of her, watching Trantor's final moments. The watch captain is on his knees, held up by the xenos with his arms outstretched, in the manner of the Imperial aquila. He is not yet dead. They are toying with him, observing how much pain and humiliation the Adeptus Astartes can endure.

Sinos clutches the icon of the Adeptus Arbites on its chain. She grips it hard, the sharp edges digging through the pad of her gauntlet.

'Faith… is my shield.'

She rolls onto her front, getting her hands beneath her chest.

'Contempt is my armour.' She climbs to her feet, both hands gripping the maul to use its head as a crutch.

'Vengeance is my sword.'

Sinos throws everything she has, every fibre of her being, into the swing. The crackling head of the power maul arcs up and over her head, trailing sparks of power.

The champion catches the maul by its haft. Alien metal clamps down on Sinos' hand, trapping her grip around the weapon. Revulsion floods through her as the thing leans its face close to hers, and speaks.

'They will avail you not, little human.'

Something punches into Sinos' chest with the force of a scattergun blast.

She groans, and her chin drops into her chest. Five knife-like fingers are embedded up to the knuckles in her armour. Red wells over black, over the xenos' vile metal and the icon of her office.

She is held upright only by the talons in her chest. Sinos' head lolls, and she finds Watch Captain Trantor beside her. His eyes are blank, the life drained from them. Sinos is glad that he is not witness to her failure to avenge him.

The alien pulls back its hand, and Solome Sinos slumps to one knee. Each breath is bubbling agony. She counts them, clinging to the impossibility that while she counts, she will not die.

The xenos kneels down beside her, head cocked in what a human would take for curiosity. It reaches out and lifts the icon of the Adeptus Arbites from Sinos' armour. Sinos groans, fighting with ebbing strength to lift her hand, to pull away.

The creature holds the scales of justice up in front of Sinos' face, ensuring that she has it in her sight.

Its metal fist clenches, and the scales are broken to fragments.

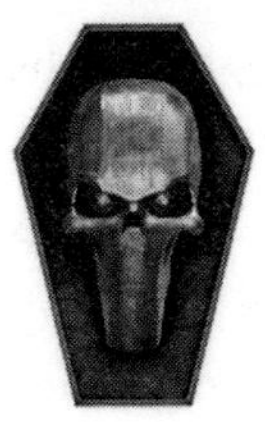

CHAPTER 9

The bridge of the *Hepherentes* is silent. All those with the capacity for attention have turned it on the scrying feeds, absorbed by the spectacle of the praetorian and her rage.

'*The Unclean have been purged,*' Khemet reports across the interstices.

'You are mistaken,' replies Kamoteph, hands dancing over a console. 'The *Hepherentes* reports that many of their auxilia have fled towards the stern. I suspect they are intent on sabotage.'

Khemet does not immediately respond. '*I saw none escape.*'

'I will believe the evidence of the ship's sensors over your testimony, praetorian.'

There is the slightest delay. '*Very well. I will pursue them.*'

This is the moment of greatest danger, yet Hekasun and his allies show no awareness at all.

The nomarch of Qeretesh sits his throne, as ever, with the scions of the Zathanor around him. They speak in interstitial whispers, as is their habit, no doubt plotting how they will carve up dominion of the world now that the champions of the humans have been dispatched.

Kamoteph abandons his place at the console, and stumps over to the base of the throne's ziggurat. He stops beside Mandulis. He gives the most minute inclination of his head, a grand display of respect for the stolid vargard.

'Victory, Kamoteph,' says Hekasun, indulgent in success.

'It was never in doubt, lord.'

Kamoteph spins, the bladed head of his staff blazing with jade energy. It describes a perfect arc of green light before it hits Mandulis in the side. The blade carves up through the vargard's torso, emerging from the far side of his chestplate. Mandulis topples to the deck, reactor core bleeding copper-orange smoke.

In the moment the vargard hits the deck, canoptek wraiths burst through the throne room's walls. They phase into being beside the lychguard who stand watch over the chamber, and grasp the deathless warriors in razor-edged jaws. Three fall instantly, severed at the waist. Wild beams of gauss fly about the chamber as others are thrown from their feet by the enormous constructs.

More canoptek creatures rush through the chamber's archways, scarabs and spyders and wyrms of every size and description. They throw themselves onto the prone lychguard, gnashing mandibles clamping around limbs and struts. A scarab pierces the gauss coil of one warrior's weapon, unleashing an explosion that paints the chamber in a ghostly green glow. The blast immolates the construct and the lychguard in an inferno that even their god-forged metal cannot withstand.

As his beasts pour in, Kamoteph hurls himself at Hekasun, leaping Mandulis' bisected body with his staff outstretched, lunging for the nomarch.

Hekasun catches the blow, his sickle blade rising at the very last moment. The glowing edge of Kamoteph's staff bites a thumb's width into Hekasun's faceplate before it is knocked back, leaving a brutal scar across the lord's face. The noble responds with a kick that throws the cryptek back down the ziggurat and over the closest console.

Battle erupts at the heart of the *Hepherentes*. Nobles arm themselves only to be swarmed by iridescent carapaces. Beams of gauss crisscross the chamber as Hekasun's warriors and brethren fight and die. On the far side of the chamber, Ptah throws back the swarm with thunderous blasts of light and sound. Hekasun contends with buzzing acanthrites that cut through the air, coiled tails alive with cutting lasers.

In the depths of the console pit, Kamoteph the Crooked straightens.

The cryptek rises from his bent-backed hunch. The overlarge segments of his spine shift, the necrodermis flowing down and into his arms and legs. The hood that casts his faceplate into shadow melts away, adding power and heft to his shoulders. He rises, no longer the stooping cripple but a forceful, dynamic paragon of necrons. He stands before Hekasun, his staff throwing out a blaze of energy that illuminates the farthest reaches of the deck.

Hekasun draws a second sickle, the twin weapons aglow with the same copper anger that burns in his chest.

'So much for Kamoteph the Crooked.'

Kamoteph rolls his newly sculpted shoulders. 'I have always despised that name.'

They come together in a flurry of blows. Hekasun leaps from his ziggurat, curved blades carving the air. Kamoteph knocks them both aside and counters with a vicious slash at the noble's face.

As they duel, every necron in the chamber feels an absence in their minds, a void that sets many of the lords of the Zathanor to flight.

'You have disabled the ship's reanimation protocols,' spits Hekasun.

'Indeed.'

'You are willing to gamble your own existence for the chance to kill me?'

Kamoteph feints the head of his staff at Hekasun, then sweeps the butt up and around to crash into his skull. Hekasun drops like a felled tree. 'I have been able to kill you since the day we met.'

Hekasun rolls away from the cryptek. He kicks out at a scarab the size of his chest that leaps for him, and uses the momentum to throw himself upright. He lands in time to catch Kamoteph's swing against the flat of his blade. He is thrown back, falling into one of the console pits. Two warriors, battling the constructs that perch atop their stations, are crushed beneath his fall.

The interstices are silent, blocked by the cryptek's malice. There will be no rescue for the nomarch, nor for the nobles who have been swamped beneath the weight of metal and piercing limbs.

But Kamoteph is no warrior. Hekasun, for all his flaws, possesses a form god-forged to rule and command. Even with his disguise thrown off, Kamoteph is slighter and weaker than the lord he seeks to kill.

Kamoteph may be no warrior, but he is a cryptek and master of the canoptek beasts. Constructs assail Hekasun in a blinding swarm. For every step and swing he makes at the treacherous cryptek, he must make another at the scarabs and spyders that seek to foul his legs. He moves in a whirling dance, never ceasing, always lashing out, defending the grasping talons and particle beams of Kamoteph's pets.

It is not a question of endurance – both could fight for centuries without tiring – but of focus. A single error will see either duellist fall.

Ptah flees. On the far side of the chamber the cryptek has steadily retreated, hurling blast after blast of pure energy into the baying mob. But his courage in the face of oblivion can only last so long. He throws up a nimbus of crackling energy and runs, following the last of Hekasun's kin who could not face the prospect of true mortality.

'Coward!' Hekasun cannot help but call out after his disloyal servant.

This is the lapse that dooms him. In the moment Hekasun's attention flicks to his fleeing cryptek, a canid-sized scarab throws itself towards him. Hekasun carves it in two, but another leaps upon his back. An acanthrite drops from its lurking hover and hacks a sliver of necrodermis from his shoulder. The constructs mob the lord, grasping the joints of his arms and legs.

He falls, as he must. More canoptek creatures add their weight to his frame and he crashes to the noctilith. He tries to rise, but a wyrm rears up beside him. Hekasun slashes a sickle across its face, but a canoptek construct cannot be blinded. The wyrm bites down, grasping Hekasun between its mandibles, pinning his arms against his sides.

Kamoteph seizes his moment. His staff rises and falls, slashing through both of Hekasun's legs, carving the limbs from his body. The wyrm shakes Hekasun's dismembered form. Under the immense pressure his ribcage cracks, venting a gout of flame into the wyrm's ruined skull. It throws him aside, sickles flying from his grasp.

Hekasun sprawls, fear settling on him for the first time. The last of his lychguard are dead, along with those of his dynasty whose loyalty outweighed their sense. They are truly dead, their engrams trapped within their sundered bodies. Shards of metal carpet the blackstone, and gauss scars blacken the chamber's stone.

Kamoteph stands above him. His metal is scarred from a dozen cuts, and his reactor core coughs a smoky residue. But he stands unbent above his broken lord.

Hekasun stares up at him. 'Betrayer.'

'Fool.'

'You cast away all that we have done for petty ambition.'

Kamoteph manages a wheeze of laughter. 'All *I* have done. You are nothing. A name. A means to obtain all that I required.' He raises his staff. 'Your use ended the moment we set foot upon Qeretesh.'

He throws back his staff, body bending into a monstrous killing blow. The shimmering head describes an arc of viridian light that flashes over and down onto Hekasun's broken body.

Khemet's rod of covenant knocks the blow aside. The staff's blade slams into the deck, sinking deep into the blackstone.

'I will not allow this.'

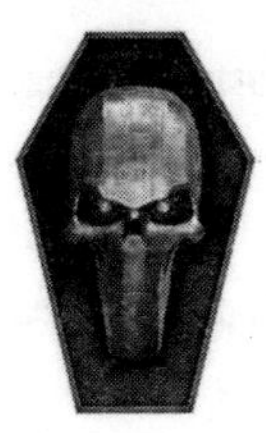

CHAPTER 10

Kamoteph whirls away, the curtain of tiles on his arm flying up to clatter against Khemet's face. She catches its trailed edge with the tip of her staff, and half a dozen shards of crystal and necrodermis fly away to skitter into the corner of the room.

'You have chosen a strange time for treachery, cryptek.'

'This is our victory, Khemet. Let us claim it together.'

She ignores his limp attempt to win her to his cause, and instead lifts a fallen blade from the deck and hurls it at him. He knocks it aside, and the blade buries itself in the blackstone at his feet.

Kamoteph backs away, retreating behind the bodies of his constructs and the fallen nobility. She can see the calculus behind his eyes. The Adeptus Astartes captain came close to ending her, and the damage to her hip is slow to mend. But despite her hindrance, and for all his new and potent stature, he cannot hope to defeat her.

As Khemet takes a step, the eternity gate set into the forward wall of the bridge blazes into sudden life. Viridian energy parts like a curtain, revealing a thing pulled from the nightmares of necrontyr children.

The tomb stalker rears up. It is a massive construct, the peak of the canoptek arts. Forty cubits of bladed limbs, a thickly armoured back, and an insectile maw. A bulbous head crowns its body, snapping mandibles on either side.

It moves like lightning, a staccato thunder of legs drumming against noctilith. It is across the chamber in the blink of an ocular, head lowered and body moving with the weight of a freight conveyor.

Khemet is smashed aside, barely avoiding the grasp of its snapping jaw, but her rod of covenant is not so lucky. The tomb stalker's razored mandible hooks around the staff, and in an instant her weapon disappears into its enormous mouth. The creature turns like a whip, flexing its body into a tight coil with Khemet at its centre. It snaps for her again and she leaps, landing atop its back. Shards of necrodermis are carved from her body by its razor spines, but she hangs on. The stalker bucks, a ripple of violent motion that runs up from its tail to whip-lash its head. Khemet digs her hands into the space between two armoured plates and holds on as the construct throws her back and forth. She flails but jams her hands deeper, seeking the column of signal relays that runs along its spine. She finds it, grips, and tears the bundle free.

The stalker's body crumples instantly, each segment collapsing against the other.

Khemet slides from its corpse. In the second she takes to assess the damage to her body Kamoteph is on her, throwing rapid thrusts at her broken torso.

Khemet jinks away, giving ground, letting the cryptek follow her across the deck and up a shallow ramp towards the scrying consoles. Her rod of covenant now lost in the maw of the tomb stalker, she is left with no option but to evade, whirling her body around Kamoteph's blade-head.

Her metal is cut in a dozen places, her reactor stressed to its maximum. There is no more ground to give, and she has no weapon. There is only one tool left in her arsenal.

Khemet reaches into the depths of her mind and awakens her chronosense.

The world lurches. Kamoteph jerks to a halt, his staff drawn back in the first motion of a swing. Across the chamber, Heka-sun ceases his twitching. The flickering orange flames rising from his cracked chest become solid, each ghost of copper and red rising and vanishing in beautiful chaos.

It is simplicity itself to catch the blow. Though she moves no quicker than Kamoteph, she has the time to perfectly compute the angle, direction, and strength of his swing. Khemet feels a part of her unclench, the release of a fear long-held and now dispelled.

The moment metal touches metal the world spins back to speed. Khemet releases her chronosense as she catches Kamoteph's staff, trapping his grip with her hand. She slams down with the other, punching into the thin struts of his wrist. The metal cracks and she continues, slamming blow after blow down against the joint of his arm.

With a final crack and a burst of sparks, Khemet tears the cryptek's hand away. Kamoteph lurches back, surprised more than pained.

Khemet seizes her chance. She steps close and clamps both hands around his skull. The jewel in her brow blazes into life, and Khemet pours herself into the cryptek's mind.

Khemet stands on black sand, with a desert wind blowing hot against her face.

She is flesh. Her metal body is gone, replaced by brown skin and warm, yielding muscle. She wears a blue robe, bound loose about her waist. Leather sandals shield her feet from the scorching touch of the sand. Her rod of covenant is in her hand, the metal smooth and cool beneath her touch. Over the crest of a nearby dune she can see low buildings, smoke rising from a cooking fire at their centre.

This is wrong. Khemet has no memory of the life she lost, but she knows that not a day passed without pain. And in this place the infirmity in her bones, the curse that haunted the necrontyr, is absent. This is a fiction, not a memory.

Kamoteph stands beside her. Kohl rings his eyes, and a dark-blue pigment stains the skin of his arms and chest. He walks with a staff, but his body is upright, his back straight and strong.

'This is how you render yourself?' She glances down at her body, as false and as fabricated as the metal form she has left behind. 'This is how you imagine we were?'

'No.'

Pain explodes throughout Khemet's being, pain that she had left behind an eternity ago. Agony throbs from within her bones, pulsing out of the diseased marrow of her limbs. Black necrotic sores bloom across her skin. The hot wind becomes a gale, driving sand with the force of a hurricane into her open wounds. Her robe rots with her flesh, falling away to reveal the metal skeleton that lies beneath. Gobbets of meat slide from her necrodermis, taking with it her memories, her sanity, her duty to–

'Enough!'

The desert is gone. Her degrading body, Kamoteph's, the black sand and the hot wind, all are destroyed in an instant, consumed by the ferocity of the azure light that blazes into being behind her. Kamoteph's twisted fiction dies in the face of Khemet's reality.

Relief pours through her like a cool river, but she can spare no runtime for it. She isolates the relevant synapses and cuts off the distracting tug of emotion.

Beneath her, caught like an insect under the glare of her authority, Khemet perceives the spectre of Kamoteph. He appears as a black mote, a sphere that swallows the light that she embodies.

'Do you mean to prolong this further?' Kamoteph's attempt at trickery has soured any impulse for mercy that might have survived his treachery.

'No,' he replies, with the false contrition with which she is so familiar. His words are not spoken, but appear in Khemet's mind fully formed.

'Had you succeeded,' she asks, 'do you imagine I would have allowed you to keep your ill-won gains?'

'You have no love for Hekasun,' says Kamoteph. 'And he despises you. Duatekh. That is his judgement. Why are you defending him?'

'I am not defending him.'

It seems to Khemet that Kamoteph's shade is weakening, shrinking by the moment. 'I see.'

'Why do this? Qeretesh is won. You steered Hekasun at every turn. Did you really need to sit upon its throne to wield its power?'

He does not reply for some time. 'I grew tired of serving,' he says finally.

She says nothing.

'I could fight you,' Kamoteph says. 'This is my mind, after all.'

'You could.'

'But the truth is, praetorian, I have no need to fight you.' The black sphere that is Kamoteph begins to grow. It expands, pressing back the cobalt rays. The interface between Khemet and Kamoteph's mental strength crackles with force, both their minds making real the struggle for dominion.

'Hekasun is venal, but he is not a fool. He knew you, before even I did. He knew your nature would threaten his desire for power.' The pretended humility that Kamoteph hides behind is gone. This is the truth of the cryptek, laid bare as it had been in the *Senusret*'s throne room when he threw off his crooked disguise.

'Hekasun feared you. And so when I rebuilt your mind, he asked me to free him from that fear.'

The beast comes from the darkness, bursting out of Kamoteph's shadow just as his tomb stalker emerged onto the command deck. It has the form of a wyrm, a spine-tipped nightmare of metal and ravening jaws.

It encircles Khemet, the segments of its body forming coil after coil. It wraps about her light, over and under, enclosing it, containing it. Squeezing tight about her, reducing the world of her mental landscape to nothing but blades and metal and snapping fangs.

But as the first of its needle spines comes close to touching her, the creature freezes.

'I am disappointed, Kamoteph,' says Khemet. 'You have under-estimated me since the moment you released me from the labyrinth.'

The beast struggles, thrashing with all its might. But she holds it with the merest fraction of her will.

'I found your wyrm long ago.'

She squeezes, and the beast crumbles, blown to dust in a jet of white-hot nuclear fire.

Kamoteph diminishes in that same fire, shrinking as violently as he grew. That he does not flee from her, attempt to hide from her, is to his credit, but only barely. He knows that there is nowhere within this realm he could hide from her.

She says no words of parting. Her mercy does not extend so far as offering a benediction to a betrayer.

The fire blazes on, ripping through his corpus, setting fire to all that was and had ever been a part of the cryptek. It takes only moments for the final mote of Kamoteph to burn to ash, and then to nothing.

Slowly, but with accelerating fury, the world collapses.

Khemet does not linger. She has been trapped in this place before.

The strength and horror of living metal cages Khemet once more.

She releases Kamoteph and steps away. His oculars are dull and lifeless, his limbs weightless. If there is anything left of the cryptek it is far afield, lost in the desolation she has made of his mind.

There was a time when she would have left him in that state, naming it a just punishment. But, for better or worse, she finds herself unable to countenance that final cruelty.

She raises a hand, and her rod of covenant erupts from the broken body of the tomb stalker. It speeds towards her across the chamber, snapping firmly into her grip. She lifts the staff in both hands and holds it level with Kamoteph's chestplate. The cryptek is unmoving. The curtain of tiles on his arm, the measure of all he achieved in life and in his life-after-life, hangs limp at his side.

Her rod of covenant glows, and Kamoteph is immolated in a rush of jade-green fire.

CHAPTER 11

She lets the charred remnants of Kamoteph's body clatter to the floor. No longer the crooked, but the cleaved.

Her own form is broken, but it will mend. That is the gift the C'tan gave the necrons, for all that they took away.

Hekasun is far more damaged. His legs are truncated stumps, sparking fitfully as his body sends signals to limbs it no longer possesses. His chestplate is a ruin, bleeding vital fluids from its cracked vents.

But he too will mend. If Khemet allows it.

She limps over to him, and he watches her approach, levering himself up on his remaining arm.

'Do you remember when I freed you from the Traveller's prison?' He has chosen spite to mask his fear. 'I do. I remember how pathetic you were. How addled were your senses.' A gout of flame erupts from his fractured chestplate, and Hekasun sprawls onto his back. He laughs, a single snarl of distortion. 'How the tables have turned.'

'Many months ago,' Khemet says after a moment's contemplation, 'you told me that I owe you gratitude for freeing me.'

Khemet stops, looming over him. She lets the staff's end strike the deck, chiming a broken note from the blackstone. 'Perhaps that is true. But I think you would agree, that debt is now paid.'

Hekasun growls, as close to bitter laughter as he can manage. 'You save me, only to slay me yourself.'

'You assume that I will kill you.'

Something has changed within Khemet. In killing Kamoteph – in executing him – something has been shaken loose, or jarred into waking. The agony of uncertainty, of self-doubt, is gone. She can sense the adamant surety on which she has built her existence, which for so long has eluded her. It is there for her to grasp. Not a splintered memory of strength but a fact, tangible and real.

'My cryptek and my nemesor,' says Hekasun, ignoring her. 'Usurpers both. Clawing for what is not yours by birth or breeding. Thieves wearing the guise of servants.'

He is pulling himself away from her with his remaining arm, crawling like a worm. Where he hopes to go, she does not know. Perhaps this is simply Hekasun's cowardice, seeking to prolong his existence in the face of destruction.

'I won your world, Hekasun. Me. As did he.' She gestures at Kamoteph's broken body. 'Without our labour, you would be lord of nothing. Nomarch of a slumbering, conquered tomb.'

'At my bidding. All you have done was in service of me.' His strength gives out, and Hekasun sprawls onto the deck. His head lands on the carcass of a spyder, propping him up so his oculars can meet hers.

'Yes,' Khemet says. 'That is our way. Kamoteph. Ptah. Even I. We are moved solely by our lords' command. All any of us do is in their name.'

'And now you will kill me, and cast off your shackles. Become a servant only to yourself.' Hekasun manages to find a new layer of contempt to add to his anger.

'No. I am a praetorian. I am a servant of the Triarch of the necron empire. My duty has never been to you.

'What is more,' she says, lifting her rod of covenant, 'it is my duty to pass judgement upon you.'

Hekasun does not flinch. He stares down his death, fury burning in the copper flames that crackle from his broken core.

'I judge you, Hekasun, to be the rightful claimant of Qeretesh, and inheritor of all that the Zathanor hold.'

Khemet lowers her weapon.

As Hekasun gawks at her, shock not yet displacing hate, Khemet reaches across the interstices and offers him all she took from Kamoteph. The command protocols for the world, for every one of its warriors, are passed to Hekasun in an instant. That is the power of a praetorian: to make and break the might of lords and nobles.

'Rule here, and rule well. Take this place that I have given you. Make Qeretesh a bastion of our people. Prove to me that you are deserving of this honour.'

Hekasun has stared in disbelieving silence, but finally his arrogance breaks through his surprise. 'I have nothing to prove to you.'

Khemet looms over his legless form. 'You have everything to prove to me, Hekasun. All that I give, I can take away. If you squander this gift I will return, and I will tear down your little kingdom and bury you within its rubble. I am your arbiter, Hekasun. You will not disappoint me.'

She leaves Hekasun where he has fallen, a final indignity to ensure her lesson is truly heeded. If he has any parting words, Khemet does not hear them. He will either learn from this moment, or he will not.

As she leaves the ruined command deck, Khemet kicks aside the canoptek wreckage of Kamoteph's creations. She ignores the broken body of their master. She is surprised to find she bears no extraordinary malice towards Kamoteph. The cryptek played his hand, and acted on the self-interest that plagues his kind. Were it not for Khemet's intervention, he would have undoubtedly succeeded in his treachery. In all likelihood, he would have been a more effective nomarch of Qeretesh than Hekasun will prove to be, for all that Khemet has warned him of her vigilance.

But that was not his fate, nor his role. For all his venality, Hekasun is the rightful heir to the Zathanor by the ancient codes of the necrontyr. And Khemet, for all her doubts, is their protector and enforcer. She is their praetorian.

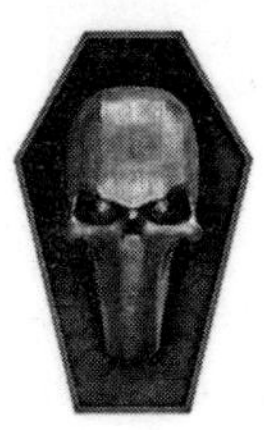

EPILOGUE

To the Imperium of Man, Orymous has ceased to exist.

Every vessel sent to investigate its fate fails to return. The benighted creatures that can look into the realm behind reality see only a lacuna. No soul-fires burn, no astropathic missives emerge. There is only emptiness.

Nothing moves across the face of the world. There are no bodies, no human refuse to pollute the atmosphere with their degradation. All have been sundered to atoms, disintegrated by the voracious, tireless carpet of constructs that have scoured an entire planet bare.

The cities remain, silent mausoleums haunted by dust and dry winds. The world's returned masters have no need of the coarse materials used in their construction, and so they are content to let them endure, for as long as they may. The works of humanity will all crumble, in time.

Beneath the world, metal figures march, and sleep, and wait.

ABOUT THE AUTHOR

Jonathan D Beer is a science fiction and alternative history writer. Equally obsessed with the 19th century and the 41st millennium, he lives with his wife and assorted cats in the untamed wilderness of Edinburgh, Scotland. He is the author of the Warhammer 40,000 novels *Dominion Genesis* and *Tomb World*, and has also written the Warhammer Crime stories 'Old Instincts', 'Service' and 'Chains', and the novel *The King of the Spoil.*

MORE FROM
BLACK LIBRARY

THE LION: SON OF THE FOREST
by Mike Brooks

The Lion. Son of the Emperor, brother of demigods and primarch of the Dark Angels.
Awakened. Returned. And yet… lost.

An extract from
Brutal Kunnin
by Mike Brooks

It had been a weird trip through the warp.

Ufthak Blackhawk knew full well that there wasn't such a thing as a normal trip through the warp, because Gork and Mork had their own senses of humour and liked to mess with the boyz every now and then. He still remembered that time he'd ended up seeing out of his own kneecaps for a while. Then there were all the interesting things you might encounter on a space hulk, like those bugeye wotsits with different numbers of arms that moved like a cyboar on nitrous. That was the great thing about space hulks – never a dull moment. Even when you thought you'd killed everything on board, you'd probably still missed a bit. And even if you hadn't, odds were you'd still have some ladz with you to have a punch-up with if everything got too boring.

This journey, though, hadn't been on a space hulk; it had been on a humie vessel, one that Ufthak and his boyz had boarded and taken, and on which Da Boffin had installed and then activated a device he'd called Da Warp Dekapitator. This had caused a katastroffic warp implosion – which was apparently a good thing, although Ufthak thought that 'catastrophic' sounded like something that should be happening to someone else – and it had dragged not only the humie ship but also all the ork ships around it into the warp and along the path of its last jump, to arrive back where it had come from.

(There was also the part where most of the bodies of the dead humie crew had merged together into a reanimated mass of flesh and steel that hungered for ork blood, and also the screaming humie faces that ran around on varying numbers of insectoid legs and spat poison, but the boyz had needed something to keep their spirits up on the way.)

Now they'd reached their destination, and had emerged from the warp again with nothing more than the sudden but quickly fading sensation that Ufthak's skeleton wasn't where it was supposed to be. And what a destination it was.

'Dat planet,' Mogrot Redtoof said, looking out of a viewport, 'is made of metal.'

Ufthak nodded sagely. Back before they'd boarded the humie ship, he and Mogrot had been rivals – two warriors jockeying for position under the command of Badgit Snazzhammer. Thanks to a series of events involving a large robot, several fatalities and a head transplant courtesy of Dok Drozfang, Ufthak's undamaged head had ended up on the decapitated Snazzhammer's undamaged and significantly larger body. After a brief meeting of the minds via a headbutt, Mogrot had settled back into a role as Ufthak's right-hand ork. That didn't mean that Ufthak trusted him, of course, but at least he was fairly certain Mogrot wouldn't try to shank him unless he was already wounded.

'Looks like a humie mekboy place,' Ufthak said. 'Humie mekboy ship, coming from a humie mekboy planet. Makes sense to me.'

'Why do dey do dat, anyway?' Mogrot asked. 'Make dere planets all shiny so ya know dey've got flashy stuff ya might want, and den when ya go to get it, dey get all annoyed an' try to kill ya?'

'Dat's da problem wiv humies,' Ufthak opined knowingly. 'Dey ain't logickal.'

'Boss!'

The shout came from the other side of the bridge, where Ufthak and his ladz had taken up residence after they'd tossed out the corpses of the crew formerly stationed there. Ufthak clumped across the deck, absent-mindedly twirling the Snazz-hammer as he went. It had been Badgit's weapon, a two-handed affair as tall as a humie with its legs still attached, with an electrified hammer on one side of the head and a choppa blade on the other. He was starting to get used to the feel of it now, and couldn't wait to krump a few more enemies with it.

'Wot?' he demanded, coming up alongside Deffrow. The other ork pointed with the few fingers that remained on his right hand, having blown most of them off by hitting a humie with a stikkbomb.

'Look at dat, boss! Dat ain't one of ours!'

Ufthak sucked his breath in through his teef as a jagged piece of darkness eclipsed the stars. The ships that made up the Waaagh! fleet of Da Meklord – Da Biggest Big Mek, and a warboss in his own right – were many and varied, but Ufthak was familiar with them, and Deffrow was correct: that wasn't one of theirs. Impressive though Da Meklord's flotilla was, none of them looked quite that… killy.

'Dat's *Da Blacktoof*,' Ufthak said in something close to wonder, as the shape of it became clear. It was a monstrous kill kroozer, bristling with guns and ordnance. And there, leering down at them from under the prow, was a single, huge glyph: a monstrous, one-eyed ork skull, with crossed bones behind it. 'Dat's Kaptin Badrukk's ship.'

The rest of his mob made suitably impressed noises. Badrukk

was a legend across the galaxy, a freebooter of infamy and renown, and his presence here surely meant that Da Meklord's own star was in the ascendancy.

Assuming, of course, that Badrukk was here because Da Meklord had arranged for him to be. If not…

'Message from da boss!' Da Boffin shouted, bursting into the bridge in a gust of fumes. At some point in the past, Da Meklord's favourite spanner had, either due to injury or simple curiosity, replaced his legs with a gyro-stabilised monowheel, and as a result he was now both much faster than a normal boy, and spectacularly poor at navigating stairs. 'All nobs are to get over to *Mork's Hammer* right now!'

Mork's Hammer was Da Meklord's flagship, and Da Meklord only called his nobs and bosses together if he had something very important to say… or, alternatively, if he wanted to yell at them all. As a new nob, Ufthak had never attended one of these Waaagh! meets before. His chest swelled with new-found pride, and he slung the Snazzhammer over his shoulder as he turned on the spot.

'Right den!' He frowned, as a thought struck him. 'Wait a minute. Do da 'Ullbreakers go backwards?' He and his mob had arrived via boarding pods, which were still locked into the side of the humie ship after they'd broken through its ferrous hide.

Da Boffin shook his head. 'Nah. Dey got just one gear – go.'

'So how're we s'posed to get back over dere, den?' Ufthak demanded. What was the good in being a nob if you couldn't go listen to your boss telling you what he wanted you to go and stomp?

Da Boffin shrugged. 'Da humies have shuttles on dis fing. We'll nick one.'

Ufthak frowned at him suspiciously. 'You know how to fly one?'

'Can't be hard,' Da Boffin grinned. 'After all, humies can do it.

* * *

The Waaagh! room of *Mork's Hammer* was crowded with orks mashed in shoulder to shoulder. Ufthak saw many faces he recognised and many more that he didn't, because every single ork of any authority under Da Meklord's command was here. Surly, black-clad Goffs glowered at camouflaged Blood Axes and blue-painted Deathskulls, while the stench of fuel from the Evil Sunz was almost overpowered, but instead just sickeningly offset, by the smell of squig dung that accompanied the Snakebites. However, most numerous by far were the yellow and black colours of the Bad Moons, which wasn't only Ufthak's clan, but also that of Da Meklord himself. They were smartest, the richest and the flashest clan of all, and the reason why the Tekwaaagh! had risen so quickly and so unstoppably. Sure, the Evil Sunz might drive a bit faster, and the Blood Axes might be a bit sneakier, but if you wanted the ladz with the best guns, you wanted Bad Moons.

This many orks in such close proximity was a pretty good recipe for a massive fight, especially given the egos involved. Ufthak could see the huge, horned helm and multiple back banners of Drak Bigfang, the Goff warboss; the collection of junk and scavenged armour plates under which was Gurnak Six-Gunz, the self-proclaimed SupaLoota of the Deathskulls; and the fur-clad bulk of Da Viper, the Snakebite Overboss, whose gargantuan squiggoth was so large it allegedly had a hold all to itself in his kroozer. Any of these orks were capable of leading a Waaagh! in their own right, but no one was starting any trouble worse than jostling their neighbour a bit. No one wanted to end up like Oldfang Krumpthunda, who'd taken Da Meklord on one on one and had been… Well, no one was quite sure *what* he had been, other than it involved getting hit with Da Meklord's shokkhammer and then ending up in lots of very small pieces in very different places. Some of the boyz said they were still finding bits of him in the stew, now and then.

Horns blared, a brassy note of challenge and conquest, and everyone shut their gobs and snapped their heads around to look at the dais built at the far end. Part of the wall behind it had been turned into a massive effigy of the face of Mork – or possibly Gork, but Ufthak reckoned it was Mork – and this was now yawning wider and wider as the mighty lower jaw dropped away. Steam and smoke gushed forth, obscuring the dais but accentuating the piercing red glare of the eyes lurking near the ceiling.

Then, first as a looming shadow in the murk, and then as a mighty figure resplendent in his yellow-and-black mega armour, Da Meklord emerged from the mouth of a god.